The Rockwood Chronicles

High upon the beautiful cliffs of the Devonshire coast, the once proud
Rockwood Castle is crumbling into ruin. Can the Carey family save
their home and their family before it's too late?

In this spellbinding six-book series, Dilly Court opens a door into Rockwood Castle -
chronicling the changing fortunes of the Carey family. . .

Book One: Fortune's Daughter

Abandoned by her parents, headstrong Rosalind must take
charge of the family. Until the appearance of dashing
Piers Blanchard threatens to ruin everything . . .

Book Two: Winter Wedding

Christmas is coming and Rockwood Castle has once again been thrown into
turmoil. As snowflakes fall, can Rosalind protect her beloved home?

Book Three: Runaway Widow

It is time for the youngest Carey sister, Patricia, to seek out her own
future. But without her family around her, will she lose her way?

Book Four: Sunday's Child

Taken in by the Carey family when she was a young girl,
Nancy Sunday has never known her true parentage.
Now eighteen years old, can she find out where she truly belongs?

Book Five: Snow Bride

The course of true love does not run straight for Nancy. Her life is filled with difficult
choices - but with Christmas around the corner, which path will she choose?

Book Six: Dolly's Dream

The eldest daughter at Rockwood, Dolly, dreams of a bigger life
beyond the castle walls. But with the family's future under threat,
will Dolly's heart lead her astray - or bring her home?

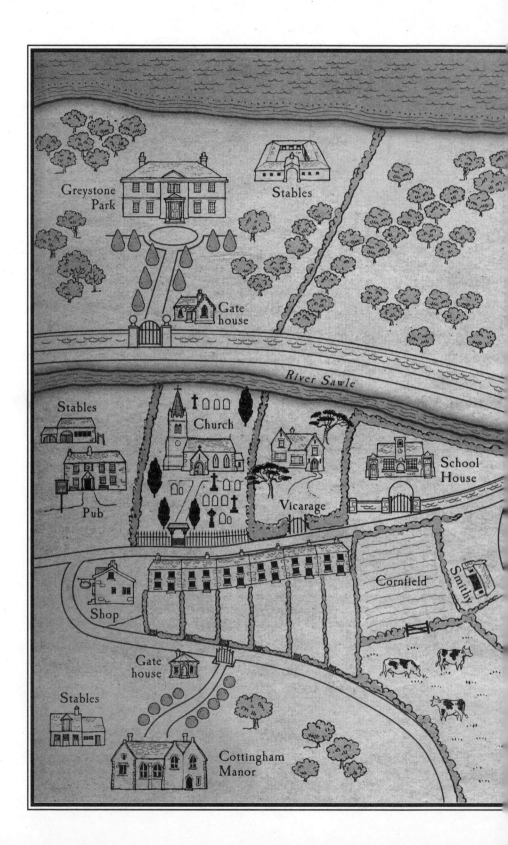

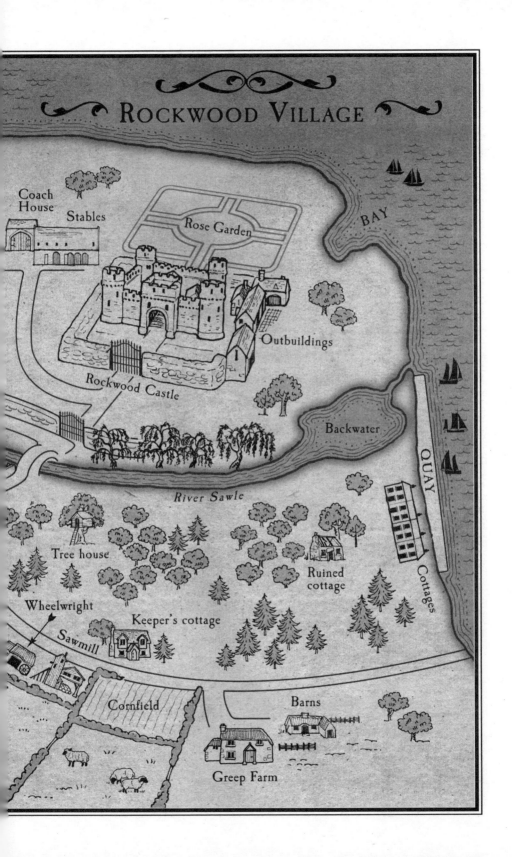

ROCKWOOD VILLAGE

Coach House

Stables

Rose Garden

BAY

Outbuildings

Rockwood Castle

Backwater

QUAY

River Sawle

Tree house

Ruined cottage

Cottages

Wheelwright

Keeper's cottage

Sawmill

Cornfield

Barns

Greep Farm

THE CAREY FAMILY

Lady Hester Carey m Vice–Admiral Sir Lucius Carey m Lady Prudence Carey
(Neé Dodridge)   (1776–1853)   (deceased)
(b. 1804)

Claude de Marney m Felicia Carey m Wilfred Carey
(b. 1805)   (b. 1806)   (1800–1851)

Sarah   m Bertram (Bertie)   Captain Alexander m Rosalind (Rosie) #—Piers   Walter m Louise   Patricia (Patsy) m 1. Sir Michael
Farthing   Carey   Blanchard   Carey   Blanchard   Carey   Shaw   Carey   Greystone
(1829–1847)   (b. 1827)   (b. 1827)   (b. 1830)   (b. 1825)   (b. 1832) (b. 1827) (b. 1834)   (b. 1806–1859)
                                                                                                                                      m 2. Leo Wilder
                                                                                                                                      (b. 1829)

Tommy Carey   Rory   Phoebe   Adela (Dolly)   Charlotte
(b. 1844)   Blanchard   Blanchard   Blanchard   Carey
                                     (b. 1856)   (b. 1858)   (b. 1854)   (b. 1859)

Dolly's Dream

Book six in

The Rockwood Chronicles

Dilly Court is a No.1 *Sunday Times* bestselling author of over forty novels. She grew up in North-East London and began her career in television, writing scripts for commercials. She is married with two grown-up children, four grandchildren and two beautiful great-grandchildren. Dilly now lives in Dorset on the Jurassic Coast with her husband.

To find out more about Dilly, please visit her website and her Facebook page:

www.dillycourt.com

/DillyCourtAuthor

Dilly Court

Dolly's Dream

Book six in

The Rockwood Chronicles

HarperCollins*Publishers*

HarperCollins*Publishers* Ltd
1 London Bridge Street
London SE1 9GF

www.harpercollins.co.uk

HarperCollins*Publishers*
Macken House,
39/40 Mayor Street Upper,
Dublin 1
D01 C9W8
Ireland

First published by HarperCollins*Publishers* 2023
1

A catalogue record for this book is available from the British Library

ISBN: 978-0-00-843568-4 (HB)
ISBN: 978-0-00-843569-1 (B)

This novel is entirely a work of fiction.
The names, characters and incidents portrayed in it are
the work of the author's imagination. Any resemblance to
actual persons, living or dead, events or localities is
entirely coincidental.

Set in Sabon LT Std by
Palimpsest Book Production Ltd, Falkirk, Stirlingshire

Printed and bound in the UK using
100% renewable electricity at CPI Group (UK) Ltd

*For Josie, a wonderful mother
and her daughter, Lisa.*

Chapter One

Rockwood Castle, March 1874

Adela Blanchard – known by all who loved her as Dolly – was bored. Born to comparative wealth and brought up in an ancient castle, surrounded by a loving family, Dolly wanted for nothing. She was officially 'out in society', having somewhat reluctantly undertaken a London season at the age of seventeen. However, the eligible young men who were paraded before her had been a total disappointment to a girl who read romances and aspired to be an opera star like her grandmother. None of her would-be suitors had matched up to her papa, who had been a dashing soldier until he was badly injured in the Crimea, or her kind uncle Freddie. Freddie Ashton, now Lord Dorrington, was her much-loved surrogate uncle. It was well-known within the family that Freddie had wanted to marry Aunt Nancy, but she had chosen Tommy Carey, her childhood sweetheart. Adela remembered their wonderful wedding in the village church one snowy Christmas. She had been a bridesmaid, along with her younger sister, Phoebe, and little May. Many years ago, Aunt Nancy had adopted May and her brother, Jack, into the family and had also rescued a dozen older boys, who had fallen into a life of crime in the backstreets of London. Nancy obviously loved children, and after her marriage she had produced three sons in quick succession. The 'Holy Terrors' Great-Grandmama Hester called them, with good reason: Edward, Oliver and Percival Carey were lovable rogues.

Dolly loved her family, but sometimes she pretended that she was an orphan, free from parental control so that she could fulfil her dreams of becoming a diva. There was a thriving theatre just a couple of miles away at Greystone Park, the estate owned by Nancy, which she had brought to the Carey family when she married Tommy. People came from far and wide to enjoy the productions put on by Nick Gibson and Grandmama Felicia, who might be an old lady now, but she still held the reins when it came to choosing plays, operas and pantomimes. It was a family business and yet she, Dolly Blanchard, was excluded. She stood up and stamped her foot. It was a childish thing to do but it emphasised the strength of her emotions.

'Dolly! What are you doing skulking in your bedroom? You're wanted downstairs in the drawing room.' Phoebe had wandered into the room unnoticed. She slumped down on the bed, pouting.

Adela sighed. At fifteen, her sister took after their aunt Patricia in looks, with violet-blue eyes and blonde hair. She had also inherited Aunt Patricia's volatile temperament, which in Phoebe's case meant that she was either in high spirits, or in the depths of despair, causing everyone to suffer. Phoebe might have a deceptively fragile beauty, but Dolly was satisfied with her own looks. Her abundant curly golden hair and perfect nose were attributes that would serve her well if she ever managed to fulfil her ambition and tread the boards. The young men who had courted her in London had often remarked on her large cornflower-blue eyes, and Dolly knew how to flutter her long eyelashes in receipt of a compliment. However, no matter how many compliments she received, she managed to keep her head and dismiss the flattery for what it was.

'I am not skulking, as you so elegantly put it, Phoebe. I just wanted a few minutes away from the family. Great-Grandmama Hester is laying down the law again. Not that anyone takes any notice of her these days, but it does get rather tiresome.'

'May and I are going to Rockwood House to see Cousin Charlotte. Why don't you come with us?'

Dolly tossed her head. 'Thank you, but I'm nineteen; I don't want to play with little girls.'

'I'm roughly the same age as Charlotte, and May is nearly sixteen, or so she thinks. It must be odd not knowing your exact date of birth or who your parents were.'

'It's not something you should talk about, at least not in her presence if it upsets her.'

Phoebe rose to her feet. 'You are a grumpy thing today. I came to give you some news.'

'What news?' Dolly asked reluctantly. She did not want to give her sister the satisfaction of seeing that her curiosity was aroused.

'Todd Taylor has returned to the village. He's qualified now and is taking over Dr Bulmer's practice.' Phoebe laughed. 'I thought that would make you sit up and take notice.'

'That's the first I've heard of it. Who told you that?'

'Tilly, if you must know. She's been visiting her mother in the village. Widow Madge knows everything that's going on and so do we, as her daughters work here.'

'What makes you think I'd be interested?' Dolly demanded, rolling her eyes. Todd was one of Nancy's street boys, rescued from a life of crime.

'You were sweet on him before he went away to St George's medical school. You know you were.'

'That was a silly, childish infatuation. I've grown up since then.'

'But you said you danced with him at a ball during the London season.'

'I may have,' Dolly said casually. 'I danced with dozens of eligible bachelors.'

Phoebe's delicate eyebrows snapped together. 'Well, none of them proposed, so you'll probably end up on the shelf and be grateful if Todd Taylor gives you a second glance.' She slammed out of the pretty bedroom in the east tower and her footsteps echoed off the stone staircase.

Dolly sank back on the window seat. Todd was the eldest of the boys that Nancy had brought to Rockwood more than ten years ago. His friend Gus had been hustled off to join the army after an unfortunate incident at Greystone Park when the house was razed to the ground by fire. Gus had later been proved innocent and the perpetrator had been sent to prison, but Gus was a career soldier now. The other boys had all found work locally and some of the younger ones still lived in the Dower House, under the watchful eye of Abel Wolfe, the fierce-looking individual who had cared for Dolly's uncle, Sir Bertram Carey, the crippled war hero, until his tragic death in a hunting accident.

Dolly went to her dressing table and seized her hairbrush, dragging it through her tangled curls. She had not seen Todd for almost a year, and she wanted to look her best. If she hurried, she would be in time to catch up with Phoebe and May, and she could stroll along the High Street, where he now lived, as if she was simply accompanying the girls. Dolly stood up and went to open the door.

'Wait for me, Phoebe. I'm coming, too.'

March winds whipped Dolly's hair from beneath her velvet bonnet as she walked on ahead of Phoebe and May. Their incessant chatter was annoying, and, if she were to tell the truth, Dolly was slightly nervous about meeting Todd again. It was true that she had been attracted to him when she was younger and had made up stories in her head in which she was the heroine and Todd was the hero. She had missed him when he went to London to study medicine, and when she met him by chance at one of the Coming Out balls, the old tug of attraction had still been there. She had become immune to the suave chitchat of her would-be suitors, but Todd was different and their relationship had changed subtly that evening. Now he was fully qualified and about to embark on a career as a country doctor. She did not want to seem too eager, but she was more than a little curious.

It was only when she reached the doctor's house in the High Street that Dolly had second thoughts. It was ridiculous for Miss Adela Blanchard from Rockwood Castle to be chasing after one of Aunt Nancy's protégés when she could have the pick of the eligible bachelors in the county. Dolly was about to walk past with her nose in the air when the front door opened and a young man in army uniform stepped onto the pavement, followed by Todd.

'Miss Blanchard. This is a pleasant surprise,' Todd said with a charming smile.

Dolly recovered her composure swiftly. 'Good morning, Dr Taylor. I was just taking the girls to Rockwood House.' She glanced over her shoulder, hoping that Phoebe would not step in and correct her, but Phoebe and May were gazing admiringly at the man in uniform.

'Don't you recognise me, Miss Blanchard? Gus Baker, now Sergeant Baker.' He swept off his military cap with a flourish.

'You've changed a great deal,' Dolly said cautiously. Gus the soldier bore no resemblance to the scruffy boy that Dolly remembered. He was taller now, with broad shoulders and a narrow waist. The uniform flattered his honed physique and his skin was tanned from exposure to the elements. He wore his pomaded auburn hair swept back to reveal a wide brow and smiling green eyes. Sideburns and a small moustache made him look older and even more dashing. Dolly tried not to stare.

'I've been on active service in India for the past ten years,' Gus said airily.

Todd sent Gus a warning glance. 'I expect you've heard that I have taken over Dr Bulmer's practice, Miss Blanchard?'

'I believe I heard some such rumour,' Dolly said casually.

Phoebe stepped in between them, dragging May with her. 'You look very smart in your uniform,

Sergeant. I can scarcely remember you before you went away.'

'You must have been a very young girl.' Gus gave her the benefit of his charming smile. 'However, I was on my way to the castle to see Nancy – I mean, Lady Carey – but perhaps I will walk with you to Rockwood House. With your permission, of course, Miss Blanchard.'

Dolly felt the colour rush to her cheeks and she looked away, suddenly shy, which was unusual for her. 'Yes, if you so wish, Sergeant.' She shot a sideways glance at Todd. 'Congratulations on your new position, Dr Taylor.'

'Todd, please. We were not so formal at the ball in London.'

Dolly frowned. It was true, but she was acutely aware of Gus, who exuded a personal magnetism that was hard to ignore. She managed a tight little smile. 'Yes, but we are at home now. I think it best to follow convention.'

'There, you've been put nicely in your place, Todd,' Gus said, proffering his arm to Dolly. 'If you'll allow me . . . ?'

'On second thoughts, I think the girls can find their own way to Rockwood House,' Dolly said firmly as she laid her hand on Gus's sleeve. 'Perhaps you'd like to escort me home, Sergeant, and then you can see Nancy and Mama. I'm sure they'll be glad to know that you are doing so well in the army.'

'What about us?' Phoebe demanded crossly. 'I thought you wanted to see us safely to Uncle Walter and Aunt Louise's house?'

Dolly shrugged. 'As I said, it's not far. And I'm sure that Gus has more important things to do.'

Todd reached into the entrance hall and picked up a large leather bag. 'As a matter of fact, my first visit is to Rockwood House. One of the maids has a fever and Mrs Carey asked me to take a look at her. I'll see the girls safely there, Miss Blanchard.'

Dolly had little choice other than to watch Todd walk off with her sister and May. This was not how she had envisaged their first casual meeting, but Gus had outmanoeuvred his friend.

'What are we waiting for, Sergeant?' She was about to walk off in the direction of home when Gus clamped his hand over her arm so that she had to remain at his side. She was irritated by his proprietorial manner and yet rather flattered.

'You really are very beautiful.'

'So I've been told,' Dolly said coldly. 'Do you always flirt so outrageously with women you hardly know?'

He laughed. 'What better way to pass the time? To be truthful, I don't meet too many lovely ladies. You'll have to forgive a brash military man.'

'I suppose we are family, in a way.'

'I don't follow your way of thinking.'

'Aunt Nancy more or less adopted you, Sergeant. That makes us cousins, of a kind.'

'Maybe, but please will you call me Gus? You were only a child when I went into the army, but I do remember seeing you up at the castle.'

'Well, I remember you, too. I was sad when they sent you away. You used to make me laugh.'

'I'm a comical fellow when I'm with friends. When I'm on duty I am someone else.'

Dolly relaxed and they fell into step as easily as if they had often walked this way. She was aware of the admiring glances at Gus from the women and girls they passed on the way to the castle.

Jarvis, the aged butler who had served the family for many years, had finally been persuaded to retire to live with his sister in a cottage on the quay, and James, the footman, had taken his place. It was James who opened the door and his eyes widened when he saw Gus. His look of surprise was replaced by one of recognition and instant suspicion. Dolly was amused to see the expressions flit across James's normally impassive face. There was not one inhabitant of Rockwood village who would not have some memory of Gus and the night of the fire at Greystone Park.

'Where will we find Lady Carey, James?' Dolly asked as she slipped off her mantle and handed it to the housemaid, Connie Tuckett, who had been polishing the oak coffers in the entrance hall.

'I believe she is in the still room, Miss Dolly.'

'Thank you, James.' Dolly took off her gloves and bonnet, handing them to Connie with a smile of acknowledgement. 'Come along, Gus. We'll give Aunt Nancy a surprise.' As she walked past the rusty old suit of armour, allegedly worn by her legendary ancestor, Sir Denys Carey during his last and fatal battle, she closed the visor with a gentle pat of her hand. 'Good morning, Sir Denys.'

Gus laughed. 'What was that about?'

'Sir Denys was killed in battle hundreds of years ago, but we all treat him as if he still lives here.' The armour rattled, making her giggle. 'Of course, you are here, Sir Denys. I was just trying to explain why we love you.' She hurried on, lowering her voice. 'He foretells disasters and the like. We try not to upset him.'

'Well, I'm blowed. I never heard the like of that before.'

Dolly quickened her pace. 'It's just superstition, but don't say things like that in his hearing – it's bad luck.'

'Well, as one army man to another, I'd better salute the old fellow every time I meet him.'

'I'm sure he will appreciate that.' Dolly smiled as she led the way through a maze of corridors to the still room.

Nancy looked up as they walked in and she smiled. 'Gus! What a wonderful surprise. You look so smart and handsome I hardly recognise you.' She held her arms out and he enveloped her in a fond embrace.

'You look wonderful, Aunt Nancy. Motherhood suits you.'

Nancy's pansy-brown eyes twinkled with amusement as she patted her belly. 'I know it does, Gus. You and Todd and the boys were my first children, but now I have three of my own and another on the way. I know it's not the done thing to talk about in front of a young gentleman, but we are family, are we not?'

'Indeed we are.' Gus held her at arm's length. 'You have been more like a mother to us than we deserved. It's so good to see you again.'

Nancy had been mixing attar of roses with almond oil and other magical ingredients to make face cream. She wiped her hands on her apron. 'How long are you with us, Gus?'

'Actually I am staying with Todd at the doctor's house. I have a week's leave.'

'Well, my dear, you must dine with us tonight, and Todd should come, too. We need to celebrate his success and you are obviously doing well. Army life definitely suit you, Gus.'

'It was Sir Bertram who saved me from a miscarriage of justice, ma'am. I owe it all to him, and nothing would give me more pleasure than to dine with you and the family.'

Nancy gave him an admiring look. 'That was well said, Gus. Oh, and before I get carried away with making this face cream, will you inform Cook that we have two more for dinner this evening, please, Dolly?'

'Very well, Aunt Nancy. Come, Sergeant. We mustn't get in the way. Let's go and find my mother.'

'Yes, dear, and don't forget to pass the message on to Cook,' Nancy called as they left the still room.

Dolly delivered the instructions to Connie, who promised to pass them on in the kitchen. Satisfied that she had done as Nancy wished, Dolly led the way to find her mother. Rosalind Blanchard was in the morning parlour, seated at a small escritoire. She looked up as they entered the room and for a moment she did not seem to recognise Gus, but then she rose gracefully to her feet and advanced on him, holding out her hands. Dolly had always thought her mother beautiful and now, in her early forties, she brought serenity and a sense of calm to everything in her daily life.

'Gus. What a lovely surprise.'

He raised her right hand to his lips. 'I owe everything to this family, Mrs Blanchard.'

'Aunt Nancy has invited Gus and Todd to dine with us tonight,' Dolly said hastily.

'Excellent. You must have many wonderful stories to tell us about army life, Gus. I'm sure that my husband will be more than interested. He may claim to be happy as a civilian but I know he misses the military, although I'm not so certain about my nephew, Tommy. As you might remember, his career was cut short by injury and illness.'

'I do, of course, ma'am. I look forward to dining with you, although I doubt if the Dowager Lady Carey will approve of me sitting at your table.'

Rosalind laughed. 'Leave Hester to me, Gus. I'm

13

sure she will be pleased to see that you are doing well for yourself.'

'Thank you, ma'am.' Gus bowed from the waist. 'I know I left Rockwood under a cloud of suspicion.'

'Proved to be unfounded,' Rosalind smiled.

'People in Rockwood have long memories,' Gus said ruefully. 'I think they will always associate me with that terrible disaster.'

'You know, of course, that my grandmother instigated the building of a theatre on the site of the old house?' Dolly eyed him curiously.

'Todd did mention it, yes.'

'Then you must go and see it for yourself,' Rosalind said enthusiastically. 'It's been very well received, even if it doesn't make as much profit as was first hoped.'

'I plan to visit it as soon as possible.'

Dolly smiled. 'I'll take you there this morning if you wish.'

'That would be wonderful. Thank you.'

'There you are then, Gus,' Rosalind said, smiling. 'You have a willing guide. I look forward to seeing you at dinner tonight. You can tell us all about army life.'

'I'll try not to bore you, Mrs Blanchard.' Gus went to open the door for Dolly.

She blew a kiss to her mother as she left the room.

'What I don't understand is why you didn't return to Rockwood sooner.' Dolly gave Gus a searching look.

'It was Captain Blanchard who suggested that I should keep my distance, even when it was proved that Jeremiah Stewer was the arsonist. I expect Mrs Cottingham still blames me. She's an unforgiving woman.' Gus fell into step beside Dolly as she made her way back to the entrance hall.

'Mrs Cottingham is too busy with her husband's ecclesiastical affairs these days. She doesn't mix much in society now, so you have no need to worry about her. Anyway, you seem to have kept in touch with Todd. You've both returned more or less at the same time.'

Gus eyed her curiously. 'He's a great chap. He stood by me from the start.'

'We've seen very little of each other since he went away to medical school,' Dolly said casually. 'Although I met him in London when I endured the Season, and then I believe he worked for a doctor in order to gain experience of general practice.' She beckoned to Connie. 'Fetch my mantle and bonnet, please, Connie. If anyone wants me I'm taking Sergeant Baker to see the theatre.'

The Pavilion Theatre never failed to impress Dolly. When she entered the grand foyer she felt shivers of anticipation run down her spine. She led Gus into the auditorium where a rehearsal for the latest opera was in progress. Felicia de Marney, the co-founder of the theatre with their late benefactor, Sir Bentley Crooke, was seated in the third row from the front, watching the rehearsal with a critical eye. She turned her head when Dolly called out to her and her brows drew together in an ominous frown.

'What have I told you about interrupting a rehearsal, Dolly Blanchard?'

'I'm sorry, Grandmama, but I've brought someone to see the marvellous things you do here.'

Felicia raised a lorgnette and squinted at Gus. 'A soldier? You do have a familiar look about you, young man.'

Gus snapped his heels together and bowed from the waist. 'It's an honour to meet you, Mrs de Marney. You won't remember me, but I was one of Miss Nancy's ragged boys.'

'I do recall something about a boy who had to be shipped off to the army to prevent him going to prison for arson. Was that you?'

'It was, except that I was innocent of the charge. Sir Bertram made it possible for me to join the army. It was the best thing I ever did.'

'That's nice to know.' Felicia turned her attention back to the stage. 'No, no, no! You sound like a frog with tonsillitis, girl. Start from the beginning and hold yourself upright. Sing from the diaphragm.'

'I have a better voice than that,' Dolly said in a stage whisper.

Felicia turned to her, frowning. 'You keep telling us how good you are, Dolly. I think it's time you got up on the stage and proved it.'

'All right, I will.' Dolly needed no second bidding.

She handed her mantle and gloves to Gus. 'Hold these, please. I'll show you what I can do.' She walked purposefully down the aisle between the rows of seats and climbed the steps onto the stage. Having taken singing lessons from her aunt Patricia, Dolly was fairly confident in her ability to perform, although acting was her real love. However, she resented her grandmother's casual dismissal of her talent and she wanted to prove herself, particularly in front of the dashing Gus.

She leaned over to speak to the pianist, giving him the title of the song. He nodded and played the introductory bars and without a moment of hesitation, Dolly sang the touching words of 'Beautiful Dreamer'. She had tears in her eyes when she finished and Gus clapped his hands enthusiastically.

'Very nice, my dear,' Felicia said in a bored voice. 'Just right for after-dinner entertainment at the castle.'

'I can do better, Grandmama.' Dolly signalled to the pianist. '"Champagne Charlie".'

'No, please, Adela,' Felicia snapped. 'We've heard enough. We have serious auditions to watch.'

But Dolly had already launched into the bright and breezy popular song, complete with actions. She could see that Gus was enjoying her performance. Dolly needed no further encouragement. She did a little dance at the end and blew a kiss to the stage manager as she walked off into the wings where she almost bumped into the girl who had been on stage before her. Dolly could see that the pretty young woman had been crying although she mopped her eyes and turned away quickly.

'I'm sorry,' Dolly said in a low voice. 'You weren't at all bad, from what I saw. I was just trying to prove a point to my grandmother.'

'It must be wonderful to be well connected,' the girl said bitterly. 'Your sort don't know you're born.'

'I beg your pardon?' Dolly glared at her. 'What do you mean by that?'

'Look at yourself, rich girl. Look at your expensive clothes and your lily-white hands that have never done a day's work.'

Dolly automatically glanced down at her own perfectly manicured nails and she clasped her hands behind her back. 'We can't help which family we are born into.'

'No, and you don't have to fight for every last penny or starve. I come down here from London in the hope of getting a part. My grannie lives here in the village. She's old and sick, living in a damp hovel with barely enough to eat and no coal nor candles.'

'Surely the Parish will help people in that position?'

'That's all you know. I gave up a lucky break at the Grecian Theatre in Shepherdess Walk to come down here and care for her. If I don't return to London tomorrow I'll lose the best job offer I've ever had, but I'm the only living relation she's got.'

'I'm sorry,' Dolly said warily. 'If there was anything I could do to help . . .'

'I'd like to see you swap places with me for a

month. You'd soon learn what real life is like, lady. Try becoming Liza Day – yes that's me name. You wouldn't last long if you had to live as I do.'

'What can I say, but I'm sorry for your troubles.'

Liza ran her hand through her tumbled auburn curls, her blue eyes cold as chips of ice. 'You think you're better than me. I heard you from the stage. Well, you go off to the Grecian and see how you get along. You try to live my life and see how clever you are then.'

Dolly met the girl's angry gaze with a cool look. 'I've never refused a dare. I'll do it and, what's more, I'll send you the money they pay me. We'll see who comes out of it best, Liza Day.'

Dolly stepped down from the stage to find Gus standing there, waiting for her with a questioning look. 'What was that all about?'

'Were you listening? It was a private conversation.'

'I think the whole auditorium would have heard it had there been anyone other than your grandmother, who was talking to the stage manager.'

Dolly tossed her head. 'It's none of your business, Sergeant.'

'I'm making it my business, Dolly Blanchard. I've known you since you were a little girl and I owe everything to your family. Were you serious about changing places with that young woman?'

'As I said, it has nothing to do with you, Gus Baker.' Dolly walked out of the auditorium, but Gus caught her up in the theatre foyer.

'Tell me you weren't serious, Dolly. Swapping

places with Liza Day is the most stupid idea I've ever heard.'

Dolly broke free from his restraining hand. 'Go back to playing at soldiers, Gus. I don't want to hear another word.'

He glared at her, holding her gaze so that she was unable to look away, and suddenly something changed between them. He wrapped his arms around her and claimed her lips in a kiss that sent her senses reeling. In her confused state she knew she should push him away and cry out in disgust, but it was the first time a man had kissed her in such a way and she found herself responding with equal fervour. She slid her arms around his neck and relaxed against his hard muscular body.

'Adela Blanchard! What is the meaning of this?' Grandmama Felicia's operatic tones rose in a crescendo that made the crystal chandeliers tinkle melodiously.

Gus released Dolly and they sprang apart.

'You were always trouble, Augustus Baker,' Felicia spat at him, the words coated with venom. 'You will leave Rockwood immediately and don't show your face here again.'

Chapter Two

'No, Grandmama,' Dolly cried angrily. 'It wasn't his fault. If Gus goes, I go too.'

'Don't be ridiculous.' Felicia grabbed Dolly by the wrist. She was surprisingly strong for a woman in her late sixties. Her hazel eyes flashed angrily. 'Go home. I will speak to your papa about this.' She turned on Gus. 'As to you, Sergeant. I meant what I said. You are not welcome here. Kindly leave now.'

Nick Gibson, the former land agent on the Greystone estate and now the theatre manager, hurried to Felicia's side. 'What is going on?' Nick stared at Gus. 'Gus Baker? You're the last person I expected to see this morning.'

'You might be pleased to see him, Nick,' Felicia said icily, 'but he's causing trouble, yet again.'

'That's not fair, Grandmama,' Dolly protested.

'Well, whatever is going on, I think you should

come with me, Gus.' Nick proffered his arm. 'We'll have a chat over a pint of beer in the Black Dog.'

Gus turned to Dolly with an anxious look. 'Will you be all right?'

'I can take care of myself, thank you.' Dolly faced her grandmother with a stubborn lift of her chin. 'We weren't doing anything wrong, Grandmama.'

'Send for my carriage before you go, Nick. I am taking Miss Dolly home.' Felicia fanned herself with her hand. 'Fetch my smelling salts, Dolly. My poor heart won't stand for all this upset.'

Dolly gazed at her grandmother, unsure whether or not it was a ploy to make her do as she was told, but the pallor on Felicia's lined cheeks was real enough. Dolly hurried to the office where she knew she would find a bottle of sal volatile. When she emerged she found that Nick and Gus had already disappeared and Felicia was reclining in her seat with her eyes closed.

Dolly opened the bottle and waved it under her grandmother's nose. Felicia coughed and gasped for breath, pushing the bottle away. 'Are you trying to kill me? Take it away.'

'I'm sorry, Grandmama,' Dolly said reluctantly. 'I didn't mean to upset you. It all happened so quickly.'

'You don't have to tell me.' Felicia rose to her feet, once again her old energetic and domineering self. 'That young man was trouble from the beginning. I blame Nancy for bringing those street urchins

22

to live amongst decent people. You will not see him again, Adela. Do you understand?'

Dolly could still feel the imprint of Gus's lips, and the taste of him lingered. The scent of his pomade mingled with a musky male odour had filled her heart and soul with unfamiliar sensations and deep longings. She was, for once, unsure of herself and confused.

'He will be gone soon,' Dolly said vaguely. She was not prepared to make a promise she knew she would not keep.

Before Felicia could respond the door to the foyer opened. 'Your carriage is being brought round to the front, Mrs de Marney.' Nick retreated before Felicia had a chance to speak.

'Where is Claude?' Felicia half rose and then sank back in the chair. 'My husband is never around when I need him.'

'Shall I go and find him, Grandmama?'

'You will not leave my side until we get home. We'll see what your papa has to say about your promiscuous behaviour.'

'It was just a kiss, Grandmama.'

Felicia held up her hand. 'I don't want to hear another word from you, young lady. Help me up. I am very disappointed in you.'

Luckily for Dolly the carriage ride from the theatre at Greystone Park to Rockwood Castle only lasted some fifteen minutes, and that included getting Felicia in and out of the vehicle. However, during that time

Felicia managed to lecture Dolly on her bad behaviour and the money wasted on her education and coming-out season. Dolly did not like to interrupt and tell her grandmother that it was wealthy Uncle Freddie, Lord Dorrington, who had paid for everything. It would have been very unwise to argue, and Dolly managed to look suitably chastened while in her head she was reliving the moments she had spent in Gus's arms. Her attraction to Todd Taylor seemed to fade into a half-forgotten dream compared to her recent experience with the handsome, dashing sergeant.

Felicia was still berating her when they entered the drawing room at Rockwood Castle. She came to a halt, glaring at Rosalind, who was enjoying a sherry with Hester, the Dowager Lady Carey.

Hester looked up to give Felicia a hard stare. 'What is troubling you, ma'am? You seem a trifle put out.'

Rosalind put her glass down and rose to her feet. 'What is the matter, Mama?'

Felicia gave Dolly a none-too-gentle push, sending her tripping over the Aubusson carpet and almost losing her balance. 'This girl has behaved like a trollop, and I don't use the word lightly, Rosalind.'

'It was just a little kiss, Mama,' Dolly said hastily. 'Nothing more than a peck, really.'

'A kiss?' Rosalind and Hester exchanged worried glances.

'They were canoodling like common villagers.' Felicia sank down on a chair by the fireplace. 'She was obviously enjoying the attention of that Gus creature. The fellow who was sent into the army to escape a prison sentence for arson.'

'You were kissing Gus Baker?' Hester stared at Dolly as if she had suddenly grown another head.

'Well, he kissed me, to be exact,' Dolly said calmly. 'Really, Mama, it was just a kiss,' she added, turning to give her mother a straight look.

'Which you obviously enjoyed.' Felicia pursed her lips. 'She had her arms around his neck. It was shocking.'

Rosalind rose to her feet. 'You shouldn't have allowed such familiarity between you and Gus, Dolly. He's a grown man and is probably used to having his way with women far more worldly than you are.'

'We didn't do anything wrong, Mama. It was over in a second and I probably won't see him again.'

'I'll make sure of that,' Felicia said firmly. 'I told him to go back from whence he came. We don't want the family name sullied by scandal.'

'That's rich coming from a woman who has made a living prancing on the public stage in revealing costumes.' Hester curled her lip. 'You were no angel, as I recall, Felicia de Marney.'

'At least I didn't claw my way up from the servants' quarters by marrying a man in his dotage.'

Rosalind stepped in between them. 'This will end in tears if you don't stop insulting each other. Dolly needs us to protect her.'

'I do not,' Dolly said angrily. 'Don't talk about

me as if I weren't here, Mama. I am a grown woman, not a child.'

'You were behaving like a spoiled brat.' Felicia rolled her eyes. 'You weren't there, Rosie. Neither were you, Hester, so you had better take note of what I am saying. That young man is after one thing and one thing only.'

'Please, Mama. There is no need for this.' Rosalind moved to Dolly's side and gave her a hug. 'Believe me, darling, we love you and simply want to keep you from harm.'

'Lock her in her room until that Gus creature has returned to his regiment,' Hester said, sinking down onto the nearest chair. 'I wash my hands of her.'

'You are not related by blood.' Felicia shot a malevolent glance in Hester's direction. 'I am the girl's grandmother and I say . . .' she paused, frowning at Dolly, '. . . I say send her down to Cornwall to stay with Lady Pentelow and Aurelia. That should keep her from harm.'

'No!' Dolly cried in alarm. 'Why are you punishing me for something so trivial?'

'From what I saw, it was anything but trivial,' Felicia said sharply. 'That young man is a fortune-hunter. You must be protected from men like him, Granddaughter.'

Rosalind shook her head. 'I wouldn't go so far as to say that. Gus is a decent enough fellow, I'm sure. However, he should have not have allowed his feelings to get the better of him.'

'I agree with Felicia.' Hester folded her arms across her ample bosom, gazing angrily at Dolly. 'You are an innocent and Gus Baker is anything but.'

'Well, you won't have to worry about me much longer.' Dolly backed towards the doorway. 'I intend to go to London and earn my own living. I'll prove to you all that I can take care of myself.'

The looks of horror on their faces made her want to laugh, but Dolly kept a straight face.

Rosalind was the first to speak. 'You, young lady, will do as your papa and I tell you. If you wish to go to London you will be under the aegis of Lord Dorrington. He will see to it that you mix in the right circles and meet eligible young men. I trust Freddie absolutely.'

'I didn't enjoy my coming-out season, Mama. I have no desire to waste my life going to parties, balls and soirées. I know what I'm going to do, with or without your permission.'

Rosalind's eyes filled with tears. 'I am so sorry, Dolly. I don't know where we've failed you, but you can't run off to London and live on your own. You are an innocent.'

'Go to your room, Adela,' Felicia said angrily. 'Your papa shall hear of this behaviour. Look how you've upset your mama.'

'No, Mama.' Rosalind turned to face her mother. 'You do not tell my daughter what to do. We will talk about this later, Dolly.'

'I don't want to upset you, Mama. You know that

I love you and Papa, but this is my life and I intend to live it to the full. I am sorry if my decision hurts you, but please don't try to stop me.'

'Dreadful girl,' Hester said, sighing. 'You are just like your aunt Patricia. She was always a handful.'

'Mind your tongue, Hester Carey.' Felicia bristled angrily.

Dolly took one look at her mother's distraught face and hurried from the room. There was no point trying to talk sense while Grandmama Felicia and Great-Grandmama Hester were needling each other. Dolly felt sorry for her mother but she was not about to be diverted from her purpose. She had made her mind up to leave home and have a life of her own away from family squabbles.

She went to her room in the tower and threw a few things in a valise. She had made a promise to Liza Day and she intended to keep it. Perhaps if she could catch Gus before he left to rejoin his regiment, they might travel together to London. She would like that more than anything else in the world. It would be the start of a wonderful adventure, and, if all else failed, she could go to Dorrington House in Piccadilly. Uncle Freddie was always ready to lend a sympathetic ear and to help if required.

Dolly left the castle through the music room, which opened out into the fragrant rose garden. She knew she would miss home, but she put all such thoughts to the back of her mind as she made her way to the village, where she hoped to catch up with Gus. She was attracting curious looks from the people she passed in the street, who eyed her case curiously as they greeted her, but were too polite to enquire where Miss Adela Blanchard might be going unescorted and without her maid. Dolly realised that the news of her escape would be likely to reach the castle before she had found Gus, and this made her bold.

She marched into the Black Dog and was met by a fug of tobacco smoke and fumes from the beer and rum being consumed at the bar. Nick Gibson and Gus were seated in the inglenook while Claude, Felicia's long-suffering husband, was at the bar ordering more drinks. There was a sudden lull in the conversation when the drinkers realised that there was a young woman in their midst, and not just any young woman but Miss Adela from the castle. Claude turned to give her a startled look. He left the bar and hurried towards her.

'Dolly, my dear, what are you doing in a place like this? Does your mama know where you are?'

'No, of course not,' Dolly said stiffly. 'I am looking for Gus, and there he is.' She waved to Gus, who leaped to his feet and made his way around the crowded tables to join them.

'What are you doing here?' he demanded, echoing Claude's question.

'I came to find you.' Dolly eyed him warily. 'I need your help.'

Claude glanced nervously over his shoulder as if

expecting his wife to materialise like a genie from a magic lamp. 'You'd best take her outside, my boy. Dolly, go home. You're making a spectacle of yourself.'

Dolly opened her mouth to retort, but Gus took her by the arm and propelled her out of the inn before she could say anything.

'What were you thinking?' Despite his serious tone, his green eyes danced with laughter and his lips quivered.

'I suppose you think it's funny. Well, this is what it's like being Miss Adela Blanchard from Rockwood Castle. I might as well be a prisoner. Anyway, I've made my escape. I'm going to London to take Liza's place at the Grecian Theatre.'

'No! By golly, you're serious.'

'Never more so. I want you to take me, Gus. I can't go on my own but I have enough money to pay for both our fares.'

'I can't do that. You don't know what you're doing, girl.'

'Yes, I do. For the first time in my life I am taking control of my life. I'm tired of doing what I am told and what is expected of me. I hated the London Season and I refuse to go to Uncle Freddie for help.'

'Do you mean Lord Dorrington? I heard that Freddie Ashton had succeeded to the earldom.' Gus laughed. 'Yes, I might have been in India for more years than I care to remember, but I did follow what is going on at home. I always thought Nancy would marry Freddie, until I realised that she was only interested in Tommy, or Sir Thomas, as I should call him now.'

'You are a constant source of surprise to me, Gus. But is that a yes or a no? If you won't go with me I shall simply have to travel on my own.'

He studied her face with a mixture of amusement and concern. 'I don't know, Miss Dolly. I suppose I should do the right thing and take you back to the castle.'

'But you aren't going to?'

'I need to think about this. Your family were very good to me. The late Sir Bertram saved me from going to prison for something I didn't do. If Mrs Cottingham had had her way I would have probably ended up in some penal colony.'

'That's all in the past. I want to go to London with you, Gus. I've never felt like this about any man I've ever met.'

He shook his head. 'Dolly, I'm a sergeant in the army. I'm not the man for you.'

'Then why did you kiss me like that? You love me, I know you do.'

'I shouldn't have done that, Dolly. Not that I didn't enjoy it – you are beautiful and desirable in every way – but you're far above me. I know that.'

'No, that's not true. I want to go to London with you. You can leave me when we get there and I take Liza's place in the theatre company, but I need your help. You aren't going to refuse, are you, Gus? Not after that kiss.'

He ran his hand through his dark auburn hair with an exasperated sigh. 'What have I done?'

'You've set me free, Gus Baker. You've shown me a way out of my dreary existence.'

'I don't know, Dolly. If I'm being honest, I think you ought to return home. You simply don't know what life is like away from the protection of your home and family.'

'Then I'll find out. Do I go alone, or are you coming with me? You can't stop me, Gus. I'm going to London with or without you.'

The warm spring weather had deteriorated during the train journey to London and it was raining when they arrived at their destination. Gus summoned a porter to take their luggage and he helped Dolly into a cab outside the station. Rain pounded on the roof and the horses' hoofs kicked up muddy water as the hackney carriage tooled through the city streets.

'Where are we going?' Dolly asked excitedly. 'I don't know this part of London.'

Gus pulled a face. 'Of course you don't, my dear. You are used to the smart part of town where the toffs live. This is what they call the East End, where people like humble army sergeants doss down in cheap hotels.'

'Oh!' Dolly gazed out of the grimy window at the even grimier streets and shabby buildings. 'Is the Royal Grecian Theatre near here?'

Gus laughed. 'London is a big place, Dolly. The theatre you want is in the City Road, at the back of the Eagle Tavern.'

'I suppose it's a bit late today,' Dolly said thoughtfully, 'but I need to go there first thing in the morning. Where will we stay?'

'You know, I have a bad feeling about this, Dolly. To all intents and purposes I have abducted you from your home and family. It wouldn't look good on my army records if the truth came out.'

She smiled. 'You could marry me, Gus. I would follow the drum. That's the right terminology, isn't it?'

'I thought you wanted a career on the stage, Dolly?'

'I do, of course. I wasn't serious. I know it was just a kiss. It didn't mean anything to a man like you.'

Gus leaned towards her, his expression grave. 'Don't say that, Dolly. I could so easily fall in love with you. If I were from your class of people I would go down on my knees and beg you to marry me, but I am not. I don't know who my parents were or where I came from. I've worked hard to attain my rank and I don't intend to ruin my life, or yours.'

'You think I would do that?'

'Not deliberately, my darling. But you will find living outside the comfort of your privileged life very hard. I am trying to be realistic, but if you look at me like that I am going to weaken and kiss you again.'

Dolly moved a little closer. She had not meant to be so forward but Gus drew her to him with an invisible force and she slipped so easily into his arms that it seemed only natural. He kissed her and she responded, ignoring the warning voice in her head that sounded like a chorus from Mama, Grandmama and Hester.

The carriage ground to a halt at the kerb and Gus released her unceremoniously. He opened the door and handed her out onto the wet pavement. The cabby climbed down to lift their cases from the back of the vehicle and Gus gave him the fare, plus what Dolly suspected was a reasonable tip.

'We'll stay here tonight,' Gus said firmly. 'It's a respectable inn, but very basic. We'll probably have to share a room, but I will be a gentleman and sleep on the floor. I haven't enough money for two rooms. Have you?'

Dolly was shocked but she did her best to look nonchalant. 'I have, but I want to save my money until I get my wages from the theatre.'

'If they take you on. And you'll have to find lodgings, Dolly. Have you thought of that?'

'I can stay with you until you return to your regiment, Gus.'

He sighed. 'I should have been more honest with you, my dear. I have only two more days and then we might be shipping out to India. I have no dependants and so I volunteered to return to Bombay. I'm sorry, Dolly.'

The rain had ceased temporarily but now the clouds opened and a sudden shower sent them hurrying into the tavern. Dolly kept close to Gus as he made his way to the bar. She was aware of the attention she was attracting and it was not flattering. The drinkers were giving Gus words of encouragement that made Dolly's cheeks flame with embarrassment. It was a relief when the landlord lifted the hatch in the counter and escorted them into a back room.

'This ain't the sort of place for a young lady,' he said tersely. 'What are you thinking of, soldier?'

'This is my wife.' Gus slipped his arm around Dolly's waist. 'We only have a couple of days before I am sent abroad, guv'nor. We'd like your best room and supper sent up with a jug of ale.'

The landlord's beady eyes flickered appreciatively over Dolly as if undressing her mentally. 'All right, sir. The very best for the honeymooners.' He cackled with laughter as he led the way into a narrow passage and up a flight of uncarpeted stairs to a room on the first floor. He flung the door open. 'This is the best I have. A fire will cost extra, although you can probably keep each other warm.'

'We'll have a fire,' Gus said stiffly. 'The room feels damp.'

'We get the miasma from the river, sir. There's nothing we can do about that, but you'll find the bed comfortable.' With a meaningful grin and a wink, he left the room, closing the door behind him.

Dolly slumped down on the edge of the bed. 'If this is his best I would hate to sleep on the worst he has to offer.'

'It's not too late, my dear. I could take you home in the morning. You would have a lot of explaining to do, but it would be better than the alternative.'

'You wish to abandon me? After all that kissing and making me feel that you loved me?'

'Dolly, my darling, what man wouldn't want to please you? But I never pretended to be in love with you. It was you who insisted on coming to London, and I wanted to show you exactly what you might be letting yourself in for.' Gus opened his arms to take in the seedy aspect of the room. 'Money counts for everything here. Without it you are just like a dead leaf tossed about by the wind.'

Dolly shivered. The room was cold and Gus had spoken the truth when he told the landlord it felt damp. Even the counterpane felt clammy, and she doubted that the sheets had been aired or even washed in between occupants. Perhaps Gus was right and she had made a dreadful mistake, but then she remembered her bold promise to Liza and her rebellious words to her mother and the family.

A tap on the door preceded the entry of a small servant girl carrying a bucket of coal and a bundle of kindling. She kneeled down in front of the grate and piled the shiny black nuggets on top of the slivers of wood and twigs, which she lit with a match. Dolly was quick to notice the child's rough, chapped hands and her ragged clothes.

'What's your name, girl?' Dolly asked tentatively. She knew it was useless to worry about a child whom she might never meet again, but the girl didn't look even as old as May, one of Nancy's many protégées.

Startled, the girl dropped a lump of coal on the hearth. 'It's Bess, miss.'

'How old are you, Bess?'

'I dunno exactly. About thirteen, I think.'

Gus put his hand in his pocket and took out a coin, which he pressed into Bess's grimy hand. 'Thank you. That will be all for now.'

Bess scrambled to her feet. 'Ta, sir. You're a toff.' She picked up the scuttle and hurried from the room as if afraid that Gus might change his mind and take the money back.

'You see how hard life is in the capital? The poor have to work or starve in the gutter. I know because I lived like that before Lady Carey took pity on us boys.'

'That's why I want to help Liza, the girl who auditioned with me. I was just showing Grandmama what I can do, but Liza was in deadly earnest.' Dolly took a deep breath. She needed to be totally honest with Gus. 'Even more than that, I want to prove to myself that I can do anything I want if I put my mind to it.'

Gus smiled. 'I'll hold you to that, Dolly Blanchard.

Although I don't think you'll find the streets of London paved with gold.'

'We'll see.' Dolly was not going to admit that she was having second thoughts. If anyone found out that she had spent a night alone in the room with Gus, her reputation would be ruined for ever. There was only one way to save face now, and that was to go to the Grecian Theatre and convince the producer that she was talented enough to take Liza Day's place. If she was successful, the rest would be easy. She did not need Gus to tell her what to do.

'Where's that food you ordered? I'm starving.'

Gus settled down in a chair by the desultory fire. 'I'm beginning to think I made a serious mistake in bringing you here, Dolly. I was carried away by your big blue eyes and your winning ways. It's a good thing I'm a gentleman, that's all I can say.'

'You can leave at any time you wish. I'm sure I don't want to be a burden to you, Gus Baker.'

He shook his head. 'Tomorrow morning, first thing, I'm going to take you to your uncle Freddie's house in Piccadilly. I'd as soon leave a lamb amongst a pack of wolves than abandon you to whatever fate has in store for you in London. I don't often admit I'm in the wrong, but this is one of those times.' Gus rose to his feet at the sound of a timid tap on the door and he opened it, taking the tray of food and jug of ale from Bess. 'Thank you. We won't be needing anything else.'

'Yes, sir.' Bess bobbed a curtsey but her shy smile

was wiped away by a look of fear at the sound of the landlord's voice summoning her to hurry downstairs.

Gus placed the tray on a small, rather rickety table under the window. 'It doesn't smell too bad. Best eat it while it's hot.'

Dolly rose to her feet and went to join him. 'I'll eat it because I'm hungry, but I can tell you this, Gus, I am going to the Grecian Theatre in the morning. Neither you, nor anyone else, is going to stop me.'

Chapter Three

Dolly slept surprisingly well, despite the uncomfortable bed and questionable cleanliness of the sheets. She was awakened early by the sound of the brewer's dray unloading barrels into the cellar, and she sat up in bed, peering at Gus. Thankfully he was sleeping soundly in the chair by the fireplace and she got up, taking care not to disturb him.

She had not pursued the argument last evening, but she had no intention of going to Uncle Freddie for help. This was a situation of her own making, even if she had confused Gus's obvious attraction to her for something deeper. She stood, for a moment, gazing down at him with a sigh. He was no doubt a fine figure of a man, totally unlike the skinny, gangly boy she remembered. It would be very easy to fall in love with someone so different from the young men she had met previously, but it was not to be, at least not for the present. Dolly had a purpose this morning, and that was to find the theatre and announce her arrival. She put on her mantle, bonnet and gloves, picked up her valise and crept out of the room, closing the door softly behind her.

The taproom was empty, except for a small figure huddled in the corner. The sound of muffled sobbing made Dolly hesitate. She knew she ought to leave immediately, but she realised that it was young Bess and she went over to her.

'What's wrong?'

Bess lifted her tear-stained face to reveal a swollen cheek, striped with red weals. 'Don't worry about me, miss.'

'Who did this to you?' Dolly asked, although she knew the answer before Bess muttered the landlord's name.

'Please don't say anything, miss. He'll kill me next time. I'll end up at the bottom of the river.'

'He won't lay a finger on you ever again. You must come with me.'

Bess cowered against the back of a chair. 'Where to, miss? I got no home to go to if you don't want me.'

'That's easy. I am looking for somewhere to lodge and you can help me. Do you know where the Royal Grecian Theatre is?'

'Yes, miss. On the corner of Shepherdess Walk and City Road. I come from Shoreditch originally.'

'Good. Then that's where we're going. You can pretend to be my maid. But on second thoughts, maybe that's not a good idea. I'll think of something. Have you got a coat and hat?'

'I got a shawl in the back room, but I daren't go and get it. He'll have me for sure. I broke a couple of plates and I'll get another beating.'

Dolly frowned. 'I don't think it's too cold outside. I have a spare shawl you can have.' She opened her valise and pulled out a woollen shawl that had been a last-minute addition. Packing her own clothes was something she had never done previously and it had been a case of flinging in whatever came to hand. 'We'd better hurry,' Dolly added as she rushed to the door to make sure that the landlord was not outside with the draymen. She beckoned to Bess. 'All clear. Come on.'

She walked off in the opposite direction to the men from the brewery, with Bess running after her. They turned the corner of the street to see a hansom cab pulling away from the kerb. Dolly waved frantically.

'Cabby, wait, please.'

Dragging her valise in one hand and grabbing Bess with the other, Dolly reached the cab before the cabby could drive off and she thrust Bess into the vehicle, throwing the case in after her.

'The Royal Grecian Theatre, please, Cabby.' Dolly climbed in and sat beside Bess, who was very pale and close to tears. 'Don't worry. We're in this together now. I'll look after you and you can guide me round the parts of London I don't know. We'll be fine.'

Bess's lips trembled. 'I've been at the pub since I was seven. Mr Warren got me from the orphans' home.'

'So you haven't got any family?'

'Not that I know of, miss.'

'Well, I can't have a maid. That wouldn't fit in with Liza Day's social standing,' Dolly said thoughtfully.

'Who is Liza Day, miss? That's not you, is it? I mean, I heard the gent calling you "Dolly".'

'That's right. I'm Dolly Blanchard. It's a long story, Bess. I think it best if we leave it now, but you could pretend to be my younger sister, if asked.'

'Why are you doing this for me, miss?'

'You should call me Dolly in private, but Liza in public if we're to get away with the deception. To tell you the truth I don't know why I've taken you on, Bess. Maybe I'm nervous about being in London on my own. Gus was right about one thing: I don't know this part of the city. In fact, I lived in luxury and was utterly spoilt. I'm beginning to realise that now.'

'So why are you here? Why not go home, wherever that is, and live like you always have?'

'I don't know, and that's the truth. There's something in me that says I can do well without my family. I'm tired of being told what to do all the

43

time. They would like to choose a husband for me, but that's not what I want.'

'He's a handsome gentleman,' Bess said wistfully. 'He was ever so nice to me. Are you going to marry him?'

'Heavens, no! Well, I did allow myself to be carried away by a single kiss, but I realise now that it wouldn't do at all. In fact, I think I used Gus to get to London. That doesn't speak well of my character, I'm afraid.'

'I think you're very brave, miss. I mean, Dolly.'

'I don't know about that.' Dolly gazed at the buildings on either side of the busy street. She did not recognise a single landmark. 'It seems like a long way to City Road. I'm afraid this is going to be expensive.'

The cab fare exceeded all Dolly's worst fears, but she was left with no choice other than to hand the money over with the minimum tip. She was in half a mind to give the grumpy cabby the exact amount, but she had seen other drivers berate mean passengers and she did not want to draw attention to herself outside the theatre.

Faced with the grand exterior and a doorman who did not look as if he suffered fools gladly, Dolly was suddenly nervous. She was no longer Miss Adela Blanchard of Rockwood Castle, about to perform in front of her grandmother; she was Liza Day, a poor girl who would have to prove herself on her own merits.

'Stage door. Don't you know nothing?' The doorman dismissed them with an impatient wave of his hand.

The older man at the stage door was also world-weary and had obviously seen many hopefuls walk past him and out again into a world of obscurity. He eyed Dolly's attire with a sceptical curl of his lip.

'Are you sure you've come to the right place, miss? You look a bit too fine for a performer.'

'Yes, I'm Liza Day. You should have my name on a list of some sort. I passed an audition a couple of weeks ago. I was told to report here.' Dolly was determined to gain admittance regardless of what it took.

He shrugged. 'Go on in, then. But the young 'un stays outside. It's more than my job's worth to let all and sundry in.'

'My sister is part of the act,' Dolly said firmly. 'The producer will be very angry if she isn't allowed in.'

'Go on then. But don't be surprised if he throws you both out.' He waved them past, and Dolly marched in with more confidence than she was feeling, Bess following her.

They entered the auditorium to find the final auditions in full swing.

'You'd best sit where they won't see you,' Dolly said, pointing to the back row. 'I'll leave my case with you.'

'All right, miss. If you say so.'

Dolly took off her gloves and mantle and left them with Bess. Taking a deep breath, she marched down the aisle to where a middle-aged man stood with a notepad in his hand.

'Name?'

'I'm Liza Day. I was here a while ago and told to return for another audition.'

He eyed her keenly. 'Funny, I don't remember you.'

'I expect you see hundreds of young ladies in a week,' Dolly said glibly. 'I can tell you, I made a good impression.'

'Hmm,' he said dubiously. 'Cocky and full of your-self. We'll see. Have you brought your music?'

'I left it in my rooms. I can sing any popular song your pianist chooses to play.'

'As I said, cocky. You'll perform your dance, too.'

'My dance?' Dolly stared at him in dismay.

'You obviously impressed us with your terpsicho-rean ability before.'

'Yes, of course I can dance.'

'Up on the stage then. We've never had such a well-dressed chorus girl before. Let's see what you can do.'

Dolly made her way onto the stage and stood there, blinking in the glare of the footlights.

'What song, miss?' The pianist's voice came out of the darkness.

'Do you know "Beautiful Dreamer"?' Dolly said in desperation.

'I should say I do.' The pianist played the introduction and Dolly launched into the song. She pretended that she was singing to Grandmama and Grandpa Claude, trying to forget that she had the most critical audience in London seated in the front row. The footlights made it difficult to see the auditorium in detail, but she could make out the shape of the producer and his assistant, and they were chatting together throughout her song. She stopped singing and performed a few steps, hoping they would look up to see why she had stopped and they did. She twirled and executed a few movements of her own, ending to dead silence.

'Next.' A voice from the front row made Dolly peer into the darkness.

'What does that mean?'

'It means: please get off the stage. Leave your name with my assistant and we'll get back to you if we decide to take you on.'

'But I need to know now, sir.'

The producer rose to his feet. 'Young lady, you are obviously not the sort of person who usually turns up for an audition, nor have you the necessary talent to be in the chorus. Please leave now, or do I have to call the doorman to escort you out of the theatre?'

'But I'm Liza Day. You told me to come back for a second audition.'

'I don't care who you are, love. You failed this one. Next.'

Reluctantly, Dolly climbed down from the stage and walked slowly to where Bess was still sitting.

'There are other theatres,' Bess said softly. 'I thought you was good, miss.'

'Not good enough, apparently.' Dolly took her gloves and mantle back from Bess and put them on. 'There's no point waiting here. Come on.'

'Where will we go now?' Bess asked anxiously. 'I can't go back to the inn. Not after leaving like that.'

'You don't have to. I'll think of something.' Dolly marched past the stage-door keeper with her head held high, but once out in the street she was not so confident. 'What would Liza Day do?' she said out loud.

'You keep on about this person,' Bess said crossly. 'Who is she?'

Dolly sighed. 'I met her briefly in my grandmama's theatre. She was auditioning for a part in one of their productions. I'm afraid I boasted about my abilities on stage, but I really thought I had a chance. I was arrogant, I realise that now. I thought I could take her place and send the money I was convinced I would earn to help her and her grandmother.'

'It seems to me that you meant well, miss.'

'Yes, I did, but that doesn't help us now. I really didn't know what I was saying and I made a promise I simply can't keep.'

'The handsome sergeant will be looking for you, miss. I think he is spiffing.'

Dolly laughed. 'I suppose he is, but I walked away from him. I can't go back.'

'I think you can. He's a real gent, in my opinion. After all, he brought you to London, didn't he?'

'Yes, but only because I made him. I'm used to getting my own way, Bess.'

'So let's go and find him. I bet he's worried sick. You should say you're sorry and he'll forgive you.'

'Do you really think so?'

'There's only one way to find out, miss.'

Dolly weighed her reticule in her hand. She knew by the lightness of the purse inside that the cab fare had made a considerable dent in the amount of money she had brought with her. Unused to paying for anything, she had no idea how much everything cost. But Bess was right – there was little choice. It was either a visit to Uncle Freddie's mansion in Piccadilly or a return to the inn in the hope that Gus would still be there.

The cab ride back to the inn was a nail-biting journey for Dolly. For a start she did not know if Gus had returned to his regiment in disgust, and, if he had waited for her, she would not blame him if he was angry.

The sight of Gus pacing the pavement in front of the inn was not encouraging, but the look of relief on his face when Dolly stepped out of the cab re-assured her a little.

'Gus, I am so sorry not to have left a note.'

'Where on earth have you been? And why did you take the servant girl with you?'

'Could we talk somewhere else?' Dolly eyed the entrance to the inn apprehensively. Warren, the land-lord, was the last person she wanted to see.

'I dare not go inside,' Bess said nervously. 'He'll beat me until I don't know the time of day.'

Gus smiled. 'Well, we can't allow that. Come with me.' He tucked Dolly's hand in the crook of his arm and walked briskly down the road towards a respectable-looking coffee house where he found them a table in the window.

'I know I owe you an explanation.' Dolly eyed him warily. 'I went for the audition at the Royal Grecian Theatre.'

'But you took your valise. That was a sign you did not intend to return if successful.'

'I told her to take it, guv,' Bess said hastily. 'Old Warren ain't above going through a guest's things for any little trinkets that might fetch money at the pawnshop.'

'It's all right, Bess.' Dolly laid her hand on Bess's skinny arm. 'I need to tell Gus the truth. You're right, Gus. I was going to strike out on my own.' She sat back on the wooden settle and sighed. 'There, I've admitted that I'm a hateful person. When I realised that you didn't want me, I was angry and hurt. I really thought I was as good, if not better than Liza Day, and I would be given her part in the production.'

Gus turned to face Dolly. 'So you didn't get it?'

She shook her head, staring down at the table. 'No. I did not. I wasn't good enough.'

'That must have been hard to admit, Dolly.' Gus's tone softened. 'I'm sorry.'

'Are you? Or are you laughing at me, Gus?'

'I've had enough rejections in my life to make me sympathetic. There's no sin in being ambitious.'

'But I promised Liza I would send the money I thought I was going to make to help her and her grandmother. Now I can't even afford decent lodgings. I know, I should have thought it out before I persuaded you to bring me to London. I've made a terrible mess of things.'

'I must take part of the blame. I should not have encouraged you to leave home. I ought to have known better, but I do care for you, Dolly. I will marry you, if that's what you want.'

'I don't think that's the answer.' Dolly met his worried expression with an attempt at a smile. 'I was carried away with a romantic idea, Gus. No one has ever kissed me like that.'

He dropped his gaze, shaking his head. 'It was unforgivable. I'm sorry.'

'Don't be.' Dolly reached out to lay her small hand on his arm. 'I could have slapped your face and sent you on your way. I wish I was a lady like Mama. She is so perfect and understanding, but I think even she would be ashamed of me.'

'I wish I had a ma like that,' Bess said, sighing.

'I doubt if I'll be welcome at Rockwood Castle after this.' Gus moved aside as the waiter brought their coffee. 'Have you any cake or pastries?'

'Yes, sir. I'll bring some for you.' The waiter hurried off, threading his way between the tightly packed tables.

Gus leaned towards Dolly. 'Be honest with me. What do you want me to do? I am responsible for your being here. I can't just rejoin my regiment and leave you on your own in London.'

'I would have come here with or without you, Gus. I must find my own solution.'

Bess eyed the plate of cakes that the waiter brought them. 'Can I have one, miss?'

'Yes, of course. Eat what you want.' Dolly frowned. 'I have to face the fact that I didn't bring enough money to live on in London. I didn't stop to think of the consequences of my decision to come with you, Gus. I can either return home, or go to Piccadilly and ask Uncle Freddie for help.'

'I'm not leaving you to manage alone,' Gus said firmly. 'Either I take you to the railway station, or to Piccadilly and Lord Dorrington's mansion. Nancy would never forgive me if I abandoned you now.'

Dolly bit her lip. She knew that Gus was talking sense, but her rebellious spirit came to the fore. She could not go home and admit she had been wrong, and it would be a similar experience if she went to Uncle Freddie. He was someone she loved and respected, but she did not want to lose face in his eyes. What she had done was the action of a spoilt child and now she must pay the price of that folly. She looked up and met Gus's troubled expression with a nod. 'All right, Gus. I'll allow you to take us both to Piccadilly and I'll do the rest.'

Gus uttered a deep sigh. 'Thank goodness. I thought you might be stubborn about this, Dolly. I remember what you were like when you were younger.'

'You hardly knew me then.'

'No, but Nancy was always very fond of you. She used to tell us stories about things you did, mainly, I think, as a warning to us boys to behave or face the consequences.'

'Well, I'm doing that now.' Dolly turned to Bess, who was munching her way through the fancies on the plate in front of her. 'I'll take you with me, if you wish. I won't let you go back to that horrible man, Warren.'

'Thank you, miss.' Bess licked her fingers one by one. 'May I have another cake before we go?'

Gus laughed. 'You may have another plateful, if you wish. I like to see a girl enjoying her food. That goes for you, too, Dolly. I'm sure they have plenty more delicacies in the kitchen.'

'I'll save my appetite for Uncle Freddie's chef,' Dolly said hastily. 'Going hungry won't be a problem.'

Gus reached out to take her hand in his. 'I would marry you like a shot, you know that. I hate myself for bringing you to this.'

'Maybe I'll take you up on that proposal one day, but not now. I won't forget you, Gus.'

They said goodbye in the hackney carriage outside the Piccadilly mansion. Dolly insisted on going on alone from there, and she sensed that Gus was relieved. He kissed her gently on the cheek before helping her from the cab. She waited until he was seated and waved him off. The busy thoroughfare seemed suddenly quiet and Dolly had never felt so alone, but she hesitated, staring at the glossy black front door with its shiny brass knocker and the troughs on the lower windowsills spilling over with daffodils and primroses. And still she could not bring herself to knock on the door.

Bess stood quietly at her side, looking round wide-eyed as she wrapped Dolly's old shawl tightly around her shoulders. 'What now, miss?'

That was a good question and Dolly had no ready answer. Dorrington House was one of several great residences in this part of Piccadilly, where only the extremely rich lived, and then usually only for the London Season. The even grander dwelling immediately adjacent was set back from the street behind iron railings and a tall gate, which swung open suddenly, making a clanging sound. A liveried footman strode out onto the pavement. He looked up and down the street before pointing to Dolly.

'Why are you loitering out here, miss? We've been waiting for you to arrive.'

Dolly shook her head. 'You must be mistaken.'

'You are Miss Jane Harding, here to interview for the position of the new lady's maid, are you not? Miss Theodora is furious.'

Dolly was about to tell him that he was making a mistake when an idea occurred to her. She glanced at Bess, who put her head on one side like a cheeky sparrow, and grinned.

'I am Miss Harding, and this is Bess Finley, the new housemaid.'

'I know nothing of that, miss. Will you come this way?'

'I arranged the appointment with the housekeeper, Mrs . . . I seem to have forgotten her name.'

'Mrs Worley, miss. I'll have to check with her and Mr Soames, the butler.'

'You may leave all that to me, James.'

'You know my name?'

Dolly knew that most footmen were called James by their employers. It saved them the trouble of remembering names of underlings. 'Of course,' she said airily. 'Will you show us the way, please?'

'Certainly, miss. It will be my pleasure.'

James led them through the main courtyard to an entrance at the side of the great house. 'I dare say Miss Theodora will want to see you first.'

Dolly entered the side door and followed the footman down a flight of stone steps and through a maze of passageways on the lower ground floor. He seemed to have forgotten Bess and she kept as close to Dolly as possible, clutching her skirt. Dolly gave her an encouraging smile.

'Don't worry. I remember this household,' she said quietly. 'Miss Theodora is a couple of years younger than me and she wasn't out when I did the London Season. But I know that Lord Bennington, her papa, is even wealthier than Uncle Freddie. They have so many servants in this household that they'll hardly notice a new girl.'

As if to underline this point, a harassed-looking woman, dressed in sombre black, rushed past them.

'Come with me, girl. Why are you loitering here? I told you to clear up the broken china in the drawing room.' She came to a halt and thrust a dustpan and brush into Bess's hand. 'I don't care what errand Mrs Worley sent you on, this is more important. Hurry, before Miss Theodora smashes another price-less figurine.'

Bess sent a pleading look to Dolly.

'Go on. This is your chance to establish yourself here.' Dolly gave Bess a gentle push so that she had little choice other than to run after the woman in black. Dolly walked on, keeping close to James as he climbed the steep stone staircase leading to the first floor.

'What is going on?' Dolly demanded in a low voice.

James glanced over his shoulder. 'Miss Theodora has gone through several lady's maids in the last month. I wish you good luck, Miss Harding.'

'Who is the frantic lady? Is she the housekeeper?'

'Mrs Brown is the assistant housekeeper, miss. Perhaps you'd better wait until she's made the going safe.'

It seemed that they were all heading for the same destination and Dolly waited with James while Mrs Brown timidly knocked on the drawing-room door. There must have been a reply from within, as the assistant housekeeper entered warily, followed by Bess. James held his finger to his lips, listening intently.

'Where is she? Where is this woman who has not the decency to arrive on time? I refuse to wait another second.' The door was flung open again and a young woman rushed out, almost bumping into James and Dolly.

'Who is this, James?'

'Miss Harding, Miss Theodora. She seemed to be a little lost when I went outside to look for her.'

Theodora brushed back her tangled mop of dark curls, glaring at Dolly. 'She can't be very bright if she gets lost in Piccadilly. Are you stupid, Miss Harding?'

Dolly was tempted to tell Miss Theodora what she thought of such rudeness, but she was curious. 'No, Miss Bennington, I am not stupid. It seems that one of us mistook the time of my interview.'

'Are you accusing me of making an error?' Theodora gazed at Dolly, wide-eyed with disbelief.

It occurred to Dolly that very few people had ever

spoken back to this spoilt young woman. 'If you don't want to hire me I have another appointment in an hour. Make your mind up, if you please. I cannot afford to waste time.'

Theodora's jaw dropped and her dark eyes narrowed. 'I should have you thrown out.'

'No need. I'm going. I don't mind what I do but I demand respect as a human being, even if I am not such a spoilt, rich person as you are, Miss Bennington.'

Dolly was not certain but she thought she heard James snigger, and Mrs Brown appeared in the doorway, staring at her open-mouthed.

James recovered quickly. 'Shall I escort this person out, Miss Theodora?'

'No. Not yet. Come into the drawing room, Miss Harding. I want to know you better before I have you thrown out onto the street. You may go about your duties, Mrs Brown, and you too, James.' Theodora marched back into the drawing room and stood with her arms folded, looking Dolly up and down. 'You are not a common servant. I'm curious.'

Bess had been left clearing the broken shards of china from the floor and her gasp alerted Theodora to her presence. She turned on her angrily. 'Get out, girl. Leave the room immediately.'

Bess scrambled to her feet and hurried from the room.

'That is no way to speak to a servant, however low in the hierarchy,' Dolly said angrily. 'Why should someone who has to earn their own living be inferior to someone like yourself, Miss Bennington?'

'You dare to question your betters?'

'I don't accept that anyone is automatically my superior. Respect has to be earned, Miss Bennington. Rudeness in any form is unacceptable.'

Theodora gave Dolly a piercing look. 'You intrigue me. That doesn't mean I am going to hire you.' She sank down onto a chair by the fireplace. 'I just want to know why you think you are as good as me.'

'Surely my opinion doesn't matter to someone like you? Either conduct this interview or let me leave now. I am not sure I want to work here anyway. It is up to you, Miss Bennington. As for myself, I could not care less whether you hire me or not.'

Chapter Four

'Who are you, Miss Harding? I don't believe you are a lady's maid.'

'I am Jane Harding and I was Miss Adela Blanchard's maid until she left home to marry.'

'I believe I've heard of Miss Blanchard. I think she was Lord Dorrington's protégée and she came out two years before me.'

'Miss Blanchard will gladly furnish me with a reference.'

'Yes, I would need that, should I decide to hire you.' Theodora frowned and for a moment her confident manner slipped and she seemed very young and unsure of herself. 'You are very forward. I'm not used to servants speaking out for themselves.'

'A lady's maid is more than an ordinary servant, Miss Bennington. If you didn't acknowledge this, it's probably why none of your previous employees has stayed with you for long.'

'That is none of your business.'

'Then I take it I am free to leave now. The interview is concluded.' Dolly walked to the door.

'No, stay. I will give you a month's trial, subject to a good reference from Miss Blanchard, of course.' Theodora rang the bell to summon a servant. 'Mrs Brown will show you to your room, which is adjacent to mine on the next floor. I insist that you are near at hand for when I need you. I take it that you are free to start right away?'

'I can see you need someone, but I have yet to be convinced that I am she.'

'You think a great deal of yourself, Miss Harding. I should send you on your way, but I confess you intrigue me.'

Mrs Brown knocked and entered. 'You rang, Miss Theodora?'

'I want you to show Miss Harding the room she will have if she takes up the position as my personal maid.'

'The one recently vacated, Miss Theodora?'

'No. She will have Essie's old room, if we come to a mutual agreement.'

Mrs Brown raised an eyebrow. 'Come this way, please, Miss Harding.'

'Come back with your reference and we will speak again.' Theodora turned away and picked up a book of fashion plates.

'Follow me, please, miss.' Tight-lipped and rigid in her disapproval, Mrs Brown led the way from the drawing room. This time they negotiated the grand staircase and not the back stairs used by the servants. Mrs Brown came to a halt. 'This is Miss Theodora's room.' She held the door open for Dolly to look at the interior.

It was a large room with tall windows, and elegantly furnished, as Dolly would have expected. Mrs Brown closed the door and moved on to the next room. She turned to give Dolly a curious look.

'This was Miss Lane's room. She was Miss Theodora's personal maid for several years.'

'Essie?'

'Yes, Essie Lane. She left to get married. After that, the subsequent maids slept in the servants' quarters on the top floor.' Mrs Brown flung open the door to the adjacent room.

Dolly stepped inside and looked round with a nod of approval. It was not as large as Theodora's room but it was a good size, well-furnished, and the bed looked comfortable. It was far superior to the room at the inn and much better accommodation than she had expected. But there was still one problem. Dolly turned to Mrs Brown.

'The young girl who came in with me is Bess Finley. She isn't actually employed here, but if I accept the position with Miss Theodora it will be part of the agreement that you take Bess on in any capacity that you see fit. She's a good girl and she'll work hard if she's treated well.'

A look of contempt crossed Mrs Brown's plain face. 'Who are you, miss? You're no servant.'

'I am Miss Harding, lady's maid. That's all you need to know, Mrs Brown. I've seen enough. Please take me back to your mistress.'

Dolly entered the drawing room, leaving Mrs Brown hovering in the doorway. 'I've decided to accept the position, Miss Bennington.'

Theodora laid the magazine carefully on the low table in front of her. 'Have you now? What would you say if I told you I had withdrawn the offer?'

'I would say you would be losing the opportunity to take on someone who understands just what a young lady in your position wants and needs.'

'You are very sure of yourself.' Theodora met Dolly's steady look with a challenge in her dark eyes. 'If you can provide me with a reference, I might take a risk on you. On a month's trial, as I said.'

'Naturally.' Dolly turned to leave, glancing over her shoulder. 'You won't regret it, I promise you that.' She marched past Mrs Brown, lowering her voice. 'I'll hold you to taking on Miss Finley.'

'It isn't up to me, miss.'

'I'm sure you have more influence than you admit to, Mrs Brown. I trust you to do this one thing for me.'

'You haven't got the job as yet, miss.'

'It's a mere formality.'

Dolly was about to head for the front entrance but Mrs Brown hissed at her, 'The servants' entrance is at the side of the residence, miss.'

Dolly decided not to chance her luck any further. She made her way out of the building and tucked her valise beneath an ornamental holly bush. There was only one way she could get a reference on headed writing paper and that was to risk knocking on the door of Dorrington House. She could only hope that Uncle Freddie was at his country estate, otherwise there would be a great deal of explaining to do. She left the premises and headed next door to Dorrington House.

Atkins, the head footman, opened the door.

'Good morning, Atkins,' Dolly said airily. 'Is Lord Dorrington at home?'

He shook his head. 'Lord Dorrington is in the country, Miss Blanchard.'

'I left some personal belongings in my room, Atkins. I wish to collect them.'

Atkins stood aside. 'Certainly, miss. Might I assist you, or would you prefer a maid?'

'No, thank you. I can manage on my own. I won't be long.' Dolly sailed past him and ascended the grand staircase as if she were still a guest in the house. She was certain that her room would have been kept in order and she was pleased to find that her assumption was correct. Nothing had changed since her last visit and she went straight to the escritoire beneath one of the windows and sat down. She found pen and ink and selected a sheet of headed paper. Theodora already knew that Adela Blanchard had been staying at Dorrington House and that made it easier to write a reference for Jane Harding, who had supposedly worked for the Blanchard family in Devonshire. Keeping as close to the truth as possible would make life more straightforward.

Dolly paused, staring at the blank sheet of deckle-edged writing paper, and she was suddenly assailed by doubts. Would life in London, serving as a lady's maid, be preferable to going home and admitting that she had made a terrible mistake? On the other hand, she would find her reputation ruined if anyone discovered that she and Gus had slept in the same bedroom, even though it was totally innocent and brought about by necessity. She chewed the end of the steel pen, running through all the possibilities in her mind. Perhaps time was of the essence. Maybe if she stuck to her plan and stayed in London for a few months, the whole scandal would blow over and everyone at home would be delighted to welcome her back into the fold. Or perhaps she would find another way to carve a future for herself. She took a deep breath and began to write her own reference.

Eventually, after wasting several sheets of expensive writing paper, Dolly was satisfied with the result. She folded the missive and tucked it into her reticule.

It would be interesting to see how a servant was treated in a great house from an individual perspective. Dolly had been brought up to consider the staff at Rockwood Castle as part of the family, but it was obvious that Miss Bennington thought differently. Dolly had sudden misgivings but she had gone too far to back out now, and she left her luxurious room with a sigh of regret, closing the door on her old life before going downstairs.

A commotion in the entrance hall made her hesitate as she rounded the curve in the sweeping staircase. To her dismay she saw Uncle Freddie with his valet, Jenkins. The under footmen were hurrying to and fro, bringing in luggage from the front entrance. Freddie looked up and his face broke into a smile of pure relief.

'Dolly. Thank God you're here.'

She descended slowly. 'You came to London looking for me?'

'Of course I did. Your family are distraught. Your papa and your uncle Walter have been scouring the countryside, but it was your mama who sent for me and I came as soon as I could.'

'I've been gone for a day,' Dolly said, torn between laughter and tears of frustration.

'Your leaving was dramatic, my dear. You marched into the Black Dog and walked out with Gus Baker, as witnessed by Claude and Nick Gibson and half the male population of Rockwood village.' Freddie shrugged off his greatcoat and handed it to his valet, together with his gloves and hat. 'What were you thinking?'

Dolly shot a wary glance in Jenkins' direction but he turned away, concentrating his attention on issuing instructions to the footmen.

'I wanted to have a life of my own, Uncle.'

Freddie took her by the arm and propelled her into the chinoiserie room. He closed the door, facing her with a questioning look. 'Really? Did you run off with Sergeant Baker, expecting him to marry you?'

'Not exactly. Well, I suppose I did in a way. I was confused and flattered by his attention. Not only that, but I made a promise to someone, which I find I cannot keep.'

Freddie sighed and motioned her to sit down. 'Start at the beginning, Dolly. You know I am always on your side, but you seem to have behaved very badly this time.'

Dolly sank onto the sofa, shaking her head. 'It must look like that, but my intentions were good. I thought I had talent, like Aunt Patricia and Grandmama. I promised Liza Day that I would send her money to help her take care of her ailing grandmother.'

'Who is Liza Day?'

'She's a girl I met at the Pavilion Theatre when I went on stage to prove to Gus that I had talent. Liza was upset because she needed the part in the production because she had come down from London to take care of her aged grandmother. They are very poor and I boasted that I could take Liza's part at the Royal Grecian Theatre. I said I would send her the money I earned.' Dolly threw up her hands. 'I know, I was vain and stupid. I assumed I could take Liza's place on stage at the Royal Grecian Theatre – I was wrong.'

'You could have asked me for help. You know that I care very much for you and your family.'

Dolly nodded. 'Yes, of course I do, but I wanted to make a mark in the world on my own.'

'I suppose I can understand that. I always knew I would have to take on the responsibility for the estate and all the people who depend upon my family for their wellbeing.'

'But that is important, Uncle Freddie. You are doing something worthwhile.'

'You were born to the life you lead, Dolly. One day you will marry and have children. You will run a household, just like your mama.'

'I have found a job,' Dolly said bluntly. 'I was mistaken for a woman who applied for a position as lady's maid to Miss Theodora Bennington and that's why I came here.' She produced the reference from her reticule. 'I forged this so that she would take me on.'

Freddie took the letter and unfolded it. Dolly waited, expecting him to react angrily but he burst into laughter. 'Dolly Blanchard, you are priceless. Have you any idea what Miss Bennington is like?'

'I think I have. She needs taking in hand.'

'But not by a servant, my dear. Theodora is a

termagant, even at her age. She's notorious for treating servants badly. Her mama died when Theodora was eight and her papa has spoiled and indulged her. I know her socially, but I wouldn't put any young woman in her path and that includes you.'

'I can handle her, Uncle Freddie.'

'You may think so now, Dolly, but you would be at her mercy. She can be quite vicious, so I've been told. I keep well away from her.'

Dolly put her head on one side. 'Has she been flirting with you? Does she have ambitions to be Lady Dorrington?'

'She is young enough to be my daughter. It would be a braver man than I am to take her on.' Freddie tore the letter in half and threw it onto the fire. 'I can't stop you if that's what you want, Dolly. But please reconsider. I am here in London at your disposal. I'm begging you to stay here with me and think carefully about what you want to do.'

'I took a servant girl, Bess Finley, from the inn where we stayed last night and I persuaded the assistant housekeeper to employ her in some menial position. I can't abandon her.'

'You stayed at an inn? With Gus Baker?'

'Yes, but it's not what it sounds like. We had to share a room but he slept in a chair.'

Freddie held up his hand. 'Don't tell me anything else. I think that part of your story should be forgotten. Where is Baker now?'

'He has to return to his regiment.'

'Then I need to speak to him before he disappears.'

'Don't make a fuss, Uncle. Really, he behaved like a gentleman. He brought me here today because I told him I was coming to stay with you.'

'A gentleman wouldn't have taken you from your family, let alone slept in the same room in a cheap inn. I'm not going to create a scene. I just want him to return to his regiment without contacting you again. Where did you stay last night?'

'If I tell you, will you promise not to harm Gus? He's a good man. He only came with me because I said I would go alone if he refused.'

'I understand, but I want you to tell me the name of the inn, and you must promise that you will remain here at least until I return. You are not to go back to the Benningtons' mansion for any reason.'

'But what about Bess?'

'Leave that to me. I'll send Atkins round to speak to their housekeeper. We'll say it was a mistake. Atkins will bring her here and find her a position in the kitchens. We always need staff.'

'All right,' Dolly said reluctantly. 'I promise to stay here, but only for tonight. I'll think about what I want to do tomorrow. But *I'll* go to the Bennington house and get Bess. I made the mistake of taking her there; it's up to me to rectify the matter.'

Freddie gave her a discerning look. 'You're going to confront Miss Theodora, aren't you?'

'I have to do this, Uncle Freddie. That woman needs to be put in her place.'

'All right. If you must. Now I'm going to see if I can catch up with Sergeant Baker. What was the name of the inn?'

Dolly waited until Freddie had left the building. She did not relish another meeting with Miss Theodora Bennington, but it was necessary to rescue Bess and set matters straight. She had left her valise under the ornamental holly bush and it contained all the items she had brought with her from home, although she had a clothes press filled with garments in her room in Dorrington House, which she had decided to leave behind when she returned to Rockwood. Dolly braced herself for an uncomfortable meeting as she left the security of the Dorrington residence and entered the grand portals of the Bennington mansion.

Soames himself answered her knock on the front door, and it was obvious that he recognised her. Dolly stepped over the threshold.

'I am not who you think I am, Soames. Please tell Miss Bennington that Miss Adela Blanchard wishes to see her.'

Soames gave nothing away by his stony expression. 'Please wait here, Miss Blanchard.' He walked off in the direction of the drawing room and returned a couple of minutes later.

'Miss Bennington will see you, Miss Blanchard. If you will follow me . . .'

Dolly marched past him. 'It's all right, Soames. I

know the way.' Despite her misgivings, she was looking forward to seeing the expression on Theodora's face when she realised that Miss Blanchard and Jane Harding were one and the same person. She opened the door and walked into the drawing room.

'Good afternoon, Miss Bennington.'

'Is this some kind of joke?' Theodora demanded angrily. 'I suppose you think this is amusing, Harding.'

'It is rather funny, Theodora. But I'm afraid your servant mistook me for the errant Miss Harding and I chose to take on the woman's identity, for a while, at least.'

'How dare you come into my home and boast about a criminal deed? I should send for the police.'

'Do that if you wish, but I have committed no crime. I came to introduce myself and to tell you that I am staying with my uncle, Lord Dorrington, for the present. Should we meet socially, which is something I doubt, I wanted to spare you any further embarrassment.' Dolly had the satisfaction of seeing Miss Theodora Bennington at a complete loss for words. 'Good day,' Dolly added amicably as she left the room.

She met Soames, who was standing very close to the door. His smug expression convinced Dolly that he had been eavesdropping.

'Will you kindly send for the girl I brought with me today, Soames? Mrs Brown was going to take her on as a maid, but I have other plans for Bess Finley.'

Soames nodded. 'Certainly, Miss Blanchard.'

Dolly thought she saw a flicker of amusement cross his face before he turned and walked off with his measured tread. She waited, gazing at the gilt-framed oil paintings that graced the walls on the wide sweep of the staircase, and the delicate plasterwork of the ornate coving. Silver urns filled with hothouse flowers were placed on pier tables in between tall mirrors in the hall itself, reflecting light from the windows. Dolly imagined the shimmering rainbows that must be cast from the crystal chandeliers when the candles were lit at night. If Dorrington House was grand, Bennington Court was even more imposing, although Hester would have called the show of ostentation vulgar.

Dolly suppressed a giggle as she imagined the rusty suit of armour that once protected Sir Denys Carey in battle moved from Rockwood Castle and placed at the foot of the stairs here. Sir Denys would keep his visor well and truly shut when faced with Theodora Bennington. The idea amused Dolly, but it also made her feel very homesick.

She turned her head at the sound of small feet pitter-pattering over the marble-tiled floor and she smiled to see Bess hurrying towards her.

'Oh, miss. I'm so glad you came for me. Are we leaving?'

'Yes, Bess. I realised this was all a terrible mistake. We'll collect my valise first, but this is the last time I will set foot in Miss Theodora Bennington's house.'

Dolly walked past Soames, who was holding the door open for them. She treated him to a gracious smile, although she was tempted to give him a saucy wink. She managed to resist the impulse. After all, she was Miss Adela Blanchard of Rockwood Castle, and years of training in good manners and etiquette were not easy to put aside.

'Where are we going now, miss?' Bess asked as they stepped outside into the sunshine. 'You aren't going to send me back to Mr Warren, are you?'

'No, certainly not. First you can pick up my valise from under that holly bush and then we'll go to Dorrington House. I have some serious thinking to do.'

Over dinner that night Dolly faced questions from Freddie. She answered them honestly, safe in the knowledge that he would give her a fair hearing.

'Well,' Freddie said, smiling, 'I think I've grasped the whole situation now, Dolly. I have to say, you are not blameless, but the talk I had with Sergeant Baker reassured me that he had behaved in a gentlemanly manner towards you, if ill-advised. I like the fellow and I can see why you were attracted to him in the first place.'

'I know what I did was foolish,' Dolly said, sighing. 'I get so bored at home. I have nothing to complain about, and I should be grateful for the love and attention I receive, but it isn't enough. I want to do something useful. Can you understand that?'

Freddie laughed. 'You remind me so much of Nancy. I know you are not related by blood, but she had the same adventurous spirit and a desire to make the world a better place.'

'You still love her, don't you?' Dolly leaned back in her chair, eyeing him curiously. In the light of dozens of candles he looked younger than his thirty-four years, and his fair hair gleamed like spun gold with the hint of silver. She could imagine how he must have looked to Nancy when they were younger and, although Freddie was not exactly handsome, he had classic, even features and a pleasant expression that charmed anyone who knew him.

'Yes, I'll always love Nancy, but from afar. She is happily married to Tommy, who is my best friend, and I suppose I love them both equally. She is part of Rockwood, whether she likes to admit it or not. I could not have taken her away from the family she loved. In the end she would have resented me and my responsibilities to my estate.'

'But you could have found someone else, Uncle Freddie. You are still a young man.'

'That is very flattering as it comes from someone who is not yet twenty.'

'I will be twenty in October.'

'Such a great age.'

'Now you're laughing at me.'

'Not at all. I sympathise with your dilemma, Dolly. I really do.'

'I know I behaved badly. They will be so worried about me at home.'

'I sent a telegram to your papa. They know you are safe with me.'

'Thank you.' Dolly reached out to lay her hand on his. 'You are so good to me. I must seem very ungrateful after all the trouble you took over my coming-out season.'

'You have my cousin Margery to thank for that. She did everything; I merely footed the bill.'

'I should have shown more gratitude to her, too. I am quite ashamed of myself.'

'Perhaps it would be best if you enjoyed a brief holiday before returning to Devonshire. What do you think?'

Dolly stared at him, frowning. 'What do you mean?'

'Well, I agreed some time ago to take Cousin Margery and her two girls to Monte Carlo, where she has rented a villa overlooking the sea. Margery loves a flutter at the card table, and the Casino in Monte is quite the place to be seen. I think she hopes to find rich husbands for Isabella and Celia as well as having some fun herself.'

'Are you including me in the husband hunt, Uncle?'

'Dolly, my dear, I know better than to try to make you do anything you don't wish to do. But it might be entertaining. What do you think?'

Chapter Five

The villa rented by Lady Margery Faraday in Monaco exceeded all Dolly's wildest dreams. It was perched on a cliff overlooking Monte Carlo and the Ligurian Sea. The white stucco walls were half hidden beneath cascades of purple bougainvillea, and the terraced gardens were punctuated by tall Italian cypress trees. Gleaming marble statues in classical poses stood between terracotta pots overflowing with scarlet geraniums, and roses filled the air with their heady scent. All this could be seen from the balcony outside Dolly's bedchamber, and it was here that she took breakfast every morning, brought to her by Bess, who had accompanied the party to Monte Carlo.

Lady Margery's twin daughters, who had shared their coming-out parties with Dolly, were in the adjacent room and their balcony was within arm's reach. However, Isabella and Celia were not early risers like Dolly. They would have lain in bed until noon each day had their mother not issued strict rules against such idleness.

Lady Margery rose early every morning and was driven by her coachman to the nearest beach, where she took a dip in the sea. She tried to persuade Freddie to join her but he laughingly refused, explaining that he had never learned how to swim, and none of his cousin's verbal bullying could make him change his mind. From the vantage point of her balcony, Dolly could see the open landau as it made its way along the twisting roads to the villa, with Lady Margery shading herself beneath a colourful silk parasol. It was a signal for Dolly to lean over the railing and call out to Anna, the girls' maid, who would then do her best to get them up and dressed before their mother appeared on the scene.

After that it was definitely Lady Margery who ran things. Their days were crammed with appointments, whether it was a visit to a modiste or sightseeing. More often than not, there were invitations to morning coffee with some of Lady Margery's many friends and acquaintances who had also travelled south in search of sun and warmer weather, free from the vagaries of the English climate. There were visits to neighbouring villas, to admire the art treasures and lush gardens, and luncheon at various clubs in the town. A siesta in the afternoon was followed by tea, taken at various exclusive hotels and restaurants, and yet more people to meet. Then it was back to the villa to rest and change in readiness for the evening functions, which included invitations to dine, card parties and visits to the grand Casino.

Lady Margery made no secret of the fact that she was husband-hunting for her twin daughters, and Dolly suspected that she would be wise to keep in the background whenever an eligible bachelor put in an appearance. In any case, she had so far not met anyone who matched up to either Gus Baker or Todd Taylor, a fact she kept to herself, even from Uncle Freddie.

Freddie himself was aware that his cousin was also keeping an eye open for a suitable bride for him. Lady Margery did not approve of Freddie's single status, telling him openly that he owed it to the family name to marry and produce an heir. Freddie took it all good-naturedly and went his own way, much to Dolly's amusement. Sometimes the two of them slipped away from parties when Lady Margery's matchmaking became tedious. If she threw any gentleman in Dolly's direction he would be someone she had discarded as a suitable husband for either of her daughters.

Even allowing for Lady Margery's determined efforts to marry off her girls, there was always the relief from her matriarchal duties offered by the card tables and roulette. She forgot everything at the turn of a card or the spin of a wheel, and she seemed to be incredibly lucky. Occasionally she lost, but more often Lady Margery won, and came away from the Casino with a heavier purse and a triumphant smile.

They had been in Monaco for almost a month and Dolly was enjoying herself more than she would have thought possible. Everything was still new and exotic, so different from home or from the hurly-burly of London. She had not forgotten Gus Baker, but she realised that her feelings for him had been mere infatuation and would have been unlikely to withstand the challenges of a closer relationship. Being married to a military man was not the future she had seen for herself, and her family would definitely disapprove of such a union. However, Dolly wrote regularly to her mother and father and sent them pen-and-ink drawings of her surroundings. In fact, she was too busy to spend much time worrying about the past, although she knew this holiday must end and then she would have to return to the tedious routine of life in Devonshire. However, at the moment it was enough to enjoy the new experiences that were heaped upon her.

This afternoon a boat trip was planned so that the party could admire the beautiful coastline. Dolly could hardly wait. Their hosts were to be Sir Bradley and Lady Stanforth. He was a business tycoon who liked to boast that he was a self-made man, and he was not above flaunting his wealth. Sir Bradley would ordinarily have been avoided by Lady

Margery, but he had a son and heir who was equally successful in business, and he was unmarried. Isabella had her eye on handsome, charming Justin Stanforth, as had her sister, Celia. If she were being honest Dolly would have said Justin's eyes were too close set, and he was too well aware of being the catch of the season. Dolly didn't care for him and preferred to sit back and watch the sisters vie with each other for his attention. So far she had not met anyone who attracted her as Gus had done, but that made life easier. She was not looking for a husband.

It was still early morning and Dolly glanced over the balustrade to see the landau approaching. She jumped to her feet, abandoning her breakfast of coffee and croissants, and leaned over the railing to call Anna.

'Lady Margery is almost home,' Dolly shouted, rattling the fronds of bougainvillaea against the glass panes. 'Can you hear me, Anna?'

The French window opened. 'Yes, miss. I'll wake the young ladies.'

'Better hurry,' Dolly added. 'Their mama will be here in less than ten minutes.'

'Yes, miss.' Anna disappeared into the shady interior of the bedchamber and Dolly could hear her calling to the girls to wake up.

Dolly resumed her seat as Bess stepped out onto the balcony. 'Would you like some more coffee, miss?'

'No, thank you, Bess. I've finished my breakfast.

You may clear the table, and finish up the croissants if you are hungry.'

Bess grinned. 'Ta, miss. I must say I like them crescent-shaped things. I never had nothing like that before, and the jam is lovely, too.'

'Well, enjoy it while you can. We'll have to return home eventually.'

Bess's smile faded. 'But what will happen to me then, miss?'

'You'll come to Rockwood Castle with me, of course.' Dolly gave her an encouraging smile. 'You didn't think I'd abandon you in London, did you?'

'I dunno, miss. I know I ain't a good servant. At least I ain't had no training, not like Anna, although she's been teaching me how to do things proper.'

'Well, make the most of it. You can be my maid at home, if my parents permit, but if they refuse I'll find something for you, so don't worry.'

'Yes, miss. Thank you.' Bess cleared the table and took the tray away. She had only just left the bedroom when the door burst open and Lady Margery stepped into the room.

'I'm glad to see that you are up and dressed, Dolly. I hope my daughters are ready because there's a change of plan. We've been invited to a garden party at the Stanforths' at midday.'

'I should really stay in and write to my parents,' Dolly said evasively. She had taken a dislike to the Stanforths at the outset, especially Justin. The girls were welcome to him.

'Nonsense, I'm sure you can do that another time. I have it on good authority that the Stanforths have invited a member of the Grimaldi family, who is unmarried, and he will have brought with him his entourage and aides. Who knows what that means? One of my beautiful girls might marry into a royal family.'

'Then surely you don't want me there, ma'am?'

Lady Margery cast her a disparaging look. 'I don't think you will be serious competition for Isabella or Celia, but you will accompany Freddie and make sure he pays attention to the marriageable young ladies who are present.'

Dolly was about to refuse, but she could tell by the martial spark in Lady Margery's piercing grey eyes that it would do no good. Her role was definitely a subsidiary one and she must not forget her place. Exactly what that was had yet to be defined, but Dolly was certain that in Lady Margery's mind she was just there to act as a go-between and a foil for the fortune-hunters who might prey on Isabella and Celia.

'Yes, ma'am,' Dolly said meekly.

'Good. I'm glad we understand each other. I will expect you to be suitably dressed and ready to leave at half past eleven. Not a minute later.' Lady Margery swept out of the room and moments later Dolly could hear her irate voice scolding her recalcitrant daughters.

Dolly waited for the arguments to cease and then,

as she had expected, Isabella rushed into the room followed by Celia.

'I suppose you know that Mama had sprung this garden party on us,' Isabella said worriedly. 'She will do these things without giving us enough time to decide what to wear, let alone to get Anna to coif our hair. She can manage one of us, but we should have a maid each.'

'Yes, we should,' Celia echoed, sighing. 'May we borrow Bess? At least she knows how to help us dress, although heaven knows which gown I should choose. Mama said that Justin will be there and a prince of the realm.' She clasped her hands together, dreamy-eyed. 'Princess Celia – can you imagine that?'

'I thought your mama said the gentleman was merely a relation of the ruling family. But, of course, it would be an honour.' Dolly looked from one anxious face to the other. She often felt impatient with the girls, but she also sympathised with their problem. Lady Margery swept everything before her, regardless of anyone else's feelings. The illustrious man related to the Grimaldi family might be middle-aged or even older. The only thing that could be relied upon was the fact that he was unmarried. Lady Margery did not waste her matchmaking talents on men who were already spoken for. Both Isabella and Celia had been brought up to believe that their sole purpose in life was to marry well. Love did not come into the equation as far as their ambitious mother was concerned.

'He would probably choose me, anyway,' Isabella said crossly. 'I must marry first as I am the eldest twin.'

Dolly stepped in between them. 'You may borrow Bess, by all means. Perhaps I can help with your hair? Maybe simple styles would be more appropriate for a garden party?'

Isabella rolled her eyes, saying nothing.

'I agree,' Celia said eagerly. 'Thank you, Dolly. You are the best.'

Isabella glanced at the mantel clock. 'Good heavens, it's half past nine. We've got so little time. What shall I wear? Do come and help me choose, Dolly. I know that Justin loves blue, but surely green is more flattering with my red hair?'

'Do calm down, both of you, I'll help you, of course, but first I want to speak to Uncle Freddie. Go back to your room and ask Anna to get out some gowns. I won't be long, I promise.' Dolly shooed them out of the door before heading off to the wing where Freddie had an apartment of his own. Lady Margery did not think it appropriate for an unmarried gentleman to have a room in close proximity to her daughters, even if he was a relation.

Dolly entered Freddie's room to find Jenkins had just finished shaving his master. He gave Dolly a disapproving look. Freddie was in his shirtsleeves, his fair hair still tousled from sleep, and as Jenkins removed the towel Dolly realised that Freddie's shirt was open at the neck exposing the upper part of his torso.

'Is anything wrong, Dolly? You don't usually walk in on me just having finished my ablutions.' Freddie buttoned his shirt, his blue eyes twinkling mischievously.

Dolly averted her gaze. 'Lady Margery wants me to accompany you to a garden party at the Stanforths' villa at noon. She expects me to steer you away from gold-digging females and throw you into the path of someone suitable, whatever that means.'

'Really?' Freddie laughed. 'So you are recruited as a junior matchmaker, with me as your subject.'

'I think that is what she has in mind. It would also serve to keep me away from the eligible young men whom she wants to flock around her girls.'

'Well, I'll go along with it if you will. We'll stand on the sidelines and watch the fun.'

'I believe there is a prince or a close relative of the royal family amongst the hopefuls.'

'Even better. What a spectacle.' Freddie's smile faded. 'But are you all right, Dolly? You take it all in good heart, but I hope my cousin's somewhat cavalier attitude doesn't hurt you.'

'No, Uncle Freddie. As long as I have you on my side I can put up with whatever Lady Margery does and says. I'm a Blanchard from Rockwood Castle and proud of it.'

'I agree entirely.' Freddie turned to his valet. 'Jenkins, will you find me something suitable to wear for a garden party? It appears that my day has been organised for me.'

Jenkins folded the towel over his arm. 'Certainly, my lord.' He strode off into the dressing room.

'I'm afraid I've offended his sensibilities by barging in here at such an early hour,' Dolly said, giggling.

'I'm sure he'll get over it. However, Lady Margery would definitely disapprove, so perhaps you'd better wait for me in the morning room.'

'I have other things to do, Uncle Freddie. I am to help Isabella and Celia get ready for their first meeting with royalty, as well as Justin Stanforth. They are all atwitter this morning.'

'I can imagine. Go then. Do your duty and I'll see you later.'

'Yes, of course.' Dolly backed towards the doorway as Jenkins marched into the room with an armful of garments. He had a way of showing his disapproval of a young woman bursting into his master's bedchamber without saying a word. Dolly left them and hurried back to the girls' room.

Two hours later, Isabella and Celia were dressed and their hair coiffed in deceptively simple styles by Anna and Dolly, with a little help from Bess. Their beds were strewn with gowns that had been tried on and then discarded for one reason or another. Anna and Bess were left with the task of tidying everything away.

Isabella gazed in the cheval mirror. 'Are you sure this is the most flattering look, Dolly? Maybe I ought to wear my hair down, like Celia.'

Dolly shook her head. 'No, Izzy. You look perfect, a real princess-in-waiting.'

Isabella's pale cheeks bloomed pink. 'Really? Do you think so?'

'Indeed I do.' Dolly turned to Celia, who was fiddling with the bows on her puffed sleeves. 'What's wrong now?'

'Maybe I look too young. I know that Izzy and I are twins, but she looks so much more sophisticated than I do. With rosebuds in my hair I look like a child.'

'Nonsense. You look like the subject for one of those romantic paintings of red-haired beauties.'

Celia's green eyes opened wider. 'You think I'm beautiful, Dolly?'

'You know you are. That's why all the gentlemen flock round you and Izzy. Now, forget about everything other than enjoying the garden party. You might fall in love with a prince or a pauper, just have a good time. I know I'm going to keep Uncle Freddie company while you two break hearts.'

Isabella smiled. 'You know exactly what to say, Dolly. You are very pretty, too. In your own way, of course. Maybe we all ought to look out for a suitable bride for Cousin Freddie. He is incredibly rich and Mama says he should marry and produce an heir. She says he doesn't take his responsibility seriously.'

'You might be surprised,' Dolly said mysteriously. 'Anyway, your mama will be sending a search party for us if we delay any longer. You both look wonderful. I'll just fetch my parasol and gloves and I'll see you downstairs.'

The Stanforths' villa was reached up a winding private road lined with cypress trees. As the carriage rounded the last sweeping curve, the view of the house took Dolly's breath away. She had been expecting a dwelling similar to the other residences on the hill, but this opulent edifice seemed to have been based on a palace suitable for an Arabian prince. A cupola formed part of the roof, with minarets at either end. Tiled steps led up to a veranda shaded by wide arches above a terraced garden filled with exotic palms and flowering shrubs. However, the lower part of the garden might well have been transported from an English country house, and it was here that colourful gazebos had been set up to protect the guests from the noonday sun. Tables and chairs were similarly shaded by large parasols. A small orchestra was situated on the far side of an ornamental pool covered with waterlilies, and liveried footmen escorted the guests from the carriage sweep to be met by Sir Bradley and Lady Stanforth. Their son was absent, which Isabella noted with a sigh.

'Don't worry,' Dolly said in an undertone. 'I expect he'll make a grand entrance later so that he can set hearts aflutter.'

Celia laughed but Lady Margery frowned. 'I hope

you won't make disparaging remarks in front of the guests, Dolly. And that goes for you, too, Freddie. I want today to go off without a hitch. Do you understand?'

Everyone nodded but no one spoke as the carriage had come to a halt and the door was being opened by one of the footmen. When everyone had alighted safely, they were all led down the twisting paths between beautifully cultivated flowerbeds to the lower part of the gardens where they were greeted by their hosts. Dolly kept close to Freddie while Lady Margery paraded her daughters around the assembled guests. They stopped and chatted to friends and were introduced to some of the many elegantly dressed people attending the party. Servants threaded their way amongst the throng serving iced champagne, and the level of conversation increased as the wine flowed.

Justin Stanforth arrived about half an hour after the last guest. He was with a party of young men, all well-dressed and seemingly full of their own importance. Lady Stanforth rushed to greet her son and she guided him towards a group of friends. It was obvious which young ladies that she hoped would attract her son's attention, and that did not include Isabella and Celia. However, Lady Margery was not one to give up easily and she managed to detach Justin from his friends with the skill of a sheepdog separating a ram from a flock of ewes. Dolly watched with admiration as Lady Margery made it impossible for Justin to ignore her daughters without appearing rude. Isabella fluttered her eyelashes and simpered, but Celia simply gazed up at him with open admiration. Justin eyed her speculatively, but they were immediately joined by two of his male companions, one of whom paid marked attention to Celia, to be obvious chagrin of her sister.

Freddie followed Dolly's gaze. 'I wouldn't worry about the girls if I were you, Dolly. They have a secret weapon, namely their mama. She will soon see off any potential roués.'

'I feel sorry for Celia,' Dolly said in a low voice. 'Isabella steals all the limelight, but this time it looks as if Celia is the one attracting the young men and Isabella isn't pleased.'

'Never mind about them. Would you like some refreshments? I see a tempting array of delicacies laid out under the pergola by the lily pond.'

'Yes, I am rather hungry. My breakfast was interrupted and I didn't finish it.' Dolly tucked her hand in the crook of his arm and they threaded their way through the crowd to the buffet. Dolly selected what she fancied and the food was served by footmen wearing white gloves.

'If you find a table I'll bring the plates,' Freddie volunteered. 'We don't want to risk a spill on that pretty gown.'

She shot him an amused glance. 'That's the nearest you've ever come to flattering me, Uncle Freddie.'

He laughed. 'I don't go in for small talk, as you

well know. It is a charming gown and it suits you. Is that what you want to hear?'

'Of course it is. All women like to be complimented from time to time, and I am a woman now, not a child.'

'Of course. I sometimes forget that you are not that sweet little girl who used to come riding with me, and always beat me in a race.'

'I'm sure I could still win, given the right horse. Maybe I'll challenge you again when we return to Devonshire.'

Freddie was about to reply but his expression changed abruptly as he glanced over Dolly's shoulder. 'Don't look now, but I think the person who has just entered the garden is someone with whom you recently crossed swords.'

Dolly could not resist the temptation to turn her head. 'Oh, no! It can't be. Not her. Perhaps she won't see us.'

'Find a table quickly, if you don't want her to see you. I'll follow.'

Dolly made her way to a table as far away from the party as possible. It was a spot sheltered on one side by pink oleander bushes and shaded by a large yellow umbrella. She sat down, making herself as small as possible. The last thing she wanted was a scene in front of Lady Margery, who was not her greatest admirer at the best of times. Dolly always had the feeling that she was here under sufferance and as a useful foil for Isabella and Celia. She would most definitely have declined the invitation if Uncle Freddie had not been one of the party. She looked up and saw him approaching, followed by a waiter bringing their meal. Forgetting everything, Dolly jumped to her feet and waved, but a familiar voice behind her made her spin round.

'I thought it was you. What are you doing here?'

'Miss Bennington. What an unpleasant surprise.'

Chapter Six

Theodora Bennington curled her lip. 'I could expose you to our host and hostess as being a liar and a fraud. You entered my home under false pretences.'

'The mistake was made by your servants, Miss Bennington. I merely went along with the farce for a while, but I admitted my error and I believe I apologised.'

'I could have had you arrested.'

Freddie hurried up to them. 'Theodora, I see you've met my ward, Miss Blanchard.'

Dolly shot him an enquiring look. Being Freddie's ward was a new idea altogether and it would have been amusing in different circumstances. She realised that he was trying to defuse the situation, although she was not sure that this was the best way. However, she was not about to contradict him.

'Your ward? She didn't mention that when she came to me with a grovelling apology for her deceit.'

'You just admitted that I apologised,' Dolly said triumphantly. 'What more do you want? Can't you see the funny side of things, Miss Bennington?'

'Not in your case. In fact I feel obliged to let all the guests here know that we have an imposter in our midst. Someone who might insinuate herself into our homes with goodness knows what intention.'

Freddie motioned Dolly to keep silent. He took a step towards Theodora, his expression forbidding. 'You have no grounds for such an accusation, Miss Bennington. I will refute anything you choose to say on the subject. I suggest that you think carefully before you cast aspersions on my ward's character, which is blameless. If you spread malicious gossip about Miss Blanchard you will have me to deal with. Do I make myself clear?'

Theodora drew herself up to her full height. 'It seems to me that your interest in this young woman goes deeper than being her guardian. You would do well to be careful what you say about me, Lord Dorrington.'

'You are threatening the wrong person, Miss Bennington.'

Theodora tossed her head and marched off, casting a withering glance at Dolly over her shoulder. 'This is not the end of the matter, Miss Blanchard.'

'It is as far as I am concerned,' Dolly called after

her. She turned to Freddie. 'How could you remain so calm?'

'Would you prefer that I had made a scene, which is exactly what that woman wanted? Keep away from her, and if you should meet her socially, don't interact with her. She is looking for trouble.'

'She will get it if she keeps on threatening you. How dare she? I don't care so much for myself because I have no reputation to keep up, but you are a peer of the realm. You have a seat in the House of Lords.'

Freddie smiled ruefully. 'Which I have yet to take up. I really prefer a quiet country life. You see how a spiteful creature like Theodora Bennington can ruin a man's life.'

'I do, and she cannot be allowed to get away with such behaviour.'

'Sit down and enjoy your luncheon, Dolly. We'll have a glass or two of champagne and observe the world around us. Unless, of course, you wish to join Isabella and Celia in the hunt for a rich husband.'

Dolly slumped down on her chair. 'No, I'm too hungry and this looks delicious.'

'That's one of the things I love about you, Dolly. You are not afraid to enjoy your food. Unlike my second cousins, who think it unladylike to have a good appetite.'

'But then I'm no lady, according to Miss Bennington. Thank goodness I didn't keep up the pretence of being poor Miss Harding. That woman had a very lucky escape.'

Freddie sat down opposite her and began eating. 'This is far too good to waste. Eat up and forget all about that wretched woman. Unfortunately, we are neighbours in London, but that doesn't mean I have to put up with her here in Monaco.'

Dolly bit into a slice of smoked salmon served on a crisp crouton. 'You're right. This is delicious. I've forgotten all about Miss Bennington.'

They chatted amicably while they enjoyed the delicious food. Dolly kept Freddie amused with witty comments about the other guests, none of them malicious, but nevertheless very entertaining. Theodora kept giving her hostile glances, but Dolly ignored her. She was enjoying herself in Freddie's company and it was a perfect setting. Sunlight sparkled off the sea in the distance, and the air was filled with the scent of champagne and flowers. Isabella seemed to have attracted Justin's attention at last, and she was smiling happily. Celia was surrounded by a group of young people, and Lady Margery was sitting with other matrons, their heads together as if they were plotting something momentous.

Suddenly the little orchestra launched into the country's national anthem, and a group of middle-aged, smartly dressed gentlemen strolled into the garden, causing heads to turn and conversation to come to an abrupt halt.

'Which one is related to the Grimaldi family?' Dolly asked in a low voice.

Freddie shook his head. 'I don't mix in those

circles, so I'm afraid I am as much in the dark as you are.'

'They look very official.' Dolly tried not to stare, but curiosity overcame manners. 'Sir Bradley seems to think they are very important and Lady Stanforth is falling over herself to appear welcoming.'

Dolly and Freddie watched the Stanforths fawning over the newcomers, but they did not introduce them to anyone. Instead they spirited their illustrious guests to a table set apart, presumably for that particular purpose. It was only then that Lady Stanforth summoned her son, and Justin abandoned Isabella to obey his mother's command.

Gradually a ripple of chitchat encouraged others to forget their important visitors and the party continued, albeit on a more subdued level. Justin seemed to have forgotten about Isabella, who pouted ominously and went to sit with the married ladies. She cast envious looks at Celia, who was obviously enjoying herself, seemingly oblivious to her sister's chagrin on being cast aside for someone of greater importance.

Lady Margery eventually rose to her feet and walked purposefully to where their hosts were sitting. Dolly and Freddie exchanged meaningful glances.

'I take it we are leaving,' Dolly said in a whisper. 'Isabella looks as if she is going to burst into tears.'

Freddie stood up. 'I think that's our cue to follow them. I think we might have a difficult journey back to the villa.'

Dolly rose to her feet. 'Poor Isabella, I really feel sorry for her, although there are other eligible young men who are probably much nicer than Justin. Just imagine having Lady Stanforth as a mother-in-law.'

'Only a little worse than marrying someone like Theodora Bennington.' Freddie fell into step beside Dolly. 'I think you should steer clear of her for the rest of our stay here. You've embarrassed her and I don't think she's the sort of person to forgive easily.'

'I really don't care.' Dolly tossed her head. 'She can tell the whole of Monaco, for all I care. I am a nobody here anyway, so it will all be forgotten in a heartbeat.'

However, Theodora Bennington's spiteful remarks circulated round the drawing rooms and parlours in Monaco with amazing speed. Everywhere that Dolly went after the fateful garden party, she received knowing looks and barbed comments, and it was obvious that she was the centre of attention for all the wrong reasons. Unfortunately the situation came to Lady Margery's attention when Lady Stanforth told her bluntly that she did not want her son associating with Isabella. She failed to give a reason, but Dolly overheard the conversation and she was uncomfortably aware that Lady Stanforth was staring in her direction. It was obvious that Theodora had done her worst. She had created a drama out of what could have been related as an amusing anecdote. Freddie was furious but there was little

he could do and Dolly begged him not to get involved.

When invitations to social gatherings failed to
materialise, Lady Margery took to the gaming tables
every evening and sometimes in the daytime, too.
After a few heavy losses it seemed that her luck had
deserted her there also. She made light of her misfor-
tune, insisting that she always won in the end, but
Dolly was not so sure. Isabella and Celia were frantic
with worry and Freddie was powerless to prevent
his cousin from frittering away the fortune left to
her by her late husband.

Night after night Dolly and Freddie accompanied
Isabella and Celia to the Casino, where they did
their best to dissuade their mother from gambling,
but Lady Margery was in the grip of gaming fever
and nothing they could say or do made any difference. She was mixing with a louche set of men and
women, who were on the edge of society and lived
by their wits. They drank too much and bet too
heavily, encouraging each other to take more and
more risks. One man pledged all his worldly posses-
sions on a single turn of the cards and lost. Next
morning the word went round that he had taken
his own life, but not even this tragic event could
dissuade Lady Margery from heading back to the
tables.

A day later Isabella and Celia were still asleep in
bed while Dolly and Freddie took coffee on the
terrace overlooking the sea.

'What are we going to do, Uncle Freddie?' Dolly asked anxiously.

'I think it's time to return to England. I've been trying to persuade Margery to see sense and go home, but the more she loses at cards or roulette, the more determined she becomes to revive her finances with the next bet. It's like an illness that has her in its grip and she simply won't listen to me.'

'Theodora has done her worst, as far as I am concerned, and that doesn't worry me. I never wanted to be part of the society here anyway, but it does affect the girls. I feel so sorry for Izzy and Cissy. They don't deserve to be ostracised because of things beyond their control.'

Freddie replaced his cup on its saucer. 'I agree. I'll speak to Margery again. I must make her see sense.'

Dolly was about to reply when she saw Bess running towards them, waving frantically. Dolly rose to her feet. 'What's wrong?'

'I'm sorry, my lord, and you, miss, but there's a man here who says we're to vacate the premises immediately. At least I think that's what he was saying. Anna translated for me.'

Freddie rose to his feet. 'I'll deal with this, Dolly. You stay here.'

Dolly was about to argue but a man in a black suit with a top hat clutched in his hands came striding down the steps from the villa.

He addressed Freddie in rapid French, and to

Dolly's surprise Freddie answered him. She could not understand the foreign language but she could see that the situation was serious.

'What's happened, Uncle Freddie? Why must we leave?'

Freddie turned to her with a grim expression. 'It seems that the rent is in arrears, and neither the servants nor the tradesmen have been paid since we moved into the villa. Don't worry, Dolly, I'll sort this out, but I suggest you wake the girls and prepare them to leave for home. This situation has got out of hand and I'm going to put a stop to it.'

Dolly followed him into the villa. She went straight to the girls' room and entered without knocking. Isabella and Celia were still asleep but Dolly pulled back the curtains and tugged off the bedclothes.

'Wake up, both of you. I need to talk to you urgently.'

Celia raised herself on her elbow, blinking sleepily at Dolly. 'Is the villa on fire?'

'It might as well be. We have to leave.'

'What are you talking about?' Celia yawned. 'We're here for the summer.'

Dolly moved to Isabella's bedside and gave her a shake. 'For goodness' sake wake up, Izzy. This is important.'

Isabella roused herself, covering her eyes with her forearm as the sunlight streamed in through the window. 'What's going on?'

'A man came to tell us to vacate the property. It

seems that nothing and no one has been paid since we arrived. Your mama has gambled away the money she should have used to pay the bills.'

'I knew it.' Isabella sat up in bed, her face crumpling as tears filled her eyes. 'I knew there was a reason why I wasn't allowed to see Justin again. It's all Mama's fault.'

'Not entirely,' Dolly said fairly. 'Theodora Bennington has a lot to answer for. She's poisoned everyone's minds against me, and that has meant fewer invitations for you girls. Your mama has taken it badly and resorted to the gaming tables. It seems that she has lost heavily.'

'You don't think she's bankrupted us, do you, Dolly?' Celia leaped out of bed.

'I hope not. Uncle Freddie is dealing with things. He won't allow you to lose everything, but we have to get your mama away from that ghastly crowd at the Casino. She thinks they are her friends but they are not.'

'I don't see what we can do about it,' Isabella said sulkily. 'My life is already ruined.'

'You would have been miserable with Lady Stanforth as your mama-in-law. Justin might be rich but he isn't a nice person.' Celia reached for the bell pull. 'I need Anna to help me dress.'

Dolly eyed them thoughtfully. 'Are you both agreed that we must get your mama away from the Casino and her new friends?'

Celia nodded. 'I am.'

'And I,' Isabella added reluctantly. 'I thought it was too good to be true when we first arrived here. It's so beautiful and London is so dirty and cold.'

'Maybe, but it's June and you could enjoy summer at home. You have a country house as well as a London residence, don't you?' Dolly looked from one to the other.

'Yes, we do, but the country is boring,' Isabella said crossly. 'There are very few balls and the local gentry are only interested in hunting and shooting.'

'But at least Mama will be kept away from the gaming tables.' Celia slumped down on the end of her bed. 'When will we be leaving here, Dolly?'

'As soon as possible. I'll go and see what Uncle Freddie has to say.' Dolly left them to get dressed and she went in search of Freddie.

She found him in the morning parlour going through a sheaf of bills. He looked up as she entered the room.

'I should have taken control from the beginning,' he said grimly. 'I knew that my cousin had a weakness for gambling when she was younger, but I really thought she was capable of running a household. It seems I was very much mistaken.'

'What did you say to that man?'

'I paid the rent and now I will have to settle these.' He waved the papers in the air with a disgruntled sigh. 'I blame myself as much as Margery. I should have stopped her when it was obvious she was spending so much time at the Casino, but I was too taken with fending off the malicious efforts of Miss Bennington. I'm sorry it has all turned out so badly, Dolly. I really wanted to take you away from all your problems and I seem to have given you more to worry about.'

Dolly smiled. 'Nonsense. To be honest, I've enjoyed most of it, if you discount Theodora's nastiness. But now it's time to go home, I think.'

'Yes, you're right. Margery will have no choice other than agree. We'll leave as soon as possible. I assume she's with her new friends at the Casino, so I'll go there now.'

'I'll come with you. It's best if Isabella and Celia are not involved. They'll only get upset if their mama makes a scene.'

Dolly entered the Casino on Freddie's arm and the first person she saw was Theodora Bennington, who was talking to a group of people. She paused when she saw Dolly and a malicious smile curved her lips.

'I'm amazed that some people have the nerve to appear in public,' Theodora said in a voice designed to echo off the high ceiling in the grand salon. 'I wonder how that woman managed to insinuate herself into the good books of an English aristocrat.'

Freddie tensed and Dolly knew he was going to leap to her defence. She squeezed his arm. 'No, Uncle Freddie. Leave this to me.' She walked up to Theodora with a measured tread. 'I see you are still spreading spiteful gossip, Miss Bennington. It's a pity you have nothing better to occupy your mind, but then you have few real friends, so I suppose you think such talk makes you interesting.'

'How dare you speak to me in such an insulting tone?' Theodora's eyes flashed, but Dolly was quick to note a flicker of uncertainty in them.

'Unlike you, I am not interested in ruining a person's reputation and defiling their good name. I could spread tales of how you treat your servants, Miss Bennington.' Dolly looked at the embarrassed faces around them. 'It was a case of mistaken identity, and I expect the servant in question was dismissed without a character for his error. I could have made myself known, and I admit it was wrong, but the deception unwittingly forced upon me was over very quickly and I apologised to Miss Bennington. However, that does not seem to be enough and she has chosen to blacken my name freely and without thinking what it might do to me or my family.' Dolly turned her attention to Theodora, whose pale lips were drawn back in a snarl. 'Take a good look at yourself, Miss Bennington. Malevolence is never attractive. It reflects as badly on the perpetrator as it does on the victim. Good day to you.' Dolly walked back to Freddie, who was standing a few feet away, waiting for her.

'I could see that you were able to handle her without my help,' he said, smiling. 'Well done, Dolly. That took courage, but I think it hit home.'

Dolly glanced over her shoulder and had the

satisfaction of seeing the people who Theodora had been addressing were slipping away, leaving her standing on her own and isolated.

'Let's find Lady Margery,' Dolly said firmly. 'Miss Bennington is unimportant. We have to look after family. Lady Margery might not be related to me, but she was kind enough to look after me in my coming-out season.'

'Margery is a good sort.' Freddie took Dolly by the arm. 'And there she is, at the roulette table. Leave the talking to me, Dolly.'

They approached the small group of people around Lady Margery, who was flushed and excited as she placed all her tokens on the corner of a line. 'My luck is in, Freddie,' she cried excitedly. 'See how much I've won this morning.'

'*Rien ne va plus,*' the croupier said, spinning the wheel.

There was a breathless silence as the ball was flung from deflector to deflector and eventually landed on black six. There was a muffled sigh and then silence as the croupier scooped all the counters away.

'All right. So your luck changed, Margery,' Freddie said gently. 'Time to go home, my dear.'

Lady Margery gave him a stricken look. 'No, Freddie. My luck *has* changed. I can't leave until I've recouped at least some of my losses. You must give me more time.'

Freddie shook his head. 'You will only lose more. Come now.'

'Lend me ten guineas, please, Freddie. I promise to repay you when I win.'

'People are looking, Lady Margery,' Dolly said gently. 'Won't you come back to the villa with us? There is something you should know.' Dolly glanced over her shoulder and was dismayed to see Theodora Bennington watching them avidly.

'I won't take no for an answer, Margery.' Freddie took her by the arm. 'Come now, please, and don't make a fuss.'

Lady Margery tried to push Freddie away but he stood firm.

'Let me go, Freddie. You're causing a scene.'

'No, Margery. It's you who are making everyone stare. If you refuse I will have to carry you and that really will create a stir.'

Reluctantly Lady Margery snatched up her reticule and allowed Freddie and Dolly to escort her from the Casino.

When they arrived back at the villa they found luggage piled up in the entrance hall, with Isabella and Celia looking woeful. The servants were rushing around gathering up trinkets and oddments that the family had collected during their stay.

'What on earth is going on?' Lady Margery demanded, sinking down on a hall chair. 'Where are we going, Freddie? This must be your doing.'

'No, Margery. I'm afraid this is entirely down to you and your gambling habit. I had a visit from the letting agent, demanding the arrears in rent. Then I had to pay the tradesmen as well as the servants. Not,' he added hastily, 'that I begrudge the money. I would have insisted on contributing fully to cover your expenditure. But what would you have done had I not been here?'

'I don't know what you're talking about,' Lady Margery said crossly. 'I am a very wealthy woman. It was just an oversight on my part.'

'We were about to be evicted, Mama,' Isabella said, frowning. 'What will the Stanforths and their friends think of us if they find out?'

'I don't care.' Celia shrugged and turned away. 'They are not nice people anyway, and Justin is stuck up and full of himself for no good reason, as far as I can see, apart from being extremely rich.'

'But to run away without saying goodbye to my acquaintances here looks like cowardice and makes me seem guilty, as if I cannot pay my debts.' Lady Margery looked from one to the other. 'You understand, don't you, Adela?'

Dolly shook her head. 'I do in a way, Lady Margery. But if the people you mention discover that we were actually evicted from the villa, it would be even worse. Most embarrassing.'

'Dolly is right,' Freddie said firmly. 'We'll leave after luncheon and take the journey in easy stages. I thought a few days in Paris might soften the blow of returning home early. What do you say to that?'

Lady Margery's answer was drowned by the cries

of excitement from Isabella and Celia. Even Dolly uttered a gasp of delight. She had read so much about Paris, but had never imagined she would visit the city.

'And before you ask, Margery, even if there is a casino in Paris, we are not going to go there.' Freddie bent down to drop a kiss on Lady Margery's forehead. 'For you own sake, my dear. Otherwise you will find yourself bankrupt and what will happen to your daughters then?'

Lady Margery bowed her head. 'You are right, of course, Freddie. I will do my best to resist the temptation from now on, and I'll concentrate on my girls. Their futures are more important to me than the thrill of the gaming tables.'

'Well said, Margery.' Freddie patted her on the shoulder. 'Why don't you go to your room and make sure that everything has been packed. Then we'll have luncheon before we set off on our travels.'

When they reached Paris late that evening, Freddie booked them into a luxurious hotel in the heart of the city. They spent the next three days exploring and seeing the sights. Lady Margery discovered a marvellous modern department store called Le Bon Marché, where she and the girls spent time and more money than was sensible on what Hester would have called 'fripperies'. Freddie insisted that Dolly bought whatever she fancied, but she hesitated to take advantage of his generosity. Even so, she did buy presents for Phoebe and everyone at home, even Hester. Isabella and Celia had no such scruples, and they purchased lace shawls, fans, dancing slippers and straw bonnets without regard as to the cost.

Every evening they dined early and went afterwards to the theatre or the opera. It was a hectic few days, and even Lady Margery said she would be relieved to go home and enjoy the peace and quiet of the English countryside.

Dolly was not so sure, but she knew she must face her family sooner or later. Her time in London and in Monaco were both eventful, and the brief holiday in Paris had been wonderful, but now she had to decide whether to follow convention and return home to her family, or to continue looking for a way of life that would satisfy her need to do something special. If only she knew what that was.

Chapter Seven

Freddie insisted on accompanying Dolly to Rock-wood, despite her protests that she was quite capable of explaining everything to her family. However, Freddie said he was responsible for taking her abroad and he had encouraged her to stay in London after her ill-fated elopement with Gus. Dolly did not think of her time with Gus as an elopement. There had been no possibility of marriage or anything of the sort, but Freddie told her that was how it would appear to everyone and it would be difficult to explain away.

Now she was returning, accompanied by her own personal maid. Quite what her parents would say to that was another matter, but Dolly could not abandon Bess. Leaving her on her own in London was unthinkable, and for her part Bess was thrilled with the opportunity to live in a castle.

They arrived in London early one morning, having travelled overnight from Paris. Freddie insisted that they had breakfast at Dorrington House before travelling on. Lady Margery, Isabella and Celia were to get a train to take them to Moonhaven Hall in Hampshire, and Freddie, Dolly and Bess planned to travel to Rockwood.

'You know you can come and stay with us, either in London or in the country, whenever you want to get away for a while, Dolly,' Celia said earnestly. 'We would love to have you, wouldn't we, Izzy?'

Isabella nodded. 'Of course. We'll miss you, Dolly. It's incredibly dull at Moonhaven, but I'm sure we can find something to amuse us.'

'Or somebody,' Celia added mischievously. 'Preferably not someone like Theodora Bennington. I'm glad we've seen the last of that person.'

'I certainly hope so.' Dolly glanced nervously over her shoulder. 'I wouldn't be surprised if she had followed us just so that she could continue to make mischief.'

'It's a pity she has nothing better to do.' Lady Margery turned to Freddie with an engaging smile. 'Thank you for everything, Freddie. You know you are always welcome at Moonhaven.'

Freddie kissed her on the cheek. 'Of course, and that goes for you and the girls. I would be delighted if you visited me in Dorrington Place, where I am most likely to be found. London holds very little attraction for me.'

At that moment, Freddie's butler, Briggs, announced that a cab had arrived for Lady Margery. There were more hugs and kisses as Dolly stepped outside onto the pavement to wave to them. She was quite sad to say goodbye to them, even Lady Margery. The trying times they had endured in Monaco had brought them all together, and Theodora Bennington had been the catalyst. Dolly stared at the imposing iron railings and gates in front of the Bennington establishment. It would be just her luck if Theodora emerged from her home ready to start another argument.

'Come in, Dolly.' Freddie appeared behind her. 'I've sent for my carriage. We'll go straight to the station and catch a train for Exeter. I don't want to keep you from home any longer than necessary.'

Dolly followed him into the house. 'Yes, of course. You must be eager to return to Dorrington Place, too.'

He smiled. 'That's not what I meant. I'm more than happy to take you to Rockwood, but I think you will need me to help smooth things over. You gave them a fright by going off like that. I hardly need to tell you.'

'No, you're right, and I'll make it up to them. I promise.'

Freddie opened the door to the morning room. 'Come and sit down. It will take Mason a while to bring the carriage round.'

Dolly perched on the edge of a spindly Sheraton

chair. 'I've caused such a lot of bother, Uncle Freddie. I'm only just beginning to realise what I've done.'

'Don't worry. They'll all be so relieved to see you again that the rest will be forgotten.' Freddie pulled a face. 'I can't speak for Hester.'

His expression made Dolly laugh. 'Yes, you're right. I'll have to do something to atone, although I can't think what it will be. I felt so bored and restless before I came to London with Gus.' She held up her hand as Freddie was about to speak. 'I know it was foolish and ill-considered, but it was a way of escaping the life I am expected to lead. Can you understand that?'

'It might surprise you to know that I do understand, perfectly. I was brought up by strict parents whose only aim in life was to see me married and producing an heir to the estate. They died within months of each other, sadly disappointed in me.'

'But you loved Aunt Nancy.'

'I'll always love her, although that's changed to something a little more comfortable now. She's a happily married woman and I'm her life-long friend.'

'So why haven't you married?'

'Perhaps because I never found anyone to take Nancy's place.' Freddie turned his head as Briggs knocked and entered.

'The carriage is outside, my lord.'

'Thank you, Briggs. We're coming right away.' He proffered his arm to Dolly. 'We'll do this together, so don't worry. Everything will go smoothly, I promise.'

The train was at the platform when they arrived at the station. A porter took charge of their luggage, with Bess keeping a strict eye on him as he deposited everything in the guard's van. Dolly settled herself in a window seat and they had the compartment to themselves for the whole journey. Freddie closed his eyes and appeared to sleep for most of the time, leaving Dolly to gaze out of the window at the countryside as it flashed past. Bess curled up in the far corner and also slept soundly, leaving Dolly to her own thoughts.

As they were approaching Exeter, her attention was attracted by a field filled with army tents and her heart missed a beat. She wondered if Gus's regiment had returned to Devonshire, but then common sense told her that there were numerous regiments in the south-west and it was unlikely that Gus would be one of the soldiers camped on that site. The train slowed down and Freddie awakened with a start.

'I think I must have dozed off. I'm sorry to be such a dull companion, Dolly.'

She smiled. 'You're showing your age, Uncle Freddie.'

He blinked and looked away. 'I suppose someone of thirty-four must seem ancient to a nineteen-year-old.'

'As I said before, I'll be twenty in October – that shortens the difference.' Dolly laughed. 'Now I've offended you. I didn't mean to be rude. You are perfect in every way and I love you.'

'And I love you, Dolly.' Freddie rose from his seat as the train ground to a halt. 'Let's hope we can hire a carriage here. I sent a telegram to Rockwood, but they might not have received it in time.'

Bess opened the carriage door and stepped onto the platform. 'I'll find a porter, my lord.' She hurried off, waving frantically to attract a porter's attention.

Dolly alighted more slowly. She was beginning to feel very apprehensive. She was looking forward to going home, but she knew she must face a barrage of questions, and Hester was unlikely to let her off easily. Dolly knew she had upset and worried them all and she was secretly quite pleased that Freddie was accompanying her. He would smooth things over. He always did. She glanced at his profile as they walked through the station concourse, having given up their tickets at the barrier. She noticed for the first time that there were small laughter lines at the corners of his blue eyes, and sometimes she caught him gazing at her with an inscrutable expression.

She put such thoughts out of her mind as she looked up and down the street. There was no sign of a cab or any other form of transport.

'What will we do, Uncle Freddie?'

He frowned. 'We'll go to the hotel and have

something to eat. Perhaps they can find us a cab that will take us to Rockwood. Maybe your family didn't get my telegram.'

Bess hurried towards them, chivvying a harassed porter who had their luggage on a trolley. 'I think I saw a carriage draw up outside the station, my lord.'

'There you are,' Freddie said triumphantly. 'I knew Alex wouldn't let us down.'

Dolly followed him into the street. It was good to see Hudson's familiar face as he reined in the horses and leaped down to help them with their luggage.

'Welcome home, miss. If I might be so bold.'

Dolly smiled. 'Thank you, Hudson. It's good to be back in Devonshire. How are the family?'

'Well, thank you, miss.'

Dolly had a sudden thought and she hesitated before climbing into the carriage. 'Hudson, you know most of what is happening in this area. Do you happen to know which regiment is camped outside Exeter?'

'I'm afraid I don't, miss. But I could find out for you.'

Freddie shot her a warning look. 'Dolly!'

She settled herself on the seat. 'I was just curious, that's all.' She patted the seat beside her. 'Get in, Bess. We'll be home soon and I'll introduce you to the rest of the servants. You'll find them a friendly bunch, I'm sure.'

'Might I ride on the box with the coachman, miss? It's a lovely afternoon and I would love to view the scenery.'

Dolly nodded. 'Of course. If Hudson doesn't mind.'

'Not I, miss. Hop up, young lady. I'll show you the sights of Devonshire on the way.' Hudson closed the carriage door, leaving Dolly and Freddie facing each other.

'What?' Dolly demanded as she met Freddie's stern gaze.

'Are you hoping that Sergeant Baker might be camped outside Exeter?'

'Of course not. I was just curious. We're an army family, unless you've forgotten. My papa was a soldier, as was Uncle Bertie, and Tommy followed in his footsteps.'

'That's true, and I don't usually interfere, but Baker isn't the man for you.'

'If you don't mind, I'd rather talk about something else. I expect I'll hear all that from my parents and Hester, anyway.'

'Yes, you're right. It isn't any of my business. I'm sorry, Dolly. It's just that I care about you and I don't want to see you ruin your life because of some dashing young military man.'

'I doubt if I'll ever see Gus again, so there's no need to worry.' The carriage moved forward and Dolly turned away to gaze out of the window.

The journey took over an hour and at first Freddie kept up his attempts at conversation, but he seemed to understand that Dolly did not feel like talking, and they travelled on in silence. She was suddenly nervous and had begun to dread what should have been a happy homecoming. She could perfectly well understand if everyone was furious with her for causing so much upset and anxiety, and she wished she had some plausible excuse. In the end, as the carriage entered the castle bailey, Dolly was resigned to the fact that the next hour or so was going to be difficult, if not actually upsetting. She was surprised and relieved to see Phoebe running to meet them. At least one person was pleased to see her.

Freddie opened the carriage door and proffered his hand to help Dolly alight. Immediately she was enveloped in a sisterly hug.

'Dolly, I'm so glad to see you. I want to hear all about your adventures. Mama said you had gone to Monte Carlo as well as London. Come indoors and tell me all about it.'

Freddie laughed. 'There, you see, Dolly. You worried unnecessarily. I'll go on ahead and reassure your parents that no harm has come to you.'

Phoebe slipped her arm around her sister's waist. 'Come along. You'll find they are all dying to see you. Well, maybe Great-Grandmama Hester is a bit miffed, but then she always is. I'm sure she's secretly relieved that you are safe and well.'

'Don't worry, Phoebe. I've returned expecting the worst. After all, I deserve everything they say to me. Let's get it over and done with.' Dolly turned to

Bess, who was standing by the pile of luggage, her hands tightly clasped and a worried frown puckering her forehead.

'Come with me, Bess. I'll ask James to take you to the servants' quarters and introduce you. One of the maids will show you where my room is and they'll find somewhere for you to sleep, too.'

Bess bobbed a curtsey. 'Thank you, miss.'

Dolly and Phoebe entered the great hall together. Dolly greeted James, the butler, with a smile.

'It's good to be home. Will you see that my maid is taken care of?'

'Of course, Miss Dolly.' James turned to Bess. 'I'll take you to meet the housekeeper, Tilly, I mean Mrs Madge.'

Satisfied that Bess would be well looked after, Dolly and Phoebe set off towards the drawing room. They had only gone a few paces when Rory strolled towards them. 'So you've decided to come home. Welcome, Dolly. I actually missed you.' He kissed her on the cheek. 'Life without you is too dull.'

'Shouldn't you be at university, Rory?' Dolly eyed him speculatively. 'Don't tell me you've been sent down again.'

He grinned. 'It was all a misunderstanding. Anyway, I was ready for a break from studying. You did me a favour by running off with the soldier. It took Papa's mind off my misdemeanours.'

'I'm glad I was some use to you,' Dolly said, laughing. Her brother had a knack of making her feel better, even when she knew she had done wrong. 'Where are they all? I expect a good telling-off.'

'They're in the drawing room, and I'm going for a ride.' Rory patted her on the shoulder. 'Stiff upper lip, Dolly. They can't eat you.' He strolled off, leaving Dolly and Phoebe in the echoing entrance hall.

Dolly braced her shoulders. 'Oh, well. I'd better get it over and done with.' She paused as she walked past the ancient suit of armour. 'Good afternoon, Sir Denys.' She patted his visor and the rusty metal clanked as if answering her. She walked on with Phoebe at her side, and as they entered the drawing room Dolly was relieved to see just her mother and her Aunt Nancy seated by the window.

Rosalind leaped to her feet and ran to hug her daughter. 'Dolly Blanchard, you gave us all such a fright by running off like that. I should scold you, but I'm so glad to see you.'

'I told you so,' Phoebe said in a superior tone.

Nancy also rose from her seat. 'You're home now, Dolly, my love. That's all that matters.'

'But your papa might have a few words to say to you.' Rosalind held Dolly at arm's length. 'We won't talk about it now. I want you to settle in and you can tell us everything when you feel you are able.'

'I agree,' Nancy added firmly. 'We've persuaded Hester to keep her thoughts to herself. You know what she's like when she has a bee in her bonnet.'

Dolly nodded. 'Yes, indeed. I was expecting a good telling-off.'

'I'm not saying you don't deserve it for the fright you gave us all,' Rosalind said, smiling. 'But I for one am just delighted to have my girl home safely.' She walked over to the mantelshelf where she tugged at the bell pull. 'I think this calls for tea and cake. Mrs Jackson has baked your favourite chocolate cake to celebrate your return.'

'It's not fair.' Phoebe's bottom lip protruded in a pout. 'I've been good and done nothing to upset anyone and I don't get chocolate cake made for me.'

'But I have a present for you, Phoebe,' Dolly said, laughing. 'Perhaps that will make up for everything.'

Phoebe's expression changed dramatically. 'Oh, really? What did you bring me?'

'Well, Uncle Freddie took us to Paris. That's me, of course, Lady Margery, Isabella and Celia. We had a wonderful time and we found this huge shop called Le Bon Marché. I bought you a present in Paris. When Bess has unpacked my valises, I'll give it to you.'

'How exciting.' Phoebe danced around the room, clapping her hands. 'A present from Paris.'

'Who is Bess?' Rosalind asked, frowning.

'She's a girl I rescued from a brutal employer in London. I took her on as a maid, Mama. I knew you wouldn't have wanted me to leave her on her own in London. I'll explain everything later. I bought something for you, too, and you, Nancy. I even remembered Hester.'

Rosalind frowned. 'I see. Well, our finance won't

run to paying for a lady's maid for you, or even for myself, but I'll speak to her before I make any decisions. We are a housemaid short since Mrs Higson retired and I promoted Tilly Madge to the position of housekeeper.'

'You know we are not the wealthiest landowners in the area,' Nancy added seriously. 'Tommy and Alex have done their best, but Rockwood Castle needs a great deal of maintenance.'

'I know, and I also realise that I was supposed to find a rich husband who would contribute to the family purse. That was what the season in London was all about.'

Rosalind and Nancy exchanged wary glances. 'It wasn't quite like that,' Rosalind said hastily. 'I married your papa for love. I wouldn't want you to sell yourself to the highest bidder. The season was supposed to broaden your outlook and introduce you into society, that's all.' Rosalind paused at the sound of someone tapping on the door. 'Enter.'

Flossie opened the door. 'You rang, ma'am?'

'Yes, Flossie. We'll have tea and Mrs Jackson's excellent chocolate cake.'

'Yes, ma'am.' Flossie left the room, and was about to close the door when Hester pushed past her and allowed the door to swing shut.

'Well, so the wanderer has returned.' She stood, arms akimbo, glaring at Dolly. 'Do you realise how much upset you caused your family, young lady?'

Dolly opened her mouth to reply but Rosalind

held up her hand. 'I'm sure that Dolly is well aware of the distress she caused us all, Hester. There's no need to labour the point. Instead we are going to celebrate her return.'

Hester sniffed and sat down in the armchair reserved especially for her. No one in the family would dare to sit in it if Hester was present, and even when she was not in the room it was the last seat that anyone else would take.

'Well, I suppose we are going to hear about all your exploits. I met Freddie in the garden. He was looking for Alex.'

Nancy smiled and stood up, smoothing down the silk of her voluminous skirt. 'I need to make sure that Freddie's usual room is ready for him. It's too late for him to set off for Dorrington Place, and I'll tell Cook we'll be two extra for dinner.'

'For heaven's sake ring the bell, Nancy,' Hester said impatiently. 'You are the mistress. The servants are supposed to wait on you.'

'Yes, Hester. I know that, but I like to do things my way. I'm sorry if you disapprove but you are not the lady of the house now.'

'Before you go, Nancy,' Hester motioned her to sit down, 'I have an announcement to make. I was going to leave it until after dinner, but I can see that Dolly will take centre stage then and we'll all be forced to listen to her exploits. When I was a girl I would have been severely punished for such wayward behaviour.'

'Dolly is my daughter,' Rosalind said sharply. 'Her papa and I decide whether or not she has done wrong. If I have my facts correct I believe you fell from grace at a very early age, if you get my meaning. You were only fifteen or so when your son was born, out of wedlock.'

Hester's face flushed wine red. 'That was not my fault, as you well know. I was taken advantage of by a ruthless butler who had his way with all the young servant girls. However, as we have brought up the subject of my status in this household, I think it's time I moved to a home of my own.'

'Really, Hester. Is that necessary?' Nancy asked anxiously.

'Yes, and I need your permission, Nancy. I want to move into the Dower House belonging to your estate.'

'But Nick Gibson has been living there for years, Hester.' Rosalind met Dolly's surprised gaze with a helpless look. 'Are you going to throw him out?'

'Nick Gibson is a bachelor. He may rent rooms from me if he chooses to stay. Mrs Banks is still the cook, so I believe, and Mrs Simpson is keeping house. His rent will pay their wages.'

'You have it all thought out, haven't you?' Nancy laughed. 'Well, I don't mind, Hester. You are welcome to live there, but I will leave you to sort out the details.'

'I thought at one time that Nick might marry Aurelia,' Rosalind said thoughtfully. 'They seemed to get on so well, and then she married Martin Gibbs, the manager of the clay mine.'

Hester pursed her lips. 'She married beneath her then and after he died she almost married that Charnley fellow. The one who owned a plantation on Barbados and forgot to tell her he already had a wife. Aurelia has no taste in men.'

'Now, Hester, that's not fair,' Rosalind protested. 'Anyway, forget Aurelia. I can't believe you want to leave us. We couldn't have treated you better had you been our blood relation.'

'Even so. I am finding the house very crowded. The nursery is overflowing with Nancy and Tommy's offspring, with another on the way. Dolly and Rory are adults and Phoebe is growing up fast. I would like some peace and quiet in my declining years.'

Dolly moved to her side and laid a hand on Hester's shoulder. 'We'll try to be quieter and more thoughtful. Please stay. The castle won't seem the same without you.'

'You are a wayward girl, just like your aunt Patricia at the same age, but you have a kind heart. No, Dolly, this is right for me. I yearn for a home that is mine and mine alone.'

'Except for Nick Gibson,' Dolly reminded her.

'Nevertheless, he will only be a lodger.' Hester turned to Nancy. 'Do I have your blessing? I will be a good tenant.'

Nancy shrugged. 'I have no doubt about that, and I'm sorry if my boys have been a nuisance, Hester. Of course you may have the Dower House. If that is what you really want.'

'It is. I will start making arrangements to move in, but for the time being I don't want you to say anything in front of the servants. I need to speak to Nick first. It's only polite.'

'Are you absolutely sure about this, Hester?' Rosalind eyed her anxiously. 'Wouldn't you like to sleep on it and see how you feel in the morning?'

'No. My mind is made up. There are too many changes here for me to cope with at my age. All I want now is a quiet life.'

'We will miss you, Hester,' Rosalind said earnestly. 'But we will visit you every day and make sure you need for nothing.'

'Yes, indeed,' Nancy added. 'Should you change your mind, you can always come home. Your room will be ready and waiting for you.'

At that moment a tinkling of china preceded the door being opened and Flossie entered, bringing a tray of tea and cake, which she placed on a side table next to Rosalind.

Hester rose to her feet. 'I will forego the tea and cake. I have much to do.' She sailed out of the room, leaving everyone staring after her in stunned silence.

Rosalind was the first to recover. She reached for the teapot and began to pour. 'Well, that's something I never expected. I still can't believe that Hester is actually going to move out. She has been at Rockwood for as long as I can remember.'

'Maybe she'll change her mind,' Nancy said thoughtfully. 'The Dower House is quite secluded.

She'll find it very quiet and probably lonely. After all, Nick is at the theatre every day and most evenings, too.'

'He's been living there for several years. He might not want to stay on if Hester is in charge.' Rosalind filled the cups and added a dash of milk in each. 'His whole life is the theatre, but he must think of the Dower House as his home.'

'He will have to sort that out with Hester.' Nancy reached out to take a cup of tea from Rosalind. She turned to Dolly. 'You are looking very thoughtful.'

'I was just thinking. If Nick has so much work to do at the theatre, I wonder if he needs an assistant. I have been looking for something to occupy my days, and I realise now that returning to London was not a good idea. I love the theatre, but I didn't have enough talent to get a part in the production at the Royal Grecian Theatre. Maybe I ought to work on stage management. I am desperate for something to interest me. What do you think, Mama? Would Grandmama and Grandpa Claude object?'

Chapter Eight

Felicia de Marney was still in her dressing robe when Dolly walked into the parlour at the former Greystone Park estate manager's house the following morning. Felicia replaced her coffee cup on a silver tray.

'So you've decided to come home, miss. You've had the whole family in a turmoil with your ill-judged adventures.'

'I know, Grandmama, and I am very sorry,' Dolly said humbly.

'Do sit down. You're making my neck ache, looking up at you.'

Dolly sat down on an upright chair, folding her hands neatly in her lap. 'How are you, Grandmama?'

Felicia eyed her warily. 'You didn't come all this way to enquire about my health. What do you want, Adela?'

When Grandmama called her by her proper name Dolly knew that she was in trouble. 'Well, Grandmama, it's like this. You know how much I admire you and how I love to watch you perform.'

'Everybody does. You are not alone in that.'

'Yes, I know.' Dolly began again. 'Well, my love for the theatre has obviously come down through you and—'

Felicia held up her hand. 'I've heard you singing. You have a sweet voice, I'll give you that, but it's not good enough for opera.'

'I do realise that, but I'm not suggesting that I work for you as a performer. I would like to assist Mr Gibson. I want to learn theatre management and everything associated with it.'

'Well, now. That's a turnaround, my dear. I never expected to hear such words coming from your young lips, but is this simply one of your fancies?'

'No, I don't think so, Grandmama. I am desperate for something to do other than to sit and wait for a suitable husband to come along.'

Felicia laughed. 'Do you know, Dolly, you are much more like me than your mama. I was so determined to make my mark as an opera singer that nothing and no one would have stood in my way. Ring the bell for Violet. I'll get dressed right away and we'll go to the theatre together. Nick will agree with me that you deserve a chance.'

*

An hour later, having been driven the short distance from the house to the theatre, they were seated in the small office off the foyer. Nick sat at his desk, having drawn up a chair for Felicia and another for Dolly. He steepled his fingers, glancing from one to the other as Felicia explained the situation.

'So you see, Nick, that's what Dolly would like to happen.' Felicia faced him with a firm set to her jaw.

Dolly knew it would be a brave person to argue when her grandmother was in this mood.

Nick smiled lazily. 'It sounds like a perfect arrangement, Felicia. The work has almost doubled since we first opened the doors. I could certainly do with some help.'

'Does that mean you are going to give me a chance?' Dolly asked eagerly. 'I promise to work very hard.'

'Why don't we give you a month's trial, Dolly? Then if you find the situation is not to your liking, you may leave without causing a problem. The same goes for me. I will not give you leeway simply because you are a family member.'

'I understand,' Dolly said, nodding. 'I don't expect special treatment.'

'You might regret those words.' Felicia laughed. 'When do you want her to start, Nick?'

'I was just about to leave for Exeter. I have to deposit a week's takings at the bank and there are the programmes for the next show to collect from the

printer. Dolly can do that while I do the banking.'
Nick turned to Dolly. 'Are you able to come with me?'

'Of course. I'm ready to go whenever you are.'

'I like to see an eager face.' Nick rose from his
seat. 'I will empty the safe and I'll drive us to the
bank in my gig. Is that all right with you, Felicia?'

She stood up. 'Yes, indeed. I will go home and
rest, but Dolly may stay here. I expect to hear good
things about you, my girl.'

'You will, Grandmama. I promise.'

Felicia swept out of the office and Dolly followed
her into the foyer.

'I told Heslop to wait for me.' Felicia faced Dolly
with narrowed eyes. 'This may all seem like a game
to you, Dolly, but I can assure you this is a very
serious business. We had some lean years at the
beginning, but with Sir Bentley's backing the theatre
survived. Since our benefactor's death we have had
to manage without his money, so it is very important
that you do everything Nick tells you.'

'Of course I will, Grandmama. I didn't realise that
things had been difficult. You always manage to
make the theatre seem to be thriving.'

'It is always a financial struggle.'

Felicia opened the door as Heslop drew the carriage to a halt. 'I wish you well, Dolly. It's nice to
have a member of the family who wants to help.'
She stepped outside, leaving a waft of expensive
perfume in her wake.

Dolly was slightly dazed by all that had happened.

She was half expecting Nick to emerge from the office to tell her that he had had second thoughts, but when he eventually joined her he was carrying a leather Gladstone bag.

'Are you ready to go, Dolly?'

'Yes, indeed I am. Although perhaps I ought to send a message to the castle to tell them that I won't be home for luncheon. They might think I've gone away again.'

'I'll send Alfie. He runs all the errands for me now and helps in the stables. You remember him, I expect. He was one of Nancy's protégés.'

Dolly smiled. 'Yes, of course. They've all done so well. They're a credit to her.'

'Alfie always loves a chance to visit the castle. Mrs Jackson has a soft spot for him and he gets the royal treatment. He's a good chap.'

It was a hot day and the sun blazed from a cerulean sky. Nick handled the reins with the ease of long practice. Dolly sat beside him enjoying the lush green of the hedgerows and the fields filled with ripening corn. Skylarks trilled their delightful song and wildlife scuttled around in the undergrowth. Dolly could not help wondering why she had wanted to swap the pleasures and fresh air of the Devonshire countryside for the stews of London.

She sat in silence for most of the journey while Nick went through the day-to-day running of the theatre. He outlined the tasks that she might take over from him when she was ready, and it seemed that they had just left Rockwood when they arrived in the centre of Exeter. Nick reined in outside the bank and climbed down to the pavement.

He held up his hand to help Dolly alight. 'The printer's shop is in the next street. You can't miss it. I might take a little while as I want to speak to the bank manager about the theatre's overdraft, but I'll meet you back here in half an hour or so.' He beckoned to a ragged, barefoot boy who was wandering idly, as if waiting to be given the task of holding the reins.

'Here's a penny for you, my lad. I'll give you the rest when I come out,' Nick said, ruffling the boy's hair. 'Take good care of my horse.' Without waiting for a reply, Nick strode into the bank with the Gladstone bag gripped in his hand.

Dolly walked on and made her way to the printer's shop, but she had only just turned the corner when she saw two soldiers in regimental uniform strolling towards her. Dolly's heartbeats quickened and for a moment she felt quite faint. She leaned her hand against the brick wall of the nearest building and steadied herself, struggling with the hope that Gus had seen her and the fear that he had not. It would be best to retreat into the printer's shop, but somehow she could not make her feet take the necessary steps. It was as if she were suddenly paralysed and unable to move an inch.

'Dolly! This is a pleasant surprise.' Gus strode

towards her with his comrade following more slowly.

'You are the last person I was expecting to see.' Dolly managed a smile.

'We're camped just outside the city.' He took both her hands in his, holding her at arm's length. 'I was so worried about leaving you in London, but Lord Dorrington told me that he would take care of you. I could hardly object to that, knowing that he's an old friend of the family.'

'Yes, it's true, he did.'

'Won't you introduce me to the beautiful young lady, Baker?' The other soldier, a man slightly older than Gus, sporting a large moustache, waxed and curled at the tips, came to stand beside them.

'Dunbar, this is Miss Dolly Blanchard. An old friend. Dolly, this is Donald Dunbar.'

Dunbar took Dolly's hand and raised it to his lips. 'Charming. How do you do, Miss Blanchard?'

Dolly snatched her hand away. His moustache tickled and she did not like the way he was looking at her. 'How do you do, sir?'

'What are you doing here on your own, Dolly?' Gus turned to Dunbar, frowning. 'Give us a few minutes, old chap.'

'Certainly, Baker. But I have to admit I'm jealous. If you'll excuse me, Miss Dolly, I'll take a short stroll.' Dunbar bowed and swaggered off, stopping to peer into a shop window a few yards away.

'Take no notice of Donald. He's a good chap, but

a bit too fond of the ladies.' Gus gave her a searching look. 'How are you, Dolly? Does your mama know you are in town without even a maid to accompany you?'

Dolly sighed. 'Really, Gus. You sound like Hester, and yet you were quite happy to leave me outside Uncle Freddie's house in Piccadilly.'

'I'm sorry, Dolly.' Gus smiled apologetically. 'I admit that I was thoughtless and I should have taken better care of you. Let's start again, shall we?'

His smile was disarming and, try as she might, Dolly could not keep up the pretence of anger. If she were to be honest, she was delighted to see him. 'Of course. I just wasn't expecting to see you here, that's all.'

'Where were you going? This isn't the part of town where I would advise a young woman to walk on her own.'

'I've found employment at the theatre, Gus. Nick Gibson had to go to the bank and he sent me to collect the latest batch of programmes from the printer.'

'What does your job entail?'

Dolly laughed. 'I'm just beginning to find that out, Gus. I only started today, and I should do what Nick asked me to do. If I'm late he'll think I'm irresponsible.'

'I remember Gibson well, of course. He looked after us boys when we were young. I seem to remember playing the Artful Dodger in the Christmas play.'

'I remember that, too. You were very good.'

'But why are you working? Surely your parents don't approve.'

'They haven't tried to stop me. You also know that I want to do something more with my life than wait around for the right man to sweep me off my feet.'

Gus pulled a face. 'It's a pity I don't fit that description.'

Dolly eyed him cautiously. She was never sure when he was being serious or if he was merely seeing the humour in a situation. She was tempted to encourage him, but she could feel Dunbar watching them. 'I must go, Gus. It's lovely to see you again.' She opened the door to the printer's shop and went inside.

The printer was overtly curious as to why a young lady had come to do something so menial. 'This box is a little heavy for a young lady to carry, miss.'

'I only have to take it to the next street.'

He rushed to open the door for her. 'Good day, miss.'

Dolly stepped out of the dim interior into the brilliant sunshine and found Gus waiting for her. He took the box from her. 'This is heavy. I'll take it to where you are meeting Gibson. I'd like to see him again anyway.'

Dolly glanced over her shoulder in time to see the printer peering curiously round the door. He closed it quickly. 'Yes, thank you, Gus,' she said gratefully.

The box was heavy but she would have managed it if necessary. She could see Dunbar loitering a little further along the street.

Gus called to him. 'Hey, Dunbar. I'll see you at the White Hart. I won't be long.'

Dunbar waved and strolled off in the opposite direction.

'Are you on leave?' Dolly fell into step beside Gus.

'No such luck. Dunbar and I have to collect a pair of horses for the colonel, but we're a bit early.'

'So you will while away the time in the public house.'

Gus laughed. 'Exactly. But seriously, Dolly, I will get some time off. I would like to visit Rockwood, but I don't want to come if it would make it awkward for you.'

'Why should it? I don't care if the gossips make something of it, Gus. You would be welcomed at the castle. Aunt Nancy would love you to visit again, you know that.'

'What about you, Dolly?'

She looked away. 'Of course I enjoy your company, Gus, but I will be working at the theatre. You know you can visit there at any time.'

They had reached the bank and Nick emerged before Gus had a chance to answer. He came towards them, smiling a greeting.

'Gus. It's good to see you looking so smart in your uniform. I missed you last time you came to Rockwood.'

Gus placed the box of programmes in the footwell of the gig. 'I would have come to the theatre to see you, Nick, but it was a very short visit. We're camped just outside the town so I hope to be able to visit Rockwood soon.'

Nick smiled. 'You know you are always welcome. You can stay at the Dower House whenever you wish.'

Dolly hesitated. She wanted to say something but she did not feel it was her place to tell Nick that he was soon to be invaded by the Dowager Lady Carey, and she knew instinctively that Gus would make light of it, thinking it a huge joke.

'Thank you, Nick. I'll do that, but I have to go now or Dunbar will have drunk himself under the table.' Gus turned to Dolly with a genuine smile. 'It's a pleasure to see you again, Dolly. I'll see you soon.' He grasped her hand and held it for a little too long.

'Of course. I'll look forward to it.' Dolly could feel her cheeks burning and her pulse was racing. The warmth of his touch sent tingles down her spine but she withdrew her hand gently. 'Goodbye, Gus.'

Nick tipped the boy holding the horse's reins before taking his place on the driver's seat. Gus lifted Dolly off her feet and set her down beside Nick. 'Don't work her too hard, Nick.' Gus saluted and backed away.

Nick encouraged the horse into a brisk walk, and Dolly turned to wave to Gus. He was standing on the pavement, watching them until the chaise turned into the next street. She sighed and sat quietly, her hands folded in her lap.

'I'm proud of Gus,' Nick said cheerfully. 'He's turned out well.'

'You had a hand in that yourself. You took the boys on and tutored them. You gave them a home after Aunt Nancy married Tommy. They are all a credit to you.'

'It was Nancy who rescued them all from a life in which they had been driven to crime simply to exist. I merely carried on where she left off, and she still takes an interest in each one of them. She treats May and Jack as if they were her own children.'

'I know. Aunt Nancy is a remarkable person. I wish I was more like her, and Mama, too. Hester tells me I am the spitting image of Aunt Patsy when she was young.'

Nick laughed. 'That's not an insult. Your aunt Patricia defied convention, that's all. You are much the same, but that's not altogether a bad trait. Live your life as you want to, Dolly. Don't be bullied into submission. I trust you to do a good job, and I know you won't disappoint me.'

'I won't. I promise to work hard. I won't complain about long hours. I'll do whatever you tell me to do and I'll do it with a willing heart.'

'I know you will, but it won't always be exciting work. A lot of what I have to do is dull routine. You will take a lot of that off my shoulders.'

'I want to learn everything about running the

theatre, and I want to prove to Grandmama that I am a person of consequence. I'm not just an empty-headed flibbertigibbet.'

They lapsed into silence for the rest of the journey. Dolly was glad of the respite and relieved that Nick did not ask her about her relationship with Gus. It must be obvious to anyone with half an eye that Gus paid her marked attention. Dolly made up her mind to warn him about it when she next saw him. There could never be anything serious between them, but Rockwood was a place where the gossips loved to make up romances and create intrigues out of the most innocent relationships.

When they reached the theatre they were met by a frantic stage manager.

'What's the trouble, Bradshaw?' Nick demanded crossly.

Bradshaw faced him, wringing is hands. 'It's only a few hours until curtain up, Mr Gibson. The leading lady has been taken ill and won't be able to perform tonight or for the foreseeable future.'

'That's annoying, but her understudy must be sent for. Why haven't you done that?'

'I did, sir. That was my first thought, but she is unwell, too. We have no one to take the part.'

Nick placed the box of programmes on his desk. 'That is serious indeed. Is there anyone in the cast who might take their places at such short notice?'

'No, sir. Most definitely not. I've been through every possibility with no success.'

Dolly had a sudden idea. 'I might know someone who could take the part at such short notice.'

Nick and Bradshaw turned to give her questioning looks.

'Who could possibly do that? You aren't offering, are you, Dolly?'

She shook her head. 'No, Nick. I learned my lesson when I tried to take this person's place at the Grecian Theatre. I'm talking about Liza Day. She auditioned for the part in this production, but for some reason Grandmama turned her down.'

'I trust Felicia's judgement.' Nick shook his head. 'If she doesn't think this girl is capable of playing the role I must agree with her.'

'Have you any choice?' Dolly met his worried look with an impatient toss of her head. 'Let me go to Liza's cottage and speak to her. I'm almost certain she knows the part. At least give her a chance.'

'It might be the answer, Mr Gibson,' Bradshaw added urgently. 'We will have to cancel the performance if she can't fill in.'

Nick sighed. 'Very well, Dolly. Go and see her. Bring her back with you if she thinks she can help out, but in the meantime I'll prepare the cancellation notice.'

'You won't need to do that. I'm sure she will leap at the opportunity to prove herself.'

It was not far to the cottage where Liza Day's grandmother had lived all her life. Dolly had only seen it in passing, but its run-down appearance had always made her shudder. She had not given much thought to the occupants and she had assumed that they would be taken care of as the dwelling was on the Greystone estate.

As she approached it from the lane she began to see it in a different light. The thatch was in desperate need of replacing and the paintwork had almost peeled away. Roses clambered over the front porch, giving it a picturesque appearance, but Dolly realised that this was a false image. The front garden, surrounded by a picket fence, also in need of repair, was laid out to vegetables and the beds cultivated in a haphazard fashion with more weeds than anything. A couple of hens waddled around, pecking at invisible insects and grubs, and a tethered goat tugged at its chain as if it wanted to rush forward to greet her.

Dolly walked up the path and the door opened. Liza Day stared at her in surprise, shielding her eyes. 'Miss Blanchard, what are you doing here?'

'So you remember me, Liza.'

'Not likely to forget you, am I? Did you take my part at the Grecian?'

'No. To be honest, I wasn't good enough. I was rude to you the day we met at the audition, and arrogant. I apologise.'

'You didn't come all this way just to say sorry.'

'No, of course not. May I come in? It's very hot out here.'

Liza shook her head. 'Grannie is asleep. She has

a bed in the parlour because she can't manage the stairs.'

'I'm sorry.'

'If you've come to look down on us you can just turn round and go away. We don't need charity or your pity.'

'That's not why I'm here, Liza. Actually, I need your help.'

'If it's cleaning work at the theatre or the castle I can do that.'

'No, it's nothing of the sort. The leading lady and the understudy of the operetta are both ill and there's no one to play the heroine. Do you know the libretto?'

'Yes,' Liza said cautiously. 'I only have to hear a song once or twice and I know it. Do you want a prompter?'

'Liza, I'm asking if you could take the lead in tonight's performance. It will be cancelled if you can't do it and the theatre will lose a lot of money.'

Liza put her head on one side, eyeing Dolly suspiciously. 'Why are you here asking this? Or is it some spiteful joke you're playing on me?'

'No, of course not. Mr Gibson has taken me on as assistant manager, and this is my first chance to do something for the theatre. Will you come with me now?'

Liza nodded. 'Let me go and tell Grannie, although she's so deaf she probably won't understand. Anyway, she sleeps nearly all day so she'll hardly notice I've gone.' Liza opened the cottage door and the smell of damp, burning tallow and smoke from the fire wafted out into the fresh air.

Moments later Liza reappeared wearing a battered straw hat with a much-darned shawl slung around her shoulders. 'I'm ready.'

They were met at the theatre by Nick. He hustled them into the auditorium. 'This is highly unusual and I am not sure it will work, Miss Day. Are you willing to do an impromptu audition? I need to be sure that you know and understand the libretto.'

'I do know it off by heart, sir.'

Nick handed her up to the stage. 'Do your best. Arnold will accompany you on the piano.' Nick jerked his head in the direction of the pianist seated at the keyboard in the orchestra pit.

'Good luck, Liza,' Dolly said earnestly. 'I know you can do it.'

Liza stood on the stage, hands folded in front of her as the pianist played the introduction. She came in at exactly the right moment and she sang from the heart. Dolly could have been jealous but she was simply filled with admiration. She was also ashamed of her previous comments to Liza on the unfortunate day when Grandmama failed to acknowledge the girl's talent. Nick was obviously impressed and also relieved. Dolly could tell by his expression that Liza would be given the part on the spot and she was not disappointed.

When the audition came to an end, Nick handed Liza a copy of the libretto. 'I've called the rest of the cast in an hour earlier than the performance is due to start. We will do a quick run-through so that you can get an idea of positioning and working with the other performers. Do you think you are up to such a challenge?'

Liza's blue eyes sparkled with enthusiasm. 'I most certainly do, sir.'

Nick beckoned to Bradshaw, who had been standing in the wings. 'Take Miss Day to the star's dressing room, please, Reg. See that she has everything she needs. I'll send a messenger to call the cast in early for a quick run-through.'

Bradshaw nodded eagerly. 'I'll do that, sir. Come with me, please, Miss Day.'

Liza sent Dolly a grateful smile before following Bradshaw backstage.

'Well, it looks as though you've saved the day,' Nick said, laughing. 'That wasn't meant to be a pun, but Liza is obviously very talented. I can't think why Mrs de Marney turned her down for the role.'

'We'll need the wardrobe mistress to make any adjustments necessary on the costumes,' Dolly said thoughtfully. 'She lives in the village, next to Dr Bulmer's house. It's not far to walk.'

'All right. That's one less task for Alfie to do.'

'I'll go right away.' Dolly went to fetch her bonnet and gloves and set off for the village. She was filled with enthusiasm for her new position and eager to prove that she could do anything asked of her. She nodded and returned the greetings of the people she met in the street but she did not stop to make conversation.

When she reached Dr Bulmer's house she came to a sudden halt. Gus and Todd were deep in conversation on the pavement outside the doctor's front door.

Gus saw her first. 'Dolly. This is the second time we've met by accident in one day.'

'I thought you had to take the horses back to your colonel.'

'I decided I'd rather visit my old friend in Rockwood. Dunbar did the necessary for me. Anyway, our paths have crossed again. That must mean something, surely?'

Dolly could feel Todd staring at her and she shot him a sideways glance. 'Gus is never serious, but we did meet in Exeter. I was there on business with Nick Gibson. I have a job at the theatre, Todd.'

'So Gus just told me. What does your papa think about that?' Todd eyed her curiously. 'I mean it's hardly the sort of thing your family would expect.'

'You are as hidebound as they are,' Dolly said, sighing. 'I am a modern young woman and I intend to earn my own living.'

'Is that why you ran off with this reprobate?' Todd was clearly not impressed.

'We didn't run off,' Dolly said angrily. 'Gus escorted me to London because that's where I was going anyway.'

'And then he abandoned you in the worst part of the city.'

'Hold on a moment, Todd,' Gus protested. 'I didn't leave Dolly; she left me.'

'Please keep your voices down,' Dolly said anxiously. 'I don't want the gossips to hear about my escapade. As it happens, everything turned out quite well and now I am home and none the worse for my experiences.' She glanced from one to the other. 'You two are the best of friends. Don't fall out over something so trivial.'

'I have a patient to visit at the hotel.' Todd started to walk away.

Dolly hurried after him. 'Would that be the leading lady from the theatre?'

'I can't discuss medical matters. You know that.' Todd came to a halt, turning to her with a steady look. 'Don't be taken in by Gus, Dolly. He'll break your heart.' He strode off, leaving Dolly staring after him.

'Dolly,' Gus called. 'What did he say to you? Don't take any notice of Todd. He's in love with you and always has been. Come back.'

Dolly was more shaken than she cared to admit. She spun round, frowning at Gus. 'Don't talk nonsense. Anyway, I can't stop now. I have more important things to do. Go back to your regiment and leave me alone.'

Chapter Nine

The performance that evening went ahead to a full house. Word that there was a new person in the leading role seemed to have spread quickly. Dolly was pleased and slightly amazed that they had managed to put the production on at all, but Nick was obviously delighted. After several curtain calls Nick took Dolly into the office and thanked her for bringing Liza to his notice.

'You certainly saved the day, Dolly, but it's getting late. I'll tell Alfie to take you home in my gig.'

'There's no need for that, sir.' Gus strolled into the office. 'I'm going that way myself. I've brought the chaise from Rockwood with instructions from her mama to take Dolly home.'

'There was really no need,' Dolly protested.

'I think there is, and so did everyone at the castle.

I went there to pay my respects to Nancy, and I was invited to stay for dinner.'

'An excellent idea. Take Dolly home by all means,' Nick said enthusiastically. 'I don't like the thought of her out on her own at this time of night.'

'I agree entirely.' Gus held out his hand. 'Are you ready, Dolly?'

She was beginning to feel like a child with no alternative but to obey her elders. She wanted to refuse but it would appear churlish and she was too tired to argue. It had been a long day and an emotional one. She had not forgotten Gus's claim that Todd loved her. It was something she had suspected but had never been able to prove. Todd was a deeply private person and had never revealed his true feelings.

'Yes, you go on, Dolly,' Nick said cheerfully. 'Come in late tomorrow morning, if you wish. You certainly earned your place here.'

Somewhat reluctantly Dolly put on her bonnet and slipped her shawl around her shoulders. It might be high summer now but it was chilly at night, particularly travelling in an open chaise. She allowed Gus to help her onto the driver's seat and he climbed up to sit beside her.

'I thought you had to get back to camp,' Dolly said stiffly.

'I'm staying with Todd at the doctor's house tonight. I'll leave first thing in the morning.'

Dolly turned her head to look him in the face. 'I made a mistake by going to London with you. I want to put it firmly in the past.'

'I enjoyed our brief adventure, even if you didn't.'

'Weren't you concerned about me after you left me in Piccadilly? You didn't even wait to see me safely inside. Anything could have happened to me.'

Gus shrugged. 'Are you trying to pick a quarrel with me, Dolly?'

'No. I'm just saying that your concern for me now is hard to accept, when you left me on a busy city street with only Bess for company.'

'All right, I admit that I'm irresponsible and unreliable. I'm everything you say I am, but if I upset you I am truly sorry.' He flicked the reins and the horse walked on, breaking into a trot when they reached the main road.

'Gus, I never know where I stand with you. I can't tell if you are being sincere or if you are teasing me.'

'I have the warmest regard for you, Dolly. I'm not sure if I know what love is, but perhaps that's what I feel for you. I know that I want to be with you. I'd like to kiss you again, but judging by your expression when you saw me just now, that wouldn't be welcome.'

'You shouldn't be talking to me like this. And why did you tell me that Todd was in love with me? What right had you to say such things?'

'I've known Todd all my life. I feel what he feels. It's as simple as that.'

'If you're his friend, why would you say things like that? You always treat everything like a joke.'

Gus reined the horse in and the chaise drew to a halt just before they reached the bridge over the River Sawle. He took Dolly in his arms and kissed her soundly, releasing her so suddenly that she had to clutch the edge of the seat to prevent herself from falling from the carriage.

'I should slap your silly face for that, Gus Baker.'

'But you didn't, did you? You and I are so similar, Dolly. We are both rebels and we need each other.'

She could still feel the imprint of his lips on hers but she was angry and confused. She stared straight ahead. 'Drive on or I'll jump off and run the rest of the way.'

'Walk on.' Gus flicked the reins and clicked his tongue against his teeth and the horse obeyed instantly. 'If only women were as easy to handle as horses.'

'You are not a gentleman, Gus.'

'I never pretended otherwise, my darling. But I'll see you safely to the door and wait until you go in this time. Perhaps it's better if you make my excuses to your family.'

'At least we agree on that.'

'I'll call on you tomorrow before I return to camp.'

'Just leave me alone. I don't want anything more to do with you, Gus. Get that into your thick skull.'

'What? And leave space for my rivals to claim you?' Gus urged the horse to a trot. 'One way or another, Dolly, you and I are bound to be together. I knew it from the first moment I returned to Rockwood and saw you all grown up and beautiful.'

'You talk nonsense, Gus. You've already said that you don't know how to love anyone – other than yourself, of course.'

He laughed. 'That was cruel, Dolly. One day you'll change your mind.' He drove on and, as promised, he set her down outside the main entrance of the castle.

James opened the door and stood aside, his expression carefully controlled as Dolly marched into the entrance hall without a backwards glance.

'Good night, my love,' Gus said loudly. 'Thank you for a wonderful evening.'

Dolly gritted her teeth, refusing to be drawn into rebuking Gus for his behaviour. She went straight to her room and rang the bell for Bess, who duly arrived, bringing a pitcher of warm water.

'We heard about the goings-on at the theatre, miss,' Bess said eagerly as she filled the wash basin. 'How did it go?'

'It went very well. Liza Day was brilliant in the part.'

'I'm glad she was a success. I was told that she came down to Rockwood to care for her sick grannie.'

'Yes, Liza deserves everything that this part will bring her. Now, I'm exhausted, Bess. Will you help me unlace my stays? I'm going to wash and put on my nightgown and fall into bed. I'll sleep without rocking tonight, that's for certain.'

Dolly fell into a dreamless sleep but she was awakened by the sound of a succession of sharp objects hitting the glass windowpanes. She sat up slowly and peered at the small carriage clock on the table beside her bed. It was five o'clock on a bright summer morning and someone in the gardens below was trying to attract her attention by flinging handfuls of gravel at her window. Suspecting the culprit, Dolly shook off the last remnants of sleep and went to the window. She flung it open and leaned out.

There standing on the grassy bank two storeys below, Gus was in full regimental uniform, grinning up at her.

'It's easier to wake up a whole battalion than you, Dolly.'

'Gus, you'll wake the entire household and have the servants running round to see what's going on.'

'You look adorable, Dolly. I love seeing you all warm and still sleepy, with your hair loose around your shoulders. I wish I could climb up there to give you a cuddle.'

'Gus Baker, you say the most outrageous things. Go away at once. I am not having this conversation.'

Gus held up his hand. 'I think I do love you, Dolly Blanchard.' He blew her a kiss and strolled off.

Dolly slammed the window shut and retreated to

her bed. She slumped down, breathing heavily. She hoped that none of the servants had witnessed his performance, and her cheeks burned at the memory of his embarrassing comments on her appearance. She was thankful that the room on the floor below her bedchamber was unoccupied at present. Gus was unpredictable and incorrigible. She could only hope that his regiment would be sent somewhere far away in the not-too-distant future. Even so, his words were flattering, and a quick glance in her dressing-table mirror confirmed his opinion that her wildly untidy hair and rosy cheeks were not un-attractive. She looked away hurriedly. Gus was not to be taken seriously. Yet again, she had almost fallen for his roguish charm.

Dolly slipped beneath the coverlet and lay down, but she was wide awake now and restless. She rose from her bed for the second time and slipped off her cotton lawn nightgown. It fell to the ground in soft white folds and she gazed at her slender figure in the cheval mirror. A sudden memory of the embrace she had shared with Gus made her turn away quickly and reach for her shift. Such improper thoughts were deeply disturbing and yet tantalisingly exciting. She dressed quickly, managing her stays as best she could without a maid to tighten them for her.

A ride before breakfast would brush away the cobwebs and give her a better start to the day. Fresh air and exercise was what Hester always ordered for a bout of the megrims, and Dolly could feel one coming on.

The stable boys were only just going about their morning routine, bleary-eyed from sleep and tousled as if they had slept in their shirts and breeches. Even so, they had Dolly's horses saddled and ready for her to ride within minutes. She thanked them, but the smell of young, unwashed bodies was too much for her. She advised them both to make use of the pump in the stable yard before Hudson or his son, Pip, the head groom, came on duty.

Dolly rode out of the bailey and crossed the bridge, heading through the village in the direction of Greystone Park. She had not gone far when she saw a familiar figure on foot. Todd had his medical bag in his hand and his feet dragged as if walking was an effort. Dolly reined in.

'Todd, you look worn out. Are you all right?'

He managed a weak grin. 'Just tired, that's all. I've been up all night with Mrs Dawson. It was a difficult delivery, but mother and baby are doing well now.'

'That's excellent news. Well done, Todd.'

'I think the praise goes to Mrs Dawson. Anyway, you are out early.'

'Yes, I felt I needed some fresh air.'

'I think Gus will have left by now. He had my bed for the night as I knew I was unlikely to get home.'

'I dare say he has,' Dolly said casually. She was tempted to tell Todd about Gus's early morning exploits, but something stopped her. He looked so tired that she wanted to put her arms around him and give him a hug, but that would never do. She could already feel eyes fixed upon them as lace curtains fluttered curiously in the terraced houses. 'Well, don't let me keep you from your bed. I'm sure you need a good rest until the next call-out.'

'Dr Bulmer is officially retired, but he has kindly offered to cover my duties this evening. I am eager to see the new leading lady.'

'Liza Day was truly magnificent last evening, Todd. She took over like a true professional. There were a few slip-ups, but the audience didn't seem to mind. In fact, they even clapped when Liza and the rest of the cast did their best to deal with the mistakes.'

'I'm pleased that you have found something you obviously enjoy doing, Dolly. Your grandmama must be delighted that you are taking an interest in her theatre.'

'Yes, I think so. For the first time in my life I seem to be doing something that she approves of. Anyway, I mustn't keep you from your bed. I hope to see you this evening.'

'I'll do my utmost to come and watch the performance.'

'I hope you get some rest. Goodbye, Todd.' Dolly rode on.

The gates to Greystone Park were open and she

decided to head for the parkland, where she could enjoy a gallop without having to jump fences or open gates. She had to pass the Dower House and she reined in at the sound of angry voices. Outside was a carter's wagon laden with furniture, which she recognised as belonging to Hester, but the driver was arguing fiercely with the housekeeper, Mrs Simpson.

'But I've been told by the Dowager Lady Carey to deliver her goods here, ma'am.'

'It's the first I've heard of it,' Mrs Simpson replied angrily. 'Take it away.'

'I can't, ma'am. I'll get the sack from my boss if I don't do the delivery.'

'I don't care. It must be some kind of joke.'

Dolly rode up to them and dismounted. 'Mrs Simpson, there has been a lack of communication, as far as I can see. I believe that the Dowager Lady Carey is going to live here, although I don't know exactly when she plans to move in.'

'Well, nobody told me anything about it.'

'It must have been a terrible oversight, but I believe the decision was taken rather quickly. However, this poor man will get the sack if he doesn't do what he came here to do. Please allow him to unload the furniture and I'll ride back to the castle and try to sort things out for you.'

Mrs Simpson scowled. 'All right, Miss Blanchard. If you put it like that I suppose I can't refuse. I'll need to have it from her ladyship if she really does intend to move in. However, you may place everything in the front parlour, my man.'

'Ta, I should just think so.' The carter began to unload the van.

Mrs Simpson turned to Dolly. 'Does Mr Gibson know about this, Miss Blanchard?'

'Is he at home, Mrs Simpson?'

'No, miss. He left a good half an hour ago. He likes to get into the theatre early. He's a very conscientious man.'

'I don't doubt it,' Dolly said hastily.

Mrs Simpson bristled as if expecting an argument. 'This has been his home for more than nine years. He looked after the boys when Miss Nancy married Sir Thomas.'

'I will make sure he is kept informed, Mrs Simpson.' Dolly backed away and led her horse to a convenient tree stump, which she used as a mounting block. She rode off, this time heading back towards the castle. She had not intended to get involved in Hester's plans, but it seemed she had little choice.

Hester was unrepentant. 'That woman has been in charge for too long. I will probably replace her with someone younger. Someone who will give me the respect due to my station in life.'

Dolly stared at her great-grandmother in amazement. Hester had always been very forthright and down to earth; very free with her opinions, and she disliked being crossed, but this person was new to Dolly. Hester had always been proud of her humble beginnings but suddenly she seemed to have changed.

'Mrs Simpson is one thing, Great-Grandmama,' Dolly said tactfully. 'But Nick Gibson has been Aunt Nancy's close friend for years. He has taken care of her boys and they still look up to him, even though they are grown men. Grandmama relies on him to run the theatre. Nick is a person of consequence, too.'

Hester sighed impatiently. 'Why does everyone think they have a right to tell me how to run my life? You are a mere child, Dolly. However, I've already said that I will see Mr Gibson. Go to the theatre now and tell him to come to the castle. I will speak to him urgently because I intend to move into the Dower House tomorrow.'

Rosalind had been sitting at her escritoire, listening intently. 'Hester, there's no need to hurry. You know we don't want you to leave us. It's entirely your decision.'

'That's right. It is my choice. I want to be mistress in my own home. At my age I need to feel secure and I want to enjoy peace and quiet. Your children are grown now, Rosalind, but Nancy's offspring are getting out of hand. In my opinion they need a strict governess and they should be confined to the schoolroom. However, I have little say in household matters. That has been made clear to me.'

'Not by me, Hester,' Rosalind said firmly. 'You

have always been given the greatest respect, and in many ways you have overstepped the limits, but we have all accommodated you out of affection for you and loyalty to Grandpapa.'

Hester sniffed. 'Then I am very sorry if I have become a tyrant. I will be out of your way very soon.'

'That's not what I said, Hester.' Rosalind shook her head. 'Whatever you choose to think, you are still part of this family.' She stood up and walked swiftly from the room, leaving Dolly to face Hester on her own.

'I'll go to the theatre and ask Nick to come here straight away,' Dolly said hastily.

'Yes, do that.' Hester assumed a martyred expression and reached for the bell pull. 'I'll send for Bertha Tuckett. I believe she works in the laundry room these days, but I have better plans for her.'

'Yes, Great-Grandmama.' Dolly hurried from the room. Bertha had worked at Greystone Park and was a notorious troublemaker, which is why Rosalind had sent her to work in the laundry room. It was only out of the kindness of her heart, and because Nancy stepped in with a good word for Bertha, that she had not been sacked for mischief-making amongst the servants.

Dolly smiled to herself as she stepped into the sunshine. Pip Hudson was walking her horse as she had requested and he helped her to mount. She thanked him and rode off, heading towards Greystone Park and the Pavilion Theatre.

She found Nick in the office and she passed on the message from Hester without going into any details. It was Hester's idea to take over the home that Nick had enjoyed for so many years, and it was up to her to break the news to him. He appeared to be mystified, but not particularly worried as he set off, leaving Dolly in charge of things at the theatre.

She was busy placing reserved tickets on the seats already booked for that evening's performance when Felicia and Claude arrived.

'Nick tells me that you are working for us in the front of house,' Felicia said warily. 'I hope you don't think this is a way to get a part in any of our productions, Adela.'

'No, Grandmama, certainly not. I've given up that idea completely.'

'It takes a clever person to know their own limitations.' Claude gave her a beaming smile. 'I admire your sense of purpose, my dear. You love the theatre, which is, after all, in your blood, and you have found a way to satisfy your creative talents.'

'Thank you, Grandpapa.' Dolly returned the smile.

'It appears that Liza Day did well last evening,' Felicia said stonily. 'I seem to remember turning her down for the part on the day you got up on stage and performed for us.'

'Don't remind me of that, please,' Dolly laughed. 'I really thought I had inherited some of your talent, Grandmama, but I realise now I was mistaken. Liza did extremely well considering she was not even the understudy. There is a full rehearsal in an hour's time, if you would care to stay and watch.'

'I think not, but we will be in our usual loge this evening. From there I can watch and make a note of any errors or improvements needed.'

'And I, as usual, will be the scribe who notes it all down,' Claude said, grinning.

'You are so hard done by, I can't imagine why you put up with it.' Felicia tossed her head and marched up the aisle towards the foyer with Claude following in her footsteps.

Dolly hurried after them. Her suspicions were correct when she reached the office just after Felicia had opened the safe and was about to count the takings.

'It's all accounted for, Grandmama. Nick showed me the figures in the book before he left this morning.'

'He should be here now. Where is he?'

Dolly hesitated. 'Well, he's gone to the castle. Hester wanted to see him.'

'That woman! What mischief is she up to now?'

Claude laid his hand on his wife's arm. 'It's probably something and nothing, my dear.'

'It's always something with Hester. She likes to think she rules the family, but she is wrong. Perhaps someone ought to remind her of her humble beginnings.'

'Dolly, my dear, how are the advance bookings?' Claude asked hastily.

'I haven't had time to study the books, Grandpapa.' Dolly gave him a grateful smile. If her grandmother started going on about Hester's many faults, as she saw it, they would be here all morning. 'Would you like to take a look?'

'Excellent idea. We have everything invested in the theatre, particularly since Sir Bentley passed away. If it fails now, we will lose everything.'

'It won't fail. I am still the main attraction,' Felicia said icily. 'I am perfect for the more mature roles, and I have many faithful devotees who are prepared to travel the length and breadth of the country to see me perform.'

'Of course you do, my love.' Claude glanced through the advance bookings, shaking his head. 'Not very good, are they?'

'I suppose not,' Dolly said reluctantly. 'I'm so new to this business that I really don't know.'

'We need to do something that will attract a wider audience. Something that will bring people to the theatre and to stay at the hotel. The trouble is that we are so far from London or any other major city.'

Dolly glanced at the pile of programmes she had collected from the printer's office. 'I see the next production is Verdi's *The Masked Ball*.'

'Yes, it's one of my favourites,' Felicia said firmly. 'What of it, Adela?'

'Why don't we hold a masked ball either before or after the performance? Everyone comes to the theatre dressed for the occasion, complete with masks. The ball could be held outside in the grounds, with marquees in case of inclement weather, although we've had a lovely summer so far.'

Claude frowned thoughtfully. 'That sounds like a wonderful idea, but would we have time to organise such an event?'

'I don't see why not. We could put an advertisement in *The Times*. There could be a prize for the best costume or a midnight unmasking – something exciting and different.'

'I think that's a very clever idea. What do you say, Felicia, my love?'

'I never thought I'd say it, but I think you might have something there, Adela. A masked ball in the theatre's grounds sound like a perfect summer's entertainment. What would the prize be?'

Dolly thought quickly. 'Perhaps you could decide upon that, Grandmama. I'm sure you would come up with something really remarkable.'

'Yes, I suppose I would,' Felicia said modestly. 'Well, go ahead with your plan, but keep me informed of every detail. Claude, we can do no more here until I have seen Miss Day in the leading role tonight. If she is as good as you say she is, Adela, I will allow her to take the part for the entire run.'

Claude frowned. 'But what about Miss Corvi, my dear?'

'According to Dr Bulmer, Carlotta Corvi is unlikely to be well enough to perform for a while and neither is her understudy. Foreigners have no stamina. Come,

Claude, I need a little sustenance. It's time to go home for luncheon.'

'Yes, my dear, of course.' Claude gave Dolly an encouraging smile as he followed his wife out of the office.

Dolly could hear her grandmother rebuking Claude for some misdemeanour, real or imagined, as they left the theatre.

When Nick returned half an hour later he looked downcast as he entered the office. Dolly closed the ledger she had been studying. 'So you know what's happening?'

He slumped down on a chair by his desk. 'Yes, your great-grandmother told me in no uncertain terms that I am no longer the tenant of the Dower House, although I may stay on if I take one of the attic rooms and eat in the servants' hall.'

'I am so sorry,' Dolly said earnestly. 'That is awful. I thought she would be more magnanimous than that.'

'It's her right to take over the house. Nancy doesn't have any objections and it was never a permanent arrangement, as far as I was concerned. I suppose it was just too easy to stay on after the boys moved out. I didn't give it a thought, but now I must.'

'What will you do?'

'Nancy said there is a cottage on the estate that I might rent from her. I'll go and take a look at it and hope it isn't too run down. Apparently it's been empty for some time.'

'I'll come with you, if that's any help, and we can talk about the idea I've had to make the next show even more spectacular and successful.'

Dolly explained her idea about the masked ball as they walked to the cottage on the far side of the deer park. At first sight it looked very dilapidated and the small enclosed garden was knee-high in weeds and brambles.

Nick opened the door and ushered Dolly inside. She was pleasantly surprised to find that the interior was in better shape than the exterior. The previous tenant had stripped the rooms of furniture and there was a thick coating of dust on the floorboards. There was a small parlour and a kitchen with a rusty range and a stone sink. Cobwebs hung like net curtains from the rafters, but as far as Dolly could see there was nothing that some energetic cleaning would not put right. Nick climbed the narrow staircase and she could hear his footsteps above as he went from one bedroom to the other. He came down again with a broad smile on his face.

'It's hardly a palace, but I think I could be quite comfortable here.'

'I'm sure we can find enough furniture to make it habitable, and Mrs Simpson will be only too happy to send one or two of her cleaners to get the cottage into reasonable shape before you move in.' Dolly eyed the range nervously. 'Do you know how to work one of these things? I'm afraid I never learned how to cook.'

'I'm a lifelong bachelor, Dolly. I was used to making my own meals before I moved into the Dower House. I'll just have to start all over again, but at least I'll be independent living here.'

'I expect you'll get plenty of help when it comes to painting the inside and outside, as well as getting the garden into shape. It's good that most of Aunt Nancy's boys have grown into useful people and have remained in the village.'

'You always see the positive side of things, Dolly.'

She smiled. 'I don't know about that.'

'You come from a remarkable family of strong women. I can see a lot of your aunt Patricia in you, as well as some of your grandmother's indomitable spirit and talent.'

Dolly pulled a face. 'Don't tell me I'm like Grand-mama.'

'She is an amazing person. She might be difficult to work with, but that's because she has genuine talent and a forceful personality.'

'I prefer to think I take after Mama,' Dolly said, smiling. 'She is always so kind and calm.'

'Your mama holds the family together. In fact, she is the person you should ask to help with a guest list for the masquerade ball.'

Dolly turned to him with a wide smile. 'So you really think it's a good idea?'

'Not just a good one, Dolly. It's brilliant. It will put the Pavilion Theatre on the map, so to speak. I suggest you go home right away and speak to your mama. Maybe Lord Dorrington would bring some of his wealthy acquaintances. We might even make it an annual event.'

'You're right. I'll go now. Leave everything to me, Nick.'

Dolly left the cottage forgetting everything other than the plans for making the masquerade ball a huge success.

Chapter Ten

Dolly had just ridden across the bridge over the River Sawle when she spotted her father and Tommy strolling towards her. They were chatting amicably but they stopped when they saw her and they waved a greeting. They had both played such a large part in her life and she adored her handsome father. Her cousin Tommy was ten years her senior and he was a much-loved friend. Dolly rode up to them, reining her horse in expertly.

'Good morning.'

'Your mama tells me that you're working at the theatre,' Alex said cheerfully. 'You aren't going to turn into your grandmama, are you, Dolly? I don't think I could stand another operatic diva in the family.'

'No, Papa. I gave that up after my experience in London. I know when I'm beaten.'

Tommy laughed. 'I don't believe that for an instant, Dolly. You are too much like both of my aunts. Although you probably take after your aunt Patsy a little more.'

'You are the second person to tell me that this morning, Tommy.' Dolly shrugged. 'I am flattered.'

'Have you finished for the day already?' Alex asked casually. 'If so, I wish we had such short working hours. What do you say, Tommy?'

'I haven't finished, Papa,' Dolly said hastily. 'Nick sent me home to speak to Mama about a very important event that was my brilliant idea. I hope to put the Pavilion Theatre on the map, and Rockwood with it.'

Tommy grinned. 'Now I'm really scared. I know that look and tone of voice. Whenever my aunts had an idea they were convinced was the best thing ever, and we all had to suffer the consequences.'

'Now you're laughing at me.' Dolly wheeled her horse around so that it was facing the castle. 'You just wait, Tommy. Wait and see, that's all I can say.' She clicked her tongue against her teeth and the animal broke into a trot, heading for the castle bailey.

Rosalind and Nancy were in the still room and they jumped guiltily when Dolly opened the door.

'Why are you in here?' Dolly looked from one to the other. 'Are you hiding from someone?'

'Shut the door quickly,' Nancy said in a low voice.

172

'We've been at Hester's beck and call all morning and we've had enough.'

'Yes, she's driving us mad,' Rosalind agreed, nodding. 'You would think she was emigrating to Africa or some far-flung outpost of the Empire. I've never heard such a fuss about moving a few personal effects from one house to another.'

'She's going through everything in each room, making sure nothing that belongs to her is left behind.' Nancy sighed. 'I'm beginning to wish that I'd refused to allow her to live in the Dower House.'

'At least we'll get a bit of peace and quiet when she's moved out,' Rosalind said wearily. 'I'm exhausted and it isn't even time for luncheon.'

Nancy held her finger to her lips at the sound of footstep, but fortunately whoever it was ran past the door. She breathed a sigh of relief. 'I hope Nick takes up my offer of the cottage. I don't know what state it will be in, but anything would be better for him than being a lodger in Hester's new home.'

'Nick is at the cottage now and he's keen to move in,' Dolly said firmly. 'I've just come from there and it only needs a good clean and a lick of paint. Perhaps you can find him some furniture that we no longer need.'

'Of course,' Rosalind said eagerly. 'I'm sure we can help out, and that goes for bed linen, too.'

'I expect Flossie will find some crockery and cooking utensils that we can give him. I'll go to the cottage later and see what he needs.' Nancy opened the door just a crack. She put her finger to her lips for hush as she listened. 'I think Hester has gone to her room. I heard Bertha calling to Jennet, asking for her help in Lady Carey's bedchamber. The poor girls are run off their feet.'

'It will all calm down when Hester is satisfied that she has everything she needs,' Rosalind said hopefully. 'Now, why did you want to see us, Dolly? Is everything all right at the theatre? I hope Mama is not making your life difficult.'

'No, really. It's not that. She is being very reasonable about Liza Day taking Carlotta Corvi's part.'

Nancy leaned against the stone sink. 'There must be something urgent that brings you here before luncheon.'

'I've discovered that the theatre isn't making as much money as it should, and without Sir Bentley's backing they need extra funds, so I suggested a masquerade ball to be held on the first night of the next production: Verdi's opera *The Masked Ball*. Nick thought that Mama would be able to help me make up a list of people who might be prepared to venture all the way to Devonshire for such an event. It would boost the theatre's takings and put the hotel on the map.'

'It sounds like a wonderful idea,' Rosalind said eagerly.

'I thought we could have a marquee in the grounds and hold the ball under the stars at the end of the performance, weather permitting, of course. There would be an unmasking at midnight and a prize for the best costume. What do you think?'

Nancy clapped her hands. 'Wonderful. I'm excited already. Just tell us what help you need.'

'You'll have to charge more for the theatre tickets, to cover the cost.' Rosalind opened the door and peeped out. 'All clear. Let's go to the morning parlour and we can make a list of prospective guests.'

'Freddie is the man to help us,' Nancy added. 'He might not enjoy mixing in high society but he knows just about everyone who is anyone. I'll send him a note.'

'He always loves an excuse to come here,' Rosalind said, laughing. 'I'm sure he spends more of the year here than he does at either Dorrington Place or his London home. Come along, but don't make a noise or we might end up helping Hester to search for things she's forgotten or never knew she had.'

Creeping stealthily, as if they were stalking deer, they went in single file to the morning parlour. Once inside, Rosalind closed the door with a sigh. 'Now then, Dolly. Let's get down to business.'

Nancy pulled up a chair. 'This is so exciting. Life was getting a little dull, especially in my condition. I need something to occupy my mind.'

'When is the baby due, Aunt Nancy?'

'In December. I hope well before Christmas, although I'm not exactly certain. But I do hope it's a girl this time. I adore my boys but it would be lovely to have a little daughter.'

The door opened suddenly and all three stiffened in anticipation, and then sighed with relief when Alex walked into the room.

'What's going on?' he demanded, grinning. 'You all look like naughty children caught scrumping apples in the orchard.'

'Shut the door, darling,' Rosalind said urgently. 'We are hiding from Hester. She has all the servants in uproar as she hunts for her belongings and supervises the packing.'

'I see. Well, all I came to say was that Tommy and I are going to Exeter after luncheon. Do any of you want anything from the town?'

'Oh, yes, please,' Dolly was suddenly alert. 'Could you go to the printer's shop and order gilt-edged tickets for the masquerade ball? I'll write it all down and you just have to give it to the printer. He always does the printing for the theatre.' She walked over to the escritoire and selected a sheet of writing paper and a pen. 'How many should I order?'

'A hundred at least,' Rosalind said slowly. 'Maybe two hundred.'

'Not everyone will reply,' Nancy added. 'Say three hundred to be on the safe side.'

'All right, I can do that,' Alex said, nodding. 'If you think of anything else, just let me know. Oh, and you don't expect me to wear some silly costume for this occasion, do you, Rosie?'

'I most certainly do, and very handsome you'll look. We'll talk about that later, Alex.' She met his agonised look with a sweet smile. 'Close the door, please, my darling. Don't forget, we're in hiding. If you see Hester, pretend you don't know where we are.'

Alex laughed. 'You can give me the ticket details when you're ready.' He left the room, closing the door behind him.

'How much time have we got to organise this event?' Rosalind turned to give Dolly a steady look. 'Don't forget it will take quite a lot of work just to get the grounds ready and organise a marquee and an orchestra, never mind refreshments.'

'I'll get my gamekeeper and gardeners to make the grounds ready,' Nancy said eagerly.

'I am quite happy to help in any way you want.' Rosalind patted Dolly's shoulder. 'Just ask and we'll help you. I'm sure that Patsy will be more than happy to be involved, and Leo used to run a pub in the London docks. He can organise the refreshments.'

Dolly laughed. 'That doesn't leave me with much to do.'

'Don't worry, darling. You'll find there's more than enough to keep you occupied.' Rosalind took the pen from her and made a few notes. 'You concentrate on drafting out the tickets for now.'

They worked together, designing the layout and writing lists of people to approach. Nancy wrote a note to Freddie, asking him to help, and she sent Pip to the village to purchase a stamp and put the letter in the post. Dolly felt that she ought to return to the theatre, but it did not take much persuasion to make her stay for luncheon.

Hester erupted into the dining room when everyone else was settled around the table.

'It's obvious you have filled my seat already,' she said crossly. 'I haven't even moved out yet.'

Alex rose to his feet and pulled out her chair. 'Nonsense, Hester. Of course you will be missed. No one here wanted you to move – it was your choice.'

'I know when I am becoming a bore,' Hester said sadly. 'I have brought this family up through good times and bad times, but now I need to have my own home.'

Rosalind sighed and reached out to lay her hand on Hester's as it rested on the white damask table-cloth. 'You were always the lynchpin of this family, Hester. As Alex said, moving out is your choice. You can change your mind, you know.'

'No. I don't think so.' Hester sat back in her chair as Flossie served her with soup. 'It's the right time for me to leave you to get on with your lives.'

An uncomfortable silence greeted this last remark. Conversation was desultory throughout the rest of the meal, with everyone carefully avoiding the subject of Hester's move. Dolly was relieved when the last plates were cleared away.

Rosalind rose from her seat. 'You'll excuse me. I need to speak to Cook.'

Nancy stood up. 'The boys will be returning for the school holidays tomorrow. I need to make sure their rooms are ready.'

Alex jumped to his feet. 'You'll excuse me, Hester. I am off to Exeter this afternoon.'

'With me, as it happens.' Tommy pushed his chair back and stood up. 'If you're gone by the time we return, I'll visit you at the Dower House in the morning to make sure you have everything you need, Hester.'

Hester shrugged. 'At least one of you has some feelings for me.'

Tommy leaned over to drop a kiss on her forehead. 'Don't be silly, Hester. We all love you and you will be missed.'

Rosalind hesitated in the doorway. 'I'll call tomorrow, too. You'll only be a mile or so away. We will probably see more of you than we do now.'

'And I'll bring the boys to visit you when they come home.' Nancy followed Rosalind out of the dining room without waiting for a response, and Dolly hurried after them. She had been on the wrong side of Hester's sharp temper more times than she cared to remember, and she was not feeling over-sympathetic now.

Everyone hurried off in different directions. Dolly returned to the parlour, where she collected the draft for the masked ball tickets. She gave it to her father, and having done that she went on to the stables to have her horse saddled.

When she arrived back at the theatre, the rehearsal was in full swing. Felicia and Claude sat in the front seats, watching as Liza Day went through her paces in the lead role. Dolly stood back, gazing at Liza in admiration. She had memorised every line and the performance was virtually faultless. Liza received a round of applause from the other members of the cast when the rehearsal came to its dramatic conclusion.

Felicia joined in, as did Claude, although he waited until his wife began to clap before he emulated her enthusiasm.

'You see,' Dolly said triumphantly as they walked back to the office. 'Liza is wonderful, isn't she?'

'I must admit that she did very well,' Felicia acknowledged reluctantly. 'She needs polish, but that will come in time, and I will make sure that she gets the correct tuition.'

Dolly could not help feeling a little sorry for Liza, but she decided that Miss Day could stand up for herself and would politely, but firmly, put Felicia de Marney in her place. Dolly looked forward to the day when that happened. In the meantime she had a lot to do. The masquerade ball would need to be a great success if it was to save the Pavilion Theatre from the threat of bankruptcy.

Dolly was on her own in the office next morning as Nick had taken time off to make the cottage habitable. Rosalind had sent her charwoman to help, as had Mrs Simpson. Dolly was satisfied that the two indomitable ladies from the village would soon dust, sweep and scrub away all the cobwebs and accumulated dirt. No doubt they would attack the rusty range with enthusiasm and delight in seeing it gleam again with a coat of black lead. Rosalind and Nancy had agreed to raid the little-used rooms in the castle turrets for furniture, rugs and a couple of beds. In fact, everyone was helping to the best of their ability.

Dolly had not been to visit Hester in her new home, but she intended to do so the minute she finished at the theatre that afternoon. She was studying the accounts ledger when the door opened and her aunt Patricia entered, bringing with her the scent of summer flowers and a wide smile.

'Darling Dolly. I've just heard about your wonderful idea for a masquerade ball. It's just what we need in Rockwood. Something to liven things up a little.' She kissed Dolly on the cheek. 'You are a clever girl.'

'I knew you'd approve,' Dolly said smugly. 'You are the very person to help me with the plans for the evening. After all, you have had experience of life in London. Mine was just a brief interlude during the season.'

'Of course. Nancy and I had many adventures in London and in Paris. But you went to Monte Carlo with Freddie. Now that's somewhere I would love to visit.'

'I'm sure that Uncle Leo would take you there if you asked him to.'

'Leo is so busy with the wretched sawmill, and now he's purchased more woodland. He says there is a building boom in London and he has a contract to supply timber. I hardly see him these days. But that's not what I had to tell you. I have an amazing piece of gossip. I thought I would tell you first, as you appreciate anything with a little mystery attached.'

'Do go on, please. I'm agog with curiosity.'

'Well, my former step-daughter, Christina Cottingham, has moved out of Cottingham Manor to be with Ossie now that he's been promoted to a bishopric in the north. I knew that she was refusing to leave Ossie's ancestral home, but apparently he has won, or rather the Church has stepped in and told her that she should support her husband in his parochial work.'

'Christina won't like that. I don't know her well, only what Aunt Nancy and Mama have told me about her.'

'All true, darling. Her sister, Sylvia, was a lovely girl, but Christina is frankly nasty. Anyway, the manor house has been sold and the new tenants have already moved in.'

'My goodness, that happened very quickly. What is the mystery? Who are the new people?'

'That's just it,' Patricia said eagerly. 'No one knows exactly who they are or where they have come from. I only found out their name this morning. It was

Tom Hannaford from the village shop and post office who told me, and even he knew very little about them.'

'Well, don't keep me in suspense.'

'The new squire is Sir Jared Mountjoy, and there is a woman. Tom didn't think it was Sir Jared's wife because she is Miss Josephine Mountjoy. Tom only saw the man, so the woman could be a sister or even an elderly aunt.'

'I don't know the name, Aunt Patsy. I've never heard of them.'

'Neither have I. They are not a Devonshire family, that's for certain. I think it's time someone paid them a courtesy call to welcome them to Rockwood.'

'We could see if they will buy tickets for the ball.'

'What a good idea. I do love a bit of a mystery.'

'We could call on them tomorrow afternoon,' Dolly said thoughtfully. 'What do you think?'

'Why not? It would seem only right and proper to pay a courtesy call on our neighbours.'

'I will have to ask Nick's permission for time off work, but I'm sure he'll agree.'

Patricia smiled. 'Now tell me more about this masquerade ball. How far have you gone in making preparations?'

'Papa took the details for the tickets to the printer's shop yesterday. Aunt Nancy has sent a note to Uncle Freddie, asking for his help in compiling a list of people he knows who might be interested, and that's as far as I've got.'

'Then we should go straight to the castle to talk it over with Rosie and Nancy. Especially the part about our new neighbours.'

'I would love to, but I should wait here for Nick to return. You know that he's moved into a cottage on Aunt Nancy's land?'

'Rosie usually keeps me abreast of the gossip, but I haven't seen her for a few days. When did this happen?'

'Hester has claimed the Dower House and Nick felt he had to leave, even though she said he might remain there.'

'I knew that Hester was talking about moving out, but I really didn't think she would do it.'

'Well, she has. I believe she is moving there today. I wonder how long it will be before she decides to return to the castle.'

'She's a very stubborn woman. I can't imagine Hester admitting that she was wrong in anything. It will be interesting to wait and see. Anyway, darling, I am going to the castle to see Rosie. Do come and join us if you can.'

Dolly followed her aunt into the foyer where they could hear Liza's beautiful voice through the open auditorium door.

'That's not Mama, surely?'

'No, there's another thing you've missed, Aunt Patsy. We have a new star now. Her name is Liza Day, and even Grandmama approves of her.'

Patsy listened intently. 'She is good. I had serious

ambitions to become an opera singer, but I didn't have the range. It was hard to admit it, but in the end I gave up. It seems we have a new diva.'

Dolly laughed. 'I think we do. She out-sang me, too. I now know my limitations. I'm going to concentrate on working front of house. It's a miracle that my parents have allowed me to go this far, so I am not about to complain.'

Patricia eyed Dolly closely. 'What happened to Gus, that young soldier you ran off with not so long ago?'

'It wasn't an elopement, Aunt Patsy. I am very fond of Gus. As a matter of fact, his regiment is encamped outside Exeter, but I don't think about him romantically.'

'Really? Are you sure about that? You're blushing, Dolly. I remember Gus. He was a cheeky boy, but very good looking. I imagine he's grown into a very attractive man.'

'Yes, he has. But he's just a friend,' Dolly said firmly. 'His regiment will be sent away soon, and that will be the last I will see of him.'

'I believe you, darling. Anyway, Robbins is walking the horse so I mustn't keep them outside in the hot sun any longer. Maybe I'll see you later if you can find time to visit your mama at the castle. I'll be there until it's time to take Charlie home. He loves being with Nancy's boys, but they are a handful in the school holidays.' Patricia swept out of the foyer and Robbins reined the horse in before leaping down to help his mistress into the carriage.

Dolly smiled to herself. She had some experience of Nancy's three boys, Hester's holy terrors, and Charlie, Patricia and Leo's son, was just as bad. The boys roamed the parkland and played in the old tree house in the woods built by Ossie Cottingham and Bertie Carey in their youth. Dolly had often been sent to bring them home when they did not return in time for supper. Leo was very strict with Charlie, but Tommy was a tolerant father and rarely punished his sons for what he called 'their high spirits'.

Dolly went back to the office but she could not settle to dull paperwork. She waited impatiently for Nick to return, and the moment he walked through the door she bombarded him with questions about the cottage.

He sat down at his desk. 'Just give me a moment to catch my breath, Dolly.'

'I'm sorry. I just wanted to know if you are definitely going to take the cottage. It must be much better now that it's clean.'

'Yes, indeed. I plan to move in this afternoon. Hudson brought me a bed and a mattress from the castle, with a bundle of bedding, and there was a box of crockery and goodness knows what else. Mrs Simpson has kindly agreed to send her housemaid to put it all straight for me. I wouldn't know where to start.'

'Let me know if I can do anything. Not that I'm very domesticated, but I can unpack things and put them away.'

Nick smiled. 'Thank you, Dolly. But you're doing a lot to help by being here so that I can get away from the office occasionally. It's not possible to lock the theatre up when there are rehearsals in progress. Did you do anything more about the masquerade ball idea?'

'Yes, I recruited Mama, Aunt Nancy and Aunt Patsy to help. They are all very excited about it and the tickets should be ready soon.'

'Then I'll leave it in your capable hands, Dolly. If it's a success it could turn the fortunes of the theatre round.'

'It will be an amazing event that people will talk about for years.' Dolly eyed him speculatively. 'Did you know that Cottingham Manor has been sold and Mrs Cottingham has gone to join her husband somewhere in the north of England?'

Nick shook his head. 'No, it's news to me, Dolly. Do you know who has purchased the Cottingham Manor?

'Tom Hannaford told Aunt Patsy that there is a new squire, Sir Jared Mountjoy. But, apparently, no one, not even Tom Hannaford, knows anything more than that.'

'I wonder if they are opera lovers.' Nick leaned back in his chair. 'It's good to have new people move into the area, especially if they are theatregoers.'

It was Dolly's turn to laugh. 'Don't you ever think about anything other than business, Nick?'

'Not for some years. Anyway, this is my livelihood.

It's a great deal easier than riding round the estate collecting rents and listening to tenants' grumbles.'

Dolly nodded. 'Aunt Patsy and I are thinking of paying a courtesy call on the new people, maybe to-morrow afternoon, if you can spare me.'

'Yes, there's nothing I can do at the cottage except get in the way. You go and make a good impression on our new neighbour. Maybe he would like to buy tickets for the masquerade ball.'

'I'll do my best to get him interested.'

'And to satisfy your own curiosity.'

Dolly smiled modestly. 'Yes, and that, too. The new owner of the manor and his family seem to be a complete mystery.'

Chapter Eleven

Next day, after luncheon at the castle, where the subject of conversation was mainly the mysterious new owner of Cottingham Manor, Dolly and Patricia sat in the Wilders' chaise as it tooled along the lane leading to the mansion.

'I haven't been here for years,' Patricia said, shading herself beneath a silk parasol. 'In fact, I cannot remember the last time I paid a call on the Cottinghams. Christina never accepted me into the family when I was married to her father. I know she disliked me, but she was furious when she discovered that Nancy was a Greystone and had inherited the estate. Poor Nancy was the innocent victim of Christina's vindictiveness.'

'I only vaguely remember Mrs Cottingham. She always ignored us children.' Dolly gazed ahead as the manor house came into view. 'I've never been here before.'

'It was all so different when your mama and I were young. We used to come here quite often. Ossie was a good friend and we got up to all sorts of pranks, which I suppose I should not admit at my age.'

'I'd love to hear about them.'

'One day, maybe, but not now.'

'We are almost at the gates,' Dolly said eagerly.

'Do you know, it's odd but I'm a little nervous?' Patricia said, sighing. 'I grew up knowing everyone in the area and it feels weird to be visiting strangers.'

'They won't be strangers for long, Aunt Patsy. Once we've introduced ourselves to them and made them welcome, they will be part of the community.'

'Yes, you're right, of course. We must make them feel that Rockwood is a good place in which to live.'

Robbins drew the horse to a halt outside the tall iron gates, and called out to the gatekeeper. When no one appeared from the cottage, Robbins climbed down to ring the brass bell. Still no one answered his summons.

'What shall I do, ma'am?' Robbins asked, frowning. 'There don't be anyone at home, so it seems.'

'The gatekeeper should be there.' Patricia closed her parasol and leaned forward. 'Try again, Robbins.'

Robbins jangled the bell energetically and shouted in an attempt to attract the attention of the gatekeeper. Eventually, after a few more minutes, the door to the gatehouse opened and a man shambled out, scowling at them.

'What d'you want?'

'Open the gates, if you please,' Robbins said politely. 'Mrs Leo Wilder has called to see the new owners.'

'I got instructions not to let no one in.'

The gatekeeper was about to retreat into his cottage.

Robbins looked to Patricia. 'What shall I do, ma'am?'

Patricia stood up in the well of the chaise. 'I suggest you consult your employer, my good man. Tell him that Mrs Leo Wilder and Miss Adela Blanchard from Rockwood Castle would like to pay their respects to their new neighbour.' Patricia sat down again. 'The mention of Rockwood Castle usually does the trick, as you will no doubt find out,' she added, turning to Dolly with a conspiratorial smile.

'I got me orders, ma'am. Castle or no castle.' The gatekeeper turned his back on them as a young woman stepped out of the shadows.

'Open the gates, Tuttle.'

'Yes, Miss Josephine.' Tuttle hurried to obey her command and the gates were swung wide open, allowing Robbins to drive through.

Patricia tapped him on the shoulder with the ferule of her parasol. 'Stop here, please. I wish to walk.'

She waited until it was safe to do so before descending to the gravelled carriage sweep with Dolly close behind her.

'I feel I should introduce myself. I am Patricia Wilder and this is my niece Adela Blanchard from Rockwood Castle.'

'I know who you are.' The beautiful young woman eyed them both dispassionately. 'I knew it wouldn't be long before someone from the castle came to inspect us.'

'It's not like that,' Patricia said hastily. 'This is a courtesy call we would pay on any newcomer to the village.'

'You may have gathered that I am Josephine Mountjoy. Spinster, now of this parish, and intent on remaining so.' Josephine flicked back her luxuriant dark hair, which she wore loose around her shoulders. 'I realise our arrival must have caused some interest in such an out-of-the-way village. Tuttle has been instructed not to allow the merely curious into the grounds.'

Dolly was instantly on guard. She did not like Miss Mountjoy's tone. She might be a wealthy and beautiful young woman, as she most definitely was, judging by the expensive cut of her elegant, sea-green silk gown, but her self-assurance verged on arrogance and discourtesy.

'We came to welcome you to Rockwood,' Dolly said, without giving Patricia the chance to respond.

Patricia sent her a warning glance. 'If our visit is

ill-timed, I apologise. Your gatekeeper made it clear that visitors were unwelcome.'

Josephine shrugged and laughed. 'You'll have to forgive Tuttle. My brother guards his privacy jealously, which is why he purchased this quaint manor house.'

'We came like good neighbours, but if our presence is unwelcome, perhaps we had better leave now.' Patricia turned to Robbins, who was perched on the driver's seat, seemingly ready to beat a hasty retreat.

Miss Mountjoy held up her hand. 'No, please stay. I apologise for our reticence in receiving guests, but it is necessary under the circumstances in which we find ourselves. Tell your man to walk your horse. We have not organised our stables properly as yet, so he might not find them ready to take care of him and the animal. But do come into the house. I can't guarantee that my brother will see you, but that is up to him. He is not the most sociable of people.'

Dolly and Patricia exchanged wary glances, but Josephine had strolled off in the direction of the front door, leaving them little choice other than to follow her. Dolly was eaten up with curiosity anyway. She could not wait to meet Sir Jared. In her mind she saw him as an ogre from a fairy tale, who kept his beautiful sister immured in a crumbling mansion. Not that Cottingham Manor resembled such a Gothic dwelling place. It had been the manor house since Tudor times and the warm red sandstone had matured with the centuries. Creeper covered one wing of the building, making it look as if the house had a green cape wrapped around its shoulders. The mullioned lattice windows reflected the sunshine from leaded glass panes, giving the building a mellow welcoming look that was not reflected in the treatment they had received from Tuttle. However, Josephine Mountjoy seemed oblivious to their discomfort and she led them into the large entrance hall, signalling to a liveried footman to close the door behind them.

'We'll take tea in the drawing room, Potter. I hope Cook isn't so drunk as to have forgotten to bake some cakes or jam tarts.'

Dolly thought for a moment that Miss Mountjoy was joking, but judging by the expression on Potter's face there was definitely a problem in the kitchen.

'I'll see that it's done, Miss Josephine. If she's in a fit state to handle a bread knife.' Potter hurried off in what appeared to be the direction of the kitchens.

'Do you allow your servants to drink on duty?' Patricia asked tentatively.

'We believe in freedom for everyone to express themselves as they see fit. She is a very good cook, when sober, but she has these occasional lapses. Come with me, please.'

Josephine led them through the wainscoted hall, which echoed to the sound of their footsteps. It seemed as though Christina had stripped the house of every stick of furniture, paintings and anything that made the mansion look like a home. Perhaps the Mountjoys had yet to furnish it to their liking, but Dolly shivered even though it was a hot summer day outside. The interior of the ancient house felt cold and unloved. She felt the hairs on the back of her neck stand up like the raised hackles on a nervous hound. Patricia reached out to take hold of Dolly's hand, clasping it firmly, but it was obvious that she too was feeling apprehensive.

They reached the drawing room and Josephine marched in without knocking. 'Jared, we have visitors.' She stood aside to allow Patricia and Dolly to enter.

Dolly gazed round at the room, which was virtually empty of furniture, although wooden packing cases were stacked against one wall. Her gaze fell upon a tall man in his early thirties; he was dark-haired like his sister and might be thought handsome by some, but Dolly felt a shiver run down her spine as she met his stony gaze. His eyes were the colour of slate and his expression was anything but welcoming. Moreover, he was standing by the fireplace with a rifle in his hands.

'Put that gun down, Jared. That is no way to greet guests.' Josephine laughed but there was no humour in the sound.

'I thought I told Tuttle not to admit anyone,' Sir Jared said angrily.

'Manners, Jared.' Josephine turned to Patricia and Dolly. 'My brother is an ill-mannered brute. You really do not want to associate with a man like him.'

Sir Jared laid his gun carefully on the carved stone mantelshelf. 'Do not listen to my sister. She thinks she is clever and amusing, but she is not. What can I do for you, ladies? A subscription to a lending library, perhaps, or a local charitable institution?'

'You are as rude as she is,' Dolly said crossly. 'We came to welcome you to Rockwood, but I see that it was a waste of time. Shall we go now, Aunt Patsy?'

'Goodbye, ladies. Thank you for calling.' Sir Jared turned his back on them.

'Jared! That's rude even by your standards.' Josephine ushered Patricia and Dolly out of the room. 'I apologise for my brother's behaviour. Now you see why we don't encourage visitors.'

'I can,' Patricia said equably. 'But that doesn't mean you have to live like a recluse, Miss Mountjoy.'

'Yes, Mrs Wilder, but you will soon learn that I live as I please. I do not allow my brother to rule me, nor do I give a fig for convention. You might not find my companionship commensurate with your way of life.'

'My aunt has never been a conventional sort of person,' Dolly said quickly. 'I doubt if anything you can say will shock her.'

'I wouldn't go so far as that, Dolly.' Patricia gave her hand a quick squeeze. 'We have obviously come at a bad time.' She turned to Josephine. 'However, there was a purpose to our visit.'

'Really? Was Jared right in that you are collecting for some village charity?'

'No, Miss Mountjoy.' Dolly faced her angrily. 'You may sneer at us if you wish, but we came to offer you tickets to a masked ball. It will be held at the Pavilion Theatre on the first night of Verdi's opera *The Masked Ball*. Although having met your brother, I doubt if he would be interested in cultural events.' Dolly knew she was being equally rude, but she was furious at the way in which her aunt had been spoken to.

Patricia opened her mouth to speak, but Josephine threw her head back and laughed. 'I like a girl with spirit, and you are quite right about my brother. He is not interested in the arts, but I am. On his behalf I would like to purchase two tickets. I take it they are not free?'

Dolly met Josephine's amused gaze with an unflinching stare. 'You would not ask such a question if the opera was to be held at the Theatre Royal, Drury Lane.'

'It will be a good chance for you to meet some of the local families,' Patricia said hastily. 'And there will be people from miles around. The theatre has gained in popularity and enjoys an excellent reputation as far away as London.'

'I will attend, even if Jared doesn't wish to accompany me. I hate being buried in the country.'

'You will come on your own?' Dolly could hardly believe her ears. Miss Mountjoy was a bold woman indeed if she dared to attend a function without an escort in a place where she was not known. Dolly eyed her with new respect.

'I told you that I don't hold with convention. I enjoy creating a stir wherever I go, although we are supposed to be living here quietly.'

'Might I enquire the reason?' Patricia asked gently. 'If it is a question of ill health, we have a very good doctor in the village.'

Josephine's laughter echoed off the ornate plaster work on the ceiling. 'I can assure you that we are both in very good health. However, our reasons for being here are nobody's business but our own.'

'I beg your pardon. I didn't intend to pry.'

'Not at all, Mrs Wilder. I have little doubt that the whole village will be agog to learn the details of our move to the manor house.' Josephine accompanied them to the front entrance, where Potter was standing to attention.

'Our visitors are leaving, Potter. Tell Cook we won't be needing refreshments now.'

'Just as well, miss. She's head down on the kitchen table, snoring and dribbling. We'll be lucky to get a meal this evening.'

'I will deal with Cook. You see these ladies out.' Josephine turned to leave them but she hesitated. 'You may bring the tickets to me tomorrow, Miss Blanchard, but don't come before noon. I am a late riser.' She walked off, heading, no doubt, for the kitchens.

'Good day, ladies,' Potter said amicably. He opened the door and stood aside to allow them to pass. 'Your man has been walking the horse up and down. You won't have long to wait before he returns.' He closed the door on them without waiting for a reply.

Patricia beckoned to Robbins, who just happened to have turned the horse in their direction. 'Well!' Patricia shook her head. 'I have never in my whole life been in such a household where the servants speak to their mistress in such a familiar tone.'

'Or a cook who is permanently drunk,' Dolly added, giggling. 'I do rather like Miss Mountjoy, though. I can't help admiring her spirit.'

'It won't get her very far in Rockwood society, Dolly. Don't form an attachment to such a woman. She will lead your into all sorts of scrapes.'

'Maybe that's what I am hoping for, Aunt Patsy.'

Patricia sighed. 'You are too much like me for your own good, Adela Blanchard. I love you dearly, but I'm very glad I am not your mama. My hair would have turned white overnight after your escapade in London.'

Robbins drew up beside them and leaped down to assist Patricia into the chaise, followed by Dolly.

'Do you want to go back to the theatre, Dolly, dear?'

'Yes, please, Aunt Patsy. I am a working woman now.'

'Of course you are. I keep forgetting. Stop at the Pavilion first, please, Robbins. Then we'll go straight home.'

'Yes, ma'am.' Robbins climbed back onto the driver's seat and flicked the reins. 'Walk on.'

Patricia leaned back in her seat. 'I suggest you send one of the stage hands to the manor house with the tickets tomorrow, Dolly. I fear that Josephine Mountjoy is not going to be a good influence on you.'

When Dolly arrived back in the office, she found Nick seated at the desk with a box of tickets in front of him. He looked up and smiled. 'I went to Exeter first thing this morning. We should get these out as soon as possible.'

'I agree,' Dolly said eagerly. 'I think I've sold two tickets to the new people at the manor house.'

'I also picked up the posters to place in the foyer and a few more to pin up in the village. I've also put advertisements in *The Times* and several local newspapers.' Nick leaned back in his chair. 'By the way, I think I saw the Dorrington coat of arms on a carriage heading for the castle.'

Dolly nodded. 'Yes, Nancy said she would enlist Uncle Freddie's help.'

'That's excellent. Dorrington has a great many friends and acquaintances – all of them wealthy. This will put the Pavilion Theatre on the map, Dolly. If our masked ball is a success, it will go a long way to reviving our fortunes – otherwise, I'm afraid, we might have to close the theatre.'

'So it really is that bad?'

'We are a long way from big cities. It's a miracle we've survived this long, and that is mainly due to your grandmother's talent and her knowledge of the

theatre world. We make more money from panto-
mimes and comedies than we do from grand opera.'

'But the hotel does quite well.'

'In summer, yes, but in the winter it's too quiet.
However, I hope we'll change all that now.'

'It won't be for the want of trying,' Dolly said
firmly. 'Would you like me to take a few tickets to
the castle? I'll show Uncle Freddie what it's all about,
and I need two for Miss Mountjoy at the manor
house.'

'That's a good idea, Dolly. You may go now, if
you wish. There's not much to do here now that
Liza has mastered her part so perfectly. I've suggested
that she studies the leading role in *The Masked Ball*.
Obviously we will have auditions, but there's no
doubt about the outcome as far as I'm concerned,
anyway. Although, of course, your grandmama
might have other ideas.'

'I don't think so, Nick. She was very impressed with
Liza. But if it's really all right with you, I'll go to the
castle and see what Uncle Freddie can do for us.'

'Yes, of course. Give him my regards.'

Dolly left the office and set off on foot for the
castle. It was a lovely day and summer heat shimmered on the cobblestones as she walked through
the village, stopping only to pass the time of day
with old friends. She had to quicken her pace in
order to catch up with Todd, who was walking
ahead of her.

'Todd. Wait for me.'

He came to a halt and turned to her smiling. 'Good afternoon, Dolly.'

She caught up with him, slightly breathless, and slipped her hand through the crook of his arm as they started walking towards the doctor's house.

'Why are you out and about on foot, Dolly? That's not like you.'

'I'm working now. I am just like you, in fact.'

Todd laughed. 'Not quite.'

'You know what I mean. Anyway, I'm on my way to the castle.' She held up the parcel of tickets. 'I'm taking these tickets for the masked ball to Uncle Freddie. I'm hoping Mama has persuaded him to ask his wealthy acquaintances to support us.'

'I heard about your plans. Nothing is secret in Rockwood for long.'

'Will you come to the ball? You don't have to attend the opera if you don't wish to.'

'It's far too grand for me. I can't afford it, Dolly. I'm a village doctor, not one of your rich London friends.'

'I do not have any friends in London. It's fancy dress. Couldn't you borrow a uniform from Gus and come as a soldier? Maybe he would like to buy tickets for both of you.'

Todd stopped outside the doctor's house. 'Is that what this is all about? You want to see Gus again. Isn't that so?'

She withdrew her hand. 'Well, not entirely. I do like Gus, but of course I'd love you to come and enjoy the ball. It will be held outside, under the stars. So romantic.'

Todd unlocked the front door and stepped inside. 'I'll pass the message on to Gus.'

'That's not what I meant at all.'

'It's all right, Dolly. You don't have to explain to me. Anyway, I have visits to make so I need to fetch my medical bag. I hope the ball goes well.' Todd stepped inside and closed the door.

Dolly stood for a moment, staring at the shiny brass door knocker. She was tempted to hammer on it and demand an explanation from Todd, but deep down she knew that he was motivated by jealousy. Perhaps she had given him false hope in the past, but it was unintentional and she was genuinely fond of him.

She sighed and walked on, quickening her pace as she headed for the bridge of the River Sawle. Life had been much more straightforward when she was simply Miss Adela Blanchard of Rockwood Castle. It was not easy trying to break through the conventions that bound young women to their families and their own social class. She hurried on, arriving at the castle hot and dishevelled. She could tell by the expression on James's face that he was shocked by her appearance, and a quick glance in one of the wall mirrors confirmed her worst fears. She took off her bonnet and gloves and made a frantic effort to tidy her tumbled curls.

'Dolly Blanchard, you look as if you've been dragged through a hedge backwards!'

Dolly turned to see her mother staring at her with much the same look that James had given her. 'I'm sorry, Mama. I chose to walk from the theatre. I didn't realise quite how hot it is today.'

'Come to the morning parlour before your papa sees you. He is very good about you working at the Pavilion, although he doesn't really approve.' Rosalind walked quickly to the morning parlour and opened the door. 'Sit down and I'll send for some lemonade.' Rosalind rang the bell and Dolly obeyed. She knew she was in no position to argue.

'Your uncle Freddie will wonder what's happened to you, too, Dolly. I'm beginning to think that allowing you to work for Nick Gibson was a mistake.'

'I work for Grandmama, too.'

'My mother would be horrified to see you in this state. You must have walked through the village and I can't imagine what the gossips will be saying.'

'Does it really matter, Mama?' Dolly could have said a lot more, but a brief knock on the door made her hesitate.

Bertha entered, bobbing a curtsey. 'You rang, ma'am?'

'Yes, Bertha. Will you bring a jug of lemonade and a glass for Miss Dolly? I'll have tea, as usual.'

'Yes, ma'am.'

Bertha left the room but the door barely closed when it opened again and Freddie strolled into the room. He took in the scene with a wry smile.

'In trouble again, Dolly?'

'Don't encourage her, Freddie. I've just been scolding her for walking on her own and arriving in such a state.'

Freddie laughed. 'She looks charming, Rosie. Don't scold the poor girl. I believe she is on a mission to save the theatre from ruin.'

Rosalind pulled a face. 'Do you know how much of my childhood and younger days were dominated by Mama being driven by her desire for recognition as an opera singer? Now it's passed on to my daughter, only in a different way.'

'Well, perhaps I can help, which is why Nancy sent for me anyway.' Freddie pulled up a chair and sat down. 'I think the plan for a masked ball on opening night is wonderful. I'm prepared to risk my sanity by going to London to see if I can drum up some interest and actual sales. It will be a new experience for me, but I need Dolly to accompany me.'

'What a lovely idea,' Dolly said eagerly.

'Can you spare her for a few days? I'm sure that Nick and Mrs de Marney will be in agreement.' Freddie turned his head as the door opened and Felicia sailed into the room followed by Claude.

'Did I hear my name mentioned?' Felicia demanded haughtily. 'Why are you here, Dorrington? You seem to live here more than you do on your own estate.'

'Mama, that is impolite,' Rosalind said anxiously.

'But I fear it's the truth.' Freddie rose to his feet

and pulled up a chair for Felicia. 'Good afternoon, Mrs de Marney. Good afternoon, sir.'

Claude patted him on the shoulder. 'Nice to see you, Dorrington. Don't take any notice of my dear wife. She's had some disturbing news from the bank.'

'I'm so sorry to hear that.' Freddie looked from one to the other. 'Can I do anything to help?'

'It's so hot today one can hardly think.' Felicia sank down on the chair, fanning herself vigorously with her hand. 'To put it bluntly, the theatre isn't paying its way. Unless we sell all the tickets for the masked ball, and can prove that takings have improved, the bank will foreclose.'

'Mama, I had no idea that matters had reached such a state,' Rosalind said urgently. 'Why didn't you tell me?'

'What could you have done, my dear? I know Rockwood keeps going in its own erratic manner, but you do not have spare funds to support my theatre. In fact, I wouldn't dream of taking money from you and Alexander. I have my pride.'

'But the theatre is your life, Mama.' Rosalind rose to her feet and moved towards her mother, holding out her arms as if to give her a hug, but Felicia held up her hands.

'I don't need sympathy, Rosalind. I need money.'

Rosalind backed away, blinking tears from her eyes. 'I wish I could help.'

'That is why I am here, as I said before.' Freddie took a seat next to Felicia. 'The reason I came today is to help raise money for the theatre. I plan to take Dolly to London, with a suitable chaperone, of course. We will do our best to encourage those who will bring their enthusiasm and their money to the masquerade ball at Greystone Park. It will give the theatre and the hotel the sort of publicity that you cannot get simply from word of mouth.'

Felicia stared at him, open-mouthed. 'You would do that for me?'

'For you, Mrs de Marney, and your whole family. I feel that I've been part of the Rockwood family since I first met Nancy in London.'

'It's a pity she didn't accept your proposal,' Felicia said acidly. 'We would not have had any money worries if she had married you instead of Tommy. Much as I love my grandson, he is very unworldly and quite content with the simple life.'

'Mama, you can't say such things.' Rosalind's cheek reddened with embarrassment. 'Freddie is a good friend to all of us.'

'Grandmama, we are trying to save your theatre.' Dolly had been perched on the arm of the sofa, but she rose to her feet. 'You understand, don't you, Grandpapa?'

Claude nodded. 'Of course I do.' He fixed his wife with a stern stare. 'You have gone too far this time, Felicia. I think you owe Freddie an apology.'

Felicia stood up. 'I never apologise for telling the truth. I don't know why you haven't made a life for yourself, Dorrington. How old are you?'

'Really, my love,' Claude began nervously, but was quelled by a look from his wife.

'It's all right, Claude. It's no secret that I am thirty-four, and a bachelor still.' Freddie smiled amiably.

Dolly could see that her grandmother's words had struck a chord and Freddie was hurt. 'No one thinks that of you, Uncle Freddie. You are not old.'

'Of course not.' Felicia tossed her head and the feathers in her hat trembled as if the bird was coming back to life. 'You could still have your pick of the eligible young ladies in the whole of the West Country, Frederick. And you have a sizeable fortune, too.'

Dolly laid her hand on Freddie's shoulder. 'I'm sorry, Grandmama. I don't wish to be disrespectful, but Uncle Freddie's marital status has nothing to do with you, or any of us. I, or any young woman, would be honoured to marry such a man as he.'

There was a shocked silence as everyone stared at her. Dolly realised what she had said, but she was determined to stand up for the man who had been such an important influence in her life.

Freddie was the first to recover and he laughed. 'I wish I could believe that, Dolly, but thank you anyway.' He stood up, holding his hand out to her. 'Since no one has raised any objections, I think it's safe to assume that this elderly bachelor has the necessary permission to take you to London on a mission to save the Pavilion Theatre.'

Dolly clasped his hand. 'I am coming with you whether they agree or not.'

Chapter Twelve

Dolly and Freddie arrived in Piccadilly with Bess, combining her duties as chaperone and lady's maid. Dolly was delighted to be back in the city and this time she had a definite mission. The only cloud on the horizon was the fact that as they alighted from a cab outside Dorrington House, they met Miss Bennington, together with a small group of friends. Dolly recognised Lady Margery Faraday with her twin daughters, Isabella and Celia, who had seemingly been out for a promenade dressed in their most fashionable clothes. Dolly felt like a country bumpkin compared to Theodora, who looked like a beautiful china doll in her afternoon gown, long gloves and a hat that must have come straight from a Paris designer. Theodora furled her parasol and looked Dolly up and down with a cynical curve to her full lips.

'Why, if it isn't Miss Blanchard, up from the country.'

'Good afternoon, Miss Bennington,' Freddie said casually. 'It's always a pleasure to see you.'

Theodora fluttered her eyelashes. 'We don't see you often enough, Lord Dorrington.'

'I prefer country living to an existence in the city,' Freddie said firmly.

Lady Margery laid her hand on his sleeve. 'It's so good to see you again, Cousin Freddie. We are in town for a few days. I hope our paths cross.'

'Yes, that would be lovely.' Isabella and Celia spoke as one.

'I see that you have brought Dolly with you.' Lady Margery frowned. 'You need to be careful, Freddie. The gossips are always looking for something or someone to talk about.'

Dolly wanted to giggle but she restrained herself. She shot Freddie a sideways glance, but he seemed oblivious to the effect he was creating.

'I will bear your good advice in mind, Margery,' Freddie said, smiling. 'Good day, ladies.' He ushered Dolly into the mansion. Mason, Briggs the butler, and Atkins, the footman, hurried out to assist Bess, who was struggling with the luggage, which was mostly Dolly's, even though she had travelled as light as possible.

'Why did they have to be outside at that particular moment?' Dolly said crossly. 'I look and feel as if I've just come in from haymaking.'

Freddie laughed. 'Have you ever tried haymaking, Dolly?'

'No, of course not,' she said, smiling ruefully. 'But you know what I mean. Theodora hates me and she makes everyone else dislike me, too.'

'I wouldn't worry about her. We are here on business, but that doesn't mean we can't enjoy ourselves.'

'Yes, you're right. I'd love to go to the theatre.'

'Agreed. We'll have supper at Kettner's or Rules, whichever you prefer.'

'Let's find a restaurant where Miss Bennington is unlikely to dine. I don't think I can face her twice in a day. She is so fashionable she makes me feel like a drab, and she never loses an opportunity to emphasise the fact.'

'Nonsense, Dolly. You are far more beautiful than Miss Bennington. She might have the advantage of gowns from Paris, but that's where it ends. I saw Isabella and Celia glancing enviously at you. I remember what it was like in Monte Carlo when you were the centre of attention and they were often overlooked.'

'That isn't how I remember it, Uncle Freddie.'

'Just forget them and remember why we came to London in the first place.' Freddie signalled to a maidservant, who hurried to his side and bobbed a curtsey.

'Show Miss Blanchard to her usual room, please, Downs.'

'Yes, my lord. Come with me, please, miss.'

Dolly followed the maid up the grand staircase with Bess following. Dolly could have found the room on her own, but she knew she must adhere to strict protocols when dealing with servants. She was very much aware that, in London, they were much more formal than in Rockwood, where the staff were treated more like family. They reached the long landing on the first floor and the maid opened the door to the elegant room that Dolly remembered so well.

Bess placed Dolly's valises on the small sofa under the window. 'Shall I unpack now, miss?'

'No, Bess. Go with Downs and she'll show you where you are to sleep. You can come back later and sort out my things. I didn't bring very much with me.'

Downs held the door open for Bess. 'Follow me, Miss Finley.'

Bess nodded and smiled. 'Ta, Nellie. I remember you from last time I was here.'

'You can share with me like we did before. I heard that you live in a castle now.' Downs closed the door and their voices faded into the distance.

Dolly smiled to herself. At least Bess would be looked after during their stay in London. However, meeting Theodora Bennington again, as well as Lady Margery and her daughters, had rekindled memories that were not all pleasant. Dolly perched on the edge of the bed, wondering if things might have turned out differently had Gus treated her more gallantly. Her cheeks burned at the memory of sharing a room with him at the inn; even though it was completely innocent, she knew the world would not view it that way. Gus had not given a thought as to what it would do to her reputation. She doubted if it had even crossed his mind. He was not for her, but she could not forget the feelings he had ignited in her.

She opened the smaller valise and took out the bundle of tickets for the masquerade ball. So much depended upon its success. Now she was back in London she was not so sure that Freddie's sophisticated friends and acquaintances would be interested in something so rural, even if they were prepared to travel so far from town. But if anyone could persuade them it was Freddie, Lord Dorrington, one of the wealthiest men in England. Despite his modesty and lack of pretention, Dolly knew that Freddie commanded respect from his peers as well as the people who depended upon him. She decided to put everything out of her mind and start enjoying herself. Freddie would do the rest.

That evening, dressed in her best silk gown and with a white lace shawl draped around her shoulders, Dolly accompanied Freddie to the Opera Comique in the Strand to see Madame Pauline Rita in the operetta *The Broken Branch*. It was a joint decision as neither of them fancied sitting through grand opera or a play that might prove disheartening.

Freddie thought that the sort of people who might brave the journey to Devonshire in order to attend a masked ball might well be those who enjoyed comic opera. Dolly heartily agreed.

During the interval they circulated amongst the other theatregoers. Freddie introduced Dolly to several young couples, who were all obviously capable of standing the expense of a trip to the country, and were eager for new experiences. Freddie invited them all to a soirée at Dorrington House the following evening, and without exception they accepted eagerly.

After the performance they decided to go to Rules restaurant in Maiden Street, Freddie having suggested that it would be more convenient than taking a cab to Kettner's, and Dolly had no objections. She was very hungry by this time and when the waiter brought them the menus she found it was impossible to pretend otherwise. She knew that it was fashionable for young ladies to eat sparingly, and no doubt some of those who wore their stays tightened too much did find it difficult to eat, but Dolly had always had a healthy appetite. She ordered what she fancied with an apologetic smile.

'I know I should eat like a sparrow, Uncle Freddie, but I'm famished.'

'It's stupid to starve oneself for fashion. To be honest, I find it quite ridiculous that some women deliberately curb a healthy appetite when, in fact, they are really very hungry.'

'I agree entirely.' Dolly took a large sip of the wine that the waiter poured for her. 'That's a good vintage. I like it.'

Freddie raised his glass to her. 'Dolly, I would be grateful if you would call me Freddie. I am not your uncle and calling me that makes me feel quite elderly.'

'I'm sorry. I had no idea. I've just grown up thinking of you in that light.'

Freddie pulled a face. 'I know, and I understand, but you're nearly twenty, Dolly. You can decide such matters for yourself.'

'I would never wish to make you feel uncomfortable. I think of you as a dear friend, not an old man.' Dolly clinked her glass against his. 'Here's to friendship, Freddie.'

'Yes, I'll drink to that, Dolly.' Freddie's smile froze. 'Don't look now, but Lady Faraday and her daughters have just walked into the restaurant.'

'Have they seen us?' Dolly held her breath.

'No, I don't think so. They're with a couple of people I don't think I know.'

Curiosity got the better of Dolly and she dropped her table napkin onto the floor, giving her an excuse to bend down and take a covert look at the newcomers. She straightened up, stifling a gasp.

'I know them. They are the people who have bought Cottingham Manor. Sir Jared Mountjoy and his sister, Josephine.'

'Mountjoy.' Freddie frowned thoughtfully. 'I know that name. There was some scandal attached to it, but I can't remember what it was. I don't usually pay much attention to gossip.'

'I called on them at the manor house. I must admit it was partly out of curiosity and I wanted to sell them some tickets for the opera and the masked ball.'

'What did you make of them?'

'He is very aloof and I didn't feel welcome. Josephine is very unconventional, but I must admit I liked her.'

'Well, she's spotted you. She's left the others and is coming this way,' Freddie said in a low voice. 'Pretend to be surprised.'

Dolly turned her head to see Josephine bearing down on them with a wide smile. 'Look who I've found. It's our pretty little neighbour from Rockwood.' Josephine pulled up a chair and sat down. 'This is a coincidence, is it not?'

'It is indeed.' Dolly tried to look surprised. 'But a pleasant one. Are you in town for long?'

'No, we'll be returning to the manor house in a day or so.' Josephine's smile faded. 'We are here to see Jared's solicitor. I expect you know all about us now.'

'Not a thing, to be honest,' Dolly said candidly.

'Maybe our reputation hasn't reached as far as Rockwood yet, which is why we chose such an out-of-the-way place.' Josephine leaned across the table to give Freddie a charming smile. 'You haven't introduced me to your beau, Dolly. You are a sly puss, coming out to dine alone with a gentleman. But when one is away from home one can get away with such behaviour.'

'This is a dear friend of the family, Lord Dorrington,' Dolly said hastily. 'Freddie, may I introduce you to Miss Josephine Mountjoy of Cottingham Manor?'

Freddie inclined his head. 'How do you do, Miss Mountjoy?'

'How do you do, Dorrington? You'll forgive the informality but I have taken a liking to your niece and I feel we are already old friends.'

'Is that so?' Freddie gave her a challenging look. 'Well, Dolly is a fine girl. You would be fortunate to have her friendship.'

'I suppose you will be purchasing tickets for the opera and the masquerade ball?' Josephine returned his gaze fearlessly.

'Of course he will.' Dolly could see that Freddie was not impressed with the beautiful and bold Miss Mountjoy. 'Freddie is a regular visitor to Rockwood Castle. We all adore him.'

Josephine turned to give her a quizzical smile. 'I think that's obvious.' She rose to her feet. 'Well, I'll leave you two to enjoy your stolen time together. Perhaps we'll meet again, Lord Dorrington, at the masked ball.' With a casual toss of her long dark curls, Josephine strolled back to the table she had been sharing with her brother and the Faradays.

'I'm sure she didn't mean anything by that remark,

Freddie.' Dolly eyed him anxiously. She could see that he was angry and it was hardly surprising. Josephine did not seem to know when to stop what she probably thought was amusing banter.

'Keep away from that woman,' Freddie said in a low voice. 'I wish I could remember what scandal they were involved in, but I do know she will cause trouble for all of us.'

Dolly sat back in her chair as two waiters appeared from seemingly nowhere to place their food on the table in front of them. 'I can look after myself, Freddie.'

He met her angry look with raised eyebrows. 'The food looks excellent. Don't let it get cold, Dolly.'

They ate in silence for the best part of the meal, but the evening was spoiled for Dolly. Each time she dared to look over her shoulder she found Josephine staring at her, and then she would turn away to say something to Lady Faraday and her daughters. Dolly had the uncomfortable feeling that they were building more into her relationship with Freddie than was true. She had always felt so safe and comfortable in his company, but now all she experienced was embarrassment. The food was delicious but her appetite had suddenly deserted her and when the plates were cleared away she declined the offer of dessert.

'Perhaps you would like me to send for a cab,' Freddie suggested with a sympathetic smile. 'I'll send one of the waiters, if you are ready to leave.'

'Yes, please. I can't eat any more. I thought

Josephine Mountjoy was very rude to you and I'm revising my good opinion of her.'

Freddie signalled to a waiter. 'Would you hail a cab for us, please?'

'Certainly, my lord.' The waiter hurried off.

Freddie rose to his feet and proffered his arm to Dolly. 'We'll walk past the Mountjoys with a gracious inclination of the head.'

Dolly stood up quickly and laid her hand on his sleeve. 'Certainly, Lord Dorrington.'

They left the restaurant, acknowledging Lady Faraday and her daughters. Sir Jared half rose, but sank back in his seat quickly and continued to scowl at his sister. Josephine blew Dolly a kiss and then resumed her conversation with Celia Faraday.

Outside in the street, Dolly took a deep breath of the cool air, despite the usual mixture of city smells. She allowed Freddie to help her into the waiting hansom cab and he climbed in to sit beside her.

'That was unfortunate,' he said, tapping on the roof to alert the driver to move on. 'I hope you weren't too embarrassed by Miss Mountjoy. She obviously delights in making people feel ill at ease.'

'I could see that. She is a mischief-maker. But quite amusing, I should imagine, providing you are not the object of her misplaced wit.'

'I, for one, was very flattered,' Freddie said, laughing. 'I am many years your senior, as we said before. I am far more suited to be your uncle than your prospective beau.'

Dolly yawned, overcome by fatigue. She reached out automatically to hold his hand. 'I told you, Freddie. Any woman, whatever her age, would be most fortunate to attract your attention.'

'Thank you, but I know you are just being kind.' Freddie patted her hand. 'Tomorrow we'll start the serious business of selling tickets for the opera and the masked ball. Don't worry about a thing, Dolly.'

'I feel confident when I'm with you.' Dolly closed her eyes.

She woke up suddenly as the cab came to a halt and she realised that she had fallen asleep, holding Freddie's hand with her head resting against his shoulder. She sat bolt upright.

'I'm so sorry. I must have dropped off.'

'You did indeed, but we're home now. You can go to bed and have a good night's sleep.'

Freddie paid the cabby through the hatch in the roof and the double doors sprang open, allowing him to alight. He helped Dolly to the pavement outside the mansion in Piccadilly and a rather sleepy-looking Briggs ushered them into the entrance hall.

'You won't think me rude if I go straight to bed, will you, Freddie?'

He smiled and kissed her lightly on the forehead. 'Of course not. We have a busy couple of days ahead of us.'

'It seems that we'll spend most of our time dodging Lady Faraday and the girls,' Dolly said ruefully. 'But thank you for doing this. You don't know how much it means to me and the rest of the family, in fact the whole of Rockwood. The theatre provides an income for many of the locals as well as bringing business to the village.'

'I do realise that, Dolly. You have my full support, you know that. Now go to bed and get some rest. Good night, my dear.'

The next three days were packed with social events. At breakfast each morning, Freddie perused all the invitations that Briggs presented on a silver salver, before passing them on to Dolly. They discussed the merit of each one while they ate, and it was Dolly's task to respond to them as they both saw fit. She discovered that, beneath his somewhat serious exterior, Freddie had a mischievous sense of humour and a sharp wit. There was no reserve between them as they chatted amicably, laughing at shared jokes as they planned their days of promoting the Pavilion Theatre and, in particular, the masked ball.

However, after a leisurely breakfast there was little time to rest; Dolly had never spent so much time changing her clothes to suit the various engagements they attended each day. When he discovered that she had brought very few outfits with her Freddie insisted on accompanying her to the fashion houses and new department stores in Oxford Street to purchase suitable garments. Dolly was reluctant at first, but he insisted that it was all part of their campaign to save the theatre and the prosperity of Rockwood itself.

Faced with such a persuasive argument, she could not disagree without appearing ungrateful.

Freddie was, if anything, overgenerous, but he seemed to enjoy spending money on her, and Dolly valued his opinion. The rather staid surrogate uncle she had always known had suddenly become a personal friend, fashion advisor and confidant, as well as an amusing companion. The gap between their ages meant nothing, and Dolly realised with something of a shock that she was actually enjoying herself. She had thought that their time in London would be a dreary round of trying to interest dull people in the opera and masquerade ball, but she could not have been more wrong.

Everything would have been perfect, had it not been for Theodora Bennington, who seemed to have a sixth sense when it came to knowing when and where Dolly and Freddie would appear next. Wherever they went, Theodora would turn up, sometimes bringing Lady Faraday and her daughters, but more often Theodora would arrive unattended. On these occasions she would head straight for Freddie and attempt to flirt with him. Freddie responded politely but without enthusiasm, which did little to deter Theodora. However, she did agree to purchase five tickets for the opera at the Pavilion and for the masquerade ball. Dolly's sales efforts had been quite successful, but she was dismayed to think that Theodora and the Faradays would invade her home territory.

Freddie laughed off her worries. Even so, Dolly was anxious, particularly when they attended a ball at Harrison House, the home of a noted banker and his wife, who had aspirations to mix with the nobility, despite their comparatively humble backgrounds. The couple were delighted to have a member of the aristocracy as their guest. They introduced Freddie and Dolly to so many people that Dolly was beginning to feel quite dizzy. They escaped to the dance floor, despite the fact that the crush was almost unbearable.

'This is hard work,' Dolly said in a whisper. 'I don't think I could do this sort of thing very often. I am a country girl at heart.'

'We've done the rounds and I'm afraid my face will crack if I have to smile at any more prospective customers.' Freddie guided her off the dance floor. 'Shall we go in to supper? I'm starving.'

'Yes, please. I thought you'd never ask.' Dolly tucked her hand in the crook of his arm as they walked slowly into the supper room. Dolly had attended many balls during her season in London, but this one was being given by a couple who were trying too hard to impress. They might be unashamed social climbers whose money opened many doors for them, but Sir Franklin Harrison had purchased enough opera tickets to fill two whole rows of the dress circle as well as a corresponding number of tickets to the masquerade ball.

Freddie gazed at the tables groaning beneath silver

platters spread with a variety of cold meats. A boar's head glared at them over the lemon stuffed in its open mouth, and terrines of every sort were garnished with every exotic fruit and vegetable available. A whole salmon lay with glazed eyes beneath an overcoat of sliced cucumber, and there were dishes of caviar nestling on bowls of crushed ice. A dazzling array of salads and crowns of jewelled rice gave way to a table devoted to trifles, jellies and ornate desserts decorated with marzipan and sugar paste.

'I half expect a footman to enter with a roasted suckling pig,' Freddie said in a low voice.

Dolly giggled. 'I can't wait to sample the Charlotte Russe. It looks delicious.'

'My mother would have considered such a spread to be verging on the vulgar,' Freddie said, grinning. 'But I say we should forget such snobbery and enjoy our hosts' hospitality.'

'It would be a pity to waste such good food,' Dolly agreed. She glanced over his shoulder. 'Oh dear. Here comes Miss Mountjoy and her objectionable brother.'

'Sir Franklin and his wife are about the only people in London who will receive them,' Freddie said in a low voice. 'I've still to discover the reason for their fall from grace. It's seldom talked about these days, which is probably why they have risked coming to London now, but I will discover it sooner or later.'

Dolly laughed. 'I've a good mind to ask Josephine.

She looks as if she's had a little too much champagne, so it might have loosened her tongue.'

'Dolly, I'm shocked. I didn't know you were so devious.' Freddie picked up a plate. 'Allow me to help you to some supper. We'll find a table in a secluded spot where we can watch the drama unfold, as surely it must.'

They found a reasonably private table shielded from view by potted palms and a large marble statue of a semi-naked goddess, which Freddie said looked as if it had been borrowed from the British Museum. Dolly settled down to enjoy her supper and had just begun to relax when Josephine bore down on them. In one hand she clutched a glass of champagne, which was in danger of being spilled on the floor as she wobbled from side to side. In her other hand was a plate of food that was likely to suffer the same fate. Sir Jared caught her up and snatched the glass from her hand.

'I think you've had enough, Josie.'

She came to a halt, facing him with a cat-like hiss of anger. 'How dare you, Jared? I am perfectly all right.'

'No, you are not. You're making a spectacle of yourself.'

'I am not. You are drunk. You can't even stand straight.' Josephine laughed uproariously and staggered as if she were about to fall.

Freddie leaped to his feet and guided her to a chair. 'Won't you sit down, Miss Mountjoy?'

'Take your hands off my sister,' Jared said in a loud voice.

It was Dolly's turn to rise. She faced Jared angrily. 'You are only making matters worse, sir.'

'What do you know about anything, Miss Blanchard? You are here unchaperoned with a gentleman who is not related to you. Perhaps you ought to consider your own behaviour.'

Freddie turned to face him. 'I think you had better leave, sir. We will see your sister safely to wherever you are staying.'

'Doubtless you've heard of Josephine's wild escapades in the past. I am trying to help her live down a sullied reputation.'

'Nonsense. The details escape me but I believe that you were the one who created a scandal. I do know that.'

Sir Jared fisted his hands. 'Step outside, Dorrington. Your title and fortune won't protect you in a fair fight.'

Josephine rose to her feet, her cheeks pale with anger. 'Jared, stop this at once. Leave the poor man alone.'

'Everyone is looking,' Dolly added anxiously. 'This isn't the way to behave. You are only making yourself look small, Sir Jared.'

'Just who do you think you are, Miss Blanchard? You can't hide behind Dorrington and his title. Your family are all but bankrupt.'

Freddie signalled to two burly footmen, who

despite their flamboyant uniforms, looked as though they should be in a boxing ring rather than the supper room of a London mansion.

'Sir Jared needs a little fresh air.' Freddie moved swiftly, twisting Sir Jared round so that the servants could each grab one of his arms. 'I'd advise you to go quietly, Mountjoy, or you'll find yourself barred from polite society yet again.'

Josephine picked up her glass and raised it as if in a toast. 'Good riddance.' She sank back onto the chair. 'I'm feeling a little unwell, Dolly.'

Dolly eyed her warily. 'Perhaps we should take you to wherever you are staying?'

'Nonsense.' Josephine staggered to her feet. 'I'm only just beginning to enjoy myself. Now Jared is out of the way I can have some real fun.' She walked off, weaving her way through the couples who had been watching the event wide-eyed.

Dolly sank down on her chair. 'I can see that life at Rockwood will never be quite the same with Josephine and her brother living at the manor house.'

Freddie flexed his fingers as he sat down. 'I'm ashamed to say that I almost lost my temper with Mountjoy. I would have gladly taken him outside and made him take back his words.'

'Freddie, I didn't know you were a fighting man.' Dolly stared at him in amazement.

'Believe me, Dolly, I am no different from any man. I will fight to protect my loved ones or anyone who is unable to stand up for themselves.'

Dolly laughed. 'I don't think Josephine comes into that category. Look at her now. She's found someone to amuse her.'

'I'm afraid she is trouble, Dolly. Far be it from me to tell you whom you might associate with, but I will say be very careful of getting too friendly with Josephine Mountjoy and her brother. I fear they are trouble personified.'

'I don't believe that for a moment, Freddie. Josephine is high spirited and her brother is miserable. Anyway, they are not our problem. We have sold so many of our opera and ball tickets. We can return to Rockwood with our mission fulfilled.'

Freddie sighed. 'Just as I was really beginning to enjoy myself.'

'What do you mean? I thought you hated London and would be eager to return home to Dorrington Place.'

'Of course. It's just that I've enjoyed our time together, Dolly. Have you?'

She smiled and reached out to lay her hand on his. 'Of course I have. You are the best friend and companion that any girl could have.'

He gazed down at her small hand. 'I wish I could believe that.'

'But I mean it wholeheartedly. I have had a wonderful time with you, Freddie.'

'Perhaps we'd better get back to you calling me Uncle Freddie when we return to Rockwood Castle,' Freddie said reluctantly.

'As you wish. But the best part is that we've created a lot of interest in our little theatre as well as the hotel. I can't wait to go home and tell everyone. The masquerade ball is going to be a huge success.'

Chapter Thirteen

Two days later Dolly, Bess and Freddie alighted from the London train at Exeter station. The late nights and hectic round of socialising were beginning to take their toll, and Dolly was tired after the journey. Freddie was about to send a porter to look for a cab when Dolly saw a familiar figure wearing military uniform, marching purposefully towards them. Forgetting decorum, she ran to meet him.

'Gus! What are you doing here?'

He picked her up and swung her round before setting her back on her feet. 'I was at the castle when the telegram arrived to say which train you would be on. Your cousin Tommy sent me to meet you. He said I might as well do something useful instead of taking up Nancy's valuable time.'

'Well, it's lovely to see you. I have so much to tell you about our time in London. Freddie – I mean

Uncle Freddie – has been wonderful. We've attended so many balls, soirées and luncheon parties that I've lost count.'

'I look forward to hearing all about it, but let's get you into the landau. You must be exhausted.' He turned to face Freddie as he walked towards them. 'I hear you and Miss Adela have had a good trip to London, my lord.'

'Yes, indeed. We've had a very pleasant time and we've sold a great many of our tickets. The masquerade ball should be a great success.'

'I've been sent to bring you back to the castle, sir. I take it you will be returning there?'

'Yes, of course. I have to deliver my charge to her family, and anyway, I left my carriage and pair at Rockwood.'

Gus signalled to the porter, who had loaded the luggage onto a trolley. 'That can be loaded onto the brake.' He handed the porter a tip before turning back to Dolly with a wide grin. 'Your papa guessed that there would be more baggage coming home than the small valise you took with you.'

'We attended so many functions, Gus. Uncle Freddie insisted on treating me to some lovely outfits, which I fear I won't have the opportunity to wear once I am back at work.'

Freddie stepped in between them. 'I think we should be on our way to Rockwood, Sergeant. Dolly must be exhausted.' Without waiting for an answer he led Dolly to the waiting landau and handed her into it.

'Was there any need to speak to Gus like that?' Dolly demanded, shooting a wary glance at Gus, who was fully occupied supervising the luggage being loaded onto the brake.

Freddie climbed in and sat down opposite her. 'Don't fall for his charms again, Dolly.'

'I'm sorry, Freddie. I respect you in every way, but I am capable of looking after myself. Gus is a friend.' Dolly leaned over the side of the vehicle and beckoned to Bess. 'Ride with us, Bess. The brake is not the most comfortable mode of transport.' She sent a challenging look in Freddie's direction as she made room for Bess to sit beside her. He had been her dear friend and mentor in London, but now they were nearing home and she felt she must take back control of her life, as much as was possible, anyway.

Gus tipped the porter and Pip Hudson drove off in the brake. Gus vaulted onto the driver's seat of the landau beside Hudson senior.

'You could sit with us, Gus,' Dolly said, frowning.

'I'm happy up here with Hudson. It gives you all a bit more room. Off we go, Hudson. Let's see if we can break the record for getting back to Rockwood.'

Hudson nodded and flicked the whip over the horses' heads. 'Walk on.'

Dolly sat back against the leather squabs and closed her eyes. She did not feel like making conversation with Freddie and she was more tired than she had realised. It was only when the carriage finally came to a halt in the bailey of Rockwood Castle that Dolly woke up. She blinked sleepily.

'Are we here already?'

'Yes, miss. You've been asleep all the way.' Bess alighted first, followed by Freddie, who held his hand out to help Dolly.

She accepted without arguing. It was good to be home, but her first concern was for Gus and she waited for him to climb down from the box.

'Will you stay for dinner, Gus? It's getting a bit late for you to travel back to camp.'

He shook his head. 'I would love to, but I'm afraid I would be had up as a deserter. I only had twenty-four hours' leave, Dolly.'

'And you wasted half of it by coming to meet us. I'm sorry, Gus.'

'Nonsense. It was worth the long drive to see you safely home.'

'When will you be able to visit us again?'

'I can't say, but be assured it won't be long. I do care for you, Dolly. I may not be the most reliable of men, but my feelings for you are sincere, if misplaced.'

'Misplaced?' Dolly met his serious gaze with a frown. 'I don't understand.'

He leaned over to drop a kiss on her forehead. 'That's another reason why I love you. But I have to leave now. There are several hours left before dark, which gives me time to ride back to camp.' He turned on his heel and strode away in the direction of the stables.

'Dolly, darling. Don't stand outside. Come in.'

Dolly looked round, staring at her mother dazedly. 'Mama?'

'What's wrong, dear? You look worn out. You're just in time for a sherry before dinner. We're all waiting to hear how you and Freddie got on in London. Your grandmama is agog with curiosity. The outcome of the masquerade ball means so much to her and the theatre.'

'I'm coming, Mama.' Dolly walked slowly into the home where she had lived all her life and allowed the peaceful atmosphere to calm her troubled soul. Gus had a way of turning her world upside down, and he had done it yet again.

The older members of the family had gathered in the drawing room, including Hester, who had come from the Dower House, driven, no doubt, by sheer curiosity. However, Walter and Louise had stayed at home with their daughter, Charlotte, and had been joined by Phoebe and May for a grown-up dinner, while Jack, Nancy's adopted son, and Rory were staying in Plymouth with a friend from university. Nancy's boys were being supervised by Wolfe in the nursery, giving Connie an evening off to spend with her gentleman friend. But Patricia and Leo had been persuaded to come for dinner, leaving Charlie with Fletcher, who had been the boy's slave from the moment he was born.

Freddie refrained from any mention of Gus's name.

He joined Dolly in recounting their experiences in London, even going so far as to add to Dolly's descriptions of Miss Bennington and Lady Faraday. The mere mention of the Mountjoys' name brought renewed interest from everyone, and the account of Josephine's behaviour at the ball brought a mixed reaction.

'Who are they really?' Hester demanded. 'I've heard all sorts of stories about the newcomers from my servants.'

'Maybe you oughtn't to listen to their gossip, Hester,' Patricia said with a mischievous smile.

'Patsy!' Leo warned, slipping his arm around his wife's waist. 'Let Dolly tell her story uninterrupted.'

Patricia tossed her head. 'I didn't stop her – it was Hester, who now listens to chit-chat from those below stairs.'

'Patsy, be quiet.' Rosalind laughed, turning to her daughter. 'Continue, please, Dolly. Tell us what you know.'

'They are a mystery,' Dolly said slowly.

'There is some scandal attached to their name,' Freddie added. 'I'm not sure I ever knew the facts of the matter, but at one time the name Mountjoy was on everyone's lips.'

'I heard that Sir Jared had embezzled a small fortune from the business he was running,' Nancy said seriously. 'I don't know if that's true.'

Tommy nodded. 'Cottingham Manor can't have been cheap.'

Patricia leaned forward, lowering her voice. 'Someone told me that they are not really brother and sister.'

Hester pursed her lips. 'She is no better than she should be. Mrs Simpson told me that Josephine Mountjoy has a love child hidden away somewhere. She refused to name the father, although some say it was a very prominent man.'

Alex stifled a yawn. 'That sounds like a yarn to me, Hester.'

She rounded on him. 'Do you know better, Alexander?'

'No. I'm keeping out of this.' Alex sent a pleading look to his wife.

Rosalind gave him a sympathetic smile. 'I think we should all mind our own business and tell the gossips to do the same.' She looked up at the sound of a knock on the door. 'Come in.'

The door opened and Flossie entered to announce that dinner was served.

'Thank goodness for that,' Freddie proffered his arm to Hester, who accepted with a regal nod of her head.

Dolly could see that it was going to be a long evening. She could not help wondering how Gus was getting on. It was a long ride back to camp, but he was a fit and healthy young man. The disturbing fact was that when he was near she forgot everything other than the hold he had on her emotions. When he smiled at her she felt as helpless as a marionette on a string and he was the puppeteer.

*

The next few days proved to be busier than Dolly could have imagined. Everyone helped to sell the theatre tickets and those for the masquerade ball. Nick had the idea of driving Liza Day to Dawlish one day and to Teignmouth the day after. They were both dressed in costume, wearing velvet masks studded with sequins. They visited all the houses owned by people likely to be interested in the performance and the ball afterwards, and returned with the last of the tickets sold just days before the opening night of *The Masked Ball*. All this was done in between rehearsals, costume fittings and the normal day-to-day running of the theatre. Dolly took on more responsibility and she enjoyed every minute. Working hard kept her mind off Gus, and Freddie was on hand to help with the preparations. He had opted to stay at Rockwood Castle until after the big event, declaring that he would not miss such excitement for the world. Dolly was glad to have his company and support, but she would not allow him to say anything detrimental about Gus. However, Gus kept away from Rockwood, and it seemed likely that his time was fully occupied by army duties. Dolly had hoped that he would attend the masquerade ball, but she never knew with Gus. He might turn up unannounced or he might not.

The whole family had thrown themselves into the event with great enthusiasm. Rosie, Patsy and Nancy had ordered costumes from a theatrical costumier in London, as had Dolly. Pip Hudson drove the brake to Exeter station to collect the parcels. Rather reluctantly, Tommy, Alex and Leo had also agreed to hire outfits suitable for the occasion, although they had refused to reveal the themes of their costumes.

'We will be the most dashing heroes you could imagine,' Alex said when Dolly demanded to know the details. She had to be content with that, but there was a general air of excitement that affected not only the occupants of the castle, but seemingly the whole village. Those who could afford to purchase tickets had done so, while others volunteered to help with the preparations, determined to take part in the event anyway.

The Pavilion Theatre was packed on the first night of the new opera. There was not a single seat available for latecomers, and all the programmes were sold, no doubt as souvenirs. Dolly and the theatre attendants wore their costumes all evening, although without the masks, which they kept for later. There was an air of anticipation and excitement during the opera performance, and the audience was most appreciative. Several curtain calls brought the house down and Liza, as leading lady, was given a standing ovation. Nick went on stage to present her with a large bouquet of roses, which Liza accepted gracefully. To the delight of everyone in the auditorium she stood on tiptoes to plant a kiss on Nick's cheek.

It had been a beautiful summer's day and the evening was balmy. Lanterns hung from the trees in the hotel grounds and the members of the theatre orchestra took their instruments to a secluded spot where chairs and music stands awaited them. Dolly saw to it that the musicians were plied with food and drink before they struck up once again.

Flares illuminated the pathway to the area designated for the ball itself, which was surrounded by small tables and gilded chairs. Marquees had been set up to provide cover for the refreshments, and trestle tables draped in white damask cloths had been laid with platters filled with tempting delicacies. There were dainty sandwiches, savoury tartlets and bite-sized pies. Jellies shimmered in glass dishes and bowls of trifle, studded with cherries and almonds, would have tempted the poorest appetite. Pyramids of small fancy cakes glistening with sugar crystals, and plates of jam tarts added to the feast. The remaining tables were groaning beneath the weight of barrels of beer and cider and huge glass bowls of fruit punch. There was champagne and fine wines to be purchased separately. As Nick said, they were out to make money, not to give it away.

Dolly did the rounds, inspecting everything before the first revellers arrived. She had donned a black velvet mask and Bess had put her hair up for her. Dolly felt suddenly mysterious and at the same time daring. The mask provided a certain amount of anonymity, which was very exciting. The orchestra were tuning up, ready to start the proceedings with a grand march. Dolly joined Nick and Liza, who were ushering in the guests at the gates to the hotel grounds. Dolly recognised some of the masked revellers, but there were many visitors from London, thanks to Freddie. Dolly had hoped that Theodora Bennington would decide against travelling all the way to Devonshire, but she arrived with a retinue of followers. Theodora was easily recognisable by the loudness of her voice and her obvious desire to attract attention to herself. She marched on ahead of Lady Faraday and her daughters and made straight for Dolly.

'I would know you anywhere by that beautiful golden hair, Miss Blanchard. Perhaps you should have worn a wig in order to disguise yourself. The mask does nothing to hide your pretty face.'

'Thank you, Miss Bennington. You will always stand out in a crowd.'

Theodora's eyes flashed. 'I'm not sure how to translate that remark, Dolly. However, I hope it was meant to be a compliment.'

'Naturally,' Dolly said vaguely. 'I see you've brought Lady Faraday, Isabella and Celia with you, as well as some other friends.'

'Of course. We are happy to support your efforts to restore the family fortunes. I am lucky that I do not have that problem.' Theodora looked round, fanning herself slowly. 'I take it that Dorrington is here in the midst of this bucolic frivolity.'

'I believe he is,' Dolly said casually. 'If you'll excuse me, Miss Bennington. I have other guests to greet.'

'Yes, I am sure you do. It must be so hard to have to earn your own living. You should look for a wealthy husband, my dear.'

Dolly was saved from answering by a loud shriek from Josephine Mountjoy, who ran towards them, arms outstretched. 'Dolly, I would know you anywhere.' She came to a halt, staring at Theodora. 'I know you, too. You are the rude and vulgar heiress whom everyone avoids because you are always boasting about your wealth.'

Theodora's eyes narrowed so that they almost disappeared into her mask. 'And you are the woman who created a drunken scene at the Harrisons' mansion in Park Lane.'

'I'm sober now, but you are still vulgar and always will be.' Josephine tossed her head. 'I see my brother. I prefer his company to yours, Miss Bennington.'

'So I've heard,' Theodora said acidly. 'You enjoy it too much, so people say.'

Dolly stared at her in horror. This was getting out of hand. She turned to Josephine with an attempt at a smile, but too late. Josephine clawed her fingers and lunged at Theodora, catching the side of her cheek with her long nails. Blood oozed from the scratches and Theodora screamed so loudly that people rushed to her aid.

Dolly held up her hand. 'It's all right. Miss Bennington has had a slight accident. I will take care of her.' She grabbed Theodora by the arm. 'Miss Mountjoy, I suggest you make yourself scarce.'

Josephine shrugged. 'She deserved it, the spiteful bitch.' She strolled off to join her brother.

Lady Margery moved closer. 'I saw what happened. Are you going to let her get away with such behaviour, Theodora?'

'She will pay for it, believe me.' Theodora held a lace hanky to her cheek. 'I'm bleeding. I need a doctor.'

'It's just a scratch or two,' Dolly said hastily. 'But Dr Taylor is here somewhere, just in case of an emergency. If you'll take care of her, Lady Faraday, I'll go and find him.'

'Of course.' Lady Faraday slipped her arm around Theodora's shoulders. 'Come with me, my dear. We'll find somewhere to sit down and wait for the doctor.'

'Josephine Mountjoy will regret this for the rest of her life,' Theodora said angrily. 'If I am scarred I will sue Josephine and her *brother* for every penny they have.'

'Take her into the hotel, ma'am,' Dolly said hastily. 'She will be taken care of there.'

'I blame you for this, Dolly Blanchard,' Theodora hissed over her shoulder. 'I think you planned this all along.'

'Come along, my dear. We'll get your injuries attended to.' Lady Faraday hustled a protesting Theodora away, heading for the hotel.

Dolly sighed. She was beginning to think that her efforts to interest wealthy patrons from London had

been misplaced. She turned at the sound of someone calling her name and, despite his disguise as an
eighteenth-century highwayman, she recognised
Freddie as he strolled towards her. He stopped and
doffed his hat with a flourish. His eyes twinkled
behind the velvet mask.

'What do you think, Dolly? Do I look terrifying?'

'I'm shaking in my shoes, sir. I have no jewels for
you to rob.'

Freddie laughed. 'We must remedy that one day,
Dolly. But until then I will have to be satisfied with
your hand in the waltz, if you will deign to dance
with a villain like me.'

Dolly laid her hand in his. 'I can hardly refuse if
my life depends upon it.'

Freddie led her to the area of grass that had been
trimmed until it was like green velvet, creating a
soft carpet underfoot. Freddie whirled her into the
dance with an expertise that Dolly found surprising.
She had always associated Freddie with country
pursuits rather than such social skills as this, and
although they had danced at the Harrisons' ball, the
floor had been too crowded to move far. Now, with
a vast expanse of lawn, there was room for everyone
to show off their terpsichorean expertise. Freddie
was rapidly proving himself to be an excellent dancer.
Dolly forgot everything other than the pleasure of
the warm summer air, redolent with the scent of
flowers and crushed grass. The night sky was filled
with stars and the light from Chinese paper lanterns

cast a magical glow on the masked revellers in their colourful silks and satins.

Dolly experienced a wave of disappointment when the waltz ended and the couples walked away into pools of shadow. Freddie still had hold of her hand.

'May I get you a glass of fruit punch?'

Slightly dazed and feeling intoxicated by the sheer excitement and romance of the evening, Dolly nodded and smiled. 'That would be lovely. Thank you, but I ought to make sure that all the guests are being looked after.'

'I think you've done more than enough to restore the fortunes of the Pavilion Theatre, Dolly. You've earned some time to enjoy yourself.' Freddie glanced over Dolly's shoulder. 'I think that's your new neighbour misbehaving, as it seems she always does at public functions.'

Dolly could hear the now familiar laughter and she turned to see Josephine standing with a group of men in army uniform. She had taken a tankard of ale from one of the men and was attempting to down it in one swallow. The soldiers were laughing but Dolly could see the more staid couples were giving the group a wide berth. It seemed that Josephine was only happy when she was causing a stir.

'I wonder where Sir Jared is,' Dolly said anxiously.

'Josephine can look after herself, I'm sure.' Freddie walked towards the marquee where the refreshments had been laid out, leaving Dolly on her own. She hesitated, torn between the desire to rescue Josephine from a situation that could get out of hand and the knowledge that Freddie had spoken the truth. Josephine Mountjoy knew exactly what she was doing – but when she snatched a cigar from one of the gentlemen and took several puffs on it, Dolly could not stand by and see Josephine making such a spectacle of herself. A small crowd of amused onlookers had gathered and were cheering her on, which only made Josephine behave even more outrageously. She took a shako from one of the officers' heads and put it on at an angle while she strutted around puffing plumes of cigar smoke into the night air, accompanied by gales of laughter.

It was obvious that Josephine was becoming very tipsy and, as there was no sign of Sir Jared, Dolly rushed forward and caught the shako before it landed on the ground. She handed it back to its owner.

'I think you've entertained the troops for long enough, Josie.' Dolly twisted Josephine around. 'You'll make yourself sick if you keep smoking that cigar. Please give it to the gentleman you took it from.'

Josephine took one last defiant puff and dropped the cigar butt onto the ground. 'It's a foul-tasting thing anyway. I prefer a cigarillo myself.' She hooked her arm around Dolly's shoulders. 'I want champagne. You could do with some as well. It might take that disapproving look off your face.'

'No, really. Freddie is getting me some fruit punch.

Why don't you go and find your brother?' Dolly wriggled free, looking round in desperation. 'He must be here somewhere.'

Josephine laughed. 'He'll have found something to make a bet on. Dear Jared loves a wager.' Josephine put her finger to her lips, lowering her voice to a stage whisper. 'That's where much of our fortune went – on the gaming tables and at the racecourse – but don't tell anyone.'

'Perhaps I should go and find him for you?' Dolly suggested hopefully.

'No, I don't need him or any man. Let's go and get a magnum of champagne. We'll drink it all ourselves.' Josephine grabbed Dolly by the hand and was about to drag her to the refreshment marquee when Freddie came towards them, clutching two glasses of fruit punch.

'Josephine wants champagne,' Dolly said urgently. 'Have you seen Sir Jared anywhere?'

Josephine seized a glass from Freddie before he could resist and she drank thirstily. 'The only trouble with drinking is that you always want more,' she said, giggling.

'I think you've had enough, Miss Mountjoy.' Freddie spoke quietly but Dolly could see that he was angry.

'Will you go and find Sir Jared, please, Freddie?'

'Are you Dolly's beau?' Josephine demanded loudly. 'You were very cosy together when we met in London. Aren't you a little old for her, sir?'

'Freddie is a dear friend,' Dolly said hastily. She could feel the colour rising to her cheeks despite the fact she was wearing a mask. She glanced round anxiously, hoping that no one had heard, but she could tell by the sudden silence that Josephine's voice had carried on the clear night air.

'If you aren't her beau, there must be something wrong with you, Dorrington,' Josephine added conversationally. 'Do you dislike women? Surely a man of your standing is in need of a wife, if only to produce an heir to all that huge fortune you inherited. I am available, sir.'

'Josephine, be quiet.' Sir Jared appeared from behind a group of interested onlookers. 'You've said enough. We're leaving.'

Josephine drained the glass and thrust it into Freddie's hand. 'I can see I've hit the nail on the head, as common people say. You should be ashamed of yourself, Dorrington. Cradle snatching is against the law, and if it isn't – it should be.' Josephine struggled as her brother clamped his hand on her arm and dragged her away. 'Beware, Dolly Blanchard. If he hasn't got honest intentions, he will take advantage of your youth and innocence. I know because I suffered at the hands of such a libertine.' Her voice trailed away as Jared marched her out of the hotel grounds.

'Freddie?' Dolly turned to him, laying her hand on his arm. 'She's drunk – she didn't mean what she said.'

He shook his head. 'If that's what people think, I am so sorry, Dolly. I would rather cut my right hand off than put you in a compromising situation.'

He turned and walked away.

Dolly's hand flew to her mouth to prevent herself from crying out. Of course what Josephine had said was nonsense, but she could tell from the covert looks of the onlookers that Josephine had succeeded in creating doubt in their minds. Dolly wanted to run after Freddie, but somehow her limbs would not move.

'Dolly, darling, I heard what that wretched woman said.' Rosalind hurried up to her daughter and gave her a hug. 'Your papa and I know that it's a pack of lies, of course.'

Alex joined them, his handsome features creased into an angry frown. 'Listen to your mother, Dolly. Everyone knows that Freddie is above reproach.'

'Then why didn't you both speak up in his defence?'

Dolly spun round to see a tall, dark-haired man standing behind them. He was wearing neither a mask nor fancy dress.

'Piers!' Rosalind clutched Alexander's arm. 'Why are you here?'

'I've come to visit my daughter. I think it's time I got to know her, and from what I just heard it seems that you need your father, Adela.'

Chapter Fourteen

'Piers, you can't just arrive unexpectedly and think that all will be well,' Alexander said angrily. 'You haven't shown any interest in Dolly for nearly twenty years. Why now?'

Rosalind glanced round anxiously. 'I don't know why you've turned up like this, Piers, but this isn't the time or the place for discussing family matters.'

'Then I suggest we take it back to the castle where it all began.' Piers turned to his cousin. 'My reasons for coming are my own business, Alex. I came to see Adela, not you or Rosie.'

Alexander took a step towards his cousin. 'You are determined to cause trouble again, Piers. I know you only too well.'

Dolly was about to speak but she saw Hester bearing down on them like a ship in full sail. She came to a halt, ripping off her mask.

'I thought it was you, Piers Blanchard. What mischief are you up to now?'

'Hester, my love. Do I detect a note of cynicism in your voice? You look magnificent, by the way. I've settled permanently in Cornwall, having made a fortune in Barbados and the Americas. However, all I want now is to get to know my daughter.'

Dolly stepped forward. 'You are all talking about me as if I weren't here. I've heard all about you, Mr Blanchard, but I can't say that I remember much about you.'

'That is why I've come to see you now, my dear.' Piers smiled. 'Not before time, I admit.'

'You've left it a bit late to take an interest in me. As far as I'm concerned *this* is my papa.' Dolly laid her hand on Alexander's arm. 'He always will be.'

Alex covered her hand with his. 'You *are* my daughter, Dolly. I couldn't love you more.'

'Where are you staying, Piers?' Rosalind asked anxiously.

'Where else other than the castle? I left my luggage there and I was told where you all were. Of course, I know all about the happenings at Rockwood. Aurelia has told me as much as she knows, so I decided to find out for myself.'

'We can't talk here,' Alexander said angrily. 'You're ruining what should have been Dolly's night. But that's what I'd expect from you, Piers.'

'I think we should go home now.' Rosalind sighed. 'It was such a lovely evening until you arrived, Piers.'

'That's not how you would have greeted me when we were married, Rosie.'

She moved closer to Alexander. 'That was over twenty years ago, Piers. You released me from our marriage during your spell in the Australian penal colony. You've never been a father to Dolly.'

Piers turned to Dolly with a questioning look. 'What do you say, Adela?'

'We've been planning this event for weeks,' Dolly said slowly. 'The future of both the theatre and the hotel depend upon tonight being a success. I'm asking you nicely, please go back to the castle. We'll talk later.'

'You heard what Dolly said.' Hester took a step towards Piers. 'You always were a troublemaker.' She glanced over her shoulder at the sound of Felicia's voice.

'What is going on? Why aren't you all mingling with the guests?' Felicia came to a sudden halt, staring at Piers. 'What are you doing here?'

Piers laughed. 'You are not the first person to ask that, Felicia.'

Rosalind moved swiftly to his side. 'Go back to the castle, Piers. We will talk about this in the morning. Now is not a good time, as you can see.'

'I think I'd rather stay and have a dance with my daughter.' Piers held his hand out to Dolly. 'Shall we?'

Alexander stepped in between them. 'Leave now, Piers. Or shall I call for assistance to have you thrown out bodily?'

'You ought to know by now that I don't take kindly to threats, Alex. I'll go but only after I've had one dance with Adela.'

Dolly grasped his hand. 'All right. This is getting ridiculous. I will dance with you, but only if I have your word you will not create a scene.'

Piers raised her hand to his lips. 'I wouldn't do anything to upset my daughter.' He led her past her outraged family and they joined in the crush of dancers, all of whom were totally oblivious of the drama unfolding around them.

'Why have you waited all these years to get to know me?' Dolly demanded in a low voice. 'I can tell by the curious stares that a lot of people recognise you. News of your arrival will be all round the village and beyond by morning.'

'I spent many years as a soldier of fortune, working for whichever side paid me the most, although I must admit my activities were almost all connected with gun-running and blockading American ports. I was never keen on bloodshed, particularly my own.'

'I seem to remember that you were in Barbados. Papa and Uncle Leo went out there to bring you home.'

'I returned to Cornwall to try to save the china clay business, which, I have to say, I did with some success, but I found it deadly dull. I think you might understand that, Adela. I see you are a rebel, too.'

'I don't know what gives you that idea.' Dolly

allowed him to lead her to a small table as the waltz came to an end. 'You know nothing about me.'

'I know that you have organised this event, quite successfully, it seems. I heard that you ran away to London with a certain army sergeant and then you were in Lord Dorrington's company abroad. Hardly the actions of a meek and mild young lady.'

'Who told you all this?'

'The landlady at the Black Dog loves to gossip. I found Mrs Causley very informative. Won't you sit down, Adela?'

She shook her head. 'No. I did what you wanted and now I'm asking you to leave. I'll speak to you in the morning.'

'You are your mother's daughter, my dear. I will go now, but we will talk again. I am not going to return to Cornwall unless you accompany me. I want you to see Trevenor, which will one day be yours.'

'What do you mean?' Dolly followed him as he made his way towards the main entrance.

'You are my only child. You will inherit the house and land as well as the mine, although I have no intention of passing away just yet. I need to make sure you are capable of taking on the responsibility.' Piers quickened his pace but Dolly ran after him.

'Just a minute. This is ridiculous. You are a relatively young man. Why don't you remarry? You could have more children.'

Piers stopped and turned to look her in the eye.

'I have tried marriage once and it didn't suit me. I shall not marry again.' He strode off into the darkness.

Dolly walked slowly back to where she had left her family, but they had all dispersed. Grandmama Felicia and Grandpa Claude were leading the country dance, with Hester sitting at a table close by, sipping a glass of something stronger than fruit punch. There was no sign of Josephine and her brother, although Lady Faraday, apparently recovered from seeing Josephine's attack on Miss Bennington, was dancing with a gentleman dressed as a Roman emperor. Isabella and Celia had been claimed by army officers, and Nick was seated at another table with Liza Day. They seemed to be getting quite close, and Dolly did not know whether to be pleased or envious. She was suddenly very much alone, despite the fact that her father had returned to claim her after all these years.

It was a relief when she saw Freddie making his way towards her. He offered her a glass of punch, which she drank thirstily.

'I saw what happened with Piers,' Freddie said gently. 'Your mama told me what he wants. How does that make you feel?'

The punch warmed Dolly's stomach but it also made her feel slightly reckless and she forgot the momentary embarrassment caused by Josephine's spiteful comments about her relationship with Freddie. 'I don't really know. I'm confused. He said a lot of things, but to be completely honest I'm not sure I believed him.'

'I think he's caused your family a lot of heartache, Dolly. I can't pretend to know him very well, but it's really up to you whether or not you choose to accept him at his word.'

'What would you do in my position?'

'I would think seriously about it. He is your father in fact, but in every other way it's Alex who has raised you and loved you all your life.'

Dolly met his earnest gaze with a smile. 'You are so wise, Freddie. What would I do without you?'

'You didn't believe all that nonsense Miss Mountjoy said, did you?'

'Of course not. You've been part of my life for almost as long as I can remember. You would have been family had you married Nancy.'

Freddie glanced at Nancy and Tommy, who were laughing at some shared joke. 'I think Nancy chose the right man and I'm happy for her.'

'You are important to me, Freddie. I feel I need someone to whom I can talk freely. My family are too involved and they all share the same opinion about Piers Blanchard. I've never heard anything good spoken about him.'

'Your mother loved him enough to marry him, so he must have some redeeming points.' Freddie took the empty punch cup from her hand and laid it on the table. 'Let's try and put everything out of our minds. This ball is promising to be a great success, in case you haven't noticed. May I have this dance?'

'Of course, but it's a polka.'

Freddie smiled ruefully. 'I am not so ancient that I cannot manage to keep in time, if you will guide me.'

'Now you're making fun of me.'

'Never. I love you for what and who you are, Dolly. Don't change for anyone, especially not for me. Now shall we show them all how it's done?'

Dolly placed her hand in his and they joined the dancers in the energetic polka. Freddie whirled her expertly around, keeping in perfect time with the music. In the end it was Dolly who was breathless and she leaned against him as the music came to an end.

'I hate to say I told you so,' Freddie said, laughing.

'You are always right, it seems. You should show off your talents more, Freddie.'

He led her to a small table and Dolly sat down, glad of a chance to catch her breath. She glanced round at the other couples, some of whom were taking advantage of their temporary disguise and behaving outrageously.

'You were right, Freddie. I think we can say that the ball is a success.'

'There will be a few embarrassed faces when the unmasking takes place at midnight.'

'I hope Nick has remembered the prize for the best costume,' Dolly said anxiously. 'Perhaps I should remind him.'

'Try to forget your responsibilities and enjoy yourself, Dolly. This is your triumph. No one else put in as much hard work as you have.'

'I've enjoyed it. I like working. I don't think I could ever simply sit at home and wait for invitations to social events.'

'I understand.'

She met his gaze with a smile. 'Yes, I know you do. You have always supported me, especially when I was in difficulties in London. I'll never forget that.'

'They're playing a mazurka now. Shall we?'

Dolly rose to her feet. 'Yes, please.'

Once again they stepped into the pool of light created by the multitude of Chinese lanterns. Dolly had not danced the mazurka since her coming-out party in London, but Freddie proved once again that he was as adept at dancing as he was at everything else. Dolly wished that Josephine Mountjoy could see them as they executed the steps in perfect time together. Josephine had a vicious tongue and Freddie was too gentlemanly to attack a lady verbally, but judging by her performance earlier in the evening, Josephine was what Hester would call a 'hoyden', and that was when Hester was being polite.

Patricia and Leo had also been enjoying the mazurka, and when the dance ended Patricia congratulated Freddie.

'I didn't know you were such an excellent dancer, Freddie.'

'Yes,' Leo added. 'You put us all to shame, old

chap. Patsy says I have two left feet and she complains that I tread upon her toes.'

'Freddie is the perfect partner.' Dolly smiled up at him. 'But I've neglected everyone. I see Todd outside the marquee, looking a little lost. I'm going to make sure he's all right.'

Leaving Freddie chatting with her aunt and uncle, Dolly made her way to where Todd was standing. He did look rather uncomfortable but his face lit up when he saw her.

'I watched you dancing, Dolly. You looked as if you were enjoying yourself.'

'I was, although it's been very up and down this evening. Did you manage to placate Miss Bennington? I haven't seen her since Josephine scratched her face. I'm assuming that Lady Faraday brought her to you.'

'Yes, she did. I put salve on Miss Bennington's cheek. The scratches were superficial, although she insisted that she would be scarred for life. In the end I had to leave her to deal with a lady who had fainted.'

'Have you had refreshments, Todd? You are just as much a guest as anyone else.'

'I wasn't sure whether I was included or whether I am just here to patch up those who fall by the wayside, so to speak.'

'Come with me. I haven't eaten a thing since breakfast and I'm starving. Let's see if there's anything left.' Dolly tucked her hand in the crook of his arm and led him into the marquee. She came to a halt at the sight of a masked man in full regimental dress uniform.

'I'm sorry, Dolly,' Todd said with a sigh. 'Gus wanted to speak to you urgently, but he's been drinking and I know how your family feel about him.'

'It's Sergeant Baker, my boy.' Gus raised his glass. 'A toast to myself for being an honourable man.'

Dolly crossed the floor and took the glass from his hand. 'I think you've had enough, Gus. I didn't even know you were here.'

He laughed. 'It is rather difficult to distinguish between the real military men and those in fancy dress.'

'Maybe I'd better get you to the doctor's house, Gus. You can't ride back to camp in that state.' Todd advanced on his friend but Gus held up both hands.

'I am perfectly sober. I'm not leaving until the party ends. I want to dance with Dolly.'

Before Dolly had a chance to respond, a loud sob made them all turn their heads as Liza Day entered the marquee and collapsed onto the nearest chair.

Dolly hurried to her side. 'Liza, what's wrong?'

'I'm so sorry. I didn't know there was anyone here.' Liza dashed tears away with the back of her hand.

'Are you ill, miss?' Todd asked anxiously. 'Can I help?'

Liza raised a tear-stained face to give him a watery

smile. 'Thank you, Doctor, but I don't think even you can mend a broken heart.'

Suddenly sober, Gus strolled over to them. 'You'd be surprised at what my friend can do, miss. Now what's the trouble? If someone has been pestering you, we'll deal with the fellow.'

'No, no.' Liza shook her head. 'I mistook his intentions. It was my fault.'

Dolly placed her arm around Liza's shoulder. 'Who was it, Liza? Can we help?'

'No, please don't say anything. I've probably been rather silly. Nick and I have been getting close but I obviously misread his intentions.'

'If I was your father I would call the fellow out,' Gus said boldly.

'Yes, if you lived in the last century.' Todd shook his head. 'You're not helping, Gus.'

'No, indeed you are not.' Dolly turned to Gus with a frown. 'Perhaps you could get some brandy for Miss Day.'

'Of course. Happy to be of service.' Gus swaggered off in the direction of the marquee where alcohol was still being served.

'Would you like me to take you home, Miss Day?' Todd asked gently. 'I know where you live.'

Liza wiped her eyes on a hanky that Dolly took from her own pocket. 'It's my grandmother's cottage. I was hoping to earn enough to rent somewhere a little bigger and less damp. She suffers from poor health.'

'Yes, I know Mrs Day well.' Todd smiled. 'She's a lovely lady. I've visited her on many occasions. I believe those cottages belong to the Cottingham estate.'

'They belong to the Mountjoys at the manor house now.' Dolly pulled a face. 'I doubt if Sir Jared will be interested in improving the lot of his tenants.'

'That's something I intend to remedy, if I can,' Todd said earnestly. 'I've been sending letters to our local member of parliament, asking for a meeting so that I can discuss such matters with him. The welfare of poor people is something that the Government needs to address with more vigour.'

Dolly stared at him in amazement. 'Todd, I had no idea that you were so public spirited.'

He laughed. 'Why would you? You live in a castle, not a hovel. Although, to be fair, the tenants on the Rockwood Estate fare better than most.'

'Aunt Patsy's first husband was a member of parliament,' Dolly said thoughtfully. 'Have you thought of standing at the next election, Todd? I think you would do well.'

'I don't imagine a poor country doctor would be considered a good candidate. You need money to do that sort of thing, and connections. I have none.' Todd proffered his hand to Liza. 'If you feel well enough I'll take you home.'

Liza laid her hand in his. 'Thank you, Dr Taylor. I would be most grateful. I don't like walking out alone in the dark.'

Todd helped her to her feet. 'I'll see her safely to

her grandmother's cottage, Dolly. I doubt if you'll need my medical assistance now, but if anything happens, send Alfie for me.'

'Thank you, Dolly,' Liza said earnestly. 'Please don't mention this to Nick. The misunderstanding was my fault.'

'I doubt that. I think Nick Gibson has made a few hearts flutter over the years, including my aunt Aurelia's, if what Nancy said is true, and I've no reason to doubt her. Nick isn't the sort of man to settle down, but he likes women. You've had a lucky escape, if you ask me.'

'I won't allow it to interfere with my performance,' Liza said stoutly. 'I am a professional artiste and that must come first.'

Todd helped Liza to her feet. 'Come along, Miss Day. Let's get you home.'

Dolly watched them leave the marquee, arm in arm. She was tempted to speak to Nick but she knew he would deny everything. In fact, he probably did not realise what he had done, and would continue to break hearts until the day he died.

She was about to leave the marquee when Gus returned, bringing a tot of brandy.

'They've gone. I suppose Todd is being the gallant gentleman and taking the poor creature home.'

'Todd certainly is a gentleman, but Liza is not a poor creature, Gus. She has been misled by a man who thinks only of himself and his own pleasure. Which category of person are you?'

Gus downed the spirit in one swallow. 'That's a little harsh, Dolly. You know I love you. I always have.'

She pushed past him. 'I know no such thing, Gus Baker. You amused yourself by taking me to London with you and then you abandoned me.'

'That's not fair and you know it, Dolly. We've been through this not so long ago.' He gazed at her, frowning. 'I admit that I was wrong in encouraging you to accompany me to London, but I left you in safe hands, or so I thought.'

'But then you always turn up unexpectedly, Gus. It seems that wherever I go you are there.'

'And that's how it would be if I had my way, Dolly.'

'I'm sorry, but I don't believe you.' Dolly shrugged and turned away. 'I should return to the party. It must be close to midnight and the prize-giving.'

Gus caught up with her before she had gone more than a few paces. 'What must I do to make you believe that my feelings for you are genuine, Dolly?'

'What are you suggesting, Gus? Are you asking me to run off with you again? Or do you just want me to tell you that I love you and I'll be your devoted friend for ever? What do you want of me?'

'I'm a soldier, Dolly. I can't buy myself out of the army to make you a good husband. Even if I could do that, I have no other profession. Your family are against me, anyway.'

'Yes, and does that surprise you? You are totally

unreliable and would probably make my life a misery if I weakened.'

'That's probably true, but I love you and I believe you have feelings for me.' Gus wrapped his arms around her and sought her lips in a kiss that was both passionate and tender. He held her so close that she could not escape, and as she succumbed to the flood of emotions that overcame her, she felt herself melting into his embrace. But the sudden hoot of a tawny owl, and the sound of raucous laughter as several drunken men staggered out of the adjacent marquee, made Gus release Dolly so suddenly that she might have fallen had he not caught her round the waist.

'Does that answer your questions, Dolly?'

She took a deep breath, gathering her scattered senses. 'No, Gus. It makes everything worse.' Summoning all her willpower, Dolly broke free and hurried away, leaving him staring after her. She could feel his gaze but she did not turn her head. To look back would be fatal. She knew she would run into his arms and fall under his spell yet again. She walked on resolutely until she came to the table where her mother and Alexander were talking earnestly to Patricia, Leo, Nancy and Tommy. It was obviously a family conference with Hester and Freddie observing intently.

Rosalind saw Dolly first. She held up a warning hand and there was a guilty silence.

'What were you saying?' Dolly demanded. 'It was about me, I can tell.'

'Darling girl, we are all concerned about you.' Alexander stood up to give her his seat. 'We don't want Piers to make your life a misery.'

'He is my father, but I have no feelings for him. You will always be my papa.'

Alexander gave her a hug. 'Sit down and join us, my love. You must decide what you wish to do next.'

'Yes, dear,' Rosalind added. 'If you want to accompany Piers to Trevenor, you must feel free to do so. No one here will stop you.'

'I would.' Hester pursed her lips. 'He's always been a troublemaker and I don't suppose he's any different now. What good will it do to send the poor girl all that way to be a victim of Lady Pentelow's ill temper? Didn't I hear that Aurelia has remarried?'

Patricia shook her head. 'I heard that she was engaged, but that was a while ago.'

'I like Aunt Aurelia,' Dolly said stubbornly. 'Maybe I should go to Trevenor and see what it's like. Apparently, it will belong to me eventually.'

Rosalind and Alexander exchanged worried glances.

'Did Piers tell you that?' Rosalind asked warily. 'He doesn't always tell the truth, Dolly, dear.'

'Just admit that he's always been a liar and a cheat,' Hester said crossly. 'Stop trying to pretend that he's changed. I, for one, don't believe a word he says.'

'Maybe that's why I should go to Cornwall.' Dolly glanced over Hester's shoulder and saw Gus watching them from a distance. She knew instinctively that he was not going to give up easily and she was suddenly desperate to put a distance between them. 'I need to visit Trevenor and find out for myself.'

Chapter Fifteen

The decision had been made quickly. Three days later Dolly alighted from the barouche outside the front entrance of Trevenor, her father's ancestral pile in Cornwall. The house itself was an elegant and eclectic mixture of periods, having been extended and modernised by successive generations of the Blanchard family. Piers had been relating the history of the property during their journey and now he proudly handed Dolly to the ground.

The door stood open, with the butler ready to greet his master.

'This is Patterson, Adela.' Piers acknowledged his butler with a nod. 'He has run Trevenor for many years. I don't know what my grandmother would have done without him when I was abroad.'

'Good afternoon, Miss Adela.' Patterson stood

aside to let them enter and a footman hurried outside to unload their luggage.

'Where will we find my grandmother, Patterson?'

'In the drawing room with Miss Aurelia, sir.'

'Come this way, Adela.' Piers strode through the wide entrance hall, his footsteps ringing out on the ancient flagstone floor.

Dolly had little time to take in her surroundings as she followed her father through the winding corridors to a room at the far end of the ground floor. Piers flung the door open and ushered Dolly inside.

'Grandmama, I've brought Adela home,' Piers said triumphantly. 'I'll leave you two to get reacquainted.' He walked away, allowing the door to swing shut behind him.

Lady Pentelow was seated in an armchair by the fire, which had been lit even though it was a hot summer's day. Dolly knew her, of course, from the long visits Lady Pentelow and Aurelia made to Rockwood Castle, but it was a shock to see how much the lady had aged. Her skin was soft but deeply lined and her snow-white hair was half hidden beneath a lace cap. She was in her late eighties but her eyes were as sharp and bright as those of a much younger woman.

'Welcome to Trevenor, Adela. It will be good to get to know you better. At Rockwood you were one of many.'

'Yes, it's lovely to see you again.' Aurelia hurried forward to kiss Dolly on both cheeks. She smelled of lavender with a hint of patchouli. At forty years of age she had retained much of her youthful prettiness, but there was a hint of sadness in her hazel eyes.

'Thank you, Aunt Aurelia.' Dolly was well aware of her aunt's rather tragic past. Her first husband had been killed during a fight at the clay mine, although it was said in the family that the marriage had not been a happy liaison. Then, some years later, Aurelia's wedding to a handsome plantation owner from Barbados had been brought to a dramatic halt by the unexpected arrival of his estranged wife.

Dolly gave her aunt a hug. 'It's lovely to be here. I'm looking forward to getting to know you better.'

Lady Pentelow picked up an ornate hearing trumpet and held it to her ear. 'What did she say, Aurelia?'

'Dolly says she is happy to be here, Grandmama.'

'So she should be. Not that I agree with a slip of a girl being first in line to inherit my beloved Trevenor. But Piers has the final say in the matter.'

'I don't want to cause any trouble,' Dolly said hastily. 'I didn't ask my father to come for me, nor do I want to take Trevenor away from anyone.'

'Grandmama is a very old lady,' Aurelia lowered her voice. 'Don't pay too much attention to what she says. You are Piers' daughter and of course you are his heir, unless he remarries, which I doubt.'

'Why do you say that?' Dolly asked. 'He's a handsome man and he's wealthy, too.'

'To tell you the truth, Dolly, I don't think he's

ever loved any woman other than your mama. But he was stupid and greedy, and he paid for his crimes in the penal colony, although I think losing your mama to our cousin, Alex, was perhaps the hardest blow of all.'

Dolly sighed. 'I don't really know much about it. No one speaks of the past, except to blame my father for just about everything that went wrong at that time.'

'That sounds like Hester talking,' Aurelia said, laughing. 'How is the old termagant?'

'She is just the same, but now she lives in the Dower House on Aunt Nancy's estate.'

'And how is that theatre getting on? Does Nick Gibson still run it? I used to like him quite a lot.'

'I believe he has an eye for a pretty woman, Aunt Aurelia. He hasn't changed, but now I work with him at the theatre. We've just thrown a masked ball to raise funds and it was a great success.'

'Really? You must tell me all about it.' Aurelia cast an anxious glance at her grandmother, who was glaring at them and waggling her ear trumpet.

'I can't hear a word you are saying. Come closer, girls.'

'Girls!' Aurelia shook her head. 'I do wish I was still a girl, but now I'm a middle-aged widow, doomed to spend my life keeping house for my aged grandmama and my ungrateful brother.'

'But I heard that you were engaged to be married, Aunt.'

'Dolly, please stop calling me "aunt". It makes me feel a hundred and one. As to my engagement, yes I thought I had met the right man at last, but when he found out that I was virtually penniless he vanished into the mist. It seems he was a fortune-hunter, and a fortune is not what I have.'

'Stop mumbling, Aurelia. I told you both to come closer. I want to hear what you have to say.'

'You'll get used to this,' Aurelia said in a low voice. 'I have to humour her, but she will fall asleep soon and that's my time to escape into the garden or to my room. I try to remember how good she was to me when I was younger, but it's not easy.' Aurelia stood up and went to sit by her grandmother, beckoning to Dolly, who followed suit.

As Aurelia had predicted, Lady Pentelow gradually dozed off until she was snoring loudly. Aurelia rose to her feet. 'Come, let me show you round the house, Dolly. Your room is quite close to mine. We are in the newer wing of the house. I rarely venture into the really old part because it's full of ghosts.'

Dolly stood up eagerly. 'Do you mean it's haunted?'

'I don't know for certain, but it feels very creepy. I don't particularly want to find out, although Piers and Alex used to go there when we were young. Goodness knows what they got up to, but I was too timid to accompany them.'

Dolly followed her from the room. 'Mama said that you and she used to explore the cellars at Rockwood.'

Aurelia laughed. 'We were convinced there was an oubliette where prisoners were left to die. But we did find a secret passageway to the sea, and we did come across real live smugglers, although luckily they didn't realise we were there. Those were the days.'

'I can't wait to hear more about it,' Dolly said hopefully. 'Mama doesn't tell me everything.'

'Perhaps some things are best forgotten.' Aurelia headed for the wide staircase. 'I'll show you your room first. You didn't bring a maid with you so you'll have to share Ada with me. She's been here for years and she knows everyone and everything. You just have to ask Ada and she will very likely have the answer.'

'Thank you, but I really only had a maid of my own in London when I was there for the season. I have Bess now, of course, but I share her with Mama and Aunt Nancy. We aren't what you would call a wealthy family.'

Aurelia led the way along a wide corridor with a high ceiling and ornate cornice. She flung open a door. 'This is my room. You are just a little further along.' She showed Dolly into a large bedchamber with a view over the cliffs and the bay. 'You can see the ships loading the clay to take it abroad. Piers will take you to the mine at some time and you'll see how it is run. I don't think his heart is really in the business, but he knows that without it we would be poor and probably lose Trevenor, so he has to knuckle down and make sure everything runs smoothly.'

Dolly gazed round the room with an appreciative smile. 'It's quite charming. I love chintz, and blue is my favourite colour.'

A maid appeared in the doorway to a smaller dressing room. 'Is it all right to start unpacking, Miss Aurelia?'

'Yes, Ada, of course. But first I want you to meet Miss Blanchard. I've told her that you know everything about our family and about Trevenor. She will ask you all sort of questions, I'm sure.'

Ada bobbed a curtsey. 'Of course, Miss Aurelia. I am more than happy to oblige.'

'I'm sure you would like to change out of your travelling garments,' Aurelia said earnestly. 'I'll be in the drawing room when you're ready and I'll show you more of the house before dinner, if you wish.'

'Thank you. That will be lovely.'

'The gardens are beautiful at this time of the year. You do ride, of course.'

'Yes, I do.'

'Then tomorrow morning, unless Piers has any-thing else planned, we'll ride around the estate. After luncheon we'll take the chaise and drive down to the village. I want you to see everything, Dolly. I'll be honest: I hope you'll fall in love with Trevenor and want to stay on.'

Dolly smiled. 'I'm sure I will enjoy my time here, but I have a job now. I can't stay away too long.'

'Yes, of course. I was forgetting, but that means I must take full advantage of you being with us.' Aurelia backed out of the room and closed the door.

'What would you like me to unpack first, Miss Blanchard?' Ada selected a blue silk afternoon gown from the valise and held it up for Dolly's inspection.

'Yes, thank you, Ada. That will do very well.'

With Ada's help, Dolly changed out of her travel-stained garments before going downstairs to the drawing room. But instead, she found herself in a huge dining hall lined with gilt-framed portraits. Having tried to retrace her steps she became even more confused and ended up in the main hall where a footman was about to take the last of Piers' luggage upstairs.

'I'm trying to find the drawing room,' Dolly said hurriedly. 'Could you point me in the right direction?'

'Of course, miss. Follow me, if you please.'

Dolly was only too happy to oblige and she wondered why she had become so lost in the first place. 'Thank you. I don't think my father mentioned your name.'

'It's Mark, miss.'

'I'll remember that. Thank you, Mark.' Dolly entered the drawing room and was relieved to find that Lady Pentelow was no longer there.

'Grandmama went up to her room for a nap,' Aurelia said in answer to Dolly's unspoken question.

'She spends most of the day in her room, or else she dozes off in her chair.'

'I'm afraid I got lost on my way here.' Dolly gave her a rueful smile. 'It is rather confusing.'

'Yes, that's the trouble with houses as old as Trevenor, but you'll soon get used to it. Now, shall we have that conducted tour? You'll find your own way easily enough after a day or two.'

Dolly nodded, although she did not imagine she would be staying at Trevenor for very long. Piers might be her father and he obviously had plans for her, but they did not coincide with what Dolly wanted for herself. One thing was becoming abundantly clear and that was her dislike for the old house. It seemed to have echoes from the past in every brick and stone. Dolly was used to ancient buildings; after all, Rockwood Castle was probably older than Trevenor, but at home she was never frightened by the lingering spirits of past residents. Here, even in broad daylight, she felt uncomfortable, as if she was being watched all the time.

Aurelia, however, seemed oblivious to the atmosphere. Dolly wondered if it was simply her imagination, or maybe she was tired after the long journey from Rockwood. Whatever the reason, she was glad to go outside into the gardens where roses tumbled over pergolas and scarlet geraniums filled terracotta pots, spilling blood-red petals onto the grass. The air was balmy and filled with birdsong with the occasional mewing of gulls as they flew overhead, no doubt heading for the village where the fishing boats were landing their catches.

Dolly took a deep breath of the salty air. 'It is nice out here, Aurelia. I don't wonder that you love Cornwall.'

'I love it and I hate it in equal measure,' Aurelia said sadly. 'My childhood memories are here in this house, but I feel that my life is withering away. Soon I'll be as dried up and lifeless as the leaves in autumn.'

'Don't say that. You aren't old and you're still beautiful.'

'Thank you, Dolly. I know it's not true, but it's kind of you to say so. I should be grateful for what I have, I know that.'

'Maybe you could come back to Rockwood with me when I return home? Perhaps a few days or so away from Trevenor might make you feel better.'

'I can't leave Grandmama, Dolly. Piers wouldn't look after her and the servants can only do so much. She's an old lady and she took care of me, Piers and Alex, when we were young. Anyway, ignore me and my megrims. I want you to enjoy your visit here, and as I promised, tomorrow I will show you the village, although I'll leave Piers to take you to the mine and give you a tour.'

'Thank you. I'll look forward to both. It's all so different from what I'm used to, and very exciting.'

Aurelia laughed. 'The novelty will soon wear off, Dolly.'

*

Dinner that evening was both formal and quiet. Lady Pentelow seemed more interested in the food on her plate than in attempting to listen to the conversation, which was desultory to say the least. Aurelia did her best to entertain Dolly, but Piers was morose and answered in monosyllables.

'I'm planning to take Dolly for a carriage ride tomorrow morning, Piers,' Aurelia said in a last attempt to encourage him to talk.

'Good,' Piers said abruptly.

'But I'm sure you will want to show her the mine and all the workings,' Aurelia added desperately.

'No. You can do that for me.' Piers rose to his feet. 'I have a meeting to attend so I must leave you now.'

'Sit down, Piers. You haven't had dessert yet.' Lady Pentelow was suddenly alert.

'You know I don't bother with the sweet dishes you love, Grandmama. I have to leave now.' He left the room before his grandmother could come in on the attack.

'He's a rude fellow,' Lady Pentelow said crossly. 'I thought I had taught him better manners.' She picked up a silver bell and rang it. 'We'll have dessert. All the more for us. What do you say, Adela?'

Dolly managed a smile, but her reply was lost as the maid, who had been standing to attention by the mahogany sideboard, leaped to attention and began clearing the plates and cutlery.

'Where has my father gone at this time in the evening?' Dolly asked in a low voice.

'Don't worry. Grandmama can't hear much without her ear trumpet,' Aurelia said, smiling. 'The truth is that my brother keeps a woman in the next village. He thinks I don't know, but it's an open secret.'

'Oh!' Dolly glanced anxiously at her great-grandmother, but Lady Pentelow was busy scolding the maid for dropping a spoon on the floor. 'Do you mean he has a lover?'

'I doubt if he has any particular feelings for her, Dolly,' Aurelia said, smiling. 'I think it's a purely business arrangement. We ladies are not supposed to know about such things, but that, of course, is nonsense.'

'Do you think he will marry her?'

'Good heavens, no. I told you, he will never remarry. If Piers ever had a heart, he lost it when he first saw Rosie.'

'That's rather sad.'

'Don't feel sorry for him, my dear. I know that Piers treated your mother badly. Piers is my brother, but your mama is much better off with my cousin, Alex. He's a good man.'

'He's certainly been a better father than I could have hoped for. I love him dearly.'

'As he deserves. Don't waste your sympathy on my brother, and don't allow him to browbeat you into doing anything against your will. Piers loves to control people and he always wants everything his own way. Stand up for yourself, Dolly, dear.'

'What are you whispering about?' Lady Pentelow demanded angrily. 'Tell me now, Aurelia.'

'Where's your ear trumpet, Grandmama?'

'What are you saying? There's no need to shout.' Lady Pentelow caught the maid by the sleeve as she was about to walk past. 'Where's my ear trumpet? Have you hidden it again, girl?'

The young maid cast a pleading look in Aurelia's direction. 'No, my lady. I haven't seen it.'

'Don't argue with me, Morwen. I know how sly you can be.'

'Oh, no, my lady. I haven't seen it.'

Aurelia rose to her feet and hurried to the head of the table. 'As I thought. It's on the floor by your chair, Grandmama.'

'I see it, Miss Aurelia.' Morwen went down on her knees and rose again, handing the ear trumpet to Lady Pentelow.

'I know you hid it from me,' Lady Pentelow said plaintively. 'My things are being taken from me all the time.' She placed the horn to her ear. 'Where's the dessert? Why are you all looking at me? Go and sit down, Aurelia. First your brother and now you. What are we coming to?'

Aurelia sighed and returned to her seat. 'Bring the desserts, please, Morwen.'

'I didn't hide it from her ladyship.' Morwen glanced over her shoulder but Lady Pentelow was busy folding and unfolding her table napkin. 'I wouldn't do anything like that.'

'I know, Morwen. Lady Pentelow gets a little be-twattled at times.'

Morwen hurried from the room.

'What does betwattled mean, Aurelia?' Dolly asked, stifling the desire to laugh.

'Confused or muddled. Anyway, I think the Cornish dialect sounds less harsh. Grandmama is like this most of the time, Dolly. You'll get used to it.'

Dolly eyed her great-grandmother warily. She had heard that Great-Grandpapa, Sir Lucien Carey, who had been a vice-admiral in the Royal Navy serving under Lord Nelson, had been a little odd at times. Aunt Patsy had once said that her grandfather had been off his chump, although that was kept within the family. Dolly was beginning to feel very sorry for her aunt, who had to put up with Lady Pentelow's idiosyncrasies and her brother's uncaring attitude. No wonder Aunt Aurelia felt sad. Dolly was at a loss as to how to make things better for her, but she was determined to try.

Lady Pentelow went straight to her room after dinner, leaving Aurelia and Dolly to take coffee in the drawing room. It was still light, although Dolly had noticed that the evenings were drawing in grad-ually. The end of summer was in sight and the golden days of autumn were not too far away.

As she sipped her coffee she found herself longing to be at home with her large and vociferous family. Nancy and Tommy's boys were allowed to dine with the adults these days when they were at home from school, and they would bicker playfully. When the meal ended everyone usually went to the music room. Nancy would play the piano and sing to them while Rory, Phoebe, May and Jack played backgammon, whist or brag, accompanied by noisy but good-natured arguments. Hester and Rosalind would sit by the fire sipping coffee, or at this time of the year, they would have chairs set by the open double doors that led into the rose garden. Tommy and Alex usually took their cigars outside, filling the air with the scent of Havana tobacco as they strolled amongst the flowerbeds, no doubt discussing the events of the day.

Dolly was homesick and all she wanted to do was sleep. Aurelia was drinking her third glass of port wine and her head was nodding.

Dolly rose to her feet. 'If you'll excuse me, Aurelia, I'll go to my bed. I'm very tired.'

'Of course you must be.' Aurelia gave her a tipsy smile. 'Sleep well, my dear. We'll have a nice day tomorrow.'

'Yes, I'm sure we will. Good night, I'll see you in the morning.'

Dolly left the room and made her way to her bedchamber. This time she did not get lost, but the light was fading rapidly, creating strange shadows on the walls. Dolly could hear whispering, as if the family portraits were talking to each other in hushed voices, although reason told her it was the wind that had sprung up from the west, whistling through ill-fitting windows and doors. It was a relief to enter her room and find Ada laying out her nightgown.

'I've brought hot water so that you can have a wash, miss. Is there anything else I can do for you?'

Dolly smiled and shook her head. 'No, thank you, Ada. Although you could unbutton my gown for me.'

'Of course, miss.' Ada's nimble fingers undid the tiny buttons.

'I can manage the rest, thank you.'

Ada bobbed a curtsey and was about to leave the room when Dolly called her back. 'Ada, do people say this house is haunted?'

'Oh, yes, miss. It's well known that there are several ghosts who roam the corridors of Trevenor.'

'Have you seen them?'

'I'm not sure. Sometimes I think I see an apparition, and then it's gone. Cook says it's my imagination, but other people have seen things too.'

'Doesn't it scare you, Ada?'

'We're used to them, miss. I always say good night to those unquiet spirits, like my grannie taught me. It seems to work and I don't get bothered by them.'

'Thank you. I'll remember that.'

'Good night, miss.'

The door closed on Ada, and Dolly was alone in the eerie room with its four-poster bed and heavy mahogany furniture. The chintz covers and curtains that had looked so fresh and inviting in the day now looked faded, with strange patterns that merged into weird shapes.

Dolly had a quick wash before taking off her stays and chemise. The curtains at one of the windows fluttered as if someone was trying to draw them aside and Dolly felt her heart miss a beat. She took a deep breath. 'Good night, unquiet spirits. I hope you will rest in peace.'

She slipped her nightgown over her head and leaped into bed, sinking deep into the feather mattress. Was it her imagination or did the room seem friendlier? She smiled and closed her eyes. Her family would think she was a tad betwattled, like Lady Pentelow, if she told them what she had done, but there was one person who would understand. She would have such a lot to tell Freddie when she went home.

Chapter Sixteen

Next morning, feeling refreshed after a good night's sleep, Dolly managed to find the dining room with little difficulty, although on her first attempt she opened the door to a large cupboard. She found Aurelia sitting in solitary splendour at the large table.

'Good morning.' Dolly eyed Lady Pentelow's empty chair nervously. 'Am I too early?'

Aurelia pointed to the silver breakfast dishes on the sideboard.

'No, Dolly. Help yourself, do.'

Dolly went to examine the contents and piled a plate with a generous helping of buttered eggs, crisp bacon and devilled kidneys. She went to sit in her place at table.

'Shouldn't we wait for Lady Pentelow?'

'I dare say she's still asleep, and anyway, she has

breakfast in bed as a general rule. There's coffee in the pot, but I'll send for a fresh pot if it's too cold.'

'Thank you.' Dolly shook out her napkin and laid it on her lap. 'I'm really hungry. It must be the Cornish air.'

Aurelia laughed. 'I expect your room is very draughty. I don't think any of the windows fit properly, but we're used to sea breezes rushing through the house.'

'And ghosts?' Dolly asked anxiously.

'Old houses are full of creaks and groans in the cool of the night. Anyway, enough about such things. You and I will have a delightful tour of the village today, as I promised.' Aurelia turned her head at the sound of the door opening and her smile froze. 'Good morning, Piers.'

'It is morning, but I don't know if it's good or not.' Piers went straight to the sideboard and piled a plate with food, which he took to the table. 'I hope you slept well, Adela.'

'Yes, thank you, Father.'

Piers nodded. 'I trust you weren't disturbed by anything.'

'What are you talking about, Piers?' Aurelia demanded crossly. 'Have you been filling her head with ghost stories?'

'Certainly not. I was merely hoping my daughter had an undisturbed night.'

'Thank you, Father. I slept like a baby.' Dolly

looked from one to the other. She sensed under-currents of ill feeling between brother and sister, which made her uncomfortable.

'I'm planning to take Dolly for a ride this morning and take the chaise to the village this afternoon,' Aurelia said stiffly. 'I suppose you have no objections.'

'As a matter of fact I have. I am going to give my daughter a tour of the mine. You can take her out this afternoon, if you wish.'

Aurelia pushed her plate away, her breakfast barely touched. 'I might have guessed that you would have different plans. All right, I will do as you wish, but I hope you will allow Dolly to enjoy her time here without bombarding her with business matters.'

'I would like to know more about the china clay mine,' Dolly said hastily. 'But I look forward to exploring the village with you, Aunt Aurelia.'

'I'll see you both at luncheon, then.' Aurelia rose to her feet. 'I need to talk to Cook, but I'll see you later, Dolly. Please don't bore her to death, Piers.' Aurelia left the dining room without giving her brother a chance to respond.

'Don't take any notice of my sister,' Piers said smugly. 'She's never been the same since she was taken in by Rupert Charnley, but then you know all about that fiasco.'

'Yes, of course. It was very sad for Aunt Aurelia, but I think you are rather hard on her, Father. If you don't mind me saying so.'

'I do mind, Adela. You will learn to understand me and my sister when you have been here longer. We might argue, but we are close nonetheless.'

'I am only staying for a while. I have a position to go back to at the theatre. I am not one of those young ladies who are prepared to stay at home until they marry.'

'We'll see about that, Adela. Of course, I can't force you to remain here at Trevenor, but it is your birthright, and I hope you will come to see it in that light.'

Dolly could see that any attempt to convince him otherwise would be futile and she concentrated on her breakfast. They finished the meal in silence.

'I'll leave in fifteen minutes,' Piers said as he stood up. 'You'll need your bonnet and shawl. Meet me in the entrance hall when you're ready. I don't like to be kept waiting.' He left the room without waiting for a reply.

Dolly shook her head. Piers Blanchard might legally be her father but it was Alex who had loved and raised her from a baby. She was even more certain now that Piers could never supplant Alex in her heart, and once again she suffered a wave of homesickness. One thing was becoming plain in her mind – she did not want to inherit Trevenor or the clay mine. She would rather work in the theatre to earn her living than take up the position as heiress to this troubled house.

*

287

The visit to the mine proved interesting and Dolly found herself to be the object of considerable interest amongst the mine workers. She was given a conducted tour by the site manager while Piers was in his office, and she learned about the process of obtaining and processing the clay. It was a great deal to absorb in such a short time but Dolly found it fascinating. She could hardly believe it when Piers told her it was time to return home for luncheon. However, he did not accompany her, saying that he had too much to do, and she returned to Trevenor on her own. Patterson was at the door and the footman hurried out to assist her from the carriage.

'Thank you, Mark,' Dolly said, smiling. She was not certain, but she thought he winked at her, something she had never experienced before in a servant. She wondered if Aunt Aurelia knew that her footman took such liberties, but she was not going to tell tales. Perhaps Mark had something in his eye, which would explain everything. Dolly walked into the house, acknowledging Patterson with a smile.

'Where will I find my aunt, Patterson?'

'I believe Miss Aurelia is in the garden, miss. She usually takes a turn around the grounds with Lady Pentelow at this time of day.'

Dolly took off her bonnet, gloves and shawl and handed them to Ada, who had been hovering in the background. At least some of the servants were well trained, although Dolly was not so sure about the footman.

'Ada, will you be kind enough to show me how to get to the garden from here?'

'Of course, miss. Follow me, if you please.' Ada led the way through the winding corridors to the far side of the house where she showed Dolly into the drawing room, which overlooked the garden. French doors led out onto a paved terrace.

'Miss Aurelia takes Lady Pentelow for a breath of air in her chair every day at this time, when the weather permits.' Ada opened the double doors and sunshine flooded the room.

'Thank you, Ada. I'll find them.'

Dolly walked outside and she could feel the heat from the stones through the soles of her boots. A marble balustrade separated the terrace from the parterre garden, which sloped down to a wide lawn surrounded by fluffy pink tamarisk trees and the dark green foliage of rhododendrons. Dolly thought the rhododendrons must be a wonderful sight when in bloom. Beyond that she caught glimpses of the sea, but more importantly, she spotted Aurelia pushing a wheeled chair. Half hidden beneath a large black umbrella, Lady Pentelow was wrapped in a plaid blanket. Dolly called out to attract her aunt's attention and Aurelia turned and waved.

Dolly crossed the wide terrace, heading for the steps that led down to a gravelled path. As she did so, she happened to look round and for a fleeting moment she thought she saw a male face watching her from an upstairs window, but it was gone so quickly she wondered if it was her imagination playing tricks on her.

She had not meant to say anything about the face she had seen, but curiosity got the better of her. 'Aurelia, is there anyone else staying here?'

Aurelia shook her head. 'No, Dolly. Whatever gave you that idea?'

'I thought I saw someone looking out of a window on the third floor. It was just a glimpse.'

'A trick of the light, I should think. That part of the house hasn't been used for years. The servants' quarters are in the north wing.'

Dolly could not argue with that, but she remained unconvinced. Despite her attempts to convince herself otherwise, she was sure she had seen someone and, if it was a ghost, it was very substantial.

'Stop gossiping and take me indoors,' Lady Pentelow said querulously. 'It's too hot out here, Aurelia, and it's time for my glass of sherry wine before luncheon.'

'Yes, of course. I'm sorry, Grandmama.' Aurelia pushed the wheeled chair towards a slope leading to the terrace. 'I'm afraid I lost track of time.'

'Well, I'm reminding you now. Just because Adela is here, it doesn't mean you can neglect me.'

'No, Grandmama. Of course not.'

'Let me help you.' Dolly joined Aurelia in her exertions and the wheeled chair shot forward, the sudden movement momentarily putting a stop to Lady Pentelow's complaining as she gasped for breath.

However, she recovered quickly.

'Don't be so rough. I could have broken my neck.'

Aurelia sighed. 'I'm sorry, Grandmama. I'll be more careful.'

'I should think so, too. I'm an old lady, Aurelia. I might not be with you for long.'

'She'll live forever,' Aurelia said in a low voice. 'She'll see me in my grave first.'

'What did you say, Aurelia? Don't mumble. Where's my ear trumpet?'

'Maybe I'll have a glass of sherry, too.' Aurelia turned to Dolly with a wry smile. 'Now you see why I enjoy a couple of glasses of port wine after dinner.'

'I quite understand,' Dolly said softly. 'And I can see how difficult things are for you here.'

'Don't sympathise with me or I might disgrace myself and burst into tears,' Aurelia said mistily. 'It's so nice to have someone to talk to. I know I'm old enough to be your mama, but I think of you as a friend.'

Dolly glanced at the upstairs window where she thought she had seen a man's face, but there was no one there. She followed Aurelia and Lady Pentelow into the house, but the image of the stranger was still in her mind. There must be a logical explanation.

Piers did not return for luncheon, which was a surprisingly quiet meal. Lady Pentelow nodding off to sleep over a bowl of junket, having enjoyed the previous course of baked salmon, peas and new potatoes glistening with butter. A glass or two of white wine to accompany the meal had stopped her from complaining, albeit temporarily. Dolly could see relief written on Aurelia's face as she instructed Mark to take Lady Pentelow to her bedchamber.

'Grandmama has a suite on the first floor,' Aurelia said cheerfully as Mark wheeled her ladyship's chair from the dining room. 'She can manage one flight of stairs with a little help, but it's been some time since she could make it to her old room.'

'Will she sleep all afternoon?' Dolly asked tentatively.

'She does usually, which leaves us free to venture into the village. We'll take the chaise. I'm very adept at handling the reins.'

'I saw a little of the scenery this morning,' Dolly said eagerly. 'It looks such a pretty place.'

'I must let some of our neighbouring families know that you are here. We don't entertain very much, but hopefully that will change now.'

'You do realise that I'm not planning to stay for long, don't you, Aurelia?'

'I know, dear, but I am hoping you will change your mind.' Aurelia rose from her seat. 'If you're ready, I'll send for the chaise.'

Aurelia might seem timid and unsure of herself nowadays, but Dolly was impressed by the way she handled the reins. When they arrived in the village they were greeted mostly by smiling faces, although some of the younger people did not seem too welcoming. Aurelia blamed Piers, admitting that her brother was not the most popular employer in the county. He had a habit of arbitrarily firing anyone who did not come up to his exacting standards, or simply if he did not like their face. It was always easy to find someone eager for work who would replace a sacked employee. Aurelia did not agree with Piers, but she insisted that she had no say in how the mine was run.

Despite the undercurrents, Dolly enjoyed the conducted tour of the pretty village and the harbour, which reminded her achingly of home. She suspected that Aurelia hoped she would decide to live at Trevenor, but Dolly was planning to return to Rockwood at the earliest possible opportunity. She realised that Piers could assert his authority as her father and prevent her from leaving Trevenor, but she hoped it would not come to that. She toyed with the idea of having a frank discussion with him, but she discarded that notion almost as soon as it popped into her head. From the little she knew of Piers Blanchard, he would not be open to debate on something so personal. She would have to be very careful and very tactful when she broached the subject of leaving.

Once again Piers left the dinner table before everyone had finished their dessert. He mumbled an excuse, which his grandmother accepted with fairly good grace. Dolly realised then that Piers could do no wrong in Lady Pentelow's eyes, despite his colourful past. It was clear that he was her favourite grandchild and nothing would change her opinion of him.

After dinner, Dolly and Aurelia sat at the back-gammon board while Lady Pentelow sipped coffee and a tot of brandy.

'Do you think my father has gone to visit his lady friend in the next village?' Dolly asked in a low voice.

Aurelia raised her eyebrows. 'Hush, don't say such things in front of Grandmama.'

'I thought it was an open secret.'

'Yes, with everyone except her. She doesn't know about Esther Pascoe, as I think I told you. Maybe I shouldn't have mentioned Esther in the first place.'

'I'm intrigued now. Who is this person?'

'She is the widow of a lawyer who had a practice in St Austell. Piers probably met her through her husband when he represented Piers in court. It was a long time ago and best forgotten.'

'But he obviously hasn't forgotten Esther. I'd like to meet her.'

'That will never happen. Your father wouldn't allow it, Dolly. Please don't mention her name in his hearing. He would be furious with me for telling you about her.'

'I don't think my father has the right to dictate to anyone, considering his background. A man who has served time in the penal colony in Australia and was involved in gun-running in the Caribbean – he has no right to tell me what to do.'

Aurelia sighed. 'I'm afraid the law is on his side this time, as you are underage, Dolly. I love my brother despite his failings, but I wouldn't advise you to get on his wrong side. Piers doesn't forgive easily.'

'I need another tot of brandy, Aurelia.' Lady Pentelow held up her empty glass. 'Send for Ada.'

Aurelia rose to her feet. 'No need, Grandmama. I'll do it.'

'Servants are there to wait upon us, Aurelia. You mustn't do their work for them.'

'Yes, Grandmama. Would you like more coffee?' Aurelia selected the brandy decanter and poured a generous measure.

'Dreadful stuff. It will give me a headache and keeps me awake all night with dyspepsia.'

Aurelia returned to her seat opposite Dolly. 'Anyway, as I said just now, please don't mention Esther's name to your father or anyone else, if it comes to that. Whatever Piers has done in the past should be left there. He's doing his best to keep the business going now.'

'I promise I won't say anything, but if he is so attached to this person, why doesn't he marry her?'

'Because she isn't a suitable wife for a Blanchard. I know it sounds hypocritical, but there you are. That's how society works, I'm afraid. When I married

Martin Gibbs, everyone said it was a *mésalliance*, as the French say. I didn't see it like that but, looking back, I realise it was a terrible error of judgement on my part.'

Dolly had no answer for this. Immediately Gus had sprung to mind and she felt the blood rush to her cheeks. If she saw him again she knew she would feel the old tug of attraction. Perhaps, like Aurelia, she had fallen for him because her family would disapprove of such a liaison. But if she closed her eyes she could recall the way her whole being had responded to his embrace. Gus was dashing, good looking and bold. He made her laugh and his kisses sent her senses reeling. He had come from nothing, and if it were not for Aunt Nancy he might still be living on the streets of London, or more likely he would be in prison. No matter which way she looked at it, Gus was forbidden fruit and that was part of his appeal.

'You're very quiet, Dolly,' Aurelia said gently. 'Perhaps you're tired and would like to finish the game now.'

Dolly dragged herself back to the present. 'Thank you. I am fatigued. Would you mind if I went to bed now?'

'Of course not. How selfish of me to keep you up with all this chit-chat. Go to bed and rest and we'll have another lovely day tomorrow.'

Dolly glanced over her shoulder at Lady Pentelow, who was falling asleep with the empty brandy goblet clasped in her hand. 'What about Grandmama?'

'I'm used to this. Mark will take her to her room and Ada will put her to bed.'

'But what about you, Aurelia? I don't like to leave you on your own.'

Aurelia smiled. 'I am not alone, Dolly. I have Mrs Gaskell's novel *Wives and Daughters* to keep me company. I used to look down on blue stockings who always had their head in a book, and now I'm one of them. Anyway, I will be fine. I'll see you at breakfast, Dolly.'

Dolly took a lighted candle with her and made her way upstairs to her room. She hesitated outside the door, cocking her head at the sound of footsteps on the floor above her. A shiver ran down her spine but she told herself it was one of the servants. However, when she worked it out, she realised that she and Aurelia had bedchambers in the east wing, overlooking the gardens and the sea. The servants' quarters were in a different part of the house altogether and were reached by a separate staircase. As yet Dolly had not explored that part of the building, even on the ground floor.

Her hand shook as she opened her door and entered her room, but once inside she began to relax and she lit the candles in a silver candelabra on the mantelshelf. The curtains had been drawn and the covers on the bed turned back with her nightgown laid out in readiness. She started to undress but a cool breeze wafted the perfume of night-scented stock and jasmine through the open window, and she went to sit on the wide cushioned seat, leaning her elbows on the sill. It was a beautiful balmy night and the sky was spangled with stars. Moonlight created a pathway on the distant sea and it looked as if she could walk upon it and pluck a star from the dark velvet sky. Dolly closed her eyes, inhaling the heady bouquet, but the sound of footsteps crunching on the gravel path made her open them again and she leaned out a little further.

Out of the shadows emerged the dark figure of a man. He came to a halt on the moonlit terrace and stood very still. Dolly could not see his face but he appeared to be quite tall, wide shouldered and he had dark hair, worn unfashionably long. Dolly was intrigued and very curious. She could not make out the details of his clothes but he did not look like a servant, and there seemed to be no reason for him to stand there. What, she wondered, was he waiting for?

The answer became apparent when another man joined him. This time Dolly knew exactly who he was. 'Father,' she said in a whisper.

Piers slapped the man on the shoulder and they moved closer together, speaking in low voices that carried on the soft night air, although Dolly could not make out what they were saying. Almost immediately they disappeared from view. It was hard to tell if they entered the house through the French doors that led onto the terrace, but suddenly all was silent and peaceful once more.

Dolly closed the window. She sat for a while, contemplating what she had seen. So her father had either not been to see his mistress in the next village, or else it had been a very short visit. But who was the stranger? Was he the man Dolly had seen at the upstairs window and did the footsteps she had heard earlier belong to him? She was not sure whether it was a comfort to find that the face she had seen at the window was a real person rather than a ghost, but it did make the likelihood of a haunting pale into insignificance. She undressed slowly, put on her nightgown and climbed into bed. This house was filled with secrets and it seemed that her father was at the centre of whatever was going on within the walls of Trevenor. Dolly closed her eyes. Maybe things would become clearer in the morning.

She awakened early. This part of the house was silent, although Dolly suspected that the servants were already going about their daily routine. She sat up in bed, recalling the strange meeting last night between her father and the stranger. She would not rest until she had solved the mystery.

Dolly swung her legs over the side of the bed and stood up. She knew she should wait until Ada brought her hot water to wash with, and a cup of hot chocolate, but she was filled with a burst of nervous energy. Minutes later, fully dressed, with her hair brushed and tied back with a blue ribbon, Dolly made her way silently down the servants' stairs to the ground floor. She was beginning to know the layout of the main part of the house and she made her way to the drawing room.

This was where she had seen her father and the unidentified man. Dolly opened the French doors and took a deep breath of the clean, salt-laden air. The sun was warm on her face but there was a faint mist over the lower lawn and a hint of a chill in the breeze. Soon the summer would be over and the dark days of winter would be upon them. She knew she must go home before then. Trevenor had many secrets hidden within its ancient walls, which were probably best left undiscovered. She had a shivery feeling every time she thought about what might be lurking there.

Dolly had not intended to go very far, but she had not yet explored much of the grounds and she found herself on the lawn, heading towards the shrubbery. Her feet were wet as dew soaked through the lace holes of her boots, but she ignored the discomfort and kept on. Suddenly it seemed important to find out exactly what lay on the other side of the thick hedge. She found a gap between a particularly dense tamarisk tree and a laurel bush. Although she had to duck down to avoid the overhanging branches it was easy enough to get through and out onto the clifftop, which fell away steeply to the beach below.

The view was magnificent and Dolly gazed over the turquoise expanse of the bay to the silvery sand of the shoreline. The village nestled in the shelter of the cliffs and beyond that were the tell-tale pyramids of waste from the clay mine. The fishing boats were just setting off from the harbour and larger ships lay at anchor, waiting to load their cargoes of clay for export. It was a calm, idyllic scene, which made the petty worries and anxieties that Dolly suffered seem superfluous. She smiled to herself and was about to turn away and retrace her steps to the house when she saw someone climbing the steep steps that led down to the beach.

She was about to beat a hasty retreat when the person looked up. His long dark hair would have alerted her anyway, but the face was that of the man she had seen looking out of the upstairs window.

Dolly was overwhelmed by panic. She turned and ran, but she had not got very far when she caught her foot in a rabbit hole and tumbled to the ground. She tried to get up but a spasm of pain from her ankle made her cry out and she fell back onto the damp grass.

'Don't move,' said a deep voice. 'You might have broken your ankle. Keep very still.'

Chapter Seventeen

The stranger kneeled down beside her, his hands gently prising her foot from the rabbit hole. 'Can you move your foot?'

Despite the pain, Dolly managed to flex her toes. 'Yes. I'm all right.'

'It's probably a sprain.' He leaned over, his damp hair sending drops of seawater onto her bare leg.

Dolly edged away from him. 'Thank you. I'm fine now.'

He sat back on his heels. 'You saw me yesterday, didn't you?'

She nodded. 'Yes, and I also saw you with my father last evening. Who are you, sir?'

'You don't need to know.'

'Are you a criminal then?'

He laughed. 'You could say that, but the less you

are told, the better. You must be Adela. Your pa has mentioned you. I'm Luke.'

'Please help me up, sir.'

Luke raised her to her feet, keeping an arm around her waist. 'Can you stand on your own?'

She nodded. 'Yes, I don't need your help now, thank you.' Dolly took a step away from him but the pain in her ankle made her groan.

Luke proffered his arm. 'Lean on me. I'll get you back to the house. I shouldn't have left my room, but I couldn't resist the temptation to go for a dip in the sea.'

'Who are you?' Dolly demanded as he helped her negotiate the tussocky grass and the gap between the bushes. 'And please don't avoid the question. I think I have a right to know if I am to keep your secret.'

He laughed. 'I can see you are your father's daughter. You won't give in until I tell you the truth.'

'No, I won't. You are taking advantage of my aunt and my great-grandmother. I think you owe them an explanation.'

'It's better for everyone if we keep this away from them, Adela.'

'Dolly. Everyone calls me Dolly, apart from my father and Great-Grandmama. How do you know him, Luke?' She winced as she attempted to put weight on her injured ankle.

Luke swung her into his arms. 'We need to get out of sight of the house as quickly as possible. I'll carry you, Dolly, so best be quiet unless you want all the servants to descend upon us.'

Dolly knew he was right, but she did not like the feeling of helplessness. 'All right, but hurry.'

'Don't worry, my dear. My life depends upon keeping away from the law. I can't say any more than that.'

Dolly was silent until they reached the relative safety of the drawing room, where Luke set her down on a chair. It was the first time she had been able to take a proper look at him, and, despite the fact that he was in some kind of trouble, she could not help liking what she saw. He was probably in his early forties and good-looking in a rugged way. His eyes were a startling blue, set beneath dark brows, with a maze of tiny laughter lines radiating at the corners so that he looked as if he had a permanent smile on his face. His skin was deeply tanned and his hands were those of a labourer, although he spoke like an educated man. His dark hair clung to his head and seawater dripped onto his shirt, darkening the cotton fabric.

'How do you know my father?' Dolly demanded abruptly. She could not allow him to go unless she had an answer.

'We were both prisoners in the penal colony in New South Wales. I arrived not long before your father earned his freedom. I escaped and you are right, I am on the run. If I am caught I will be sent back to the colony for life.'

'Did you kill someone to have such a harsh sentence?'

Luke laughed but there was no humour in the sound. 'No. I'm not a violent man. It's a long story and I should be going back to my room. Your father is sheltering me but I will only stay for a while. I don't want to get your family involved, Dolly.'

She shrugged. 'It seems to me you've done that already.'

'You're right, and I truly regret that.' Luke headed for the doorway, pausing before he opened it. 'I hope to leave here very soon, but I'll always be grateful for the help your father has given me.'

He was gone before Dolly could think of anything to say. However, she was not going to leave things as they were. No matter what this man had done, he was putting her aunt and great-grandmother at risk. Dolly rose from her seat and made her way carefully across the room. She did not attempt to negotiate the stairs but went straight to the dining room, where, to her surprise, she found her father seated at the table, reading a copy of yesterday's *Times*.

'Good morning, Father.'

He lowered the paper, staring at her over the top of it with eyebrows raised. 'Adela? You are up early.'

'I went for a walk on the cliffs, but I fell and twisted my ankle.'

'You shouldn't go out on your own. The paths close to the edge are treacherous.'

305

The aroma of bacon and hot toast made Dolly's stomach rumble and she realised that she was hungry. She went to the sideboard and helped herself to a generous amount of bacon, buttered eggs and black pudding, before returning to the table. Her father had disappeared once more behind the newspaper and she settled down to enjoy her food. One of the younger housemaids brought more toast and a fresh pot of coffee, which she placed on the table in front of Dolly.

'Will there be anything else, miss?'

'Miss Adela,' Piers said sharply. 'Address her properly.'

'I beg your pardon, sir.' The girl, who was little more than a child, blushed rosily and backed out of the room.

'Was that necessary?' Dolly asked angrily.

'Yes, it was. Don't question my authority, Adela. I am the head of the house and the servants do what I say.'

His arrogant tone annoyed Dolly even more. Piers Blanchard might be her father but he was almost a complete stranger to her. She had no feelings for him, at least none of the loving emotions she would have expected herself to experience in the company of the man who had fathered her. She pushed her plate away. 'And yet you bring trouble into your own home, Father.'

Piers dropped the paper. 'What are you talking about?'

'I saw you talking to him last night, and this morning he was coming back from the beach when we met in broad daylight. You know who I mean.'

'Have you been spying on me, Adela?'

'Why would I even consider something like that?' Dolly said boldly. She could see that he was discomforted and she pressed her point home. 'Luke told me very little except that he was on the run from the police. He escaped from the penal colony, which is why you are hiding him. That's the truth, isn't it?'

'You have no right to question me. It has nothing to do with you.'

'It has while I'm under your roof, and it certainly does affect Aunt Aurelia and Great-Grandmama. What happens if the police come here looking for that man?'

Piers rose from the table and began to pace the floor. He came to a halt beside Dolly. 'I will tell you this in confidence, Adela. But if you breathe a word to anyone it could get me into serious trouble, which would have repercussions on the business and my family.'

'I won't say a word. I promise.'

Piers pulled up a chair and sat down beside her. 'I met Luke when he first arrived in New South Wales more years ago than I care to remember. I took him under my wing and we became friends, or should I say fellow sufferers. It wasn't an easy life.'

'So why is he here now?'

'Luke received a life sentence for embezzlement, which he claimed he had not committed, and I believe him. The authorities took a different view and he lost his appeal against the sentence. Luke Gilpin comes from a wealthy family. His brother accused him of misappropriating funds from the family business for his own use. Luke is adamant that it was the reverse. His brother used the money for his own purposes and blamed him. The judge took Luke's elder brother's word for it, and Luke received the harsh sentence.'

'So why did he return to England, Papa? He must have known he would be arrested.'

'He received word that his mother was dying. By that time Luke was a ticket-of-leave man, which enabled him to work and he made a fortune in construction. Unfortunately his mother had died by the time he arrived in England. His brother immediately notified the authorities, no doubt fearful that the truth might come to light. Luke had no option but to run and hide. He came here because he knew I would help him.' Piers broke off, turning his head at the sound of the door opening.

Aurelia entered the room, gazing at her brother in disbelief. 'I heard most of that, Piers.'

'You were eavesdropping,' Piers leaped to his feet. 'You were always doing that as a child. It's not an attractive quality.'

'It's the only way to find out what's going on in

this household. You were always secretive, Piers. You remember Ewart Blease and the trouble that man brought to this family? Well, it seems that you have involved us in something almost as bad.'

'I've met him, Aunt Aurelia,' Dolly said hastily. 'Luke doesn't seem like a bad person.'

'Why am I always the last to be told these things?' Aurelia turned on Piers angrily. 'How dare you expose your daughter to a criminal on the run, Piers?'

Dolly felt compelled to put matters straight. 'I saw them out of my window last night. Luke was the man I spotted looking out of the upstairs window yesterday. I met him this morning when I went out for a walk. I ran away and fell. He brought me home.'

'Even so, he is still running away from the law. You can't shield him here, Piers. Think what it would do to Grandmama if the police came here looking for your friend.'

'Grandmama has faced worse than that in her life, Aurelia. But I will get Luke away as soon as possible. I intend to put him on the next cargo ship due to sail, but unfortunately there's been a delay in loading. He will have to go on at the last minute.'

'How long will that take?' Aurelia demanded crossly. 'You shouldn't have put us in this situation.'

'I know and I'm sorry, but Luke is a decent fellow. If you met him you would agree, Aurelia.'

She stiffened and then relaxed slightly. 'All right. I will see him. I heard what you said about him being wrongly accused but I want to judge for myself.'

Dolly stared at her aunt in surprise. Aurelia seemed meek and mild, but this was a different person and Piers seemed suddenly in awe of his younger sister.

'Very well. Have your breakfast, Aurelia. I'll bring him to the music room before luncheon. You may judge him for yourself.'

'What will happen if I don't approve of your criminal friend?'

'I will have to find somewhere else to hide him.'

Aurelia smiled sweetly. 'I'm sure that Esther Pascoe will be only too happy to oblige.'

'That was uncalled for,' Piers said angrily. 'Esther is a friend.'

'A very good friend, so I've heard.' Aurelia walked over to the sideboard and lifted the lid of a silver breakfast dish. 'No devilled kidneys. What a shame.'

Piers shrugged and left the room.

'Were you going to tell me, Dolly?' Aurelia demanded as she brought her plate to the table. 'Or were you going to join your papa in this deceit?'

'I only stumbled on the truth by accident. But, having met him, I don't think he's a bad person. You might even like him.'

'I doubt that. Anyone who would put others at risk is not a good person. But as you seem to like the fellow I'm prepared to reserve judgement.'

Dolly filled her cup with coffee, eyeing her aunt warily. 'Will you tell Great-Grandmama?'

'Heavens, no! She would never shelter a felon in Trevenor. It would be like asking St Peter to allow the devil to enter through the pearly gates.'

Dolly laughed. She had thought Aunt Aurelia was rather stiff and starchy to begin with, but now she was seeing her in a completely different light. She had caught a glimpse of the lively, outgoing person her aunt must have been before her unhappy marriage, widowhood and being jilted at the altar.

'I'd take you to him, but I don't know where he's hiding exactly.'

'I think I do,' Aurelia said thoughtfully. 'If you saw him staring out of the window one storey above the music room I know exactly where he is. I'm not going to wait for Piers to arrange a meeting. We will catch the man unawares.'

'Do you mean to go now?' Dolly asked eagerly.

'He can wait until I've had breakfast. Then we'll find the fellow and I will decide whether or not he can hide here until Piers gets him to safety.'

'My father said it's only until there's a ship leaving port.'

'Let's hope that happens soon.' Aurelia settled down to enjoy her meal, leaving Dolly little alternative but to wait until she had finished.

Luke Gilpin jumped to his feet when Aurelia burst into the room, followed by Dolly.

'I know who you are, Mr Gilpin,' Aurelia said coldly. 'And I know why my brother has chosen to shelter you under our roof.'

Luke eyed her curiously. 'You are not what I expected, Miss Blanchard.'

'It's Mrs Gibbs, and I'm a widow. Not that it's any of your business, sir. I suppose you realise that you are putting us in jeopardy by being here. I don't know what the penalty for harbouring an escaped criminal is, but it will be significant, I'm sure.'

'I understand your concerns, Mrs Gibbs. I never wanted to involve your family, but I was desperate when I came to see Piers. I promise you I will leave at the first possible opportunity.'

'It can't be too long before there's a ship leaving the harbour.' Dolly could see that her aunt was weakening and she pressed her point home. 'Father will make it happen soon, I'm certain.'

'I will leave now if you are worried, ma'am,' Luke said humbly.

Aurelia relaxed visibly. 'You are here now, sir. All I ask is that you are circumspect in your behaviour. No more early morning swimming.'

Luke smiled ruefully. 'That was a mistake, for which I apologise. It was such a beautiful morning I succumbed to temptation.'

Aurelia walked to the window and gazed out at the view. 'I will speak to my brother, but the longer you remain here, the more difficult it will be to keep your presence a secret from the servants.'

Dolly frowned thoughtfully. 'I have an idea, Aunt Aurelia.'

Aurelia turned to give her a searching look. 'Speak up then, Dolly.'

'If Mr Gilpin was a guest in this house no one would think anything of it.'

'That's ridiculous, Dolly.' Aurelia shook her head. 'You know how tittle-tattle gets around in small towns and villages.'

'That's exactly what I was thinking,' Dolly said, warming to her theme. 'If Father takes the carriage to the nearest railway station he could tell the servants he was meeting a friend, who would be staying here for a while. He could bring Mr Gilpin back with him and no one would be any the wiser.' Dolly turned to Luke. 'You don't come from Cornwall, do you?'

'No. My family have an estate in the wilds of Essex.'

'Then who would know anything about your history?' Dolly smiled triumphantly. 'I believe they call it hiding in plain sight. I read something of the sort in a short story.'

Aurelia met Luke's questioning look with a frown, which melted into a smile. 'I think Dolly could be right, Mr Gilpin. I'll discuss it with Piers.'

'Thank you, ma'am. I am very much obliged.'

'We will have to give you a new name and make up a story about you that sounds convincing,' Dolly said eagerly. 'How exciting. And I thought my stay here would be so dull.'

Luke laughed. 'I am glad to have provided you with some entertainment, Dolly. Perhaps you would like to invent my new persona for me.'

'That would be marvellous. It will be like being in a theatrical production at the Pavilion Theatre, where I am employed. You will be able to swim in the sea every morning if you so wish.'

'Just a minute, Dolly,' Aurelia said firmly. 'Piers hasn't agreed to it yet. Leave your play-acting until I have spoken to your father.'

'All right, but if he wants to keep his friend safe I know he will agree.'

'We'll take the chaise and drive to the mine office, Dolly.' Aurelia walked to the door and opened it. 'In the meantime, Mr Gilpin, please keep very quiet and don't give the servants cause to come looking for an intruder. I'll let you know what Piers says when we get back.'

Chapter Eighteen

Piers was annoyed at first. He was angry with Luke for being careless and he obviously resented what he considered to be Dolly's interference in his affairs. However, after a few minutes of consideration, during which time he paced the office floor, he acquiesced, admitting it was probably the safest and easiest way out of a difficult situation, as it might be several days before the next ship sailed. Dolly tried not to look too pleased with herself, but Aurelia clapped her hands and congratulated Piers on his good sense. That did not seem to please him much either, but he agreed to smuggle Luke out of the house first thing next morning. The rest of the plan would fall into place as the day wore on. Piers refused to say more than that.

'But,' he said, as Dolly and Aurelia were about to

leave the office, 'don't think I condone your spying on me. That goes for both of you.'

Aurelia straightened up to look him in the face. 'Don't be ridiculous, Piers. Why would either of us do that? Your friend betrayed himself. It was fortunate that Dolly and I are reasonable people, otherwise we might have had hysterics and sent for the constable. If you had confided in me in the first place, none of this would have happened. Come, Dolly. It's time we returned home to give Mr Gilpin the good news.'

Dolly shot her father a wary glance as she followed her aunt out of the office.

'You were brave, Aurelia.'

'I used to stand up to Piers and Alex when we were younger. I've allowed myself to be browbeaten into submission by my own brother. You've shown me how wrong I was, Dolly. I will stand it no more.'

'I'm really proud of you,' Dolly said with feeling. 'I hardly know my father, but he is not an easy person to like.'

Aurelia beckoned to the young boy who had been walking the horse while they were in the office. 'You are right, Dolly. I'm afraid it's true. I had hoped Piers would change when he married your mama, but it was not to be. However, we have to put up with our families, no matter what.'

'I suppose so,' Dolly said reluctantly. She had not come to Cornwall with any great expectations of getting closer to her father, but she could not help feeling disappointed that her feelings for him were so far removed from those she had for Alex, whom she had always considered to be her papa. She climbed into the chaise to sit beside her aunt.

'One day all this will be yours, Dolly,' Aurelia said as she took hold of the reins.

'I suppose it will.' Somehow the thought of inheriting the clay mine and all its problems, as well as Trevenor, with its ghostly echoes of the past, did not thrill Dolly. She could not imagine burying herself in the countryside so far from Rockwood Castle and the people she loved. Until this moment Dolly had not realised how much the success of the Pavilion Theatre meant to her. She missed Nick, with his wry sense of humour and kind disposition. She even missed her bombastic grandmother and dear Claude, the peacemaker. Dolly sighed. At least the unexpected arrival of Luke Gilpin had livened up what had been a rather dull stay in Cornwall. Even so she could not wait to go home to Rockwood, the place she loved most in the whole world.

'Walk on,' Aurelia said with a gentle flick of the reins. The horse plodded on, heading automatically for home. 'You may give Mr Gilpin the good news, Dolly. I think it best if I keep away from that part of the house. I don't want to make the servants suspicious.'

'No, of course not,' Dolly agreed, nodding. 'We'll go to his room when we're sure no one will see us.

I'm sure he will be relieved to have a little more freedom.'

'Yes, but he must stay in the house or the grounds. We must make that clear to him, Dolly.'

'Of course.'

'It's not going to be as easy as it sounds.'

'We need to give him a new name,' Dolly said eagerly. 'Great-Grandmama will want to know all about him, so we will have to make up a convincing story as to how he came to know my father.'

'We'll discuss this with my brother after dinner tonight, but we'll have to wait until Grandmama has gone to bed. She says she is deaf but it's amazing how much she actually hears when she's a mind to listen.'

Dolly laughed. 'I will be very careful.'

That evening, after dinner, when Lady Pentelow had retired to bed, Dolly and Aurelia sat down together to create a new persona for Luke Gilpin. They had asked Piers to join them but he declined, saying he was going to the village to check on a sick employee. Aurelia had mouthed the words 'Esther Pascoe' to Dolly, who had difficulty in controlling the desire to giggle. However, it was more entertaining to make up several past histories for Luke, all of which turned out to be amusing but too far-fetched.

In the end they decided that it would be best to keep his first name in order to avoid confusion, and Dolly suggested they pick a common surname.

So Luke Johnson gradually came to life in their inventive minds. He was born into a good family, of course. Aurelia said that Lady Pentelow would object to a guest who came from a poor background, and Dolly agreed. After discarding all their more outrageous suggestions, they opted for the simplest. Luke Johnson, the eldest son of a wealthy family from the east coast, which was virtually true, was on his way to Santander in Spain where he had business connections. They could not decide exactly what this entailed, but perhaps Luke or Piers might have some good ideas. Anyway, as Aurelia said, it was vulgar to discuss business in company.

'Shall we give him a wife and children?' Dolly asked, sipping her rapidly cooling coffee.

Aurelia frowned. 'No, perhaps not. We don't want too many complications. We've decided that he's known Piers for many years, but they haven't seen each other for a long time.'

'Yes, and they met again by chance when Luke was in St Austell on business. Although that sounds rather dull, and Luke is a long way from home.'

'Maybe he needed to get as far away as possible after the tragic death of his fiancée, who succumbed to lung fever. She died in his arms and he's recovering from his broken heart.' Aurelia brushed a tear from her cheeks. 'So sad.'

'I don't know why you are crying,' Dolly said crossly. 'You just made it up, Aurelia.'

'I know, but the poor man must have suffered terribly.'

Dolly laughed. 'I think we'd better leave Luke Johnson's past rather vague. Shall we go and tell him what we've decided?'

'I don't know about that, Dolly. Do you think it's proper to visit a gentleman in his room, especially in the evening?'

'I think he needs to know that we've given him a new name and a broken heart.'

'I suppose you're right. I feel quite cruel for making the poor man suffer.'

'It's not real, Aurelia.'

'I know, but I still feel mean. I don't want to make him sad.'

Dolly placed her cup and saucer on the table at her side. She stood up, holding out her hand. 'Come with me. We'll put our ideas to Luke and let him decide.'

If Luke was surprised to see two ladies when he opened his bedroom door, he was too polite to make any comments. 'How nice to see you both,' he said, smiling. 'Won't you come in?'

Aurelia entered the room and then hesitated, as if having second thoughts, but Dolly pushed past her.

'This isn't the time for false modesty, Aurelia,' Dolly said severely. She turned to Luke. 'You must wonder why we've come here so late in the evening, Mr Gilpin.'

'Luke, please. Won't you take a seat?' He motioned to two rather uncomfortable-looking upright chairs. 'I am not really set up to entertain guests,' he added, smiling.

Aurelia took a deep breath. 'Mr Gilpin . . . Luke. I know my brother told you of our plans to bring you to the house tomorrow as a guest.'

'Yes, he did and I'm very grateful, but I don't want to put you and your family to any inconvenience. I realise that my presence here is placing you in a difficult situation.'

'It's only until there's one of my father's ships ready to take you to Spain,' Dolly said firmly. 'In the meantime, Aurelia and I have been trying to decide on a new name for you and a past that sounds convincing, but doesn't excite comment.'

'Fascinating. I can't wait to know my new identity.'

'It's not funny, Luke,' Aurelia said stiffly. 'As you said, you are placing us in a very difficult position. But my brother is head of the household and therefore we have no choice other than to do as he wishes.'

'I'm sorry, Mrs Gibbs. I didn't mean to offend you.'

'I just don't want any of this deceitfulness to get to my grandmother's ears. She's a very old lady and has set ideas. This is her home and she would be horrified if she knew the truth.'

'I understand.' Luke took Aurelia's hand and raised it to his lips. 'If this situation is too uncomfortable for you, I will leave. I'm sure I can find somewhere to hide until a berth is found for me.'

Dolly shook her head. 'Please don't go. Let me tell you our ideas and you can say whether or not you wish to go ahead with the story. Maybe you have a few notions of your own.' Dolly sent a meaningful look in Aurelia's direction. 'Will you tell Luke, or shall I?'

Aurelia cleared her throat. 'Well, these are just ideas. Please feel free to reject them.'

Luke listened intently until Aurelia finished speaking. 'So I am broken-hearted Luke Johnson, am I?'

Dolly nodded enthusiastically. 'Yes, but you can choose any name you fancy. We just thought something not too unusual might be best.'

'Oh, I agree. Luke Johnson is a fairly dull fellow, but add the tragic tale of my broken heart and I suddenly become much more interesting. And I'm waiting for a berth on a ship heading for Santander, is that right?'

'Yes,' Aurelia said tentatively. 'But you can make up another destination if you wish.'

'Santander sounds reasonable. Did you both decide on a trade or profession for Mr Johnson?'

Dolly and Aurelia exchanged worried glances. 'No, not exactly,' Dolly said slowly.

Luke laughed. 'Don't look so anxious. I think I can add to the story myself.'

'Does that mean you agree with us?' Dolly asked eagerly.

'I'm touched that you've gone to so much trouble for a stranger. From now on I will be Luke Johnson heading for Santander on business.'

Aurelia made a move towards the door. 'We'd better let Mr Johnson get some rest, Dolly. He'll have to rise early tomorrow morning.'

'Of course.' Dolly followed her reluctantly. 'I must say, this is all very exciting.'

'Good night, Mrs Gibbs,' Luke said, smiling. 'Good night, Miss Blanchard.'

Aurelia held the door open for Dolly. 'Come along. We should go straight to our rooms, Dolly. Ada will be wondering where I am and we mustn't arouse suspicion among the servants.'

Next morning Dolly and Aurelia were walking in the garden after breakfast when the sound of carriage wheels on the gravelled drive made them both hurry to the end of the terrace.

'We'd better try to look surprised,' Dolly said in a whisper. 'Do you think we ought to go inside and greet Luke, or would it be best for Father to bring him to us out here?'

Aurelia sighed. 'I don't know, Dolly. Maybe we should wait. After all, we aren't supposed to know that Luke is coming.'

'You're right, but we would be curious, wouldn't we?'

'We don't get many visitors here, so I suppose it would be quite natural for us to go inside and see who Piers has brought home.'

Dolly grabbed her by the hand. 'What are we waiting for?' She dragged Aurelia through the open French doors, but then common sense took over and Dolly released her aunt's hand. 'Curious, but not too eager.'

'Yes, Dolly. Slow down. Try to look casual.' Aurelia walked on ahead at a stately pace, and it took all Dolly's willpower to follow slowly. She had been worried that her father would not enter into the spirit of things and might give Luke away, but she was pleasantly surprised when Piers greeted them warmly.

'Aurelia, Adela, I want you to meet my good friend Luke Johnson. He's hoping to get a berth on one of my ships.'

'Aurelia Gibbs.' Aurelia extend her hand with a gracious smile. 'How do you do, Mr Johnson? Welcome to Trevenor.'

'How do you do, Mrs Gibbs?' Luke said, raising her hand to his lips.

'And this is my daughter, Adela,' Piers added. 'She's come to live with us.'

Dolly was about to argue, but a warning glance from Aurelia made her remember her part. She shook Luke's hand. 'How do you do, Mr Johnson?'

'How do you do, Miss Blanchard? It's a pleasure to meet you and your aunt.'

'Have you come far, Mr Johnson?' Aurelia asked conversationally.

'From London, Mrs Gibbs. Piers met me at St Austell station.'

Aurelia beckoned to Morwen, who was hovering nearby. 'Take Mr Johnson's coat and hat. We'll have coffee in the music room. Have you had breakfast, Mr Johnson?'

Piers shook his head. 'We stopped at an inn, Aurelia.'

'Coffee would be most welcome, Mrs Gibbs.' Luke rewarded her with an engaging smile.

Dolly was quick to see that her aunt was rather taken with Luke and he was equally attracted to her. Dolly sensed a budding romance, but the thought filled her with dismay. A mild flirtation with an attractive man on the run from the police was one thing, but a serious attachment could spell disaster for both of them. She was beginning to think perhaps this was not such a good idea, but it was too late to back out now. Luke was a guest in their house and Lady Pentelow was making her slow but majestic way down the wide oak staircase.

'Piers! Who is this? Have we visitors?'

Piers spun round to stare at his grandmother. 'Grandmama, may I introduce an old friend of mine? Luke Johnson from East Anglia.'

Lady Pentelow walked slowly towards them, leaning heavily on an ebony cane. She eyed Luke suspiciously. 'Why wasn't I consulted when you invited a friend to stay, Piers?'

Dolly held her breath. This was one complication that neither she nor Aurelia had considered.

'Because I didn't know myself until late last evening. I received a telegram saying that Luke would be arriving at St Austell early this morning. He's headed for Santander and he wanted to book a passage on one of our ships. However, we have no free berths at the moment, so I invited him to stay. I knew you would extend Trevenor's hospitality to a traveller.'

'Of course. You are welcome, Mr Johnson.' Lady Pentelow nodded graciously. 'I will be in the drawing room if you need me, Aurelia.'

Luke bowed and opened his mouth to speak but Lady Pentelow had walked on, tapping her ebony cane on the floor as she went.

'Yes, Grandmama,' Aurelia called after her.

'See to it that a guest room is prepared for him, Aurelia.'

'Yes, Grandmama.' Aurelia smiled. 'Please come to the drawing room, Mr Johnson. I'll have a room made ready for you.'

'I think your grandmother is suspicious,' Luke said in a low voice.

'Grandmama takes time to get used to people, old chap.' Piers marched on ahead. 'I think I need something stronger than coffee. Come to my study, Luke. I have a bottle of Armagnac that I'd like you to sample.'

Luke nodded. 'Maybe later, Piers. It would not be

polite to refuse coffee with your sister and daughter, especially as I need your grandmother to tolerate my presence.'

'Suit yourself,' Piers said huffily. 'I'll be in my study if you would care to join me later.'

He marched off, leaving Dolly to stare after him. She could not think why her father was so annoyed. Surely this was all part of the conspiracy to keep Luke safe until he could safely leave the country? Father had brought about this situation by sheltering a fugitive. He had involved his family whether or not they were agreeable.

'Ignore my brother's lack of manners, Luke. Dolly and I will be eager to learn more about you.' Aurelia beckoned to Dolly. 'I suggest we enjoy our guest's company while he's staying here. I'll go to the housekeeper's office and arrange for a room to be made ready for you, Luke. I'll order coffee, too. Dolly will show you the way to the drawing room.' Aurelia walked off in the direction of the servants' quarters.

'Come with me then, Mr Johnson,' Dolly said, smiling.

There was a strained atmosphere in the drawing room as they waited for Morwen to bring the coffee.

Luke walked towards the French doors, which had been flung open to allow the late summer sunshine to warm the room. He stood, looking out across the terrace to the parterre gardens below.

'This is a beautiful old house. I don't wonder that you love it, Mrs Gibbs.'

'Aurelia, please. But you're wrong, Luke. I hate Trevenor.'

Dolly stared at her in surprise. 'I thought you loved it, too.'

'No, indeed. I've had to live here for most of my life, but it's a miserable house, with sad memories etched into its stones. I doubt if any Blanchard has been happy living here.'

'Father loves it, Aurelia?'

'Does he? I doubt it, Dolly. Your father has spent more of his life away from Trevenor than he has living here. He enjoys owning it, but that doesn't mean he's content to live here. Given the opportunity and the money, I think he would gladly sell up and move away permanently.'

'And yet he made such a fuss about bringing me here so that I can get to know the home I will inherit one day.'

'Don't ask me why he had that sudden whim. I think you are a possession as much as this house and the land. I don't wish to be cruel, Dolly, but your father never gave a thought to you until recently.'

Luke turned to face them. 'In his defence, I have to say that life in the penal colony was more than tough. Existing in those conditions does something to the men and women who underwent deportation, too. Perhaps that goes some way to explaining why Piers is so attached to this house and the estate.'

The rattle of china stopped the conversation while Morwen brought in the tray of coffee and a plate of biscuits, which she placed on a table beside the sofa where Aurelia was seated.

'Thank you, Morwen,' Aurelia said, smiling.

Morwen bobbed a curtsey and slipped silently from the room.

Aurelia poured the coffee. 'Do sit down, Luke. We might as well enjoy your visit, no matter what the circumstances. It will be so interesting to learn more about you.'

He took the cup and saucer she offered him. 'Thank you, Aurelia. I doubt if you'll find my story very exciting.'

'I'm sure we will,' Dolly added eagerly. 'But only if you feel like confiding in us. Perhaps you would rather forget your past experiences, especially those in the penal colony.'

Luke sat down, resting his cup and saucer on his knee. 'As a matter of fact, although I railed against deportation for something for which I was not guilty, the events I suffered made me who I am today. I survived all the hardships, largely thanks to Piers guiding me through the first dreadful months. Eventually I became a ticket-of-leave man, which meant I could work, earn my own living, marry and even bring relatives from Britain to New South

Wales. I started a construction business and I made a fortune. The only thing I was not allowed to do was to return home.'

'But you did,' Aurelia said slowly. 'May I ask why you risked everything to return to this country?'

'My story is not as romantic as the one you made up for me, but it is very simple. I received a letter from my sister informing me that our mother was suffering from a serious illness, and might not survive. She had been asking for me and my sister begged me to return before it was too late.'

'So you risked everything to see your mother?' Aurelia's eyes filled with tears. 'Were you in time?'

Luke shook his head. 'Sadly I was too late. I knew that seeing her before she died was a vain hope, due to the time the letter had taken to reach me and the length of the passage back to England, but I couldn't let Jane down. She had looked after both my parents even though she suffered the loss of her husband during that time. I needed to sign over everything I had inherited to her, so that she could bring her children up in comfort.'

'She must have been relieved to see you,' Dolly said gently.

'She was, and the children, too. In fact we decided that she should sell the family home and book a passage to Sydney. I'll build a house for her and the children. We'll be a family again.'

Aurelia clapped her hands. 'How wonderful. That must mean so much to you, Luke.'

'Are you married, Luke?' Dolly asked boldly.

'Dolly! You don't ask questions like that,' Aurelia said, blushing.

'It's all right. I am happy to answer any questions you have, Dolly.' Luke gave her an amused smile. 'And no, I am not married. I have never found a woman who could put up with me. I work long hours and I am away from home often.'

Dolly nodded wisely. 'Ah yes, but the right woman would not mind all that. If she truly loved you, she would help you in your endeavours to make a good life for yourself.'

'I think we've put Luke through enough, Dolly,' Aurelia said, smiling. 'We should let him drink his coffee in peace.'

'I can't thank you both enough for what you are doing for me.' Luke sipped his coffee.

'You can stay as long as you like,' Dolly said eagerly. 'I'm sure you have many interesting stories about your life in Australia. We can all relax and enjoy your company.'

'Dolly is right,' Aurelia added. 'Now your presence is out in the open, I hope we will be able to treat you like an ordinary guest.'

Luke finished his coffee and set the cup back on its saucer. 'Perhaps I should join Piers in his study. He's been telling me about the mine and I might have some ideas to boost his business. I learned a lot after I left the penal colony and started my building company.' He rose to his feet.

'I'll show you the way,' Aurelia said hastily. 'Trevenor is very confusing at first but you'll soon find your way around.' She walked with him to the door and he held it open for her.

Dolly could hear Aurelia chatting to him until their voices faded away. She drank her coffee and nibbled a biscuit. It occurred to her that they had not questioned him about the crime that warranted the harsh sentence that had sent him halfway around the world, and lifelong banishment from his native country. Dolly waited impatiently for Aurelia to return.

'What do you think of him?' Dolly asked eagerly.

'He seems like a very nice person. I think he was treated very badly and he did not deserve such a cruel sentence. I believe him when he said he is innocent of all the charges against him.'

'Yes,' Dolly said softly. 'He is either an honest man, or a very good liar. I wonder if we'll ever know the whole story.'

Chapter Nineteen

Whether Luke had lied or not, he was a charming house guest. After the first difficult hour or two, Lady Pentelow warmed to him, and by the end of the first week she made it plain that Luke Johnson was high in her esteem. He had great patience and would sit with her after dinner, telling her stories of his travels abroad and making her laugh at some of his anecdotes. Every morning Piers took him to the mine office and Luke was enthusiastic about the future of the china clay company. Somehow, in spite of being kept busy, Luke found plenty of time for Aurelia and Dolly, although Dolly suspected that it was Aurelia's company that Luke really sought. On her part, Aurelia seemed equally smitten, but she refused to admit any attraction for the man who would soon be leaving them, never to return.

Lady Pentelow wanted to hold a soirée so that

she could introduce their guest to local society, but it was here that Piers put his foot down, very firmly. Lady Pentelow was surprised and then angry, but nothing she could say would change his mind. Dolly understood perfectly, as did Aurelia, and both of them tried to smooth things over, but Lady Pentelow was furious and refused to speak to Piers for several days. However, in the end diplomacy won and Luke managed to clear the air by suggesting that they all go for a picnic on the cliffs.

Dolly held her breath, gazing at Lady Pentelow, who was frowning as she considered the proposition.

'I'm too old for such an outing,' Lady Pentelow said at last. 'I can't walk very far.'

'I was thinking more of a carriage ride to a local beauty spot, my lady,' Luke said, smiling. 'The servants would bring chairs and a table, as well as a sunshade to protect your delicate complexion.'

Lady Pentelow blushed and giggled like a girl. 'You shouldn't talk about such personal things, Luke.'

He held his hand to his heart. 'I only speak the truth, ma'am. Now, what do you say?'

'Yes, Grandmama,' Piers added hastily. 'Do agree. It would be a shame to miss the opportunity to enjoy the last of the hot weather. Autumn will be here soon enough.'

Aurelia took a hint from her brother. 'Piers is right, Grandmama. It would be lovely to picnic with the sun shining on the sea and the warm breeze caressing our cheeks.'

'Oh, well. I can see you are all intent on such an outing. Perhaps it would be rather enjoyable. You will travel with me in my barouche, won't you, Luke?'

'Of course, my lady. I will run alongside it, if you prefer.'

Lady Pentelow laughed, a very rare occurrence, which made both Dolly and Aurelia stare at her in surprise.

'That's settled then.' Piers rose from his seat by the window. 'I'll leave the arrangements to you, Aurelia. If you need any help from me, just ask.'

'Of course, Piers.' Aurelia smiled angelically.

Dolly suspected that Aurelia and Luke had planned the picnic and had simply been waiting for a chance to suggest it to the family. The growing attraction between the two of them was obvious, although Dolly did not think her father suspected anything. She could not help wondering just what he would make of a romance between his sister and someone who was literally on the run from the police. So far it seemed as though they were safe from detection, but Luke was becoming increasingly a part of the family. Dolly was afraid that Aurelia would be deeply upset when he eventually found a berth on one of the company's ships. To Dolly's knowledge, Aurelia had always been unlucky in love and if she had deep feelings for Luke her loss this time would be even greater.

*

Aurelia threw herself into making arrangements for the proposed picnic with such enthusiasm that Dolly was even more worried. She noticed that Aurelia and Luke took long walks in the grounds at every opportunity, and when they returned Aurelia was glowing with happiness. There was no one in whom Dolly could confide and she felt quite helpless. She was moved to ask her father when the next ship would sail for Santander, or anywhere that would set Luke off on his return to Australia, but Piers' answer was vague, leaving Dolly frustrated and even more worried for her aunt. She had grown fond of Aurelia during the weeks she had been staying at Trevenor and she did not want to see her suffering yet another broken heart.

The day of the picnic dawned fine and warm. Aurelia had everything planned to the last small detail. She and Luke were to travel in Lady Pentelow's barouche and Dolly had chosen to ride with her father. The servants were to follow in two vehicles, one of which carried the table, chairs and sunshades, and the other was packed with delicacies to tempt the fussiest eater. Lady Pentelow was not among that set; she enjoyed her food and made no secret of her liking for a good sherry and vintage wine. In fact, she did not approve of young ladies pretending to eat like sparrows when in reality they were starving themselves.

Dolly and Piers left first, riding on ahead of the barouche. Piers knew all the back lanes and Dolly was content to follow him at a safe distance. Her horse was spirited and eager to be off, but her father's black hunter was a powerful animal and it took a good horseman to master him. Dolly had a sneaking admiration for her father, but that did not equate to loving him. There was no emotion in the way in which he treated her, which should have hurt, but somehow it was easier to accept than an overt display of affection. They treated each other with polite civility and Dolly had come to the conclusion that this was all there would ever be between them. However, she was determined to enjoy the day.

The fields were golden with ripe corn and the harvest was under way, with whole families turning out to bring the crops in before the weather broke. Heat haze shimmered above the dusty lanes, and the hedgerows were heavy with leaves, some of which were just beginning to change colour.

The chosen picnic spot was less than a mile from Trevenor and Dolly dismounted, tethering her horse to a stunted tree that was twisted and gnarled by the prevailing winds. Fortunately, there was only a warm breeze today and the sea below the steep cliffs was deep turquoise with a band of ultramarine at the horizon. But there was little time to enjoy the view before the servants arrived and began to set up the table, chairs and large sunshade, while others began laying out the food on a trestle covered in a white cloth.

Dolly stood back waiting for Lady Pentelow's

barouche to come into view. She could not help comparing this luxurious form of picnicking to the simple packs of jam sandwiches wrapped in cheese-cloth and slabs of currant cake that comprised the meals she and her brother and sister had shared with some of Nancy's boys in the tree house. The memory came with a pang of homesickness for Rockwood Castle and her family. She pushed all such thoughts to the back of her mind as Lady Pentelow's carriage drew to a halt and the footman leaped to the ground to assist the passengers to alight.

It seemed that Aurelia had thought of everything, including bottles of chilled champagne, although as Dolly sipped hers from a crystal glass she remembered the lukewarm lemonade they had drunk with such enjoyment all those years ago. Lady Pentelow sat on a chair like a throne beneath the sunshade. She drank champagne and gazed out to sea with a contented smile.

Piers had gone off on his own somewhere, but Dolly was getting used to her father's need for solitude. There was no sign of Aurelia and Luke. They had slipped away unnoticed while the servants were clearing away the debris left after the meal. Dolly was about to ask Lady Pentelow if she would like her glass refilled with champagne when she realised that her ladyship was sound asleep. Dolly rose from her seat and took the delicate crystal glass from Lady Pentelow's hand before it fell to the ground and smashed. She placed it on the table and stood for a moment, undecided as to what she should do next.

She could simply sit and enjoy the sunshine or she could walk off in the same direction as her father in the hope of catching up with him. However, in the end she decided to explore a little on her own and she made her way over the hummocky grass to the shade of the bushes and stunted trees where she spotted a narrow path, winding into the cool greenery. The sun blazed down and a skylark whose nest she had almost trodden on wheeled above her head singing its glorious song. It was surprisingly hot for the time of year and it was a relief to step into the shade.

The heady scent of crushed grass alerted her to the fact that others had trodden this path before her and, as she entered a small clearing, she was shocked to see Aurelia and Luke clinging to each other in a passionate embrace. Aurelia's bonnet had fallen to the ground and her lace shawl was snagged on a thorn bush. Luke had also lost his hat and his appearance was dishevelled. Dolly backed away but a twig snapped beneath her feet and the lovers sprang apart.

'Dolly, it's not what it looks like,' Aurelia said breathlessly.

'It's exactly what it appears,' Luke added firmly. 'I love Aurelia and I believe she loves me.'

'You mustn't say that, Luke.' Aurelia backed away,

holding up her hands. 'Please, I don't want Piers or Grandmama to find out. They will make you leave the house, and then what will you do?'

Dolly joined them reluctantly. 'It's been obvious you two have feelings for each other. At least, I could see it, although I don't know about my father. I'm not going to say anything, I promise.'

'We shouldn't put you in that position, Dolly,' Aurelia said tearfully. 'It isn't fair.'

'What will you do?' Dolly asked anxiously. 'Luke, you will be leaving us very soon. I heard Father say that a ship is due to sail in two days' time.'

'I want Aurelia to come with me. I can give her a good life in New South Wales where I'm a reasonably wealthy man, and I intend to build my business even bigger. With a wife like Aurelia at my side, I could accomplish anything.'

'You really want to marry me?' Aurelia said in a voice that shook with emotion. 'You didn't say so, Luke.'

'I didn't want to take advantage of you in your own home, my darling. I knew when I first saw you that my heart was lost for ever. But if you come with me, it's almost certain that you won't see your family again.'

'You will be my family, Luke,' Aurelia said softly. 'Nothing else matters to me.' She turned to Dolly with a pleading look. 'You do understand, don't you?'

'I think I do.' Dolly threw her arms around her

aunt and hugged her. 'You must do what makes you happy, Aurelia. Never mind anyone else.'

'But Grandmama is an old lady. I can't abandon her.'

'My father should look after her now, Aurelia. You have done your share while he was away.'

'I agree,' Luke said hastily.

Dolly stepped away. She sensed that Luke had something very important to say.

'I don't know,' Aurelia said miserably.

Luke went down on one knee and took her hand in his. 'My dearest Aurelia, I realise we have only known each other for a very short time, but I love you with all my heart. If you will do me the honour of becoming my wife I will love and protect you until the day I die. Will you marry me, Aurelia?'

'Yes, Luke. I will.' Aurelia's voice broke as he rose swiftly to his feet and folded her in an embrace.

Dolly turned away to hide the tears that coursed down her cheeks. She had no doubt that Luke spoke from the heart and that Aurelia's response was sincere. Dolly was about to walk away when Aurelia called out to her.

'Dolly, you won't say anything to anyone, will you?'

'No, of course not.' Dolly stopped and turned back to face them. 'But what will you do? Will you sail with Luke on one of the company's ships? Will Father allow it?'

Aurelia's happy smile faded and she glanced

anxiously at Luke, who had his arm around her waist. 'What will we do now, Luke? This is all so sudden.'

Luke kissed her on the forehead. 'We'll think of something, but Dolly is right. I'm afraid Piers will try to stop us, and I can't really blame him. He knows that life is harsh where we were in the prison colony.'

'But you are not there now,' Aurelia said desperately. 'You have a home, you said so.'

'I built a small house for myself and I will build a mansion for you, my love, but it will take time. If you would rather remain here until I can reasonably provide you with the home you deserve, that is what we will do.'

Dolly held her breath. She would not blame her aunt if she chose the safe option, and their feelings for each other might change over the period of a few months or even a year.

Aurelia smiled up at Luke. She clutched his hand and raised it to her cheek. 'I will go wherever you go, Luke. I've never been so certain of anything in my life. I lived in a small cottage when I was married to Martin. I can do the same again. I'm not afraid, just so long as you are with me.'

Luke kissed her again, this time on the lips and she wound her arms around his neck.

Dolly backed away. She knew she was not needed here and she retraced her steps, emerging into the bright sunshine on the cliff top. She realised that it would not be easy for Aurelia and Luke, but she had a feeling they would overcome all the obstacles in their way.

However, their first major difficulty would be getting away from Trevenor. Dolly could only imagine the opposition they would receive from her father and from Great-Grandmama. The obvious answer would be an elopement, but with the police looking for Luke it would not be easy to leave the country. It seemed that a berth on one of the company's ships would be out of the question when Father discovered that his sister had fallen in love with a ticket-of-leave man.

Lady Pentelow was still asleep beneath the sunshade and there was no sign of Piers. Dolly resumed her seat as if nothing had happened, but she realised that their safe little world at Trevenor was about to be turned upside down. The scandal would reverberate around the county and reach as far as Rockwood and even beyond.

Dolly picked up her glass of champagne and raised it in an imaginary toast to the determined lovers. She wondered if she would have the courage to give up everything for love like her aunt. A sudden vision of Gus brought a rueful smile to her lips. The champagne had gone straight to her head and the tingling on her lips reminded her of the intoxicating kisses she had shared with Gus. Was it love she felt for him? Maybe she would never know, but one thing was becoming clear: she wanted to go home to

Rockwood, where she truly belonged. Trevenor had never felt a particularly friendly place and it would become unbearable if Aurelia left with Luke. Dolly knew what she had to do.

That evening, Lady Pentelow retired to her room immediately after dinner. She had complained about her aches and pains throughout dinner, and did not seem at all grateful for the trouble that Aurelia had taken in arranging the picnic outing for her. It was a relief when she finally went upstairs, aided by Morwen and Ada, who looked as though they might buckle beneath Lady Pentelow's weight as they mounted the stairs.

'Should I go with them?' Dolly asked anxiously.

Aurelia shrugged. 'Don't worry, Morwen is stronger than she looks, and so is Ada. Grandmama is quite capable to ascending the stairs on her own, but she enjoys creating a scene. You ought to know that by now, Dolly. Let's go into the drawing room and wait for Luke and Piers to join us.'

Dolly waited until her great-grandmother had reached the top of the stairs before following Aurelia to the drawing room. Daylight was fading and the candles had been lit, casting flickering shadows on the walls.

'What are you and Luke going to do?' Dolly asked in a low voice as she sat beside Aurelia on the sofa.

'I don't know, Dolly.' Aurelia filled a cup with coffee and passed it to Dolly. 'We haven't had a chance to discuss it fully. I'm still reeling from the speed with which it's all happened. I can hardly believe I accepted his proposal and I'll be travelling halfway around the world to live in another country.'

'Are you having second thoughts?'

'Oh, no. I have never been more certain of anything. I would go tomorrow if it were possible.'

'I'm glad you are so sure. It's a long way to go if you should change your mind.'

'Do you doubt me, Dolly?'

'No, not for a minute. It was obvious from the beginning that you and Luke were attracted to each other, despite all the difficulties.'

'The main one being how do we get out of the country if we can't travel on one of our own vessels? We have to leave quickly before Piers discovers our secret.'

'Luke is wanted by the police. Don't forget that.'

'How could I? It's uppermost in my mind, although they won't be looking for Mr and Mrs Johnson. We need a marriage certificate to prove who we are.'

'A secret wedding? Is that possible?'

'Highly unlikely, given the circumstances. We would need a special licence, which is, I believe, very expensive, and then we would have to find a priest willing to conduct the ceremony.'

'There must be a way,' Dolly said, frowning.

'Don't say another word. I hear voices. I don't want Piers to find out yet. He would throw Luke out on the street, I know it.'

The door opened and Luke entered, pausing on the threshold. 'Well, good night, then, Piers. I'll see you in the morning.'

Piers put his head round the door. 'I have to call in at the mine office, Aurelia. I'll say good night.' He did not wait for an answer.

'We all know where my brother is going,' Aurelia said as the door closed. 'Come and sit down, Luke. We have so much to talk about.'

Dolly rose to her feet. 'I'll give you some privacy.'

'No, don't go, Dolly,' Aurelia said hastily. 'You know everything so far.'

'Yes, but this is between the two of you. I think I'll take a walk in the garden. It's not dark yet.'

Dolly left the room before either Aurelia or Luke had a chance to respond. She was happy for them, but she could not quite dispel the niggling worry that Aurelia had fallen in love with a dream, and that reality might prove quite different. Luke was a good-looking, charismatic man, but he was an escaped convict, and life in New South Wales would be a complete contrast to the way Aurelia had lived since childhood.

Haunted by these thoughts, Dolly went into the scented rose garden. The late blooms nodded their heavy heads in the slight breeze and the perfume of night-scented stock filled the air. Bats zoomed crazily overhead and the sound of the waves on the shore was both rhythmic and soothing.

Darkness had swallowed up the garden in great

greedy gulps and a cold wind blew up off the sea. Dolly wrapped her shawl around her shoulders and retreated into the drawing room. She did not want to disturb the lovers, who were seated together on the sofa, and she tiptoed past them, but Aurelia jumped to her feet, slightly dishevelled but smiling as she followed Dolly out of the room.

'I'm so glad I caught you before you went to bed, Dolly.'

'Why? What's happened?'

'Luke has found a fisherman who is willing to take us to France. We'll be free there to get married and find a ship to take us to Australia with no questions asked.'

'That was very sudden, Aurelia. When did this happen?'

'I didn't ask. Luke managed it somehow and we're leaving tomorrow.'

'So soon?'

'Why wait? I know my own mind. I don't want to dwindle into widowhood with Piers using me as a housekeeper and Grandmama expecting me to be her nurse as well as her companion.' Aurelia clutched Dolly's hand. 'You do approve, don't you? I am doing the right thing, aren't I?'

Dolly slept little that night. She was even more worried about Aurelia's future now. She had promised not to tell anyone about the planned elopement, but it weighed heavily upon her conscience. When she did manage to doze off she had disturbing dreams and awakened soon after dawn. She rose from her bed and splashed cold water on her face from the flower-patterned bowl on the washstand. She dressed hurriedly, brushed her hair and tied it back with a blue ribbon. It was too early for breakfast although she could hear the servants moving from room to room as they made the house ready for the family above stairs. Aurelia had not mentioned a time for her departure with Luke, and there was nothing Dolly could do other than to wait. She had reached the main hall when she saw Ada coming towards her carrying a large ewer, filled with hot water for the bedrooms.

'Good morning, Ada.'

Ada stared at her in amazement. 'Good morning, miss.'

'Are you taking that to Mrs Gibbs's room?'

'Yes, miss. She asked me to wake her early.'

'Thank you, Ada.' Dolly walked on. So Aurelia was planning to get up earlier than usual. Perhaps it was not too late to make her change her mind, even if it was just to wait until she had had time to get to know Luke a little better.

Dolly smiled to herself. It would be ironic if she were to be the voice of sense, when usually it was someone else giving her advice.

A flurry of activity at the front entrance attracted her attention as Mark hurried outside onto the forecourt. Dolly could hear the rumble of wheels on the cobblestones and the clatter of horses' hoofs. She hurried to the door. The carriage drew to a halt and she recognised the coat of arms in the cartouche on the door. She ran to greet the new arrival.

'Freddie! I don't believe it. What brings you here?'

Freddie greeted her with a smile. 'I've come to bring you home, Dolly. That is, if you wish to leave Trevenor. Your mother and stepfather sent me.'

'Is anything wrong?' Dolly asked anxiously.

Freddie shook his head. 'Don't upset yourself, Dolly. If you wish to remain here with your father, they will understand. To be honest, it was I who suggested that it might be a good idea to check on you.'

Dolly turned to Mark, who was standing in the doorway, trying to look as though he was not listening. 'Mark, will you go to the kitchen, please? Ask Cook to prepare breakfast early as we have a visitor who has been travelling for days, or so I imagine. Oh, and coffee in the morning room would be a good idea.'

'Yes, Miss Adela.' Mark abandoned Freddie's cases and hurried off in the direction of the kitchens.

Dolly tucked her hand in the crook of Freddie's arm. 'Come with me. We'll wait in the morning parlour until breakfast is served.'

Freddie gave her a searching look. 'What's wrong, Dolly? I can tell that something is worrying you.'

'Is it so obvious?'

'Only to someone who has known you since you were a child. Is Piers treating you properly?'

'He barely seems to know that I'm here. He isn't unpleasant, but he just doesn't seem to see me as a person. I think I'm more of a possession to him.'

'I'm sorry, but I'm not surprised. I don't know him well, but what I've learned about him isn't to his credit.'

'And yet my parents were happy to let me come here.'

'I don't think they had much choice, Dolly. Piers is your father and you are not yet twenty.'

'I will be in a few weeks, but that's not the point. Mama could have warned me what my father was like.'

'Rosie would not want to influence you unduly. She's too fair minded for that. But if you wish to leave here there is nothing to stop you.'

'Not even my father?'

'He can hardly hold you prisoner, Dolly. You are a grown woman, even if you haven't reached your majority. Just say the word and I'll take you home.'

They had reached the morning room and Dolly took a seat on the sofa.

'I will take you up on that offer, Freddie, but not until I'm sure that Aurelia is doing the right thing.'

Freddie smiled. 'Aurelia Blanchard has lurched from one disastrous relationship to another. Who is it this time?'

'Someone we are not supposed to be helping, Freddie. He is wanted by the police.'

'A criminal?'

'Well, to be exact he is a ticket-of-leave man, but he came back to England for family reasons, so I believe. Anyway, he is on the run from the police and waiting for a ship to take him back to Australia.'

'And of course Aurelia has fallen in love with the fellow.'

'Yes, and they plan to elope today. They have found a fisherman willing to take them to France, and from there they plan to make their way to Australia. Luke has promised Aurelia that she will have a big house and want for nothing, but I'm worried, Freddie.'

'It sounds as if you have good reason to be alarmed. I suppose Aurelia is convinced that this is true love at last.'

Dolly gave him a searching look. 'What do you mean?'

'From what I know of Aurelia, she falls in love very easily. I believe at one time she was infatuated with Nick Gibson and he was quite seriously involved, but she let him down.'

'I didn't know that. Nick is a lovely man. He deserves to find happiness.'

A loud rap on the door made Dolly look up as Ada rushed into the room. It was obvious from her distressed expression that something had upset her.

Chapter Twenty

'What is it, Ada?' Dolly asked urgently. 'What's the matter?'

'I don't know if I should say anything, Miss Adela, but Mrs Gibbs asked me to pack her things. She's about to leave with that gentleman who has been staying here.'

Dolly leaped to her feet. 'Thank you, Ada. I'll deal with this.'

'I'll come with you.' Freddie followed her as she rushed from the room and made her way to the entrance hall.

Aurelia was standing by the main entrance amongst a pile of luggage. She appeared to be having a heated argument with Luke. She stopped talking and her hand flew to cover her mouth when she saw Dolly and Freddie.

'What's going on?' Dolly demanded. 'Surely you weren't going to leave without saying goodbye?'

'We won't be going anywhere unless Aurelia agrees to travel light,' Luke said angrily. He pointed to the bulging valises, bandboxes and a steamer trunk. 'How do you expect to get all this to the harbour, Aurelia? There's enough luggage here to sink the fishing boat.'

'If I am to travel halfway around the world with you I will need my things, Luke.'

'I will buy you what you need as we go along. You cannot take all this. One small valise will have to suffice.'

Aurelia's eyes filled with tears. 'How can you be so unfeeling? I am leaving everything I hold dear to marry you and live in a foreign country.'

'You will do no such thing.' Lady Pentelow's querulous voice rang out across the hall.

There was a sudden hush as everyone turned to see Lady Pentelow slowly descending the stairs. A white lace nightcap covered her hair and her dressing robe flowed around her with the rustle of silk accentuating every step she took.

'Grandmama,' Aurelia began haltingly. 'I didn't expect you to be up so early.'

'I was awakened by the sound of a carriage on the forecourt.' Lady Pentelow sent a chilling look in Freddie's direction. 'I don't know what you are doing here, Dorrington, but I suspect it's not Aurelia you are after.'

'I came to make sure that Dolly was content to remain here, my lady.' Freddie stepped forward, proffering his hand to assist her down the last few steps, but she brushed it away.

'I don't need your help. I am not yet in my dotage.' Lady Pentelow marched past him. She came to a halt at Aurelia's side. 'You are going nowhere, Aurelia. I was beginning to doubt Mr Johnson's sincerity. I don't know who you are, sir, although I suspect you have not been entirely honest with me.'

'I assure you my intentions are honourable, Lady Pentelow,' Luke said hastily. 'Please believe that. I love Aurelia and I want to marry her.'

Lady Pentelow gave him a withering look. 'Maybe, but I can assure you that Aurelia has no fortune to call her own.'

'Grandmama, how could you?' Aurelia's lips trembled. 'What a dreadful thing to suggest. Luke and I love each other. I am going to Australia with him.'

'You are going nowhere, Aurelia. Just wait until your brother comes down. I sent Morwen to wake him when she told me you were about to leave without a word.'

'If you treated me like a grown woman, I wouldn't have to elope,' Aurelia said tearfully. 'I am forty years old, Grandmama. This might be my last chance for happiness.'

'Balderdash!' Lady Pentelow closed her fingers around Aurelia's thin arm and propelled her towards the morning room. 'Mr Johnson, you will make your explanations and apologies to my grandson. I hear his footsteps on the stairs now. Aurelia, you will come with me and we will have a sensible discussion about your future.'

Dolly exchanged worried glances with Freddie. She hurried after Lady Pentelow and Aurelia. 'Wait . . . please allow Aurelia to make her own decision, ma'am.'

Lady Pentelow came to a halt outside the morning room. 'You are a troublesome girl, Adela, and I've no doubt you encouraged Aurelia to behave so recklessly.'

'Aurelia is a grown woman, ma'am,' Dolly said angrily.

Freddie laid his hand on Dolly's arm. 'Let them talk it over on their own, Dolly.'

She glanced up at him, frowning. 'But Aurelia will be browbeaten into submission.'

'It's time Aurelia stood up for herself.'

Lady Pentelow opened the door. 'Wait out here, Adela, and you, too, Dorrington. I have a few words to say to Aurelia.' She gave her granddaughter a gentle shove and Aurelia stumbled into the room. The door closed on them, but raised voices coming from the entrance hall made Dolly turn to see her father at the foot of the stairs, berating Luke in a loud voice.

'My father doesn't sound as if he approves either, but he must take the blame for this situation. It was he who brought Luke to this house in the full knowledge that he was evading detection by the police.'

'I'm sorry, Dolly. I don't know what else to say. Piers should not have placed his family in jeopardy. I will be more than happy to take you home today, if you so wish.'

'I don't think I can stay here any longer, Freddie. Lady Pentelow has never approved of me, although I can't think why. Perhaps Aurelia will choose Luke – who knows?'

'We can leave immediately. You have only to say the word.' Freddie stroked her cheek with the tip of his finger. 'However, I am absolutely starving,' he added, smiling. 'Do you think it would be terribly insensitive of us to have breakfast while the family sort this out between themselves?'

'I don't suppose there's anything I can say or do that will make any difference, so, yes. I think I might manage a slice or two of bacon and some buttered eggs. Come with me, Freddie. I'll show you to the dining room.'

Dolly ate sparingly but Freddie obviously enjoyed his breakfast.

'I haven't eaten since yesterday evening,' he said ruefully. 'And I left the inn where I was staying in the early hours this morning so that I could get here in plenty of time.'

'Time for what?' Dolly eyed him over the rim of her coffee cup. 'Why did you come in such a rush?'

'I don't know exactly. I had a feeling that you might need someone on your side, Dolly. You know I am always on hand, if necessary.'

Dolly sighed. 'Well, there doesn't seem to be much point in my staying on here. Father may think he needs me, but the truth is that he doesn't need anyone. He takes a brief interest in someone and then moves on to someone or something else. He would be quite happy for me to live here and dwindle into an old maid so that I can inherit this old house and all its ghosts. I don't feel that anyone was ever happy living here. Perhaps that is why Aurelia is so eager to leave.'

'We can take her to Rockwood with us, if she wishes, Dolly.' Freddie rose to his feet as the door opened to admit Aurelia.

'Don't get up, Freddie.' Aurelia's eyes were red and swollen but she seemed calm.

Dolly jumped to her feet and gave Aurelia a hug. 'Are you all right? What did your grandmama say?'

Aurelia returned the embrace and then broke away. 'She was quite kind, considering how she must feel about us planning to elope.'

Dolly sank back onto her seat. 'Are you still going with Luke?'

'Piers spirited him away. I don't know where they have gone, but Luke did not put up a fight. I don't think he can have loved me truly if he gave up so easily.' Aurelia pulled up a chair and sat down. She reached for the coffee pot and filled a cup.

'I am so sorry,' Dolly said gently. 'You could go after them. Maybe Father has forced Luke to leave.'

'Luke is younger and I dare say he is stronger than my brother. I think he cares more for his freedom than he does for me. Maybe I fell in love with a romantic dream.' Aurelia added several lumps of sugar to her coffee and stirred it, staring moodily into space.

'Again, I am so sorry.' Dolly reached out to lay her hand on Aurelia's. 'Freddie has come to take me home and I've decided to return to Rockwood. I was hoping you might come with us.'

'I don't know, Dolly. I can't really think of anything at the moment. I would be a burden to your mama and Alex.'

'I'm sure they would be delighted to see you,' Freddie said firmly. 'I know Alex would. He's very fond of you, Aurelia.'

'Maybe, but we've been apart for too many years. I am set in my ways now, like an old maid.'

'Nonsense,' Dolly smiled, shaking her head. 'You are still a lovely woman, especially when you are your normal happy self. If you come with us I could take you to the theatre and show you what I do there. I'm sure Nick would be delighted to see you.'

Aurelia pulled a face. 'I didn't treat him very well all those years ago. I expect he has a new love now, unless he is married, of course.'

'Nick isn't married. He has shown interest in our opera star, Liza Day, but I think she is very ambitious. I would not be surprised if we lost her to one of the major opera houses.'

'You are already packed and ready to leave,' Freddie added. 'Come with us, Aurelia. You can return to Trevenor when you wish, but some time away from here would help you to recover from your disappointment.'

'You don't think Luke was sincere in his affection for me, do you?'

Dolly and Freddie exchanged worried glances.

'I don't honestly know.' Dolly patted Aurelia's hand. 'But, in any event, he will have to give himself up sooner or later.'

'And he will probably be sent back to prison,' Freddie added. 'If he's caught now it doesn't bode well for him.'

'I need to speak to Piers,' Aurelia said, rising to her feet, but she swayed dizzily and collapsed back on her chair.

'You need to eat something,' Dolly said severely. 'Stay here with Freddie and I will see if I can find Father and Luke.'

'All right, if you're sure.' Aurelia closed her eyes. 'I will have some toast in a minute.'

Dolly rose from the table. 'Look after her, Freddie. I won't be long.' She hurried from the room and made her way to the stables, which seemed like the obvious place to look for Luke and her father.

They were seated in the chaise, about to leave, when Dolly caught up with them.

'Where are you taking him, Father?'

'One of our ships is ready to sail. I was going to take him to the harbour anyway, but this madness has made it even more urgent.' Piers raised the whip to encourage the horse to walk on.

Luke leaned over, fixing Dolly with a pleading look. 'Please tell Aurelia that I do love her. But I was being selfish in wanting to drag her into my world. It's no place for a woman like her.'

'Walk on,' Piers flicked the whip over the horse's head.

'Tell her I am sorry,' Luke called as the chaise moved off at a brisk pace.

Dolly walked slowly back to the house. She knew in her heart that Aurelia had had a lucky escape, but it would take time for her to recover from yet another broken heart.

She went first to the morning room where Lady Pentelow was taking coffee.

'Oh, so you've decided to tell me what was about to happen?' Lady Pentelow glowered at Dolly, replacing her cup with a thud on its saucer.

'I am sorry, ma'am. I couldn't betray a confidence.'

'Your loyalty is misplaced. I have met men like Luke Johnson before and they always cause trouble. Aurelia may be over forty, but she is still an innocent when it comes to worldly matters. She goes from one disastrous romance to another.'

'Lady Pentelow, I know you don't like me very much, but I am very fond of Aurelia. I've asked her to accompany us today when we leave for Rock-wood. I think a few weeks away from Trevenor might help her to recover from this sad situation.'

'I do not dislike you, Adela. I disapprove of you and your modern behaviour. In my day a young woman remained at home with her parents until an eligible man offered for her, but you have chosen to work in a theatre, of all places. Of course, I blame Felicia for that.'

'I am sorry you feel like that, of course, but this is about Aurelia, not me. She will come to Rockwood whether you give her your permission or not, but it would be so much more pleasant if you were to agree, and send her off with a smile.'

Lady Pentelow fixed Dolly with an inscrutable stare. 'I won't try to stop her,' she said after a brief pause. 'You may tell her that, even though I do not approve of her leaving. Pentelows do not run away. I have no idea what Piers will say to all this.'

'Aurelia is a Blanchard, ma'am. It seems to me that my father has done a great deal of running away in the past. I am thankful that I do not take after him.'

'There are times when I doubt very much if you are Piers' daughter, and this is one of them.'

Dolly stared at her in amazement. 'What do you mean by that, ma'am?'

'It doesn't matter, but just watch your tongue, young lady.'

'No, ma'am. You can't say something like that and expect me to forget it immediately.'

'You must ask your mother. I will say no more on the subject.' Lady Pentelow rose to her feet. 'I suggest you leave as soon as you have gathered together your belongings. Take Aurelia with you and be damned to the Careys and all who live at Rockwood Castle. I will never set foot there again.' She marched out of the room, leaving the air crackling with her displeasure.

Dolly shook her head. She had not expected to release so much anger, but she realised that resentment of that nature must have been building up for years. It had now found a way to escape and Lady Pentelow had said her piece. The inference that Piers Blanchard was not her father was disturbing, and yet believable. Dolly knew the answer lay with one person only and she was determined to speak openly to her mother. She could not wait to return to Rockwood. It was definitely time to go home.

Two days later Dolly, Aurelia and Freddie arrived at Rockwood Castle to an enthusiastic welcome. Dolly was still struggling with the spiteful things that Lady Pentelow had said, although in her heart she suspected that it was the truth – Piers Blanchard was not her real father. It would explain why she had such a bond with Alex, but it was a difficult subject to broach. If true, it meant that Mama had been unfaithful to her first husband. Somehow the right moment to seek the truth did not happen during the first heady days of being welcomed home. Besides which, Mama was always busy.

Rosalind took Aurelia under her wing and Alex refrained from teasing his sister. In fact, everyone went out of their way to be kind to Aurelia, so much so that she begged Dolly to tell the family that she would rather be treated as if nothing untoward had happened. It was then that Dolly decided to take Aurelia to the theatre. Nick would know how to handle the situation better than almost anyone.

It was a warm and mellow September day. A golden sun shone from a cloudless sky, and the leaves on the trees were beginning to change colour. The warm earth smelled of plum pudding as Dolly reined in the horse outside the theatre. She tossed the reins to Alfie, who emerged at the sound of their arrival. He had been a small, sickly child when Nancy brought him from the backstreets in London, together with the rest of the gang, but now he was tall, broad shouldered and a picture of health. His infectious grin always made Dolly respond with a wide smile. Alfie always seemed cheerful, no matter what.

'Good morning, Miss Dolly. It's a pleasure to see you back here.'

'Thank you, Alfie. I think you know Mrs Gibbs. She's staying at the castle for a while.'

Alfie tipped his cap. 'Yes, of course. Good morning, ma'am.'

Aurelia smiled and nodded.

Dolly could feel the tension that had built up within Aurelia during the short carriage ride from Rockwood. She gave her an encouraging smile.

'Well, we're here. Is Mr Gibson in the office, Alfie?'

'Yes, Miss Dolly. Shall I announce you?'

Dolly laughed. 'No need, thank you. Just take care of the horse and trap for me.' Dolly alighted and Aurelia followed more slowly. 'Come on, Aurelia. I'm sure Nick will be delighted to see you.'

Aurelia murmured a muffled response as they entered the building. She came to a halt in the foyer, gazing round, wide-eyed. 'I'd forgotten how grand this is. It's years since I was last here.'

'Dolly, you've come home.' Nick strolled out of the office, but he came to a sudden halt when he saw Aurelia. 'Aurelia . . . I mean, Mrs Gibbs. This is an unexpected pleasure.' His smile was genuine as he stepped forward to take Aurelia's hands in his. 'Welcome to the Pavilion Theatre.'

'Thank you, Nick. It's good to see you again.' Aurelia smiled, visibly relaxing as she squeezed his fingers. 'I'd forgotten what a lovely theatre this is.'

'I'm ready to start work again, Nick,' Dolly added earnestly. 'You haven't replaced me, have you?'

Nick laughed. 'You are irreplaceable, Dolly. You can come back as soon as you are ready.'

'How about this afternoon? I can't wait any longer.'

'This afternoon would be wonderful. I'll let you settle in while I give Mrs Gibbs a conducted tour of the theatre. Did you tell her about our masked ball?'

'She did indeed,' Aurelia said, finding her voice at last. 'It sounds wonderful. Maybe you should do something similar while I am here.'

'Will you be staying long?'

'I have no immediate plans to return to Cornwall,' Aurelia said with an arch smile.

Dolly tried not to gloat. It was obvious that there was still mutual attraction between the two of them. She had never understood why a handsome, kind-hearted man like Nick Gibson had never married. Perhaps the answer lay here?

'Shall I take a look at the bookings, Nick?'

'An excellent plan. Come with me, Aurelia. I'll point out the improvements we've made since you were last here.'

'I think I owe you something of an apology for the way I treated you, Nick.'

'Nonsense. The time was not right for us then. We will always be friends.'

Their voices died away as Nick led Aurelia into the auditorium.

Dolly was smiling as she entered the office but her smile faded when she saw the chaos created during the time she had been away in Cornwall. If she had required anything to convince her that she was needed at the Pavilion, this was it. Papers were strewn everywhere: flyers advertising the next production were jumbled together with bills, invoices and notes in Nick's handwriting. It seemed as if he needed to make lists of all the things he had to do and then discarded them. The floor was barely visible beneath a carpet of screwed-up or torn paper, and unwashed teacups littered the desk and shelves. Flies buzzed around the dregs of sour milk in a jug that had been long forgotten.

'Thank goodness you've returned, Dolly.' Liza Day stood in the doorway, shaking her head. 'Look what happens when you go away.'

'I can see this will take some time to sort out.'

'You are back permanently, I hope.'

'Yes, I am. Living in Cornwall is not for me. But what about you, Liza?' Dolly eyed her warily. 'You look very smart, I must say.'

'I know, I do. In fact I have had the most wonderful luck, Dolly. I've been offered a season at Covent Garden, and I've come to tell Nick.'

'He doesn't know yet?'

Liza produced a letter from her reticule. 'This only came today. I did an audition for Garson Thorne last week. I didn't tell Nick in case nothing came of it, but Garson said in all the years he's been directing opera singers, my voice is the purest and my range is amazing. I can't turn this down.'

'I think I've heard his name mentioned before. Wasn't he the man who gave Aunt Patricia a chance in his opera company?'

'I don't know about that. All I know is that this is his last season at Covent Garden. I am so fortunate to have him to direct me in a leading role.'

'Does this mean you will be living in London?'

'Yes. I need to find a lodging house near the theatre.'

'What about your ailing grandmother?'

'Nick helped me to find better accommodation for her. I've been able to see that she has proper meals and she's quite recovered now. Her next-door neighbour is going to keep an eye on her for me and I'll come down to see her whenever I can.'

'I'm very happy for you, Liza. But I'm sure that Nick will be sad to lose you.'

'He won't stand in my way and he'll find some-one to take my place,' Liza said airily. 'I enjoy his company, but I know he has never been serious about me.'

Dolly laughed. 'Lady Pentelow would say you are a bold young woman. She thinks that young ladies should remain at home waiting for a gentleman to sweep them off their feet.'

'Really?' Liza tossed her head. 'She does sound very old-fashioned.'

'Yes, and you can't say that of *my* grandmama. She will be sad to see you go, Liza, but I think she'll be pleased for you, too.'

'Your grandmama is someone I admire whole-heartedly. Felicia has defied convention very suc-cessfully and I hope to do the same.'

'I am sure you will. Good luck, Liza.'

'Thank you for everything, Dolly. If it weren't for you I would not be in this position today. I'll leave now. Say goodbye to Nick for me.' Liza strode out of the office with such an air of confidence that Dolly was convinced nothing would stop her march to fame and fortune. Dolly sighed and returned to the task of tidying up the mess that Nick had made.

It took an hour to sort everything into neat piles and by this time Dolly was feeling hungry. There was no sign of Nick and Aurelia, and the auditorium was empty apart from two cleaning women from the village. Dolly greeted them cheerfully and returned to the office, but she had lost concentration on the very dull work in hand and she left the theatre, heading for the stables.

Alfie met her in the doorway. 'Are you ready to go home, Miss Dolly?'

'Yes, Alfie. But I can't find Mrs Gibbs or Mr Gibson.'

'They drove off in Mr Gibson's trap about half an hour ago.'

'Did they leave a message?'

Alfie scratched his head, frowning. 'I don't think so, miss.'

'Oh, well. You'd better drive me home, Alfie. I will come back this afternoon and finish off the task I started this morning.'

'Of course, Miss Dolly. If you would wait a moment while I harness up Jubilee? It won't take me more than a few minutes.'

Dolly waited patiently, enjoying the warmth of the sun on her face. She loved this particular part of the Greystone estate. It brought back memories of the masked ball, although they were bittersweet. She had not seen Gus since then and, for all she knew, his regiment might have been shipped out to a conflict almost anywhere in the world. She knew it was for the best, but a small part of her still longed to be with him and she could not forget the sweetness of his kisses or the excitement she felt in his company. She had once imagined herself to be in love with Todd, but that was a girlish fancy. Todd was everything that Gus was not, but still her heart yearned for the swaggering, unreliable, undeniably attractive soldier.

She turned her head at the sound of carriage wheels on the dusty surface of the road and saw Freddie driving a gig that belonged to Rockwood stables. He reined in beside her.

'I thought you might wish to be at home in time for luncheon.'

'How did you know I was here? I might have gone off with Nick and Aurelia.'

'I saw them outside the Black Dog. I assumed that they were going to sample some of Mrs Causley's excellent steak pies. I believe she uses her mother-in-law's recipe, so they are bound to be delicious.'

Dolly waved to Alfie, who had just led Jubilee from the stables. 'Thank you, Alfie. I'm going home with Lord Dorrington. I won't need you after all.'

Alfie touched his cap and walked Jubilee in a wide circle so that he could lead him back to the stables.

Freddie handed Dolly into the gig. 'I would have

come earlier had I known that you were abandoned here.'

Dolly settled herself in the gig. 'Nonsense, Freddie. I could have walked. I've done it dozens of times in the past.'

'You are a very independent young lady.' Freddie climbed into the gig and picked up the reins. 'Are you determined to resume your job at the theatre?'

'There was never any doubt of that, Freddie. I love working here.'

'Would you give up your work to get married?'

Dolly shot him a sideways glance. 'I might. If the right man proposed to me.'

'Walk on.' Freddie flicked the reins and the horse ambled off towards the main gates of the Greystone estate. 'You know I hold you in great esteem, Dolly.'

She laughed. 'You sound very serious. What has brought this on?'

'I am thirty-four, Dolly. Years older than you.'

'I don't think that matters, Freddie. I enjoy your company. I never think about the age difference.'

'But I expect you would wish to marry someone nearer to you in age.'

'I hadn't given it much thought. I suppose I would.'

They lapsed into silence as Freddie concentrated on guiding the horse through the gates onto the lane that led to the village. He urged the horse to a fast trot.

'But you would consider me too old to marry someone of your age?' Freddie said tentatively.

'Have you met someone much younger than yourself? Don't tell me that you have fallen in love with Theodora Bennington?' Dolly laughed. 'Or one of her friends?'

'It was a rhetorical question, Dolly. Forget I said it.'

Dolly leaned forward. 'Look, Freddie. Army uniforms. I'd swear that is Gus and his friend Dunbar. What on earth are they doing in Rockwood? Please stop.'

Chapter Twenty-One

'No! Wait.' Dolly leaned forward, staring at the elegant young woman who had just emerged from the small haberdashery owned and run by Nurse Betts', sister, Iris. 'It's Josephine Mountjoy. She's stopped to talk to them. I didn't know she was acquainted with Gus.'

Freddie slowed the horse to a sedate walk. 'She seems to know him well.'

They were too far away to hear what was being said, but Josephine had linked arms with Gus.

'She's flirting with him,' Dolly said in disgust. 'Donald Dunbar seems to be amused, but I doubt if Josephine's brother would think her behaviour acceptable.'

'Dolly, you sound like Hester,' Freddie said, smiling. 'Do you want me to drive on and ignore them?'

'No. Stop, please.' Dolly barely waited for the vehicle to come to a halt before alighting.

Gus had seen her and he waved. 'Dolly . . . Miss Blanchard.'

Josephine turned to give her a beaming smile. 'Dolly, dear. How nice to see you again. I thought you had moved permanently to Cornwall.'

'No, Miss Mountjoy. I was just visiting.' Dolly shot a wary glance at Dunbar.

'Good afternoon, Miss Blanchard.' Dunbar swept off his peaked cap, acknowledging her with a theatrical bow.

Dolly was inwardly fuming, although she was at a loss as to why she felt so annoyed. Gus was nothing to her and Josephine was a very attractive woman.

'It's good to see you all,' Dolly said, forcing herself to smile. 'You'll forgive me if I don't stay to chat. I am expected at home for luncheon.'

'How fortunate you are.' Josephine clutched Gus's arm even tighter. 'Our cook serves the most dreadful meals, even when she's sober. I envy your family at the castle, Dolly.'

'We were toying with the idea of eating at the Black Dog,' Gus said hastily. 'Won't you join us, Dolly?'

'Thank you but as I said I have to go home. It's good to see you.' Dolly turned on her heel and walked quickly towards the chaise where Freddie was waiting for her. She sensed that Gus was staring after her but she forced herself to look straight ahead.

Freddie leaped to the ground and helped her into the chaise. 'Are you all right, Dolly? You look rather pale?'

'I'm rather hungry. I will feel better when I've had something to eat. It was a very busy morning.'

Freddie climbed up to sit beside her. 'Did that fellow say something to upset you?'

'I hardly spoke to him. Miss Mountjoy took centre stage, as always. I'm surprised she doesn't audition for a part in Grandmama's next production at the theatre.'

'I doubt if Mrs de Marney would approve of Josephine Mountjoy. There are very few people who have anything to do with the Mountjoys.' Freddie urged the horse to a trot. 'No one seems to have any details of the scandal that made them flee from London to hide away in Cottingham Manor, but whatever it was seems to have followed them here.'

'I remember the scene at the masked ball. I can't say I like either of them, especially having seen Josephine throw herself at Gus. Has she no pride?'

'Forget her, Dolly. As to Gus Baker, you know he's not for you, especially after the way he compromised your good name by taking you to London. Perhaps he is the ideal partner for Miss Mountjoy. They seem to be cut from the same cloth.'

'She is welcome to him,' Dolly said icily. 'Let's go home.'

*

No matter what anyone said, Dolly could not forget the way Josephine had clung to Gus's arm or the way she had smiled up at him. Gus himself had not seemed to mind; in fact he had obviously enjoyed being treated like a god by someone as beautiful and wealthy as Miss Mountjoy.

Dolly returned to the theatre after luncheon but she found it difficult to concentrate.

It was mid-afternoon by the time Nick appeared. He was smiling happily and he seemed very pleased with himself.

Dolly faced him, unsmiling. 'Liza Day called in after you left with Aurelia this morning.'

'Really? What did she want?'

'She's leaving Rockwood when the season ends. She's been offered a leading role in one of Garson Thorne's productions.' Dolly could see from his expression that this remark had upset him, and she wished she had broached the subject more tactfully. 'I'm sorry, Nick.'

He sighed. 'Don't be. I suppose I was expecting it. Liza is too talented to be buried here in the country. We do reasonably well considering we are so far from the big cities, but she has a wonderful voice. One day she will be as famous as your grandmother was in her heyday.'

'Will we have to arrange auditions for a replacement?'

'I suppose so, Dolly. I hadn't thought she would leave quite so soon. I was hoping she might stay for one more season.'

'Would you like me to set up the auditions, Nick? I'll be only too happy to help.'

He nodded vaguely. 'Yes, please do. You can arrange it to suit your grandmama. She always had first choice.'

'Of course. I'll go and see her at the hotel when I've finished tidying up in here.'

'Thank you. As a matter of fact I offered to take Aurelia for a carriage ride.'

'Excellent idea. She needs something to raise her spirits.'

'Thank you, Dolly. I knew you'd understand. I'll be back before the beginning of this evening's performance.' Nick hurried from the office, leaving Dolly to finish what she had begun before luncheon.

When she was satisfied that everything was in order, Dolly put on her bonnet and shawl and walked to the hotel where her grandmother and Claude had a suite of rooms. They had given up the cottage they had rented from Nancy, and had moved into the hotel where the staff waited on them hand and foot. Felicia had attempted to persuade Hester to give up the Dower House and move into the cottage, but had met with a firm refusal. Hester knew what she wanted and what was due to her as the widow of Vice-Admiral Sir Lucius Carey, Baronet. Felicia had to admit defeat and now she terrorised the staff at the hotel. Dolly made her way up two flights of stairs and knocked on the door of her grandmother's suite.

Claude smiled with genuine pleasure at the sight of her. 'Come in, my dear. I didn't realise that you had returned from Cornwall.'

Dolly stood on tiptoe to kiss his whiskery cheek. 'I couldn't stay away a moment longer, Grandpapa.'

Claude led her into the large drawing room, tastefully furnished with the addition of Felicia's knick-knacks and souvenirs of her travels abroad displayed on every available surface. Felicia was relaxing on a chaise longue beneath a tall window overlooking the deer park. She raised a languid hand.

'So you've deigned to visit us, have you, Adela?'

'I've only recently returned from Cornwall, Grandmama. I am just catching up with events at the theatre.'

Felicia snapped into a sitting position, eyebrows raised. 'What events? What haven't I been told?'

'Do take a seat, my dear,' Claude said gently. 'Would you like me to send for some tea or a glass of lemonade?'

'No, thank you.' Dolly perched on the edge of an upright chair. 'I'll come straight to the point. There's no easy way to say this, but Liza Day has accepted a leading role in Garson Thorne's last production at Covent Garden. He's retiring at the end of the next season.'

'No! Why didn't he inform me?' Felicia demanded crossly. 'Sometimes I hate being buried in the countryside, Claude. I think it's time we had a few weeks in London.'

'I'm sure that would be lovely,' Dolly said hastily. 'But first we need to find another prima donna. Would you like me to set up an audition, Grandmama?'

Felicia rolled her eyes. 'How tedious. I was hoping that Liza would stay on for the next few seasons. She needs the experience.'

'Would you have turned down the opportunity to take a leading role in a London production at her age, my love?' Claude smiled benignly. 'You don't need to answer because I know very well that nothing would have stopped you. You have proved yourself world-wide. Now it's Liza's turn.'

'Well, if you put it like that I suppose I have to agree.' Felicia lay back against the cushions, fanning herself with her hand. 'Ring for a servant, Claude. I will have a tray of tea and some of those little fancies that Chef makes especially for me.'

Claude smiled and went to the mantelshelf to tug the bell pull. 'It shall be done, my love.'

'Grandmama, what do you say with regard to the audition?' Dolly could only hope that if she persisted she would get an answer. 'We may need to have two or even three auditions if we cannot find a suitable person.'

'I would take the leading role myself,' Felicia said with a heavy sigh, 'but it's time to give the younger singers a chance to prove themselves.'

'Then you don't mind if I arrange auditions for next week?'

'No, I suppose not.' Felicia turned to her husband. 'Claude, have we any events booked?'

'No, my love. Our diary is empty.'

'I remember a time when every page was filled with appointments, engagements and costume fittings. However, it seems we are free. Just let me know the day and time and we'll be there.' Felicia lay back, closing her eyes. 'I am a little fatigued. Claude will see you out, Adela.'

Claude beckoned to Dolly and she jumped to her feet. 'Thank you, Grandpapa. I'll let you know as soon as I've made the arrangements.'

He led her to the door and opened it. 'It's good to have you back at home where you belong, my dear.'

Dolly smiled. 'It's lovely to see you, too. I'll let you know when I have a day and a time.' Dolly left the room, passing the maid who was scurrying towards the private suite as if her life depended upon getting there as fast as possible. Dolly headed for the staircase. She did not envy the staff at the hotel having to be at Grandmama's beck and call day and night. However, she had more important things to worry about now, the main one being setting up the auditions. She would definitely have to ask Nick to help her with this task.

Dolly left the hotel and was about to walk back to the theatre when she heard hoofbeats and Gus rode up to her. He reined in the frisky animal, controlling it with expertise.

'Are you following me, Gus?' Dolly demanded angrily. 'It seems that everywhere I go you appear.'

He dismounted and walked beside her, leading his mount. 'Pure coincidence, Dolly. But a very pleasant one.'

'I've been home for less than two days and this is the third time our paths have crossed. Now that is a strange coincidence.'

He laughed. 'Perhaps I helped fate a little. I've missed you, Dolly.'

'You seemed very friendly with Miss Mountjoy.'

'Are you jealous, by any chance?'

Dolly tossed her head and quickened her pace. 'You flatter yourself, Gus. I made a mistake of trusting you once, but I soon realised how foolish that was when you chose to abandon me in London.'

'You knew that I had to return to my regiment, Dolly. You were only interested in making a name for yourself on the stage. That was your mistake, not mine.'

'Maybe, but I should never have let you persuade me to accompany you in the first place. You and I have nothing in common, Gus. If Nancy hadn't brought you to Rockwood when you were a boy we would never have met.'

'That would have been a tragedy for both of us.' Gus took her by the hand and closed his fingers around hers. 'You do care for me, don't you?'

Dolly snatched her hand free. 'You are so full of your own self-importance, Gus Baker. Go and charm

Miss Mountjoy. Leave me alone.' She marched off towards the theatre entrance, leaving Gus standing with his horse. He did not attempt to follow her.

At home that evening, the ladies had retired to the drawing room, leaving Alex, Tommy and Freddie to enjoy their brandy and cigars.

Aurelia talked about nothing other than the enjoyable time she had spent in Nick's company and how much she appreciated being at Rockwood, especially after being immured in Trevenor for years. Rosalind and Nancy listened sympathetically, but Dolly found her thoughts drifting in another direction entirely. However, the mention of Josephine Mountjoy's name made her pay attention.

'What did you say, Mama?'

Rosalind smiled. 'I didn't think you were listening, Dolly. You were far away.'

'I have to organise auditions for the next production, Mama. I was wondering how I should go about it. Grandmama was not much help and Claude dared not offend her by adding his suggestions.'

Rosalind sighed. 'Poor Claude.'

'What were you talking about just now, Mama? I thought you said something about Josephine Mountjoy. I saw her recently, chatting to Gus and Sergeant Dunbar.'

Rosalind and Nancy exchanged meaningful glances.

'Josephine Mountjoy isn't the person she claims to be,' Rosalind said cautiously. 'That is gossip you will hear eventually, so I don't feel the need to keep silent.'

'Go on, Rosie.' Nancy sipped her coffee. 'Tell Dolly what you told me.'

'Yes, do please, Mama.' Dolly leaned forward eagerly.

'Well, I had this from a very trustworthy source. Apparently, Josephine Mountjoy was born Giuseppina Bougie, in the slums of Milan. She sang on street corners until she was spotted by an impresario who took her under his wing.'

Dolly gasped. 'Was that Jared Mountjoy?'

'Yes,' Nancy said excitedly. 'And Jared's real name is Jared Conti. He had an Italian father and an English mother. We had all this from Fletcher, who has struck up an unlikely friendship with the Mountjoys' gatekeeper, Tuttle.'

'I remember him,' Dolly said thoughtfully. 'He is rude and grumpy. Not the sort of person I would wish to employ.'

Nancy laughed. 'He sounds the ideal partner for Fletcher.'

'You don't mean that, Nancy,' Rosalind said, smiling. 'I know you're fond of Fletcher really.'

'Of course I am, but you must admit she hasn't the sweetest nature. Anyway, I'm sure she's devoted to Wolfe, and Tuttle is a passing fancy.'

'Aunt Nancy, you're being very mischievous.' Dolly tried hard to keep a straight face. 'Do go on, Mama. How does Tuttle come into the story?'

'Apparently he's been with the Mountjoys ever since they fled to America.'

'Why did they leave Italy?'

'Let me tell her,' Nancy said eagerly. 'Josephine had an affair with a well-known politician. Jared tried unsuccessfully to blackmail the man and it ended up in a fight. The politician died and Jared was a wanted man. He and Josephine fled to America, where they changed their names.'

'But why did they come to London?'

Nancy shook her head. 'I don't know, but apparently they made a lot of money in California during the gold rush. They went to London first, and then they came to Devonshire and ended up purchasing Cottingham Manor.'

'So Jared is still wanted in Italy?'

'I assume so,' Nancy said, frowning. 'Fletcher couldn't get any more information from Tuttle. But it seems that Jared and Josephine are actually man and wife.'

'They're married?' Dolly looked from one to the other.

'So Fletcher said,' Nancy said with a wry smile. 'I suppose they thought it looked less suspicious if they were simply brother and sister. It seems we have a murderer in our midst.'

'It could have been a fair fight with a tragic ending, Nancy.' Rosalind shook her head. 'We don't know all the facts.'

'We do know they lied to us,' Dolly said angrily.

'But it does not sound as if they are wanted by the police in this country.'

Nancy put her head on one side. 'What are you thinking, Dolly? I know that look and it usually means trouble.'

Dolly laughed. 'Well, if Josephine is such a wonderful singer she might be interested in auditioning for the leading role in the next production.'

'Surely not?' Nancy reached for her cup of coffee and took a sip. 'She would not want to draw attention to herself.'

'I don't know about that.' Dolly frowned thoughtfully. 'She has gone out of her way to make everyone notice her. I believe she is too much of a diva to want to retire gracefully, even for the sake of her husband.'

'Given the circumstances, I doubt if he would allow her to perform,' Rosalind said slowly. 'I think you ought to be very careful about what you suggest to Nick and Mama. You don't want to bring the theatre into disrepute, do you, Dolly?'

'No, but if the scandal should become public it would be wonderful publicity. I think people would flock from far and wide to see the production.'

'Be very careful, Dolly,' Rosalind said anxiously. 'I don't think Sir Jared would take it kindly if you tried to interfere in their lives.'

'He has obviously given himself a title. Isn't that a crime in itself?' Nancy replaced her cup on its saucer. She clutched her swollen belly and laughed.

'Oh, dear. I'm afraid my baby has woken up and is kicking me.'

'I expect it's another boy,' Dolly said, smiling.

Nancy sighed. 'I was hoping to have a girl this time, but this baby is as restless as his three brothers were. He is just starting his evening clog dance. It seems he cannot bear me to sit quietly for any length of time.'

'If you continue to produce boys you will have to send them to a public school with a football team,' Rosalind said, smiling.

'This is definitely the last one.' Nancy stood up and stretched. 'Anyway, there's no need to be smug because you had two girls. I love all my boys, whether I gave birth to them or not.'

'Don't forget May,' Rosalind said quickly. 'She is also one of your protégées.'

'May is a darling,' Nancy agreed, nodding. 'But she is more yours than mine, Rosie. I have had no experience of bringing up a girl, but you have done wonderfully. She's devoted to you, Dolly, and to Phoebe as well.'

Dolly laughed. 'Thank you, Aunt Nancy. I'll take that as a compliment to me as well as to my mama.' She rose to her feet. 'I feel like a stroll in the rose garden. I love it at night with the sound of the waves breaking on the shingle at the bottom of the cliffs.'

'Would you like me to come with you?' Rosalind was about to rise but Dolly motioned her to remain seated.

'No, thank you, Mama. I need to think about the

auditions. I'm certainly not going to complicate matters by letting Josephine know that we need a new prima donna. The less we see of her, the better, in my opinion.'

'All right, Dolly. But put your shawl on. It's getting colder in the evenings now.'

'Yes, Mama.' Dolly picked up her lacy woollen shawl and headed for the doorway.

'She's a grown woman now, Rosie,' Nancy said severely. 'She's no longer your baby girl.'

Dolly did not wait to hear her mother's response as she headed towards the music room and the French doors leading out into the rose garden. She had reached the pergola where climbing roses trailed over the woody stems of wisteria where the flowers had turned into seed heads. She thought she was alone but the breeze carried a waft of cigar smoke mingled with the heady perfume of the flowers. A man's outline was blurred by the cascading greenery, but when he turned his head she knew at once that it was Freddie.

She breathed a sigh of relief and walked towards him. She had not been ready to talk to Alex, for the simple reason that he might ask her about her relationship with his cousin, and she did not want to lie. She loved her papa, Alex, with all her heart but she did not want to tell him that she actually disliked the man who was her father by blood. Piers Blanchard would never match up to Alex, no matter how hard he tried.

'Freddie, it's you.'

He stubbed out the butt of his cigar, grinding the tobacco into the flowerbed. 'Dolly, it's getting cold. You should be indoors.'

'I'm not a hothouse bloom, Freddie. I love the night air, especially at this time of the year.'

'I know what you mean, and I agree.'

Dolly could not see his features clearly but she could hear the smile in his voice. 'I knew you would understand. I like to come out here when I have a problem to solve.'

He proffered his arm. 'Shall we walk? It's a little chilly to stand about.'

'Gladly.' Dolly tucked her hand in the crook of his arm. Freddie was so familiar and his presence so comforting. He was the kind uncle of her child-hood and now an even kinder friend.

'What is the problem? Can I help?'

'Your advice is always welcome, but this is about the theatre. Liza Day has accepted a leading role in Garson Thorne's last production before he retires. That leaves us without a leading lady for the new season and I have to arrange auditions.'

'Surely that's Nick's job?'

'Ordinarily, yes, but he's only interested in Aurelia at the moment. Apparently they were quite close some years ago.'

'And now they're rekindling an old flame?'

'It would seem so, although they've only just met again after years apart. Anyway, it leaves me in charge of auditions.'

'I thought that your grandmama would be the person to arrange them.'

'I went to see her but she expects me to do it, although of course she will be there to choose Liza's successor. I have to make everything ready.'

'Would you like me to have a word with Nick? He is the theatre manager, after all.'

'No, Freddie. Thank you, but I have to sort this out myself. I'll give it more thought.'

'I'm afraid I am not much help.'

'Just talking about it makes things clearer in my mind.'

'You know, Dolly. You don't have to do this. I mean you could stop working in the theatre and . . .' Freddie paused, gazing down at her.

'What are you suggesting? That I give up and wait for an eligible man to propose marriage?'

'Something like that.' Freddie took both her hands in his. 'I know I'm a lot older than you, but we've always got on well together, haven't we, Dolly?'

'We talked about this before, and yes, you've always been wonderful to me.'

Freddie cleared his throat nervously. 'You know how much I care for you, don't you?'

'Of course I do.' Dolly withdrew her hands swiftly. 'I don't know what you're trying to tell me, Freddie. But I think it's time to say good night.'

'Dolly, if I don't say this now I doubt if I'll ever have the courage to speak up again.'

A sudden feeling of panic made Dolly back away. 'Please don't say any more.'

'I can't stop now I've gone this far. If you could consider me as a husband, I would love you and give you anything you wanted, Dolly. You would share everything I have.'

Dolly shook her head. 'No, please, Freddie. I understand that you are lonely and you need a wife to produce an heir, but you could have your pick of the marriageable women in the whole country.'

'I've put this badly. I don't want anyone else – that's what I'm trying to tell you. In my clumsy way, Dolly, I am telling you that I love you.'

'Please don't, Freddie. I want things to be as they always were.'

Dolly turned and ran. She could hear Freddie calling to her but she closed her ears to his entreaties. The moon had hidden behind clouds that obscured the stars and a sudden flash of lightning was followed by a crash of thunder. Dolly did not stop until she reached her bedroom and she locked the door.

Freddie had ruined everything. She might have flirted with him occasionally, but that had been in fun; now it was spoiled and she would never think of him in the same way again. She was angry with Freddie and furious with herself for being so blind. She wondered how she would ever face him again after tonight's humiliating episode.

Chapter Twenty-Two

Dolly was up early next morning. She left for the theatre before the rest of the family came down to breakfast, and when she returned home late that afternoon she discovered that Freddie had left for Dorrington Place. A feeling of relief swept over her and she managed to avoid the enquiring glances from her mother and Aunt Nancy. They seemed to sense when she was troubled, no matter how hard she tried to hide her feelings, and the last thing Dolly wanted was a cross-examination from the two women she loved most in the world. However, she had to admit that united on a difficult subject, they made the Spanish Inquisition look like a tea party.

In the end she received help from the most unexpected source when her uncle Walter came across her in the library, frowning over an advertisement she was attempting to write.

'No matter how I try to word this, it doesn't come out as I wish,' Dolly said, sighing.

'I am well up in the literary world.' Walter puffed out his chest. 'In fact I am going to London tomorrow to see my publisher. If you like I can take the advertisement to *The Times* office and make sure it goes in the correct column.'

'Oh, would you? Thank you so much. I haven't had any help with regard to arranging the auditions and we haven't much time before the start of the next season.'

Walter frowned. 'Nick is being very lazy. I know he's fallen head over heels for Aurelia, yet again, but he still has his job to do.'

'Aurelia has that effect on gentlemen,' Dolly said ruefully. 'I would like to see her happy, and Nick is a lovely person.'

'It was the best day of my life when I married Louise. I can't think of any other woman who would put up with me. Most of the time I am working on my novels or poetry, and if I am not actually writing I have the themes going round and round in my head.'

'I think the answer is simple – she loves you for who you are.'

Walter laughed. 'So young and yet so wise. And what about you, Dolly? Do you have dreams of marriage and children, or are you going to be a woman with a career? Don't tell me you are planning to become one of those tiresome women who demand emancipation?'

'Of course I sympathise with their aims, but I am too caught up with the theatre to have time for anything else.'

'Or any one person? A gentleman we know very well, for instance?'

Dolly stared at him in surprise. 'You know about Freddie?'

'My dear girl, it stood out a mile. I might appear to be in a world of my own – although to tell the truth that is often the case – but I do sometimes see things that others miss. It's been obvious for some time that Freddie has a very soft spot for you.'

'I didn't see it myself and now I feel awful, Uncle Walter. He tried to propose to me and I handled it very badly. I was too shocked to be kind.'

'Don't blame yourself. Freddie is old enough to take a rejection or two, even from someone on whom he obviously dotes. But he will get over it in time. You must not allow yourself to become involved more deeply from pity. That would be a disaster. It has happened in this family before.'

Dolly eyed him warily. 'Are you referring to my mother and Piers Blanchard?'

'You don't refer to him as your father?'

'I tried to love him, but I feel nothing for him. Am I a bad person? I don't love my real father and

I don't love Freddie, at least not in the way he wants me to.'

Walter stroked a wayward strand of hair from Dolly's forehead. 'I am going to tell you something now, Dolly. As I said, people don't think I take much notice of what is going on around me, but I don't believe Piers is your father.'

'You don't? Why do you say that?'

'Piers should never have married your mama. He made her very unhappy. I'm sure you know about the time that Piers and Alexander were injured and taken to a convent hospital in Northern France.'

'Yes, I did hear something of the sort.'

'I'm very fond of Rosie. I know her better than Patsy or Bertie did, and I could see the change in her when she returned from France. I knew then that she and Alex had fallen in love. They tried to hide it from the family, but I could see it in the way they looked at each other and the different tone of voice that Alex used when he spoke to Rosie. I can't prove it, of course. The only person who knows for certain is your mama, but I would stake my life on the fact that your papa is truly Alexander Blanchard.'

'I always felt that he was my father. I love Alex and I really don't like Piers. I think it's time I was told the truth.'

'I agree, but it would have consequences for everyone, not least you.'

'What do you mean?'

'Put simply, if what I suspect is true, your parents

were not married to each other when you were born. You know what that means. Of course.'

'I am a love child. How romantic – but I do see that it makes me less of a good marriage prospect. I have no fortune to make up for my deficiencies.'

'The right man will not care for any of that, and those who do care are not worth bothering about.' Walter kissed the top of her head and sat down beside her. 'Now what about that advertisement for a prima donna? What have you written so far . . . ?'

With Walter's help Dolly managed to produce an advertisement that was both brief and to the point. Walter tucked it into his breast pocket and promised faithfully to deliver it in person to the newspaper office.

When he had gone, Dolly rose slowly to her feet. She had pushed the subject firmly to the back of her mind while she was concentrating on the advertisement for a new star, but now her uncle's words came flooding back to her. There was only one person who could tell her the truth about her parentage and that was Mama. Dolly went in search of her mother.

Rosalind was in the music room with Phoebe, who was looking mutinous.

'Ask your sister, Phoebe,' Rosalind said, sighing. 'Dolly, please tell Phoebe why she is not allowed to go shopping in Exeter without a chaperone.'

Dolly shrugged. 'You know why, Phoebe. Stop

being a brat. Your trouble is that you are spoilt. You always get your own way.'

'You are being horrid,' Phoebe said, pouting ominously. 'May and I want to go together. We don't want Fletcher walking behind us like a prison warder.'

'Maybe you would prefer Wolfe.' Rosalind sighed. 'Be reasonable, dear.'

'I won't go then.' Phoebe flounced out of the room, slamming the door behind her.

'May I have a word with you, Mama?' Dolly asked nervously. 'Or is this a bad time?'

'No, of course not, Dolly. I always have time for you. What is it?'

'I was glad to come home from Trevenor, Mama. I didn't enjoy my stay there.'

'I'm so sorry. What went wrong?'

Dolly walked over to the French doors, breathing in the scent of the fading roses. 'I don't get along well with Piers.'

'He is your father, Dolly. Maybe if you knew him better . . .'

'He abandoned you, Mama. He spent years in the penal colony and even when he was pardoned he chose to pursue his own ambitions.'

'No one is perfect, Dolly. You'll find that out as you get older.'

Dolly turned to look her mother in the eye. 'Will you answer one question? I want the truth.'

'Of course. What is it?'

'Is Piers really my father, or is it Alex?'

Rosalind's cheeks paled and she did not answer immediately.

'Please, Mama. I think I have a right to know.'

'Come and sit beside me, Dolly. I can't shout across the room.'

Dolly hurried to her mother's side. 'I want the truth, please, Mama.'

'I was in love with Piers when we married, or I thought I was. At first it was fine and I think we were happy, but he was involved in criminal matters about which I knew nothing.'

'And Alex?'

'Alex and I always got on well together. We were close friends before I married Piers, and after that Alex became engaged to Aunt Patsy. Anyway, it seemed that fate was determined to throw us together. When I heard that Piers had been seriously injured in a shipwreck and he and Alex were in a hospital in France, naturally I packed my things and set off for France. Hester accompanied me and we rented a rather creepy villa close to the hospital where Piers lay unconscious. Alex was in another room with a badly broken leg.' Rosalind paused with a faraway look in her eyes.

'So what happened then?'

'When he was well enough, we moved Alex to the villa. Piers was still in hospital and gradually Alex and I realised that we were in love.'

'And so Alex *is* my father.'

'It wasn't deliberate, Dolly. It only happened once, but when I discovered that I was going to have a baby I was so happy. I'm sorry, Dolly. Perhaps we should have told you sooner.'

'But you were content to allow me to think that Piers Blanchard is my father.'

'No, that's not true. Neither Alex nor I wanted the deception, but we both knew that the world is a cruel place, especially for someone born out of wedlock. The disgrace, if you wish to call it that, was ours. We did it to protect you.'

'I don't know what to think,' Dolly said slowly. 'But I am glad that Alex is my real father. I've always thought of him as my papa.'

'And he loves you, Dolly, make no mistake about that. I hope you will forgive us for keeping the truth from you.'

'Does Freddie know?'

Rosalind's eyes widened. 'Why would we tell Freddie?'

'He's always been so close to you and Nancy.'

'Has something happened, Dolly? You would tell me, wouldn't you?'

'He asked me to marry him.'

'Freddie wants to marry you?'

'There is nothing between us, Mama. At least not on my side. I've always thought of him as family, as a dear friend. I didn't realise that he was thinking otherwise.'

'Poor Freddie. He's doomed to fall in love with

the wrong women. You didn't accept him, did you? I mean, he's a wonderful person and you'd be a very rich woman if you were fond of him.'

'I didn't accept him. I do love him but not in the way he would wish. I feel dreadful for causing him pain.'

'You mustn't feel like that. Come here and let me give you a hug, my poor girl.' Rosalind held out her arms.

'I don't know what to do, Mama.' Dolly allowed her mother to comfort her as if she were a small child. 'He's been so good to me.'

'Marrying him out of pity would be a great mistake. Freddie will recover eventually. Besides which, he must know that he's too old for you.'

'Yes, and that makes it worse.'

'Nonsense, Dolly. It isn't your fault. Freddie is a wonderful person and a dear friend, but he isn't for you, of that I am sure.'

'Thank you, Mama.' Dolly extricated herself from the warmth of her mother's arms. 'I feel better having told you, and I'm glad I know who my real father is. I dislike Piers and I hate Trevenor. I don't want to inherit it.'

Rosalind laughed. 'I wouldn't worry too much about that. Piers is a relatively young man. I don't think he will die in the near future. You must concentrate on your own life, Dolly. I want you to enjoy working at the theatre. The right man will come along but, in the meantime, you should do what you want to do. Now, I suggest you change for dinner and put all this behind you, if you can.'

'Thank you, Mama. All I have to do now is to make sure that the auditions are arranged in time for the next season.'

'I've always thought you should do more panto-mimes,' Rosie said thoughtfully. 'It might be a good idea to suggest that to your grandmama.'

'A pantomime?' Dolly gazed at her mother in ad-miration. 'You know your talent is wasted, Mama.'

'Oh, no. I have no talent for the theatre. Now your aunt Patsy was an opera singer for a while, and Nancy is a wonderful pianist.'

'Mama, that's it! We don't have to look too far for talent. We have it right here at Rockwood Castle.' Dolly rushed out of the room, wrapping her shawl around her shoulders as she crossed the entrance hall. 'James, send to the stables for the trap. I have an urgent errand to run before dinner.'

Dolly drove herself to Nick's cottage and hammered on the door. She could only hope she was in time to catch him before he left for the theatre.

Nick opened the door, staring at her in surprise. 'Dolly? What has happened? Has the theatre burned down?'

Dolly stepped over the threshold without waiting to be asked. A keen wind had numbed her hands and feet and her lacy shawl offered little protection from the elements.

'No, but I need to talk to you about the next season. It was Mama's suggestion, but I think it might solve all our problems. Can I come in?'

'You are in. Come and sit by the fire. There's a definite chill in the air this evening.'

Dolly took a seat on a rather saggy armchair by the fire. 'Liza is leaving us at the end of the month . . .'

'Yes, it's come as a bit of a shock but her big opportunity is in London.' Nick sat down opposite her.

'And after that I believe we have a month of orchestral concerts.'

'That's right. That has been booked for some time. It's the next opera season that worries me. Have you done anything about arranging auditions?'

'Yes, but that's not really my job, Nick. I had some help from Uncle Walter. He's taking the advertisement to *The Times* tomorrow.'

Nick frowned. 'I'm sorry, Dolly. You're right, of course. That should have been my job. I expect too much from you.'

'I don't mind, really. I'm glad to help, and Aurelia needs someone like you to take her mind off what happened in Cornwall.'

'She's been treated so badly by all the men she trusted. She deserves better.'

'She does indeed. But that's not why I'm here. The next opera season would include Christmas. The theatre put on a pantomime once when I was much younger and I loved it. Why don't we do that again? Mama reminded me that Aunt Patsy has a very good singing voice and Nancy plays the piano. Why not make use of the family? Maybe Grandmama might like a part in the production, too.'

'A family pantomime? I don't know how they would feel about performing, but in general it's a good idea. Until we can find a new prima donna to match Liza Day, I can't even plan another opera.'

'Why not throw the auditions open to everyone, Nick? We might find some hidden talent in the village.'

'The theatre should be here for everyone,' Nick said thoughtfully. 'Perhaps we have been too exclusive in our choice of programmes until now.'

'I think you're right. After all, we cannot compete with Covent Garden or the other opera houses. We might even have a season of music-hall acts.'

Nick laughed. 'I can't imagine your grandmama agreeing to that.'

'I think she might surprise you. Grandmama knows that theatre depends upon box office sales. She is a good businesswoman at heart, although she would rather die than admit to anything so vulgar.'

'Well, vulgar puts money in our pockets and keeps the theatres from bankruptcy. I think we should put this idea to her, Dolly.'

'Will you do it, or shall I?'

'It was your idea, Dolly. I think you ought to take

the credit for it.' Nick glanced at the brass clock on the mantelshelf. 'Is that the time? I should have been at the theatre ten minutes ago.' He rose to his feet. 'You'll have to excuse me, but we'll talk more about this in the morning. I'll endeavour to get to the theatre early.'

'This is so exciting. If Grandmama agrees to the plan we could attract an even wider audience. There would be no question of having to spend time and money on masquerade balls, although that was a great success.' Dolly stood up. 'I should go home before I'm missed.'

'Didn't you tell anyone you were coming here?'

'I didn't, but they'll think I've gone for a walk in the gardens, which I do sometimes before dinner.'

'I should see you home.'

'No, indeed. Go to the theatre. It's only a short drive to the castle.'

'Well, if you are sure.' Nick reached for his hat and gloves. 'I really should go now.'

'Goodnight, Nick. I'll see you tomorrow.'

Nick ushered her out through the front door and handed her into the chaise before walking off in the direction of the theatre. Dolly flicked the reins and the horse obeyed eagerly as if keen to get back to a nice warm stable. It was completely dark now. The sound of the horse's hoofs on the packed earth road, and the rumble of the carriage wheels, startled small creatures, sending them scurrying for shelter in the woods. Dolly wished she had stopped to light the carriage lamps and she encouraged the animal to a brisk trot.

It was a relief to reach the gates and drive out into the lane. She could see the lights from houses and cottages in the village across the River Sawle. It was a tranquil sight, but just as the bridge came into view, Dolly was aware of a gang of rowdy youths staggering towards the vehicle. It was too dark to see them clearly, and they did not seem familiar, which was odd as she knew everybody in the village. They were obviously drunk and looking for trouble.

At first she thought she could get past them, but a particularly tall, gangly youth leaped in front of the horse. Startled and terrified, the horse bucked and reared, almost tipping Dolly from the driver's seat. She raised the whip and cracked it over the aggressor's head.

'Get away from my horse.'

'Leave her alone, Snapper.' One of the more sober youths pushed the one he called Snapper so that he staggered against the chaise.

Dolly struggled to keep the horse calm, but it was snorting and trying everything it could to get away from the noisy crowd. Some of them were laughing while others cursed loudly as they had to leap to safety from the horse's flailing hoofs.

Dolly stood up in the well of the chaise, brandishing the whip, but Snapper had recovered and he seized her round the waist, lifting her clear of the chaise.

'Look what a pretty fish I've caught, boys. Who'll be the first to have a go?'

Dolly screamed and kicked but he was too strong for her. There was chaos all round and she was flung to the ground. She barely heard the sound of galloping horses, but the rider leaped from his horse and grabbed Snapper from behind.

'Gus? Is that you?' Dolly's pulse was racing so fast that it was difficult for her to speak.

'Are you hurt, Dolly?'

'No,' she said shakily. 'I don't think so.'

Gus hoisted Snapper over his shoulder. 'Shall I throw this tiddler back in the river?'

Dolly could only look on as Gus strode to the edge of the river and tipped the struggling Snapper into the water. Dunbar charged his horse at the remaining youths, who fled in all directions.

Gus held out his hand to help Dolly to her feet. 'What on earth were you doing driving alone at night?'

'I've been to see Nick about business. I wasn't expecting to be set upon.' Dolly glanced at the churning water where Snapper was struggling to keep afloat. 'I don't think he can swim, Gus.'

'He'll soon learn.' Gus helped her back into the chaise and climbed up to sit beside her. 'I'm taking you home. Dunbar, will you bring my horse?'

'Yes, of course,' Dunbar said calmly. 'I'll follow on.'

Gus took the reins. 'I don't think your parents will be too pleased when they hear about this.'

'You are not to tell anyone, Gus.'

He shot her an amused glance. 'So how will you explain your torn gown and the bruises that you are bound to have after what I witnessed?'

'I'll think of something.' Dolly laid her hand on his arm. 'Why are we heading along the high street? This isn't the way home.'

'Dunbar and I are staying with Todd at the doctor's house. I think Todd should take a look at you to make sure nothing is broken.'

'I don't want to be examined, Gus. I am quite all right. I want to go home. Please.'

'Well, at least allow Mrs Lloyd to clean you up before I take you back to the castle.'

'All right,' Dolly said reluctantly. 'I don't want anyone at home to find out. I wasn't supposed to go out on my own.'

Gus was suddenly serious. 'Now you know why. Even in a safe place like Rockwood there can be unexpected hazards. Those youths were in the Black Dog earlier today. They were drunk then and Causley threw them out. Dunbar and I were just returning from Cottingham Manor when we saw you.'

Dolly stiffened. 'You've been to see Josephine Mountjoy?'

'At her invitation. Why? Don't you approve? I thought you didn't care what I do.'

'You are free to mix with whom you please, but perhaps you ought to be more careful in your choice of friends.'

'Don't tell me you are jealous, Dolly?'

'Of course not.'

'Then why are you so angry? I've just saved you from a gang of drunken louts.'

'You really are impossible, Gus Baker. Give me the reins.'

Gus laughed as he handed them to her. 'Are you kidnapping me, Dolly?'

She reined in and the horse came to a standstill. 'Get out, Gus. I'm taking myself home. I don't need the doctor's housekeeper to clean me up. I have a maid to help me with my toilette.'

Gus turned to look at her with such a tender, teasing smile that Dolly almost relented.

'Dolly, you know I love you, don't you?'

She took a deep breath. 'You say a lot of things, Gus. I never know when you are serious or simply amusing yourself.'

'I wouldn't joke about anything so important. I've loved you since we were both children, but you never even noticed me.'

'I'm sure I did. You were always in trouble.'

'I was desperate to make you look at me. You were starry-eyed when it came to Todd.'

'I was not.'

'Yes, you were. I know you better than you know yourself, Dolly Blanchard.'

Dolly struggled against the almost irresistible urge to believe him, but a sudden vision of him with Josephine Mountjoy hardened her heart. 'And I know you, Gus. You are a flirt and you'll say anything to get what you want.'

'What do you think I want from you?' Gus was suddenly serious and he reached out to take hold of Dolly's hand.

'Maybe you think I'm an heiress, simply because I am a Blanchard. Well, I am not, so you are wasting your time.' Dolly snatched her hand free. Her heart was beating so fast she could hardly breathe, but she could see from Gus's expression that her words had hurt him. She wanted desperately to apologise, but she knew it would be fatal. 'I need to go home. Please get down from the chaise now.'

'You're setting me down in the middle of the High Street?'

'Dunbar is following with your horse. Anyway, it's only a couple of hundred yards to the doctor's house. Give my regards to Todd.'

Gus climbed down to the ground. 'You are a hard woman, Dolly Blanchard. But I spoke the truth. I love you and I always will.'

Dolly wheeled the tired horse round, almost over-turning the chaise in her efforts to escape a situation she knew very well she could not handle. She wanted to get away – she needed to get as far away from Gus Baker as she could. She needed to go home.

Chapter Twenty-Three

Dolly managed to get into the castle through the servants' entrance. As the family were all at supper in the dining hall, she was able to creep in unseen. As Gus had predicted, she did suffer some bruising, but it was covered by her clothing and no bones were broken. She undressed carefully and slipped on her nightgown.

As she lay in her bed, unable to sleep, she realised that she had been too hard on Gus. After all, he had saved her from the group of drunken ruffians and she had not even thanked him. She did not want to admit it, but the mention of Josephine Mountjoy's name had made her jealous, and that was why she had been so mean to Gus. But he should not be associating with the Mountjoys. Perhaps now was the time to tell him the truth about the couple.

It would give her a certain amount of satisfaction to see his face when she revealed that Josephine and Jared were husband and wife, but in the end she decided that it would be best if she kept well away from Gus Baker. The tug of attraction was still there, and every time they were together it seemed to grow stronger. It would only take a small detour on her way to the theatre in the morning, and she could make things right with Gus. It was a tempting idea but it might also be a fatal mistake. The last time she had given way to her feelings for him she had ended up alone in London. No matter how attractive she might find Gus, he was not the sort of man her parents expected her to marry.

Then there was Freddie. Dear, loyal, kind and loving Freddie. She sighed and curled up in a ball, closing her eyes and forcing the memory of his proposal to the back of her mind. Why was life so complicated?

After a restless night, Dolly rose early next morning. She ate breakfast alone in the dining room and set off for the theatre, brimming with determination to put the past behind her. The prospect of the auditions and the idea of a family pantomime were uppermost in her mind. It was a surprise when she reached the theatre to hear the sound of a fine contralto voice singing, unaccompanied, on the stage. The doors had been left ajar and the two cleaning women from the village were listening, spellbound.

'Who is that, Mrs Brewer?' Dolly asked in a whisper.

Mrs Brewer turned to her with an excited grin. 'It's that there new lady from Cottingham Manor. I never heard a voice like that, miss. Not even your grandmama, if you'll pardon me saying so.'

'It's Miss Mountjoy,' Mrs Trent said knowledgeably. 'Looks like she'll be taking Miss Day's place.'

Dolly stared at her in surprise. 'How did you know that Miss Day is leaving?'

'I lives next door to her grannie, don't I? The whole village knows it by now, miss.'

Dolly edged past them, and made her way down the aisle to stand beside Nick. Josephine was on stage, singing with such a powerful voice that the melodious sound filled the auditorium.

'It looks as if we've found our future prima donna without the need for an advertisement,' Nick said, smiling.

Dolly shook her head. 'You don't know the whole story, Nick. Anyway, how did this happen? Why is Josephine Mountjoy auditioning for you?'

'She isn't. At least not officially. She was here when I arrived and she insisted on demonstrating her talent, which is considerable. How someone could have such a beautiful, well-trained voice and be ignored by the operatic world is beyond me.'

'I need to talk to you urgently.' Dolly took him by the arm. 'Please, Nick. This is important.'

Nick moved closed to the stage. He held up his

hand and Josephine stopped singing. 'That was amazing, Miss Mountjoy. Won't you take a seat for a few minutes? I'll be back quickly and we can have that discussion you want.'

Dolly practically dragged him to the office, much to the surprise of the cleaners, who moved away swiftly and recommenced sweeping the aisle.

'What is this all about?' Nick demanded as Dolly closed the office door.

'Josephine Mountjoy is not her real name, Nick. I only learned about her history recently. Apparently she was born Giuseppina Bougie in Milan, where she rose from humble beginnings to becoming a prima donna.'

'How do you know all this? It sounds like a fabrication.'

'Tuttle, their gatekeeper, told Fletcher, who passed it on to my mama. It doesn't stop there, Nick. Apparently Josephine married her manager, one Jared Conti. At the height of her fame she had an affair with a prominent Italian politician. Jared found out and was blackmailing the man. Anyway, it all went wrong and the politician was killed. I don't know the details, but Jared and Josephine fled to America, where they changed their name to Mountjoy.'

Nick eyed her warily. 'It sounds more and more like the plot of a cheap operetta. How did they come to buy Cottingham Manor?'

'Jared struck it lucky in the Californian gold fields,

411

but for some reason they decided to come to London. I don't know if the Italian police are still looking for Jared, but that could be why they hid themselves away under aliases in Cottingham Manor.'

'In that case it doesn't make sense for Josephine to make her debut on the stage, even in such an out-of-the-way place as Rockwood.'

'I agree, but I don't know any more than I've told you. Maybe she can't abide life out of the limelight. Perhaps she finds living in the country a bore. Who knows?' Dolly turned her head as the door opened and Josephine stopped on the threshold.

'Are you talking about me?'

Nick stepped forward and pulled up a chair. 'Won't you take a seat, Miss Mountjoy?'

'You were discussing me. I can always tell. I hope it was flattering.' Josephine sat down, arranging her skirts around her.

'You have a wonderful voice,' Dolly said hastily.

Josephine eyed her with a wry smile. 'I know that, but this is something different. What is being said about me?'

'There is always gossip about newcomers,' Nick said tactfully.

'Tuttle has been talking, hasn't he? I knew that bringing him here was a mistake, but Jared insisted on it.'

Dolly perched on the edge of Nick's desk. 'So there's no truth in what he said?'

'That depends.' Josephine glanced from one to the

other. 'I admit that I have a well-trained voice, but you already know that. I was a prima donna in my home city of Milan, but events forced me to leave.'

'And Jared is your husband, is he not?' Dolly was not in a mood to pander to the woman who had lied to everyone and taken them all for fools. 'You did not come to Rockwood because you wanted a quiet life, did you?'

'I can see that I'll have to be frank with you. Jared is my husband, and we do not use our former names, but there is no law against that.'

'No, but I understand your husband was in some sort of trouble in Italy, Mrs Mountjoy,' Nick said warily.

'It was a fair fight, but the man who died was wealthy and influential. We had to leave rather quickly.'

'You went to America.' Dolly eyed her closely. 'But it seems you left there in rather a hurry, too.'

'I was recognised,' Josephine said modestly. 'It happens all the time when I am out in society. It wasn't safe to remain in California.'

'America is a big country.' Nick folded his arms, frowning. 'Why didn't you move to another state?'

'We thought it safer to come to England. I do not have to explain myself to you, Mr Gibson, or you, Dolly Blanchard.'

'You thought you could hide away here in Devonshire.' Dolly tried hard to keep the annoyance she was feeling from her tone. 'So why do you want to appear on stage again? Why don't you keep out of the public eye?'

'My dear Miss Blanchard, I have a God-given talent that must not be hidden away in a tiny village like Rockwood. I am tired of pretending.'

'But your husband is still wanted by the police. Won't you be putting him in jeopardy?'

'We are the Mountjoys. No one need know the rest. It would not benefit your little theatre if the truth were known, but my voice will bring audiences flocking to Rockwood. You need me more than I need you.'

Nick met Dolly's sceptical glance with a worried frown. 'She is right in a way, Dolly. We need an outstanding attraction in order to fill the theatre. We are miles from the nearest big city. The late Sir Bentley Crooke might have wanted to bring culture to the masses, but it has proved difficult to make the experiment profitable. Miss Mountjoy has a truly amazing voice and I think people would travel a long way to hear her sing.'

'Yes, I have a magnificent voice,' Josephine smiled triumphantly. 'You need to be realistic, both of you. I will sing for you providing you keep my past out of the press. As far as anybody need know, I am Josephine Mountjoy and Jared is my brother. I am a new talent, discovered by you, Nick. But I insist on top billing and I want to pick and choose which roles I will take.'

'You won't get away with it,' Dolly said flatly.

'Someone will recognise you one day and you will have to flee again.'

'Very likely, but until that time comes I will be back on stage where I belong. I should really be performing in the most famous opera houses in the world, but for the moment I will settle for the Pavilion Theatre, Rockwood. Are we in agreement?'

Dolly shook her head but Nick proffered his hand to Josephine. 'We are. If you are prepared to take the risk, then so am I. The future of this theatre is continually at stake, but with a voice like yours we might be able to make the Pavilion famous.'

'But we were going to do a pantomime for Christmas,' Dolly protested.

Josephine laughed. 'No, not pantomime. I draw the line at that.'

'Nick, you can't agree to anything unless you talk it over with Grandmama,' Dolly said anxiously. 'It is her theatre, after all.'

'I am quite prepared to sing for Mrs de Marney.' Josephine made her way to the door and waited for Nick as he hurried to open it for her. 'Just let me know when she is available and I will be sure to impress someone who was once almost as famous as I.'

'If you say that to her, she will never accept you,' Dolly said in a low voice. 'You need a little humility, Miss Mountjoy.'

Josephine tossed her head. 'Humility is for the

poor and talentless. I am neither. Good day to you. I will let you know which opera I wish to star in next.' She sailed out of the office and made a grand exit through the foyer.

Dolly stood up, facing Nick angrily. 'Do you really want to work with that woman? Have you lost your mind?'

'We have to put the theatre first, Dolly. A family pantomime is well and good but it won't bring in the audiences that Miss Mountjoy will attract. If I give her the chance to prove herself it will be good for my career, too.'

'I don't see that, Nick.'

'Dolly, I want to marry Aurelia. I've loved her for years but she was always too far above me to consider such a match. Now I believe she needs me and if I am a successful impresario she will be much more likely to accept my proposal.'

'Love isn't about money and position, Nick. I thought you of all people would know that.'

'Isn't it? Wouldn't your family be far happier if you were to marry Lord Dorrington rather than Sergeant Baker?'

'I don't know what you're talking about.'

'Don't you? Would you accept Gus if he were to propose to you today? Would you be prepared to follow the drum with the other wives of ordinary soldiers?'

'You are talking nonsense. I don't want to marry either of them.' Dolly picked up her shawl. 'I am

416

going to tell Grandmama what has happened. She needs to know, Nick, so don't try to stop me.'

'I agree, but I think she will be impressed with Miss Mountjoy's presence, not to mention her wonderful voice. Your grandmama has the best interests of the theatre at heart, Dolly. Have you? Or is this personal dislike for Josephine that you are experiencing?'

Dolly did not dignify this question with an answer. She left the theatre and walked to the hotel.

Felicia was dressing to go out, but she allowed Dolly five minutes of her time. Dolly told her about Josephine's impromptu audition and her ambition to become the next prima donna, but she omitted to mention the more sordid details. However, Felicia was unimpressed. 'Are you telling me that parvenu Josephine Mountjoy thinks she can succeed me? I am one of the most famous prima donnas in the world, or at least I was before I decided to retire.'

'Of course you were, my love,' Claude said gently. 'Your talent is undeniable.'

'Yes, it is. Thank you, Claude.' Felicia fixed Dolly with a hard stare. 'What makes this woman think she can outdo me?'

'She does have a very good voice, Grandmama. But I was thinking more along the lines of doing a pantomime this Christmas, not a series of grand operas. I thought you might like to have a part in it yourself.'

'Me? In pantomime?' Felicia's eyes bulged and her lips worked soundlessly.

'A guest appearance, Grandmama,' Dolly added hastily. 'Saving the best until last, of course. I thought Aunt Patsy might like to have a part and Aunt Nancy, too. She can play the piano so beautifully.'

'I suppose Wolfe and Fletcher will be in starring roles,' Felicia said acidly. 'I am not sure that an amateur production is something to consider.'

'But you are not against a pantomime, Grandmama?'

'I think it would be an excellent idea, my love.' Claude filled a glass with port and handed it to his wife. 'People would travel a long way to see something like that, and if they bring their young ones it will introduce a new generation to the theatre.'

Felicia sipped the wine thoughtfully. 'When you put it like that, I have to agree, Claude. You do sometimes have a good idea.'

'Then it's settled. We have a pantomime for the festive season,' Dolly said triumphantly. 'Now what about Miss Mountjoy, Grandmama? We need a really good programme to start the New Year. Would you consider hearing her sing?'

'As Miss Day is leaving so soon, I suppose we need to do something quickly. You may instruct Miss Mountjoy to be at the theatre tomorrow at midday. I will make an exception for this person, although, from what I've seen of her so far, I do not approve. She is vulgar and seeks attention.'

'You are right, Grandmama. I agree entirely, but she does have a fine voice and we need a new prima donna when Liza leaves us for London.'

'I'll see this woman tomorrow, as I said. Your time is up, Adela. I am lunching at Sutton Hall. Lady Bromfield has invited some of her friends to meet me.'

'Some of her very wealthy and influential friends,' Claude added, smiling. 'Perhaps a word in the right ear might further the new era at the theatre, my love.'

Felicia drained her glass and handed it back to him. 'I am above using my status to advertise the Pavilion, Claude. It would be extremely vulgar. You sometimes forget that I was a Carey of Rockwood Castle before I married you.'

Claude stared into the empty glass. 'I hate to remind you of this, my love, but you married into the Carey family. You were born Felicia Gaunt and your father was a stage hand at the old theatre in Covent Garden. Your mama was in the chorus.'

Felicia threw her silver-backed hair brush at him, narrowly missing his head. 'I told you never to mention that, Claude. Take no notice of him, Adela. Claude's mother took in washing and his father was a notorious gambler.'

Dolly backed towards the doorway. 'You are both wonderful people, Grandmama. I don't think it matters who your parents were. You have made your own way in the world.'

She ducked as Felicia hurled a slipper at Claude with such a bad aim that it almost hit Dolly. She left the room and closed the door before another such missile flew through the air.

The knowledge that her grandmother had come from humble beginnings was something of a shock. Dolly had never thought about it before, but she had always assumed that everyone in the family came from similar backgrounds. But Grandmama had risen above her origins and made her own way in the world. Claude seemed to have done the same. Perhaps birth and lineage were not as important as the rest of the family made out.

Instead of going back to the theatre, Dolly walked to the village. She had an apology to make and she went straight to the doctor's house, where she rattled the doorknocker.

Mrs Lloyd opened the door and her wrinkled face creased into a welcoming smile. 'Good morning, Miss Blanchard. I'm afraid Dr Taylor is out on a call.'

'It's all right, Mrs Lloyd, I am not unwell, I wanted to have a word with Sergeant Baker, if he is still here.'

'I'm so sorry, miss. Sergeant Baker left for Exeter an hour ago, and Sergeant Dunbar, too.'

Dolly tried to look unconcerned. 'Thank you. I'm sorry to have bothered you.'

'No bother, miss. I believe the regiment are breaking camp today. Sergeant Baker said he didn't know where they would be posted next. He's such a lovely young man. I remember him when he was a naughty young fellow, but he's grown up to be a worthy citizen, as have all Miss Nancy's boys.'

'Yes, thank you, Mrs Lloyd.' Dolly backed away. Her desire to see Gus again had become so pressing that it was all she could think about. She should have returned to the theatre, but it was almost midday and she found herself walking in the direction of the castle. She needed to go home and feel the warmth of the family around her while she struggled with her inner demons.

It was a chilly October day and a slight drizzle cooled Dolly's cheeks as she walked briskly in the direction of the castle. However, the refreshing effect of the rain soon wore off and she was beginning to shiver as the dampness seeped through her shawl and the bodice of her fine woollen gown. Quite what she intended to do next she had not decided, but when she entered the bailey and saw Freddie's carriage about to be driven to the stables, she had a moment of panic. She almost turned and ran, but Freddie was standing in the entrance, talking to James and he seemed to sense her presence. He turned and greeted her with such a warm smile that she forgot her initial reaction and hurried towards him. This was the Freddie she had known and loved for most of her life, not the stranger who proposed marriage to her in the rose garden.

'Freddie, I didn't know you were expected.'

He ushered her into the entrance hall, handing his hat, gloves and cane to Bertha, who was waiting in the background. 'It was a spur-of-the-moment decision, Dolly,' Freddie said calmly. 'I had business in Exeter so I thought I would come the extra distance to see my favourite family.'

'They will be delighted to see you, as always.' Dolly turned to James with a smile. 'Where will we find everyone, James?'

'I believe they are still at luncheon, Miss Adela.'

'I'm hungry. Shall we join them, Freddie?'

'Yes, of course.' Freddie fell into step beside her. 'How are you, Dolly? You look rather flushed.'

'I've been very busy. I'll tell you all about it at luncheon when I go through it for everyone else. It's theatre business, so not terribly interesting.'

'Nonsense. I love being kept up to date.' Freddie drew her to a halt outside the dining room. 'We are all right, aren't we, Dolly? I know I spoke out of turn when we were last together. I hope you can forgive me.'

'Don't mention it, Freddie. It's all forgotten.'

He sighed. 'Of course. Anyway, let's join the family. Rockwood has always been my second home, and I am keen to hear their news.' He opened the door and they were greeted with smiles.

Alex rose to his feet. 'Freddie, this is a pleasant surprise. Come and sit down.'

'Yes,' Tommy said, patting the empty chair on his left. 'Sit by me.'

Rosalind gave Dolly a searching look. 'You look as though you ought to change your clothes, Dolly. Did you walk home in the rain?'

'Yes, I got caught in a shower, Mama. But I'm drying out nicely. I'll be all right as I am.'

'Well, dear, don't blame me if you come down with a chill.'

'Don't worry about me, Mama.' Dolly sat down beside her mother and ate sparingly of the dishes that were put before her, but her mind was elsewhere. She only heard fragments of the conversation. Freddie was amusing everyone by recounting an argument with a neighbouring landowner, but Dolly could not concentrate for more than a minute or two. Her mind kept straying to her conversation with Gus and the fact that his regiment were on the move. If only she could relive the past twenty-four hours and do things differently.

'Are you staying with us, Freddie?' Nancy asked during a lull in the conversation.

'I was planning to return to Dorrington Place later today, although I do have unfinished business in Exeter.'

'Then you must stay with us at least for tonight, old chap,' Alex said firmly. 'You know you are always welcome.'

'That's kind of you, but I don't want to impose.'

'It's always a pleasure to have you with us,' Rosalind said, smiling. 'Do say you'll stay.'

'Well, of course I would love to. I can go to my solicitor on my way home tomorrow.'

Dolly eyed him speculatively. She had been trying to think of a way to get to Exeter and back without arousing suspicion, but she might be able to persuade Freddie to take her tomorrow. She would have to think of a good excuse.

'You look very thoughtful, Dolly,' Nancy said curiously. 'Is everything all right at the theatre?'

Dolly glanced round at their expectant faces. She knew she could not get away with an abridged version of the recent events and she launched into a detailed description of how Liza Day's sudden departure would affect future plans for the theatre. She finished by recounting her recent conversation with her grandmother.

Tommy slapped his hand on the table and laughed. 'Dolly Blanchard, I can't believe that you asked Grandmama to appear in a pantomime. I would not have had the nerve.'

Dolly smiled modestly. 'She was a little horrified at first, but I assured her it would be a guest appearance, and she did not seem to mind that.'

'I think a pantomime with members of the family in it would be wonderful,' Rosalind said thoughtfully. 'Patsy will jump at the chance to perform again.'

Nancy pulled a face. 'I don't mind playing the

piano, if needed. At least we won't get rotten tomatoes thrown at us in Rockwood, unlike some of our performances in London.'

'Nothing is settled, as yet,' Dolly said hastily. 'Everything depends upon whether or not Grandmama agrees that Josephine can take Liza's place.'

Chapter Twenty-Four

Dolly had managed to persuade Freddie to take her to Exeter next day, but she had not thought through what it might be like travelling on her own with him for the first time since his unsuccessful proposal of marriage. Now, seated beside him in his luxurious carriage, she was unsure of herself. She stole a sideways glance at his strong profile. He turned to look at her as if aware of her scrutiny.

'Are you all right, Dolly? I mean, I know you said it didn't upset you, but I don't want what happened on my last visit to come between us.'

'No, Freddie. It's not that, although I still feel dreadful for the way I treated you. I don't know what you must think of me.'

'Dolly, if anyone is to blame it is I. You are far too young for me. I love you dearly, but I was deluding myself in thinking that the difference in our ages meant nothing.'

'I do love you, Freddie. But not in the way you want.'

'I know and I understand. Now, Dolly, please tell me what you are up to. I have the feeling you were not telling me the complete truth about needing to visit Exeter so urgently. If it was to do with the theatre, surely Nick would have gone himself?'

Dolly took a deep breath. There was nothing for it but to be brutally honest. 'I'm afraid I lied to everyone, Freddie. Nick didn't ask me to visit the printers again. The truth is that I'm desperate to see Gus before his regiment moves out. I was horrid to him the other evening, even though he'd saved me from a gang of drunken ruffians.'

Freddie stared at her in dismay. 'You were attacked?'

'Yes, but I wasn't hurt, thanks to Gus. Yesterday morning I felt terrible because I had been horrid to him, so I went to the doctor's house to apologise. Gus had been staying there with Todd.' Dolly paused as the events of earlier came back to her with heart-stopping clarity. 'Mrs Lloyd told me that Gus and Dunbar had returned to Exeter as their regiment was breaking camp, and I don't know where they will be sent next. I may never see him again.'

Freddie was silent for a moment, staring out of

the carriage window. He sighed. 'It was always Gus, wasn't it, Dolly? You ran away with him once and now you are prepared to risk everything to do it again.'

'No. Yes – I don't know. I just need to see him and tell him that I was mean to him because I was jealous of Josephine.'

'Josephine Mountjoy?'

'I saw them talking – well, flirting – and I couldn't help it, I was furious and jealous.'

'I'm sure he would be flattered if he knew why you were so angry.'

'It was more than that. I was already in a state because I had discovered that Alex is my real father, not Piers. It came as a shock, even though I've always thought of Alex as my papa, and I don't get on very well with Piers. Try as I might, I can't warm to him, so in that way it wasn't a surprise.'

'I'm so sorry, Dolly. I've always suspected that you were Alexander's daughter, but it was none of my business. He certainly has loved you and raised you as his own child.'

'It was still a shock to find out the truth. Let's say I was not thinking straight when I decided to drive home from the theatre after dark on my own.' Dolly held up her hand. 'Don't say anything, Freddie. I know it was stupid. Anyway, there was a group of drunken men loitering close to the bridge and one of them dragged me from the chaise. I struggled but he was very drunk and I was really frightened.

Then Gus appeared as if from nowhere and he set about the fellow. Dunbar rode his horse at the rest of the gang and they ran away.'

'It sounds as if you had a lucky escape, Dolly.'

'I know, and I ought to have been grateful to Gus. I should have thanked him for saving me, but I picked a quarrel with him about Josephine. Then I insisted on driving myself home alone. I set him down in the middle of the High Street, so that he had to walk to the doctor's house. It was a childish and petty thing to do, and I wouldn't blame him if he never wanted to see me again.'

'I'm sure he would understand if you were to explain everything to him as you have to me, Dolly, my dear. It's obvious that young man has deep feelings for you.'

'I don't know about that, Freddie. It all seems hopeless, and he left without telling me.'

'He must be aware that your family would disapprove of such a match.'

'I don't think he wants to marry me,' Dolly sighed. 'We would probably make each other miserable, even if it were possible. Anyway, I can't allow him to leave without saying goodbye. I need to make him understand why I treated him as I did.'

'Then we must do something about it. I will take you to the encampment and I'll wait while you put matters straight with Gus. I'll make sure you get home safely afterwards.'

Forgetting her initial shyness, Dolly gave Freddie

a hug. 'You are so kind to me. I can't thank you enough.'

'You need to tell him how you feel, but I'm sure there is nothing between him and Josephine Mountjoy. That young woman seems to cause trouble wherever she goes.'

'She is not who she pretends to be, Freddie. She was an opera singer in Italy and Jared isn't her brother. They are husband and wife.'

'Why would they pretend otherwise?'

'Apparently, Jared fought and killed a prominent politician who had been having an affair with Josephine.'

'It seems we are never to get away from grand opera. How do you know all this?'

'Fletcher is friendly with Tuttle, the Mountjoys' gatekeeper and manservant. He told Fletcher that Jared and Josephine fled from Italy. They went to California where Jared struck lucky in the goldfields. Then, for some reason, they decided to come to England and they purchased Cottingham Manor. I imagine Jared thought they could lead a quiet life in the country.'

'They have a strange way of going about it,' Freddie said with a wry smile.

'I agree, and now Josephine wants to perform on stage at the Pavilion Theatre.'

'That sounds reckless to me. Particularly so if there is still a warrant for Jared's arrest in Italy.'

'I don't know about that, Freddie.' Dolly frowned.

'Maybe that's what Josephine wants. Perhaps she would like to be free from her husband. They don't seem to be very happy together.'

'But what about you, Dolly? I personally don't give a fig for Miss Mountjoy or whatever her name is, but I do care about you. I agree that you should see Gus, but please think carefully before you do anything rash.'

'All I know is that I am not the person I thought I was. Maybe you would have hesitated before proposing marriage if you had known that I was born out of wedlock.'

'It wouldn't have made the slightest bit of different to me, nor would it to any decent man who had the good fortune to love you and be loved in return.'

Dolly turned away to gaze out of the window. 'Now I feel even worse about rejecting you.'

Freddie took her hand and held it in a firm clasp. 'You must put all such feelings aside. You did absolutely the right thing in rejecting the proposal of someone you knew you could not love, and I'm grateful for your honesty.' He raised her hand to his lips before releasing it gently. 'We will forget all about me and concentrate on getting you to see Gus and sorting things out with him, one way or another.'

They settled down in companionable silence for the rest of the journey.

For a moment Dolly thought they had come to the wrong site when they reached the large field where

Gus's regiment had been encamped. The only evidence that the army had been there was circles of blackened soil where fires had been doused and dug over. The farmer was already at work ploughing furrows in preparation for sowing spring crops.

Freddie tapped on the roof of the carriage and ordered the coachman to bring it to a halt.

'Hey, there. A moment of your time, sir,' Freddie called from the open window.

The farmer reined in his horse and stopped ploughing. 'Can I help you, master?'

'The regiment who were here – can you tell me where they have gone and when they left?'

'They left early on, sir. I dunno where they be going. I am not in the know, so to speak.' The farmer tipped his cap and urged the sturdy plough horse to walk on.

'Thank you, sir.' Freddie called after him.

'I'll never see Gus again.' Dolly bit her lip to prevent herself from bursting into tears. She was not the sort of person who resorted to tears in order to gain sympathy. She tried to convince herself that she was simply tired and emotionally exhausted, but she knew that was a lie.

'The regimental headquarters are in Exeter,' Freddie said thoughtfully. 'The staff there should know.' He leaned out of the window. 'Mason, drive back to town and stop at the barracks.' Freddie closed the window. 'Don't worry, Dolly. We'll find out where they have gone.'

'Even if we do, I cannot go chasing after the regiment,' Dolly said sadly. 'I have work to do at the theatre. In fact, I should be there now. I'm sorry for dragging you on a wild-goose chase, Freddie.'

'I can take you back to Rockwood, if you wish, or do you want me to take you straight to the theatre?'

'Yes, please.'

'I will, but first I'll see if I can find out where Gus is being posted. That way at least you will know where he is.'

Dolly said little on the way into town. If only she had come straight to Exeter yesterday when she discovered that Gus was being sent away. She waited in the carriage while Freddie went into the office at the regimental headquarters, and he emerged minutes later with a serious expression. He climbed into the carriage.

'I'm sorry, Dolly. They wouldn't tell me anything. The best I could do was to ask for a message to be sent to Sergeant Baker, asking him to contact you as soon as he was able.'

'Thank you, Freddie.' Dolly managed to murmur the words without bursting into tears. She had feared as much and, after the way she had behaved, she did not hold out much hope of Gus ever wanting to see her again. 'I'd be grateful if you would take me to the theatre now. I need to get back to work.'

'Where have you been, Dolly?' Nick demanded when she walked into the office two hours later. 'It's past midday and your grandmama was asking for you when she came to audition Miss Mountjoy.'

'I'm sorry, Nick. I had urgent business in Exeter.'

Nick frowned. 'You were not here when you were needed. Mrs de Marney gave me a long lecture on keeping her informed of events at the theatre. Although she always seems to know about things before I do. However, that's immaterial.'

'But did she like Josephine as a performer?'

Nick rolled his eyes. 'You know how your grandmama hates to admit that anyone has a talent matching hers?'

'Yes, of course. But did she accept Josephine as our next prima donna?'

'Reluctantly, but I think Mrs de Marney is too shrewd to allow personal feelings to affect her judgement, especially when it comes to theatre business.'

'And did Josephine accept your offer?'

'She said she would, but she seemed quite casual about the whole business. I never know what ladies are thinking. I am a very poor judge of their reactions.'

Dolly smiled as she took off her bonnet and shawl. 'Are you talking about Aurelia now?'

'How did you guess?'

'You have devoted yourself to her ever since she arrived back in Rockwood. You follow her round like an adoring spaniel, Nick. You have eyes for no one else, and you have left things at the theatre to me that you would normally have done yourself.'

'Have I been so remiss?'

'Yes, to be honest, you have. But I don't blame you for one moment. Aurelia is a lovely person and she needs someone like you. Have you told her how you feel?'

'I'm afraid she will walk away, just as she did years ago.'

'You know the old saying, Nick. Faint heart never won fair lady.'

'But I have nothing to offer her. Aurelia is used to living in grand houses and being waited upon hand and foot.'

'You love her, Nick. You can provide her with a pretty little house and I expect you can afford a cook and a maid. If not, you need a larger salary and I'm sure Grandmama would agree to that.'

'So you think I should tell Aurelia how I feel?'

Dolly laughed in exasperation. 'Just do it, please, Nick. Go now and find her. Take her for a walk while the sun is shining. Tell her how you feel before she gets tired of waiting and returns to Trevenor.'

'Do you think she would do that?' Nick's eyes widened in alarm.

'It's a possibility,' Dolly said firmly. 'Go now, while you are feeling bold.'

'All right, I will.' Nick jumped to his feet, grabbed his hat and gloves and left the office. His footsteps echoed on the marble floor of the foyer and the double doors creaked on their hinges as he left the theatre.

Dolly took a seat at the desk. At least someone would be made happy today. She had no doubt as to Aurelia's answer. As to her own problems, she would have to get used to the fact that Gus had gone away and might never return. It was her own fault and she had no one else to blame. She threw herself into the routine business of running the theatre and did her best to forget her own problems.

When Nick returned to the theatre late that afternoon his triumphant grin gave him away.

'Aurelia said yes.' He did a little dance of sheer joy.

Dolly leaped to her feet and enveloped him in a hug. 'What did I tell you? Congratulations, Nick. That's really wonderful news.'

That evening there was a festive atmosphere at a hastily convened family dinner in honour of Aurelia and Nick's engagement. Aurelia was all blushes and smiles as she showed off the ring that had belonged to Nick's late mother. Tommy sent for champagne so that everyone could toast the happy couple. Dolly joined in enthusiastically, although she could not shake off a feeling close to despair. She had encouraged Nick to speak up and claim his future bride, but she, Dolly Blanchard, had turned her own love life into a disaster. She had refused Freddie's offer of marriage, a title and a fortune, as well as sending the man she loved to possible death on the battlefield. Dolly realised that this was a slight exaggeration as, to her knowledge, the regiment was not being sent to war, but even so, the life of a soldier was often a short one. She could have shared it with Gus had she been strong enough to defy convention and her family.

At one point during the conversation she looked up and met Freddie's eyes across the table. He gave her an encouraging smile and she knew that he understood and empathised with her confused emotions. At least there was one person who was on her side. She returned the smile and raised her glass to him.

Rosalind was quick to notice. 'Are you celebrating something else, Dolly? Freddie?'

'I am happy for Aurelia and Nick,' Dolly said hastily.

Freddie nodded in agreement.

'Thank you, everyone.' Aurelia smiled and clutched Nick's hand. 'I can hardly believe that this has happened.'

'I will do my utmost to make you happy, Aurelia.' Nick raised her hand to his lips. 'I count myself as the most fortunate man in the world.'

A round of clapping was followed by yet more toasts.

At the end of the meal, the ladies retired to the drawing room as usual, leaving the gentlemen to their brandy and cigars.

Aurelia fluttered around the room like an excited

butterfly. 'I want to be married from here, if you don't mind, Nancy?'

'Of course not,' Nancy said, smiling. 'But what will Lady Pentelow say to that? Surely she will want you to have the ceremony at Trevenor?'

'No. I don't want to go back to that miserable house. Piers will certainly disapprove of Nick. My dear brother has become so pompous lately that I really don't know him any more. Isn't that true, Dolly?'

Hester frowned. 'He was always difficult. Better keep him away. That's my considered opinion.'

'I agree with you,' Rosalind said, nodding. 'It's not as if this is Aurelia's first wedding. I mean it's a very exciting occasion,' she added hastily, 'but you don't need your brother's permission, Aurelia.'

'No, indeed.' Aurelia sank down onto the sofa next to Dolly and Patricia.

'We'll organise it for you,' Patricia said eagerly. 'Rosie, Nancy and myself will arrange everything.'

'I'll help.' Louise glanced round anxiously. 'I can decorate the church. Mama will be only too pleased to help.'

'Might Charlotte, May and I be your bridesmaids, Aunt Aurelia?' Phoebe asked excitedly. 'Do say we may.'

'Of course you may. That would be delightful.' Aurelia clasped her hands together, her eyes sparkling with pleasure. 'Perhaps Edward, Oliver and Percy would like to be page boys, Nancy?'

Nancy laughed. 'You might be able to persuade Percy, but Eddie and Ollie would consider themselves far to grown-up for that. I'll speak to Percy anyway. He's the easiest of my sons.'

'If your family doesn't stop growing you will have to add another wing to the castle,' Patricia said, laughing. 'One son is quite enough for me.'

Dolly could see that Nancy was upset by this remark and she rose swiftly to her feet. 'I think it's wonderful that Aurelia wishes to get married in the village church and to have her wedding breakfast here. I'll do anything I can to help, but if no one objects I am very tired and I need to get some sleep. Will you all excuse me, please?'

'Of course,' Nancy said hastily. 'You do look a little peaky. Perhaps you are working too hard at the theatre?'

Dolly was about to answer when the door burst open and Felicia marched into the room, followed by Claude.

'Why wasn't I invited to this gathering?' Felicia demanded crossly. 'The whole family is here, apart from Claude and myself.'

Rosalind rose to her feet. 'Come and sit by the fire, Mama. I'm sorry for the oversight, but this was arranged in rather a hurry.'

'An oversight, am I?' Felicia took Rosalind's seat with ill grace. 'What is the cause of this celebration?'

Aurelia giggled girlishly. 'It's to celebrate my en-gagement to Nick, Mrs de Marney.'

'You and Nick? Why wasn't I told about this sooner? Nick works for me at the theatre. I have a right to know.'

Claude cleared his throat. 'My love, this is Aurelia and Nick's business. It has nothing to do with us.'

'It will affect us if Nick chooses to move to Trevenor and play at being a country gentleman.'

'No, no. I can assure you that isn't the case, Mrs de Marney,' Aurelia said anxiously. 'We will reside in the village.'

Felicia curled her lip. 'And you think you would be happy living on Nick's meagre salary? You are either blind or stupid, Aurelia. Although I've always thought your head was stuffed with rags instead of a brain.'

Aurelia's bottom lip drooped and her eyes filled with tears. 'You cannot talk to me like that, ma'am.'

'I simply speak the truth. This marriage would be a disaster for both of you.'

'Mama, that is quite enough.' Rosalind had remained standing and she glared down at her mother. 'You are being very unfair. I am sorry we forgot to invite you to dinner, but it was a rather spur-of-the-moment arrangement. However, that does not give you the right to hurt Aurelia's feelings.'

'Yes, Grandmama,' Dolly added with feeling. 'Nick is a fine man. I think they will be very happy.'

Felicia rounded on Dolly. 'And what do you know about it, miss? You dally with Freddie Dorrington and I hear that you've been seen once again in the company of one of Nancy's delinquents, a rough army sergeant.'

Hester rose majestically to her feet. 'Felicia Gaunt, you have no cause to look down on anyone. I remember the day that Master Wilfred brought you home as a young bride. Sir Lucien was not best pleased about the match his son had made, but you've survived and prospered. Leave Aurelia and Nick alone.' She subsided back onto her chair, picked up her glass of port and downed it in one gulp.

Felicia stared at Hester, open-mouthed. 'I – I . . .'

Claude reached for a decanter and filled a glass with port, which he handed to his wife. 'There you are, my love. Maybe you should think before you speak.'

'Claude?' Felicia stared up at him, her sense of shock palpable.

'I love you dearly,' Claude continued firmly, 'but it's time you learned to accept others for what they are. You cannot control the world.'

There was a sudden silence in the room with everyone gazing in horror at Felicia, as if waiting for the inevitable explosion of rage.

'Well!' Felicia's mouth worked and her eyes flashed, but she subsided into a sulk.

It was at that moment the door opened once again as Tommy strolled in, followed by Alex, Leo, Nick and Freddie. They were laughing and chatting, oblivious to the tense atmosphere in the room.

Dolly chose this interruption to slip out unnoticed.

She made her way to her bedroom and closed the door.

Freddie left for Dorrington Place early next morning, having first promised to return for the wedding, the date of which was to be in three weeks after the last of the banns had been called. Later that day, Nick and Aurelia left for Trevenor, where they planned to give Lady Pentelow and Piers their good news, although Dolly doubted if either her ladyship or Piers would approve. However, Nick was adamant that no matter what Aurelia's closest relatives said, it would not prevent them from getting married as soon as possible.

Before he left for Cornwall, Nick had given Dolly a list of instructions to follow in his absence. Felicia was at the meeting in the office and she seemed uncharacteristically subdued. After Claude's unusual outburst, the rest of the evening had gone surprisingly well, and Dolly had applauded him silently. It was high time someone had put Grandmama in her place. However, it would be best to keep on the right side of her from now on. They would have to work together to keep things going during Nick's absence. One thing had already been decided and that was Josephine's part in the next operatic production.

With Nick and Aurelia temporarily absent, the rest of the family became involved in the production of the pantomime, including Rory and Jack, who promised to do anything they could to help when they came home at the end of the Christmas term. Walter was given the task of writing the script, and Nancy admitted a hitherto hidden talent for composing music. Between the two of them they were confident that they could work together and get the pantomime scenario completed in time to begin rehearsal for the short Christmas season.

Dolly had an almost impossible amount of work to cope with at the theatre. There was the current production to deal with, and rehearsals to be arranged for the new opera starring Josephine Mountjoy. But to Dolly's surprise it was Felicia who came to her aid and they worked together in perfect harmony. Dolly naturally deferred to her grandmother when it came to the present production and the choice for the next season, although Josephine insisted on having her say. However, even more surprisingly, it seemed that Felicia and Josephine actually agreed on the final choice of opera, and the resident company were to begin rehearsals the moment the present run ended.

What with the theatre business and the arrangements for Aurelia and Nick's wedding, Dolly had little time to brood on her own problems. She had not heard from Gus and there seemed to be no way she could find out where he had been posted. He might be gone but he was definitely not forgotten.

Aurelia and Nick were away for just less than a week, suggesting that their stay at Trevenor had not been a comfortable one. However, they were both glowing with happiness when they returned and Aurelia was at once absorbed in the arrangements for her forthcoming wedding.

Dolly was relieved to have Nick back at the theatre and glad to be able to hand over some of the more tedious parts of management to him. She had thrown herself into her work during his absence, but now it was time to become more involved with the pantomime as well as the wedding preparations. The church had been booked and the hymns chosen, although it was Nancy and Louise who had taken on the latter task as Aurelia had not left any instructions as to the form of the service. When asked, she smiled happily and told them she was quite sure she would love their choices.

Dolly had not particularly wanted to be one of the bride's entourage but, having returned from Cornwall with fresh ideas, Aurelia insisted that Dolly should be her chief bridesmaid. Dolly did not want to cast a shadow on what promised to be a wonderful event and so she agreed, albeit reluctantly. That meant more dress fittings, which necessitated trips to Exeter. Dolly was tempted to visit the army barracks to enquire as to the whereabouts of Gus's regiment, but she managed to resist the temptation. For one thing she doubted if they would tell her, and if she discovered that he was somewhere abroad the information would make her feel even worse. She pushed all such thoughts to the back of her mind and concentrated on the matter in hand. Aurelia's wedding was going to be wonderful, and maybe that would make up for the disaster she had experienced at the hands of Rupert Charnley.

Chapter Twenty-Five

Everything was finally ready. The wedding guests had arrived at Rockwood Castle and were settled in their rooms. Of course, Freddie was there. No family occasion would be the same if he was absent. Lady Pentelow had deigned to come, accompanied by her maid, her butler, her coachman and two footmen. Her decision to bring such a large entourage brought criticism from Alex, but Rosalind, as always, smoothed things over and welcomed Lady Pentelow and all her servants. Relations that Aurelia had not seen for years had accepted their invitations, probably more out of curiosity than affection, Alex said wearily. Rosalind made light of it and each new arrival was greeted warmly. Alex and Tommy escaped to the Black Dog with Leo, leaving Freddie to stand in for them. Freddie accepted the responsibilities thrust upon him with his usual good humour.

'I don't know many of these people,' Dolly said in a low voice as family and guests filed into the great hall, where two dining tables had been put together in order to accommodate everyone. 'I don't think Aurelia has met half of them.'

Freddie laughed softly. 'They are here for the free food and wine, I suspect. Also they can go back to their normal lives boasting they have stayed in a castle.'

'I hope they don't catch cold from the draughts that whistle through their ill-fitting windows,' Dolly said, giggling. 'And if it rains, the rooms in the west wing leak. Maybe they would think twice about the romance of living in an ancient pile like Rockwood.'

'Allow me.' Freddie pulled out a chair for Dolly and she waited for Nancy to sit down before she took her seat.

Freddie was placed next to her, which was a relief. She had feared she might be paired with the overweight man with mutton-chop whiskers and yellow teeth, who claimed to be Aurelia's cousin Humphrey. He had been giving her leery smiles ever since he arrived from Cornwall that afternoon, and his breath reeked of whisky with a hint of lavender cologne, with which Dolly suspected he had gargled before joining the party.

There was a clattering of chairs on the polished floorboards and a rustle of damask table napkins as the diners anticipated the arrival of the food. The soup was being served when James made his way to the head of the table and whispered something in Tommy's ear. Tommy rose to his feet at the sound of booted footsteps and all heads turned to stare at the newcomer who strode into the great hall.

Piers gazed dispassionately at the curious guests as he made his way purposefully to where Aurelia was seated beside Nick.

Aurelia gazed up at him nervously and Nick half rose from his seat.

'Piers, this is an unexpected pleasure.' Alex stood up and beckoned to his cousin. 'There is a chair here. You are just in time for dinner.'

'I've dined, thank you.' Piers turned his attention to Aurelia. 'I am the head of the family, Aurelia. I forbid you to marry this commoner.'

Nick straightened up, facing Piers with outthrust jaw. 'This is none of your business, Mr Blanchard. Aurelia and I are to be married tomorrow and there is nothing you can do about it.'

'Hear, hear,' Humphrey, the whiskery relative said loudly. 'Where's the soup? I'm starving.'

Rosalind rose to her feet and hastened to Piers' side. 'Please don't do this. All we want is a pleasant family meal. Don't make a scene.'

'You never could manage a household properly, Rosie. Go and sit down. This is my business, not yours.'

'This is my home, Piers. Tommy is head of the family at Rockwood Castle. You have no connection with us now. Please sit down or leave us in peace.'

Alex joined them, taking Piers by the arm. 'Come on, old chap. This isn't the time or the place. We can discuss this after dinner, in private.'

'I'm not staying here, Alex. I've booked a room at the inn. I will have my say now, in front of these relations, who have appeared, no doubt for the free food and wine.'

A ripple of dissent went round the people concerned. Lady Pentelow banged her soup spoon on the table. 'Piers Blanchard, go away. This is not good form.'

'You should have stopped this ridiculous match when they visited us at Trevenor,' Piers said angrily.

'Why didn't *you*, if that's how you feel?' Lady Pentelow bristled with outrage. 'I am an old woman and you are supposed to be the head of the house, but that did not stop you from giving shelter to an escaped convict.'

Another even louder wave of concern swept round the table.

'That is over and done with, Grandmama. This is my sister's future we are talking about. I was too busy keeping the mine in profit to attend to matters when they visited Trevenor. I am here now and, Aurelia, I forbid you to marry this fellow.'

Dolly held her breath. She longed to leap to Aurelia's defence but she knew she must not interfere.

'Piers.' Aurelia stood up, tossing her table napkin to the floor. 'I won't allow you to speak to me in that tone.' She laid her hand on Nick's arm as he was about to step between her and her brother. 'No, Nick. This is my family at the moment. When you are my husband you may speak for both of us, but this is my business. You are a horrible person, Piers Blanchard. You married Rosalind and made her miserable. You ended up in the penal colony in Australia, and now you try to tell me how to live my life. Well, no more. I am a grown woman and I am telling you to leave me alone. Go away. Look after Grandmama; I neither want you nor need you.' Aurelia came to a halt, leaning heavily on Nick's arm.

A moment of stunned silence was followed by a round of applause when Dolly started clapping, and the rest of the diners joined in. Piers threw up his hands and stamped out of the great hall, pushing past James who opened the door for him. James closed the heavy oak door with a resounding thud.

A buzz of conversation erupted but Alex held up his hand for silence. 'I apologise for my cousin Piers. Forget what just happened and enjoy your dinner.' He turned to Aurelia and kissed her cheek. 'You were splendid. I was never more proud of you. Look after her, Nick. She's a wonderful woman.'

'I intend to. Don't worry.' Nick slipped his arm around Aurelia's shoulders. 'Tomorrow I'm going to be the proudest man in the whole world.'

*

The next day dawned cold, with an icing of frost on the grass and berried hedgerows as the carriages containing the wedding party left the castle grounds for the short drive to the village church. Dolly, as chief bridesmaid, travelled in the open landau with Aurelia, who was wrapped in a cloak of blue velvet, trimmed with white fur. Her silk gown had been lovingly created by Meggie Brewer, the talented dressmaker from Exeter, who was now aided by her two daughters. They had also made Dolly's gown, which was ivory satin, trimmed with bugle beads and sequins, which caught the light and, as Phoebe said, made Dolly shimmer like a snow queen.

Phoebe, May and Charlotte were in the next carriage, together with Percy, who had been persuaded to wear crimson velvet breeches and a white ruffled shirt for the occasion. Nancy had not revealed her promised reward for Percy if he wore the old-fashioned garments, although Dolly thought it might have something to do with his father's military dress sword. It had hung below antique weapons in the great hall, close to Sir Denys's suit of armour, and Percy had coveted it for as long as Dolly could remember.

Whatever the means, it had worked and Percy was part of the bride's retinue. His brothers had been threatened on pain of death not to tease him until after the ceremony.

When they arrived at the church, the guests were already assembled and many of the villagers had turned out to line the streets. Aurelia stepped from the carriage to a smattering of cheers and applause, and once inside the church she slipped off her cloak and handed it to Dolly.

'You'll freeze,' Dolly whispered anxiously.

'I don't care. I want Nick to see me looking radiant in my beautiful gown.'

Nick was standing in front of the altar with his best man, Alfie, who looked very self-conscious in a borrowed frock coat and pinstripe trousers. Louise had excelled herself when it came to decorating the church, but Dolly suspected the hothouse roses and lilies had come from the greenhouses on the Dorrington estate. Freddie was always ready to contribute anything, including his own time, when the Blanchard and Carey families needed his help. He was seated in the front row in between Felicia and Lady Pentelow. Dolly hid a smile. It looked as if he had been placed there to prevent the two dowagers from falling out. Hester sat beside Claude, who could be relied upon to calm her if she found something to grumble about.

The organist struck up the Wedding March and Alex stepped forward to escort Aurelia up the aisle. Percy followed them, holding up Aurelia's train, with Dolly leading the younger bridesmaids. She took the bouquet from Aurelia and stepped back as the ceremony commenced. Dolly sat next to Hester in the front row, praying silently that Piers would not make another sudden appearance to declare his objections to the marriage. But she need not have worried. The ceremony went off without a hitch, the vows were made and George Shaw declared the couple to be husband and wife. Dolly could have cried with relief, although any tears shed that morning were tears of happiness. Having signed the register, Aurelia and Nick processed down the aisle and the wedding party returned to the castle ready for the celebrations to begin.

The wedding breakfast took a couple of hours and was followed by speeches, which Rosalind had insisted be kept reasonably short. When the last toast had been drunk, the guests retired to the music room while the servants cleared and removed the long refectory tables in order for the dancing to commence. The orchestra had arrived and took their places and once the music started the floor began to fill with couples whirling around to the strains of a Viennese waltz. Percy had undergone some teasing from his brothers and his cousin Charlie, but when Tommy took the sword from the wall and presented it to his son, the other boys could only look on with envy. Percy unsheathed the weapon with difficulty as it was far too big for him, but he made everyone laugh by pretending to challenge Sir Denys's armour to a duel. Tommy took the sword from him and replaced it in its sheath, warning Percy gently that it would be taken away from him if he tried to unsheathe it again.

Freddie moved to Dolly's side. 'That boy will go

far,' he said, laughing. 'Another male Carey who will join the army when he's old enough.'

'It seems we cannot get away from the military,' Dolly said sadly.

'You still haven't heard from Gus?'

She shook her head. 'No, and to be honest I doubt if he will contact me, Freddie. I made it clear that I was not interested in romance, and I sent him away. It's my fault.'

'I'm genuinely sorry, Dolly.' Freddie proffered his hand. 'May I have this dance, Miss Blanchard?'

'Yes, indeed.' Dolly smiled. Freddie was always there when she needed him most. She allowed him to whirl her into the midst of the dancers, temporarily forgetting Gus and the pain he had caused.

When the dance ended Freddie went to fetch them both some champagne. Dolly leaned against the wall, watching the start of a country dance with enjoyment. Everyone seemed happy, not least the newlyweds. She had never seen Aurelia looking so well, and Nick was every inch the proud husband. Then, to her dismay, Dolly saw whiskery Humphrey heading towards her. His flushed cheeks and red nose warned her that he had been drinking heavily and was unlikely to take no for an answer. Luckily, she spotted Alfie and Todd, chatting together a little apart from the rest of the guests. Normally Nancy would have been ensuring that they were able to mix freely but she was busy with Tommy and their sons. Dolly made a swift detour to join her old friends.

'Why aren't you dancing, Todd? And you too, Alfie.'

Todd grinned. 'I'm not much of a one for the country dances, as you might remember from the days in London.'

'Please don't remind me of my awful coming-out balls. How you must have laughed at us young ladies in our white gowns with our noses permanently stuck in the air.'

Alfie eyed her in amazement. 'I'm sure you were never like that, Miss Dolly.'

'Yes, she was,' Todd said before Dolly had a chance to argue. 'Miss Adela Blanchard was very much aware of her social standing.'

'That's unfair, Todd,' Dolly protested. 'I was simply nervous. I didn't fit in with the other young ladies and I wasn't sure how I should behave.'

Alfie glanced over her shoulder. 'Do you know that big fat chap with the mutton-chop whiskers, Dolly? It looks as if he is coming over here and I don't think he wants to dance with Todd or myself.'

Dolly followed his gaze. 'Oh heavens! He is such a priceless bore.' She flung herself into Todd's arms. 'Dance with me, Todd. I don't care if we get into a tangle with the steps. Save me from whiskery Humphrey.'

Todd took her by the hand and led her onto the floor. 'Don't say I didn't warn you, Dolly.'

They managed to get by with a minimum of mistakes and, anyway, the champagne was beginning to take effect, as even the most proficient dancers were able to laugh when things did not quite go to plan. At the end of the dance Dolly could see her would-be suitor still waiting for her.

'Todd, please. This is a polka. Take me to the other side of the hall, away from that awful man.'

'Can't you put him in his place, Dolly?' Todd took her in his arms. 'You seem to be quite good at that, so I hear.'

Dolly met his quizzical smile with a murmur of alarm. 'If you mean Gus, I made a terrible mistake. I know I treated him badly but I was jealous of Miss Mountjoy.'

They slipped into the energetic dance and were unable to speak for a while, but when the floor became too crowded to move quickly, Todd gave her a searching look. 'Why was that? Gus isn't interested in that woman.'

'Isn't he?'

'No, Dolly. You ought to know by now that the only woman he's ever wanted is you.'

'I didn't know that, Todd.'

'You are both as difficult as each other.'

'How was I to know how he feels? He's so bad at talking to me.'

'You made your feelings very clear. He knew he had lost you when he took you to Lord Dorrington's mansion in Piccadilly.'

'That was out of necessity, Todd. I had nowhere else to go and no money for the fare home.'

Todd rolled his eyes. 'You are so far above him, Dolly. He thinks he's crying for the moon in wanting you.'

'He does?'

'What else can I say?'

'I don't know where he is or how to contact him.' Dolly came to a halt in the middle of the dance floor. 'But you know, don't you?'

'I can get in touch with him, but why should I when you two can't talk to each other? Anyway, Gus has just been promoted to sub-lieutenant. He's being sent abroad, possibly to India – he was not sure where.'

'So far away? I will never see him again. Please, Todd, you must help me. At least write and tell him I am so sorry for what I said and did. I will regret it for the rest of my life.'

Todd led her back into the dance, holding her tightly. 'I'll do what I can, but I can't promise anything.'

'I understand, and I'm very grateful. I always thought that you and Gus were the best of Nancy's boys, and Alfie, of course. He's sweet and lovely.' Dolly reached up to brush his cheek with a kiss as the dance came to an end. 'I can see May and Charlotte are without partners. Come with me and I'll make sure that you and Alfie do not lack for company.' She dragged him by the hand. 'May, Charlotte. Why are you being wallflowers? Todd is too shy to ask you to dance, May. And Alfie is over there on his own, Charlotte. I think you might be kind and take pity on him.'

May slipped her hand into Todd's and they joined in a lively mazurka, but Charlotte eyed Alfie nervously. 'I can't ask a man to dance with me.'

Dolly grabbed her by the hand. 'Come with me. I am not so shy.' She led Charlotte to the other side of the great hall.

Alfie needed only a little encouragement to ask Charlotte to dance with him and they joined the dance eagerly. Dolly sighed with satisfaction. She had just found partners for Todd and Alfie, and there was a chance that Todd might be able to get in touch with Gus on her behalf. She turned to find whiskery Humphrey standing so close behind her. There was no way of escape.

'Miss Dolly, would you do me the honour of being my partner for this dance?'

'Why not?' Dolly allowed him to take her by the hand. She might soon be reunited with Gus. She could afford to be nice to this unlikeable man for one dance.

Chapter Twenty-Six

After the excitement of the wedding, everything slipped back into routine at the castle. Although there was still the pantomime to finish writing and rehearsals to begin. Nick and Aurelia spent their honeymoon secluded in their cottage on the Greystone estate, leaving Dolly in charge of the theatre. However, the production was almost at the end of its run and there was little to do other than count the takings and keep the books up to date.

Josephine and Felicia seemed unlikely partners, but they met regularly to discuss the programme for the new season. Dolly was surprised to find that Josephine had good sense and a sound idea of what was commercial. Even Felicia had to agree that beneath the outward show of bravado, Josephine Mountjoy had a serious side to her nature. She most certainly knew what she was doing when it came to matters concerning the theatre. Jared kept himself so much in the background that he almost disappeared. He apparently spent his days hunting and fishing on the estate and was content to live a quiet life, leaving his wife to enjoy the limelight.

One thing that Felicia insisted upon was that the pantomime, written and performed by members of the Carey and Blanchard families, should run for only two nights. After that she insisted that a professional company should take over. It was not to be expected that rank amateurs could keep up the standard required for more than a couple of performances: the novelty would wear off and the audiences would feel cheated. It might be amusing to see the local gentry giving their all on stage, but there was a thin line between success and embarrassment. Dolly was disappointed at first, but she had to admit that it made sense.

Walter and Nancy produced the finished score and libretto, and the great hall was turned into a rehearsal room so that the running of the actual theatre was not compromised. Patricia threw herself into the part she was playing with enormous energy and enthusiasm. The pantomime was Walter and Nancy's version of *Dick Whittington*, and the costumes were hired from a theatrical costumier in London.

There was a somewhat undignified scramble for the part of Dick Whittington's cat, as the suit was made of real fur. When Rory and Jack arrived home from university, they both wanted to dress up and play the part. Dolly had volunteered, as had May and Phoebe, but Felicia crushed their enthusiasm by saying it was unladylike to show off one's legs. Even in such a disguise it would encourage salacious comments from the gentlemen in the audience. In the end it was decided that Alfie should be the cat as he was small enough to fit into the suit. Rory and Jack suddenly lost interest and took themselves off to the Black Dog.

Patricia was to play Dick Whittington, although Felicia insisted that she wear breeches instead of the tights favoured by bold professional actresses. Wolfe was persuaded to play King Rat and Leo was Alderman Fitzwarren with Dolly taking the part of his daughter, Alice. Phoebe, Charlotte and May were desperate to be included and Walter hastily added three good fairies to sing in the chorus. Nancy's boys and Charlie were to be the rats that plagued the ship, of which Tommy was the captain. Alex decided he would rather be backstage, and Felicia declined to add her name to the cast other than taking credit for being the producer. The rehearsals were chaotic and usually ended up with the entire family falling about with laughter.

Nick was back at work and in a supremely good mood. He was enthusiastic and had worked hard with publicity for the pantomime. He announced that all the seats were sold for both nights and people were queuing up for any cancellations that might occur.

Dolly had only a few lines. All she had to do was to look pretty and smile or cry in the right places. She did not wish for a larger part and she was glad she did not have to sing. Patricia made the most of playing the principal boy and she strutted around the stage in tights and breeches, freed from corsets and long skirts. Hester was horrified when she discovered that Patricia would be wearing such a costume. She did not approve of a woman playing the part of a man and she took every opportunity to make her opinion felt. However, Patricia had been in the audience of several London pantomime productions when she was married to Sir Michael, and she knew exactly how the professionals performed.

'It's liberating, Dolly,' Patricia confided while they waited for their cue to go on stage. 'I wish women could wear breeches like men.'

'Maybe they will one day,' Dolly said hopefully. 'I'm surprised that Grandmama allowed you this much freedom.'

'Mama knows what the audiences like. We'll be a great success, Dolly. Just wait and see. We might even make a yearly event of the Carey–Blanchard production. I rather fancy being Prince Charming next time.'

Dolly giggled. 'Let's wait and see how this one goes down. We might get rotten tomatoes thrown at us, as you did in London.'

'Don't remind me of that incident. Anyway, it

was in a street market. I don't think that country people would waste good food by throwing it at us.'

'And tomatoes are out of season,' Dolly added, giggling. 'I suppose the worst that could happen is being booed off the stage.'

Dolly need not have worried. The first night of the family pantomime was played to a packed house and received a rapturous ovation at the finish. There were so many curtain calls that in the end Felicia went on stage to thank the audience for their enthusiastic support.

'We should be having a party to celebrate,' Nancy said eagerly as she helped Patricia and Dolly to take off their costumes in the dressing room.

'That would be wonderful, Nancy,' Phoebe said enthusiastically. 'We deserve something after all our hard work.'

'Not tonight,' Patricia said firmly. 'We'll celebrate tomorrow after the last performance. We all need to have a good rest and sleep well so that we are fresh tomorrow.'

'I agree,' Dolly said, yawning. She glanced anxiously at Nancy. 'You look tired, Nancy. You are the one who should be resting. It can't be much longer before the baby comes.'

Nancy shrugged. 'Thank you for worrying about me, but I think I have a week or so before I need to take things quietly. Baby Carey was dancing in time to the music this evening. I think he or she is destined for the stage.'

'Well, don't do too much.' Dolly slipped her shawl around her shoulders. 'I'm going to check on the office. I want to see the bookings for tomorrow night.'

She did not wait for an answer as she walked out of the dressing room and made her way through the auditorium. For a moment she thought she saw a flash of scarlet dress uniform as the audience filed into the foyer. She hurried as fast as she could in an attempt to get a better view, but when she finally reached the foyer there was no sign of any military men. She took a deep breath, telling herself that it was her imagination playing tricks on her. She had tried to put Gus out of her mind, but he had a habit of creeping in when she was off guard. His regiment had moved on and she must also, or she would face a desperately dull and lonely life. She crossed the floor and entered the office, where Nick was stowing the evening's takings into the safe.

He looked up and grinned. 'A full house means a good profit, especially as all the performers are not expecting payment, and the hotel is fully booked for the next few days.'

'The pantomime went down well, Nick. You should be proud of yourself for promoting it.'

'I did very little, as it happens. It was the combined efforts of the Careys and the Blanchards that made the evening such a success.'

'And the de Marneys,' Dolly added, smiling. 'Don't leave Grandmama out or she will be very angry.'

'Of course. Felicia is always the leading light in anything we do at the Pavilion. I can't wait to see how her collaboration with Josephine Mountjoy evolves.'

'I will watch with interest.' Dolly toyed with a pile of programmes on the desk. 'I don't suppose you noticed any military uniforms in the audience, did you, Nick?'

'I didn't, I'm afraid. Do you think Gus saw the performance?'

'I probably imagined it. I thought I saw red coats, but it was probably a trick of the light.'

'Or wishful thinking?'

'Now you're laughing at me.'

'No, of course not, Dolly. I would never be so unfeeling. I know you are fond of Gus. He was always one of my favourites when it came to Nancy's boys. I do know that Todd bought tickets, although I didn't actually see him in the auditorium. Why don't you ask him?'

'I might. Anyway, it's not important. I'm sure Gus would have come backstage had he been in the audience.' Dolly was about to leave the office when Nick caught her by the sleeve.

'If he's the one you want, don't give up, Dolly. I almost lost Aurelia, but I was lucky enough to have a second chance. You deserve to be happy, and if the opportunity arises don't be afraid to grasp it with both hands. Do you understand what I'm saying?'

Dolly managed a watery smile. 'Yes, I do. Thank you, Nick.' She hurried into the foyer and found Freddie waiting for her with Phoebe and May.

'Are you ready to come home with us, Dolly?' Freddie asked, smiling. 'You were wonderful tonight. All of you,' he added hastily.

'Why did you hurry off like that?' Phoebe demanded crossly. 'I'm tired and I want to go home.'

'I had work to do.' Dolly hurried past Phoebe and May. She knew that they would tease her mercilessly if they found out why she had made such a speedy exit. It was ridiculous to harbour feelings for someone whom she might never see again. 'Thank you for waiting for me, Freddie. What would I do without you?'

Chapter Twenty-Seven

Dolly had intended to call upon Todd next day before she started work at the theatre, but to her surprise the whole family were up early, including Freddie, and she found everyone in the dining room enjoying their breakfast.

'Good morning, Dolly,' Freddie said, rising from his seat. 'Did you sleep well after all that excitement last evening?'

Dolly smiled. 'Thank you, yes. I was very tired.' She glanced round the table. 'I'm surprised to see everyone up and about.'

'We have a busy day ahead of us.' Rosalind filled a cup with coffee and handed it to Dolly. 'I'm glad it went so well last evening. The audience loved the show.'

'I tore my beautiful fairy costume,' Phoebe said,

wiping her lips on her table napkin. 'Would you be a dear and mend it for me, Dolly?'

'I don't know if I have time.' Dolly helped herself to buttered eggs from the salver on the sideboard. 'I have things to do.'

'Like what?' Phoebe demanded.

'Darling, those costumes have to be returned to the theatrical costumiers tomorrow,' Rosalind said hastily. 'They will fine us for sending back a torn gown. I'm sure you could find time to mend the tear for your sister.'

Dolly realised that Aunt Nancy was staring at her as if she could read her thoughts. Nancy had an uncanny knack of sensing a lie. Maybe that was what came from having three boisterous sons who were constantly involved in pranks of one sort or another. Dolly knew she could not win. 'All right, Phoebe. I'll do it when I've had my breakfast.'

Phoebe grinned triumphantly. 'I knew you would. You're the best sister, Dolly.'

'I'm your only sister.'

'I am a sort of sister,' May said wistfully. 'I think of you both as my sisters.'

'Of course you are.' Dolly reached out to pat May's hand. 'I'm sorry, I didn't mean to leave you out. Have you any mending for me to do?'

May shook her head. 'No. I was more careful than Phoebe.'

'Now girls, please don't start a fight,' Rosalind said wearily. 'We have one more performance of the pantomime to get through and then we can concentrate on decorating the castle ready for Christmas. It's only a couple of weeks away.'

'I need to go shopping in Exeter. It will probably be my last opportunity before the baby arrives.' Nancy reached for the coffee pot. 'Will you come with me, Rosie?'

'I'll take you,' Tommy volunteered. 'We can have luncheon at the White Hart. I want to make sure you don't overtire yourself, my darling. As you said, you are very close to your time.'

Alex rose to his feet. 'I'll be in the study if anyone needs me. Someone has to keep the estate running. Although I could do with some advice from you, Freddie, if you can spare me the time.'

'Of course. I'll be glad to help in any way I can.' Freddie stood up. 'I was going to return to Dorrington Place today, but I think I might stay on to see the final performance.'

'You know you're always welcome here, old chap.' Alex patted him on the shoulder. 'Go on ahead, Freddie. I won't be a moment.' Alex leaned over to drop a kiss on Rosalind's forehead. 'Go to Exeter whenever you like, my love, but please don't ask me to accompany you. I hate shopping.'

Rosalind laughed. 'I haven't been married to you for twenty years without discovering that, Alexander Blanchard. I will go with Nancy and Tommy.'

'I'll see you all later.' Alex followed Freddie from the room, closing the door behind him.

'Would any of you girls like to accompany us to Exeter this afternoon?' Rosalind asked.

It was on the tip of Dolly's tongue to say she would like to go, but Phoebe spoke up first.

'Yes, please, Mama. I expect May would like to come, too.'

May nodded vigorously. 'Yes, please.'

Rosalind turned to Dolly. 'What about you, Dolly?'

Dolly shook her head. She wanted desperately to visit the regimental headquarters, but she knew she would never be able to shake off her inquisitive sister. 'No thank you, Mama. Perhaps another time. I have to go to the theatre when I've mended Phoebe's costume.' Dolly sipped her coffee, avoiding Nancy's curious gaze. She finished her breakfast, barely listening to Phoebe and May's excited chatter about the shopping expedition, and as soon as she had finished she rose from the table. 'Phoebe, I'll deal with your costume now, if you'll fetch it for me, but please hurry. I don't want to be late for work.'

'Oh, all right.' Phoebe stood up, brushing toast crumbs from her skirt. 'You are a misery, Dolly. You should forget the theatre for five minutes and come with us.'

'I would if I could, but you will have a lovely time with May. I have things to do, so please fetch the gown and bring it to the morning parlour. My work box is there.'

The tear, when Dolly examined the gauzy material, was very small. It took only a few well-placed stitches to mend it so that only the closest examination would reveal where it had been torn. When she had finished she folded the garment and left it for Phoebe to take to the theatre. It was hard to believe that tonight would be their second and final performance after the weeks of planning and rehearsing, but the professional company would take over and complete the pantomime season until after Christmas. Then it would be Josephine's turn to shine in the next production.

Dolly was about to leave the morning room when a tap on the door made her jump. 'Come in.'

'I was told you were in here, Dolly.' Freddie entered and closed the door. 'May I have a word with you?'

'Yes, of course.'

Freddie walked over to the fireplace and stood with his back to it. His serious expression made Dolly nervous.

'What is it? You look anxious.'

'I just wanted to tell you that I am going home, Dolly.'

'Yes, I believe you said that before. Is anything wrong?'

'No . . . well, yes. Dolly, I know there is no hope for me.' He held up his hand as she was about to answer. 'We've had this conversation before, but I just wanted to tell you that your happiness is all that matters to me. I will always love you, but I realise that your heart belongs to someone else.'

'Oh, Freddie. I'm sorry.'

He smiled. 'Don't apologise. I want the best for you, and, odd as it may seem, I think a certain military man might be that person. I'll say no more, my dear girl. But I claim the first dance at your wedding, after the bridegroom, of course.'

Dolly's eyes filled with tears. 'Thank you, Freddie. Your opinion really matters to me and it always will.'

'We understand each other, Dolly. I'm going home, but I will be back in time for Christmas.'

'It wouldn't be the same without you, Freddie.'

He nodded wordlessly and hurried from the room. Dolly struggled with feelings of guilt and relief. Freddie was the last person in the world whom she wished to hurt, and in different circumstances she might have weakened and agreed to marry him. Despite everything that had gone before, she knew that Freddie would always be there for her, no matter what the future held. He had made it easy for her and she loved him for that.

Half an hour later, Dolly set off on foot for the theatre, wrapped up against the cold in a fur-lined cape with a matching bonnet and warm woollen mittens. It was a frosty morning and a pale, buttery sun burned off the early mist. There was the last performance of the pantomime to look forward to as well as the preparations for Christmas. It was the time of year that Dolly had always loved but, try as she might, she could not dispel the feeling of sadness and loss she had experienced since last evening. It must have been wishful thinking when she thought she saw Gus leaving the auditorium, but even if he had been at the theatre, he obviously had no intention of contacting her, and who could blame him?

She was tempted to stop off at the doctor's house to see if Gus was there, but she forced herself to walk on until she came to the tall wrought-iron gates at the entrance of the Greystone Park estate. The theatre was at the end of the tree-lined avenue where once the Greystone mansion had stood, and the Palladian façade was bathed in sunlight. This, she decided, was where her future lay and a *frisson* of excitement rippled through her veins at the thought of the next performance. She had achieved her ambition of performing on stage and the enthusiastic applause from the audience was a memory she would treasure. It was a pity that this would be the beginning and the end of her acting career, but she could continue in management, if allowed. However, she was painfully aware that the odds were against her as a woman in business – she would always be Nick's assistant and to rise any higher was unlikely. She quickened her pace.

Perhaps she ought to have accepted Freddie's proposal. After all, nothing was expected of her other than that she married well. If she produced a healthy heir she would have fulfilled her destiny, and she would spend her life supporting her husband, rearing his children and entertaining his family and friends. She would have servants to wait upon her hand and foot and an unlimited income so that she could enjoy the best that money could buy. She knew that she should be grateful for such an opportunity, but if she were honest the prospect filled her with dread. A chilly wind had sprung up and the clouds met together, blotting out the sun and sending a sharp, sleety shower to make Dolly run the last few yards. She burst into the foyer and came to a sudden halt as she found Nick and Aurelia in the middle of a fierce argument.

'What's the matter?' Dolly asked anxiously. 'Is anything wrong?'

'Alfie has had an accident.' Nick sighed. 'He was bringing my horse to the cottage when something must have startled it and Alfie was unseated. He fell badly and broke his arm. I've just brought him back from the doctor's house.'

'Oh, poor Alfie,' Dolly said, frowning. 'Is he all right?'

'Todd set his arm, but Alfie won't be able to play the cat this evening.'

'I've told Nick that I could take over Alfie's role,' Aurelia said sulkily, 'but he won't hear of it.'

Nick shrugged, frowning. 'It's not that I don't want you to, my love. But you haven't been at many rehearsals and you don't know the part.'

'I can pretend to be a cat. Everyone will help me. I want to be involved in this, Nick. The whole family are in it and as your wife I think I should be, too.'

'My darling, you are too tall. I'm afraid the cat costume won't fit you. That's why Alfie got the part in the first place.'

Dolly thought quickly. 'I'm small enough to get into the costume, Nick.'

'Yes, I agree, and you know what to do, but who will play Alice? You can't do both.'

'Isn't it obvious?' Dolly exchanged meaningful glances with Aurelia. 'Of course Aurelia will make a lovely Alice Fitzwarren. It's not as if she will have to learn many lines.'

'You can teach me today,' Aurelia said excitedly. 'I can do it. You agree, don't you, Nick?'

He looked from one to the other. 'Well, if you are both sure?'

Dolly took off her gloves and bonnet. 'Come into the office with me, Aurelia. I'll give you the script and we'll go through it together. You've seen the show so you have an idea how it goes.'

'Yes, indeed. I've always wanted to go on the stage. What Grandmama would say I hate to think, but she need never know. This is so exciting.' Aurelia followed Dolly into the office.

'I'll leave you two to work it out together,' Nick said vaguely. 'Let's hope nothing else goes wrong.'

*

When the family returned from Exeter late that afternoon, they were all surprised and amused to discover that Dolly was going to stand in for Alfie as the pantomime cat. Nancy, who had taken the position as dresser for the girls, was pale and tired, but she insisted on accompanying them to the theatre despite Tommy's pleas for her to remain at home and rest.

There was an air of excitement backstage that had been missing the previous evening. Perhaps they had been too nervous to enjoy the experience, but whatever it was this time they were all bubbling with energy and eager to get on with the show. Aurelia was quietly confident and Nick wished her good luck before leaving them to man the office. He was assisted by Fletcher. She had a way of dealing with later-comers who had not had the forethought to make a booking. One fierce look from Fletcher, especially when she rolled up her sleeves to show her tattoos, would make them back away and apologise for their shortcomings.

Dolly was eager to play the part of the cat. She had watched Alfie carefully and she knew his every move. The furry cat costume was close-fitting, hot and itchy, but the disguise was perfect. She knew that no one would realise who was inside, and that gave her the courage to give a performance that made the audience laugh and cheer every time she came onto the stage.

Everything went exceptionally well and the theatre rocked with laughter and applause. When the final curtain went down there were calls for more, but eventually Nick turned the lights on in the auditorium and the audience filed out, albeit reluctantly.

Dolly took off the headpiece, taking deep breaths of air. She was hot and uncomfortable, but she had the comfort of knowing she had done well. She had fulfilled an ambition. However, she could not resist peeping out through the curtains just in case there was someone whom she might recognise in the audience.

She saw him as he rose from his seat, and she tried to call out but she had suddenly lost her voice. She pulled back the curtain just far enough to see him better and waved, but even as she did so a loud cry of pain made her spin round to see Nancy collapsed, clutching her belly.

Suddenly the stage was filled with family, who were crowding around Nancy. Tommy pushed past everyone to kneel at his wife's side. 'We must get you home, darling. I knew you shouldn't have come tonight.'

Nancy leaned her head against his shoulder, her face contorted with pain. 'I'm not sure I'll get that far, Tommy.'

Forgetting everything other than Nancy's plight, Dolly opened the curtains. 'Is Dr Taylor in the theatre? We need a doctor.' She spotted Todd and Gus, who had stopped and turned to look at her. She beckoned frantically. 'Todd, please. We need you.'

He made his way up the steps, followed by Gus,

but by now Dolly was too concerned for Nancy to worry about herself. 'Nancy's baby is coming, Todd.'

He crossed the stage, ordering everyone to stand clear while he examined Nancy.

'Is that really you in a cat costume?' Gus said, grinning. 'I would never have guessed, Dolly.'

'Well, it is. You can laugh, but I was filling in for Alfie. He broke his arm and he couldn't perform.'

'And you stepped in.' Gus stroked the fur around Dolly's neck. 'I've never seen such a lovely cat.'

'Gus.' Todd rose to his feet. 'We haven't got time to get Lady Carey home. I'll need my doctor's bag, towels and carbolic soap. You'll have to get them from my house, but hurry.'

'I'll be as quick as I can.'

Dolly grabbed his hand. 'I'm coming with you. You'll need me to help carry everything.'

'Take my horse,' Todd said urgently. 'And hurry.'

Gus lifted Dolly bodily from the stage and set her down on her feet. 'You'll have to come like that, Puss.'

In spite of everything, this made Dolly laugh. She ran after him as he ploughed through the stragglers to get out of the theatre. The horses were tethered not far away and Gus threw Dolly onto the saddle of Todd's animal. He mounted and urged his horse to a trot and then a canter, which evolved swiftly into a gallop. Dolly did not have time to register the expressions on the faces of the people leaving the theatre when they saw the pantomime cat riding hell for leather towards the village.

If Mrs Lloyd was shocked or surprised to see Gus with Dolly dressed in a fur suit, she was too accustomed to desperate situations to show any emotion. She knew exactly what was needed and she handed a bundle of towels and necessary items to Dolly, while Gus took the doctor's leather bag. They set off again and reached the theatre just as the last of the audience were leaving. Forgetting everything other than Nancy's plight, Dolly leaped from the saddle and raced back into the theatre with Gus not far behind.

Tommy was pacing the floor in front of the orchestra pit while the rest of the family sat in the front stalls, waiting anxiously and shuddering with every agonising cry from behind the curtains. Rosalind and Patricia were on stage when Dolly slipped behind the curtains with the towel bundle. Gus passed the doctor's bag to Dolly and he stepped away.

Todd was attending to Nancy, who lay on cushions taken from the dressing rooms. Dolly did not look too closely. This was her first experience of being close to a woman in labour and she was trembling with concern for Nancy.

'You can't do any more than you've already done, my love,' Rosalind said gently. 'Take her to join the others, please, Gus. We can look after Nancy.'

Gus took Dolly by the hand and led her down the steps to join the rest of her family.

Alex gave her a hug. 'Well done, Whittington's cat. I'm proud of you, Dolly.'

'It's Gus you have to thank. I just followed suit.'

'We did it together,' Gus said firmly. 'You should have seen the faces of everyone we passed. A cat riding a horse will go down in Rockwood history.'

Alex slipped his arm around Dolly's shoulders. 'You are so like your mother, Dolly – loyal and brave.' He glanced at Gus's dress uniform. 'You're a sub-lieutenant now then?'

'Yes, sir. I'm making my way up the ranks. One day I hope to rise to adjutant.'

'You've come a long way,' Alex said, nodding. 'You've proved yourself, Sub-Lieutenant Baker.'

Gus smiled. 'Gus will do, sir. I was intending to pay a visit to Rockwood in order to see you tomorrow.'

Alex eyed him curiously. 'Perhaps this is not the time or place, but you can say your piece now.'

Dolly clutched Gus's arm. 'Maybe not now, Gus.'

He looked at her with a smile that made her heart miss a beat. 'I was going to ask your permission to pay court to your daughter, Captain Blanchard. I know what you thought of me in the past, and I realise I'm not the sort of suitor you might choose for Dolly, but I love her and I always have.'

A rending cry from the stage made everyone rise to their feet and Tommy rushed onto the stage.

Patricia met him, clutching a tiny squalling bundle

wrapped in a towel. 'You have a daughter, Tommy. She is beautiful, like her mother.'

Tommy leaned over to kiss the baby's head before hurrying behind the curtains. 'Nancy, my darling.' Moments later he put his head round the curtains. 'Somebody send for the carriage. I'm taking my wife and daughter home.'

'I'll go.' Rory headed for the foyer, followed by Jack.

May, Phoebe and Charlotte hugged each other and Nick put his arm around Aurelia.

'You were a wonderful Alice,' he said softly.

Alex grasped Gus by the hand. 'Come and see me at the castle in the morning. We are all too tired and emotional to think rationally tonight.'

'Yes, sir. I will.' Gus turned to Dolly. 'Would you allow me to escort you home, Puss in Boots? I have a serious question to ask you.'

'Todd will need his horse,' Dolly said, frowning.

'He'll travel in the carriage with Nancy and the baby. I'll take him home later. For now, my darling cat, all I want to do is to be with you and tell you how I feel, which I should have done from the start.'

'Why didn't you?'

'Because I knew I wasn't good enough for you. I can't give you the life you're used to.'

'That's for me to judge, not you, Gus. You never asked me what I wanted.'

'Will you forgive me for being such a fool?'

Dolly laid her hand in his. 'It was always you, Gus.'

They left the theatre together. Gus took her in his arms and kissed her. There was no need for words as he lifted her onto the saddle. He vaulted onto his horse and they rode slowly this time, side by side, holding hands. A full moon illuminated the long straight drive through the trees, which stood to attention, their bare branches forming a triumphal arch over the riders' heads. Frost sparkled on the grass and the air was charged with icy particles.

When they reached the castle, Gus lifted Dolly from the saddle, holding her close. 'I thought I had lost you to Dorrington.'

'I do love Freddie, but not in the way I love you, Gus.'

'Even so, you could do better than me, Dolly. But I can promise you that no man could ever love you more than I do, and always will.'

'I doubted you once, but not any more, Gus.'

He went down on one knee. 'I should wait until I have your father's permission, but I can't go a day longer without knowing your answer. Dolly, I love you now and for ever. Will you do me the honour of becoming my wife?'

She looked into his eyes and saw her past and her future. 'Yes, Gus. I will marry you. No matter where the army sends us, I will enjoy the adventure. I will be by your side for as long as I live.'